DEAD WEIGHT

ONI
PRESS

AN ONI PRESS PUBLICATION

DEAD WEIGHT

MURDER AT CAMP BLOOM

WRITTEN BY TERRY BLAS AND MOLLY MULDOON
ILLUSTRATED AND COLORED BY MATTHEW SEELY
LETTERED BY FRED C. STRESING
COLORING ASSISTANCE BY TAIT HOWARD AND SANDRA LANZ

DESIGNED BY KATE Z. STONE
EDITED BY ROBIN HERRERA

PUBLISHED BY ONI PRESS, INC.

JOE NOZEMACK founder & chief financial officer
JAMES LUCAS JONES publisher
CHARLIE CHU v.p. of creative & business development
BRAD ROOKS director of operations
RACHEL REED marketing manager
MELISSA MESZAROS publicity manager
TROY LOOK director of design & production
HILARY THOMPSON senior graphic designer
KATE Z. STONE junior graphic designer
ANGIE KNOWLES digital prepress lead
ARI YARWOOD executive editor
ROBIN HERRERA senior editor
DESIREE WILSON associate editor
ALISSA SALLAH administrative assistant
JUNG LEE logistics associate

ONIPRESS.COM
FACEBOOK.COM/ONIPRESS
TWITTER.COM/ONIPRESS
ONIPRESS.TUMBLR.COM
INSTAGRAM.COM/ONIPRESS

FIRST EDITION: APRIL 2018
ISBN 978-1-62010-481-1
EISBN 978-1-62010-482-8

Printed in China.

Library of Congress Control Number: 2017952715

10 9 8 7 6 5 4 3 2 1

For Sonja, who taught me how to love myself,
and for Scott who loved me when I started to.
—TB

For my parents, who have been way more supportive
than I probably deserve.
—MM

For my dad, mom, and Sandra. Thank you for all your support,
I LITERALLY could not have done this without you.
—MS

CHAPTER ONE

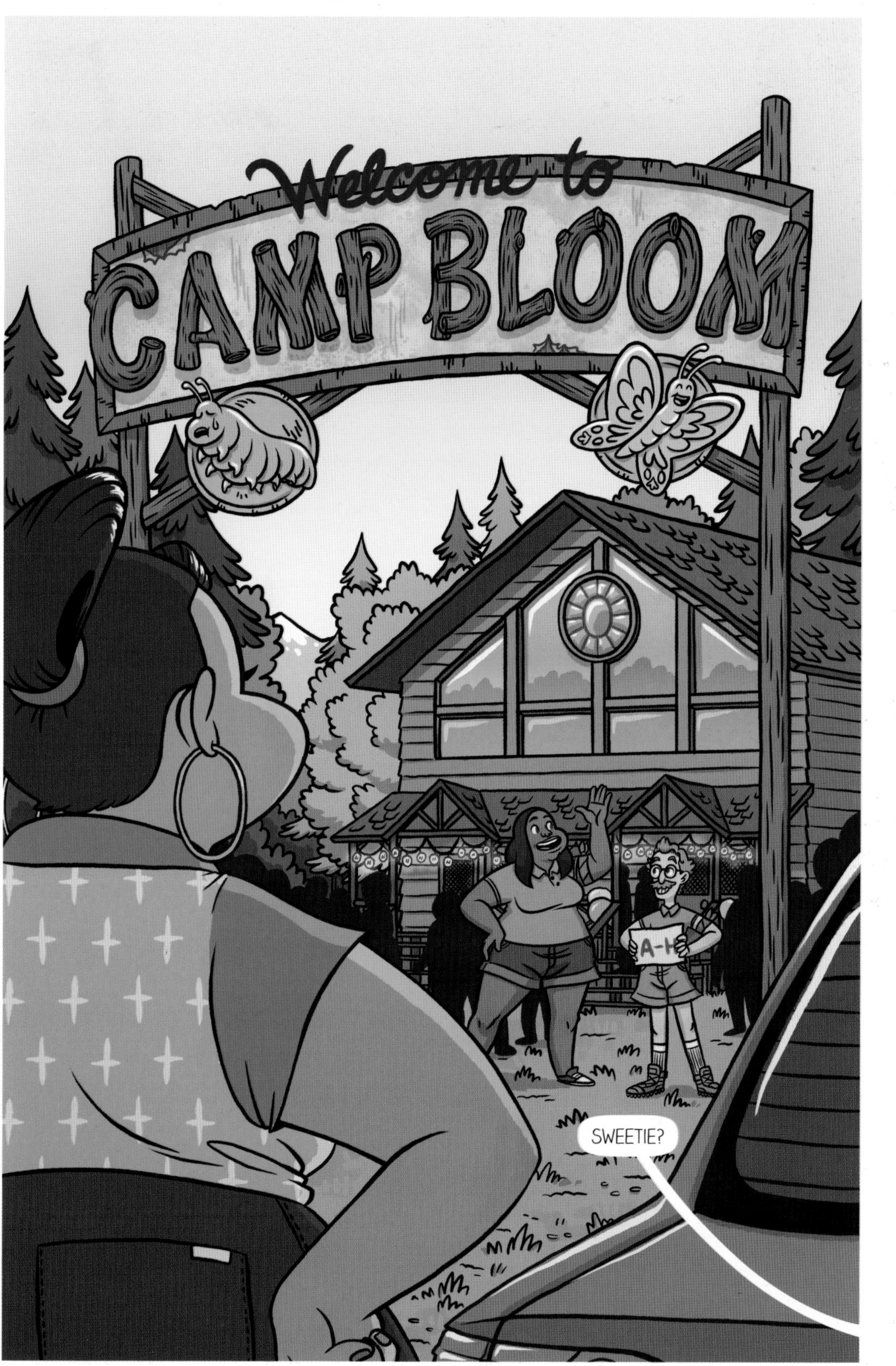
Welcome to
CAMP BLOOM
SWEETIE?

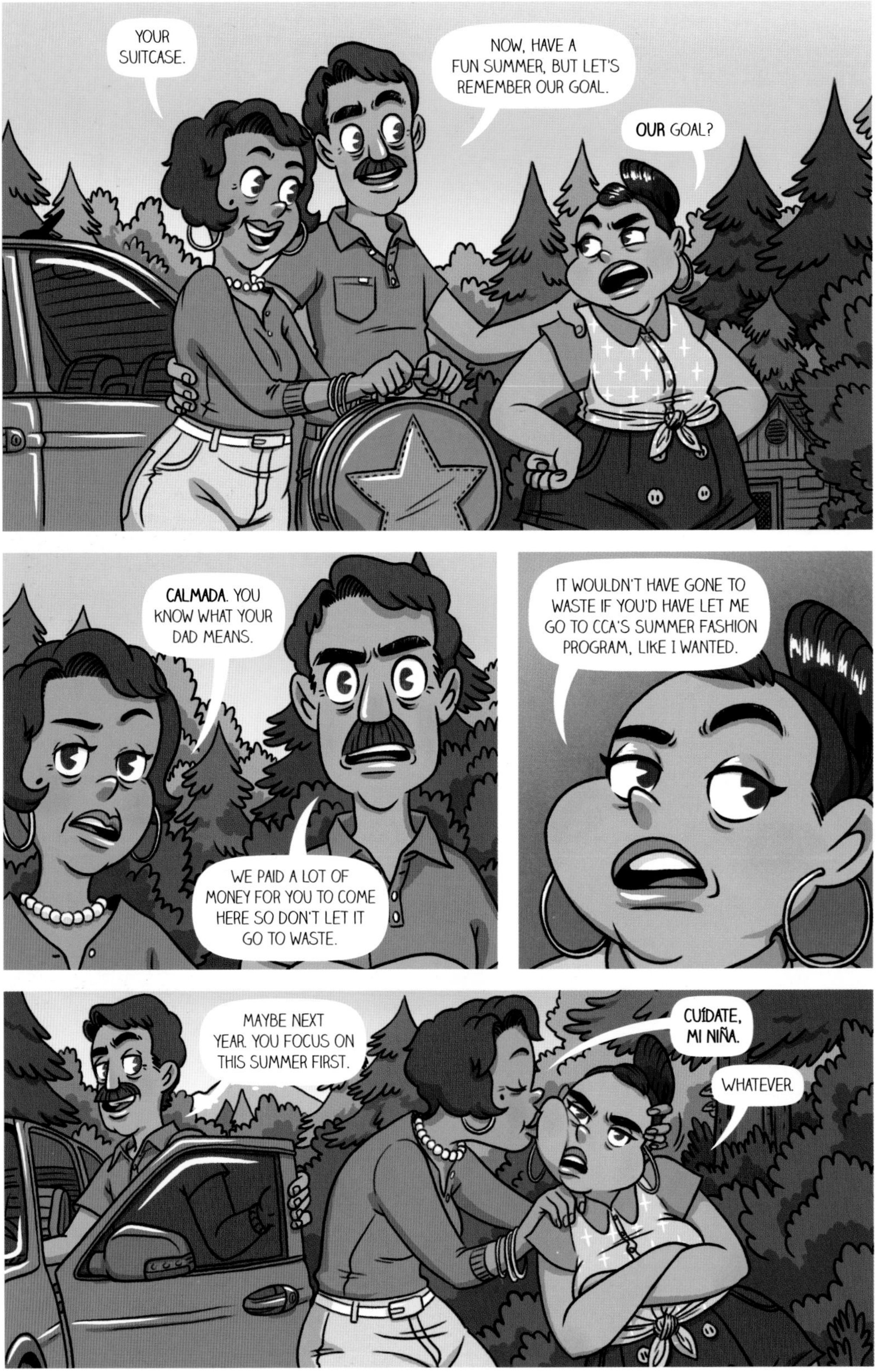
YOUR SUITCASE.
NOW, HAVE A FUN SUMMER, BUT LET'S REMEMBER OUR GOAL.
OUR GOAL?
CALMADA. YOU KNOW WHAT YOUR DAD MEANS.
WE PAID A LOT OF MONEY FOR YOU TO COME HERE SO DON'T LET IT GO TO WASTE.
IT WOULDN'T HAVE GONE TO WASTE IF YOU'D HAVE LET ME GO TO CCA'S SUMMER FASHION PROGRAM, LIKE I WANTED.
MAYBE NEXT YEAR. YOU FOCUS ON THIS SUMMER FIRST.
CUÍDATE, MI NIÑA.
WHATEVER.

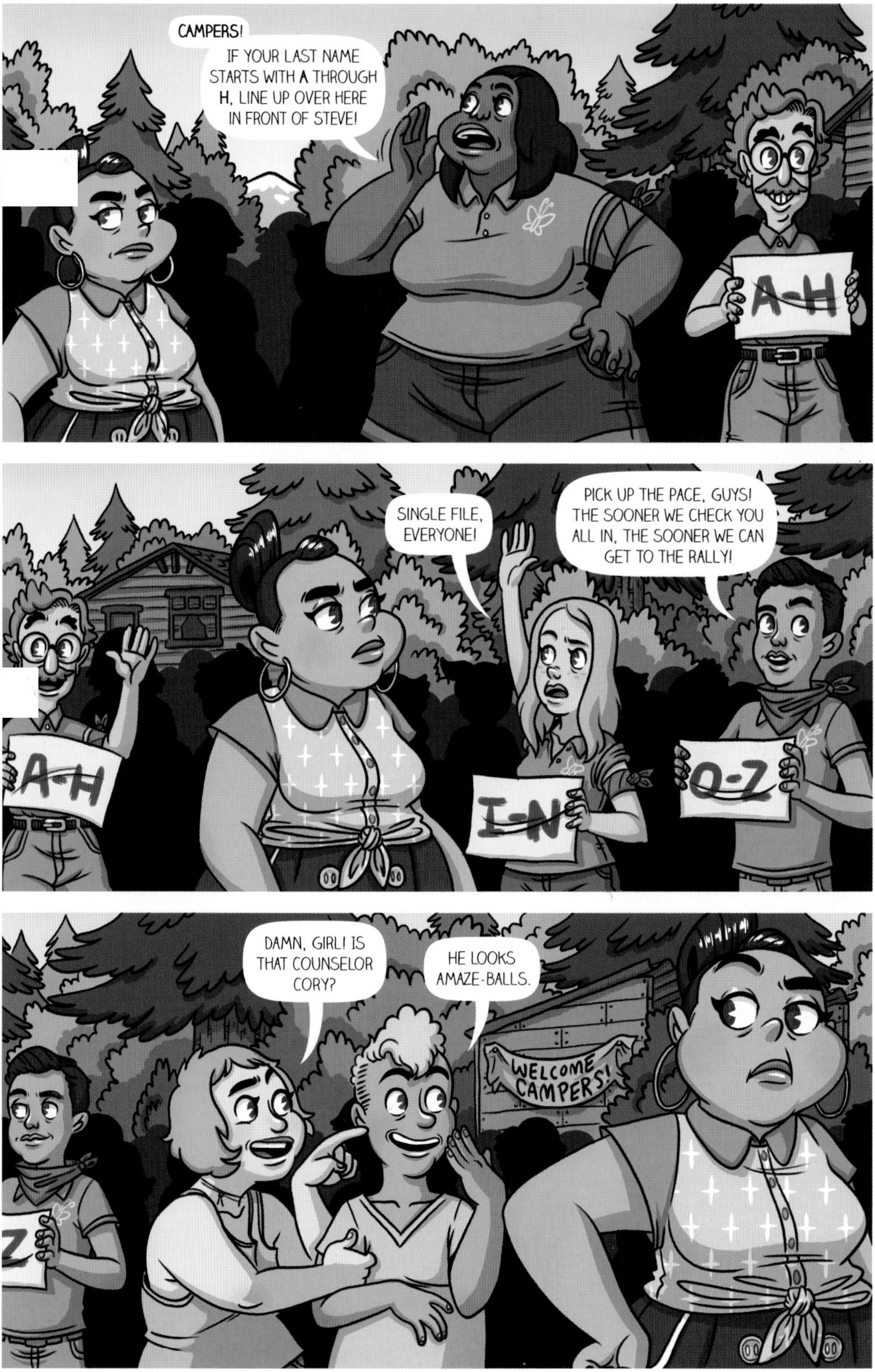
CAMPERS!
IF YOUR LAST NAME STARTS WITH A THROUGH H, LINE UP OVER HERE IN FRONT OF STEVE!
A-H
A-H
SINGLE FILE, EVERYONE!
PICK UP THE PACE, GUYS! THE SOONER WE CHECK YOU ALL IN, THE SOONER WE CAN GET TO THE RALLY!
I-N
O-Z
DAMN, GIRL! IS THAT COUNSELOR CORY?
HE LOOKS AMAZE-BALLS.
WELCOME CAMPERS!

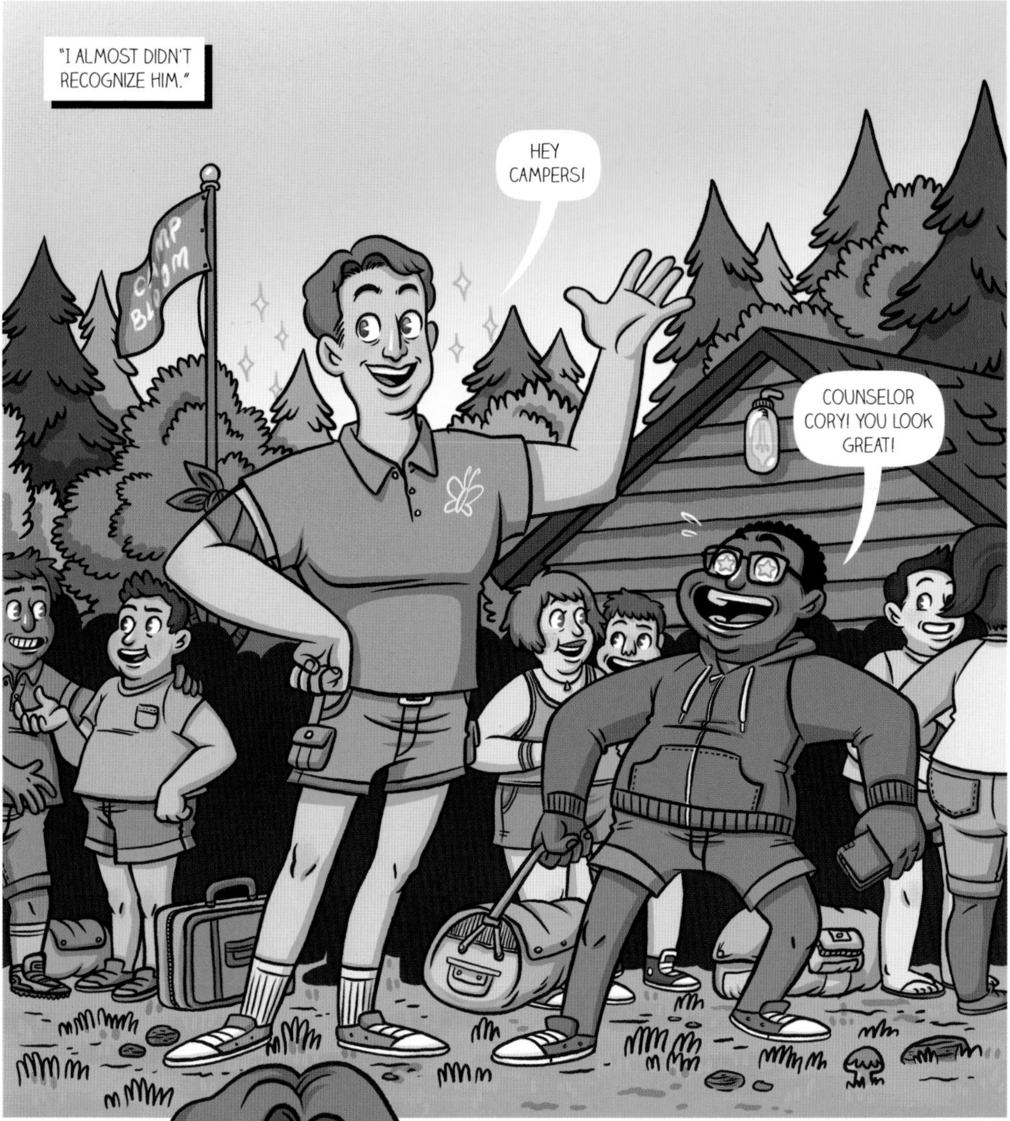
"I ALMOST DIDN'T RECOGNIZE HIM."
HEY CAMPERS!
CAMP BLOOM
COUNSELOR CORY! YOU LOOK GREAT!

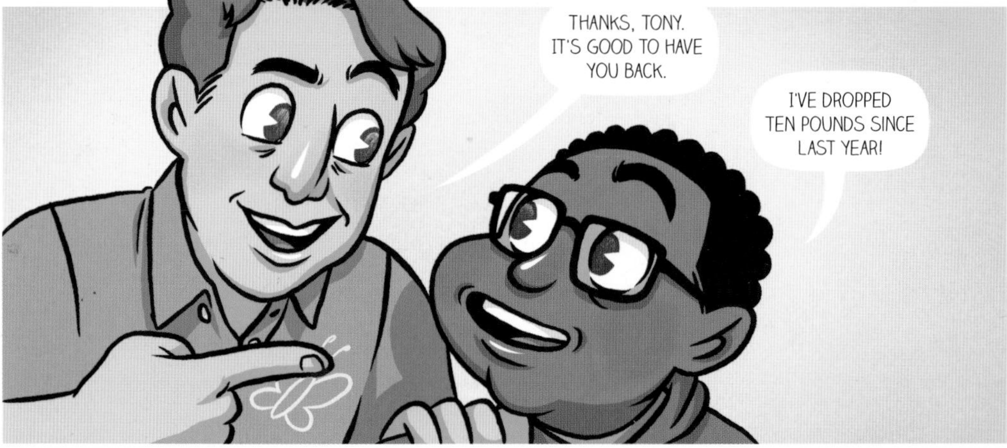
THANKS, TONY. IT'S GOOD TO HAVE YOU BACK.
I'VE DROPPED TEN POUNDS SINCE LAST YEAR!

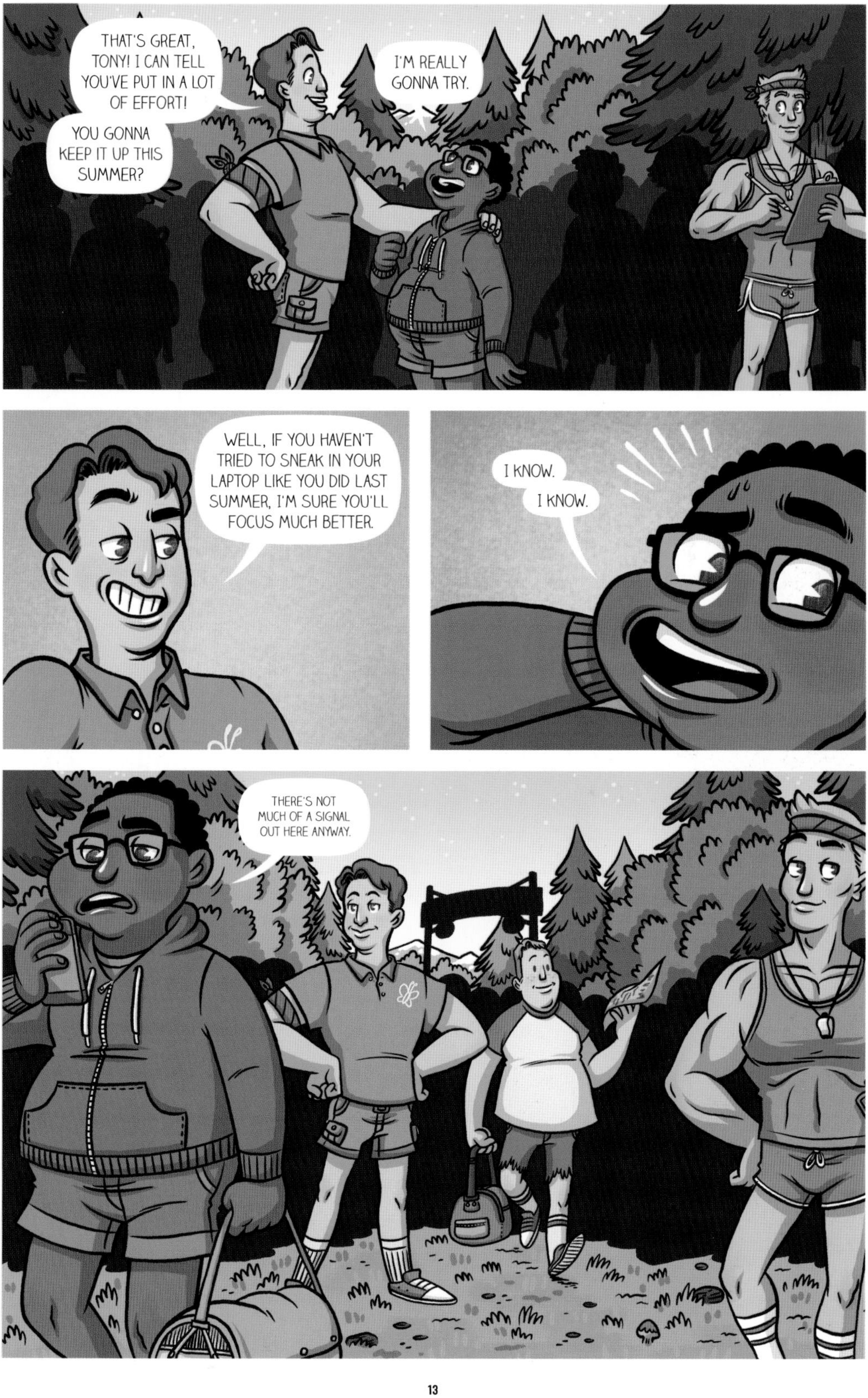
THAT'S GREAT, TONY! I CAN TELL YOU'VE PUT IN A LOT OF EFFORT!
YOU GONNA KEEP IT UP THIS SUMMER?
I'M REALLY GONNA TRY.
WELL, IF YOU HAVEN'T TRIED TO SNEAK IN YOUR LAPTOP LIKE YOU DID LAST SUMMER, I'M SURE YOU'LL FOCUS MUCH BETTER.
I KNOW.
I KNOW.
THERE'S NOT MUCH OF A SIGNAL OUT HERE ANYWAY.

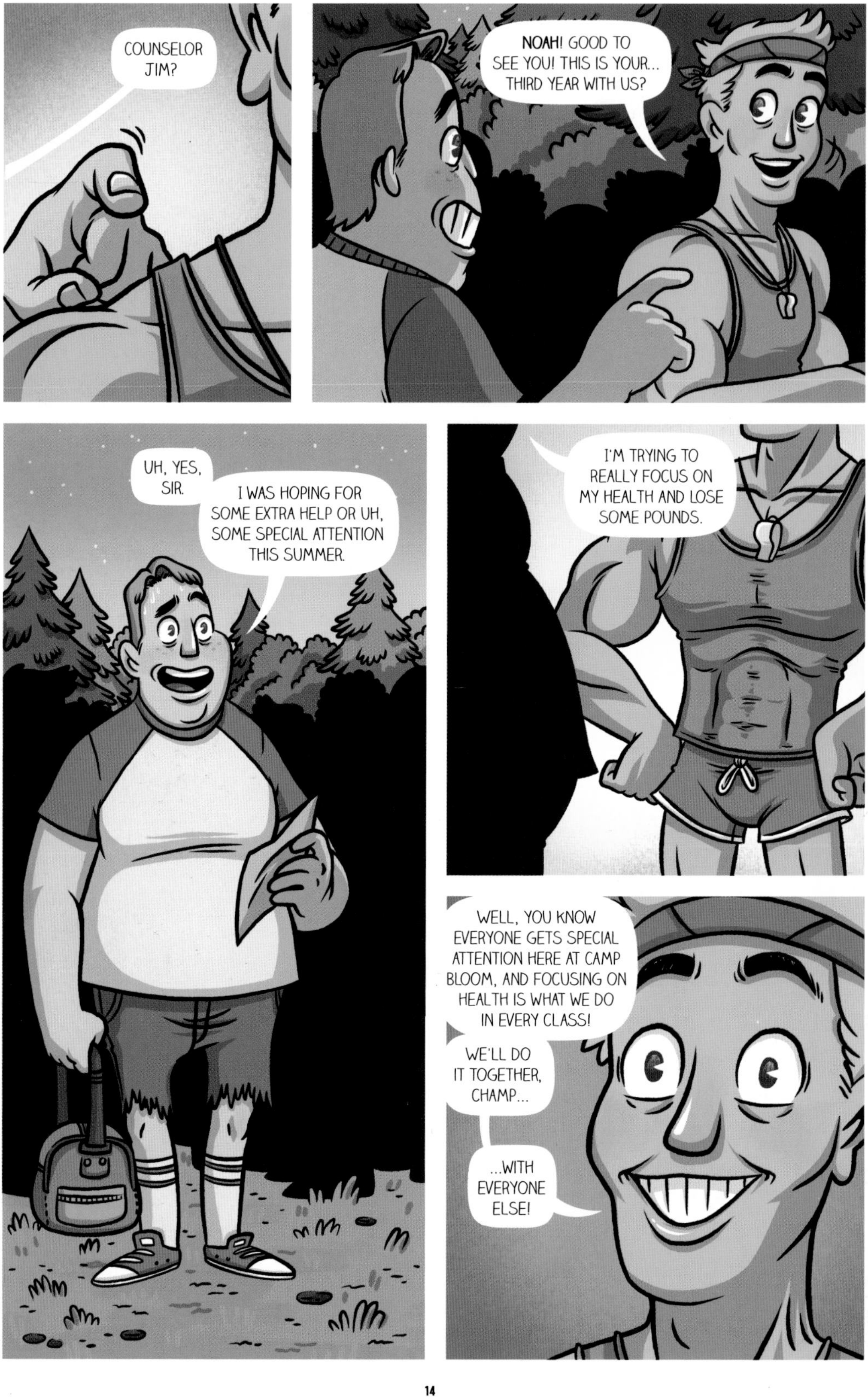
COUNSELOR JIM?
NOAH! GOOD TO SEE YOU! THIS IS YOUR... THIRD YEAR WITH US?
UH, YES, SIR.
I WAS HOPING FOR SOME EXTRA HELP OR UH, SOME SPECIAL ATTENTION THIS SUMMER.
I'M TRYING TO REALLY FOCUS ON MY HEALTH AND LOSE SOME POUNDS.
WELL, YOU KNOW EVERYONE GETS SPECIAL ATTENTION HERE AT CAMP BLOOM, AND FOCUSING ON HEALTH IS WHAT WE DO IN EVERY CLASS!
WE'LL DO IT TOGETHER, CHAMP...
...WITH EVERYONE ELSE!

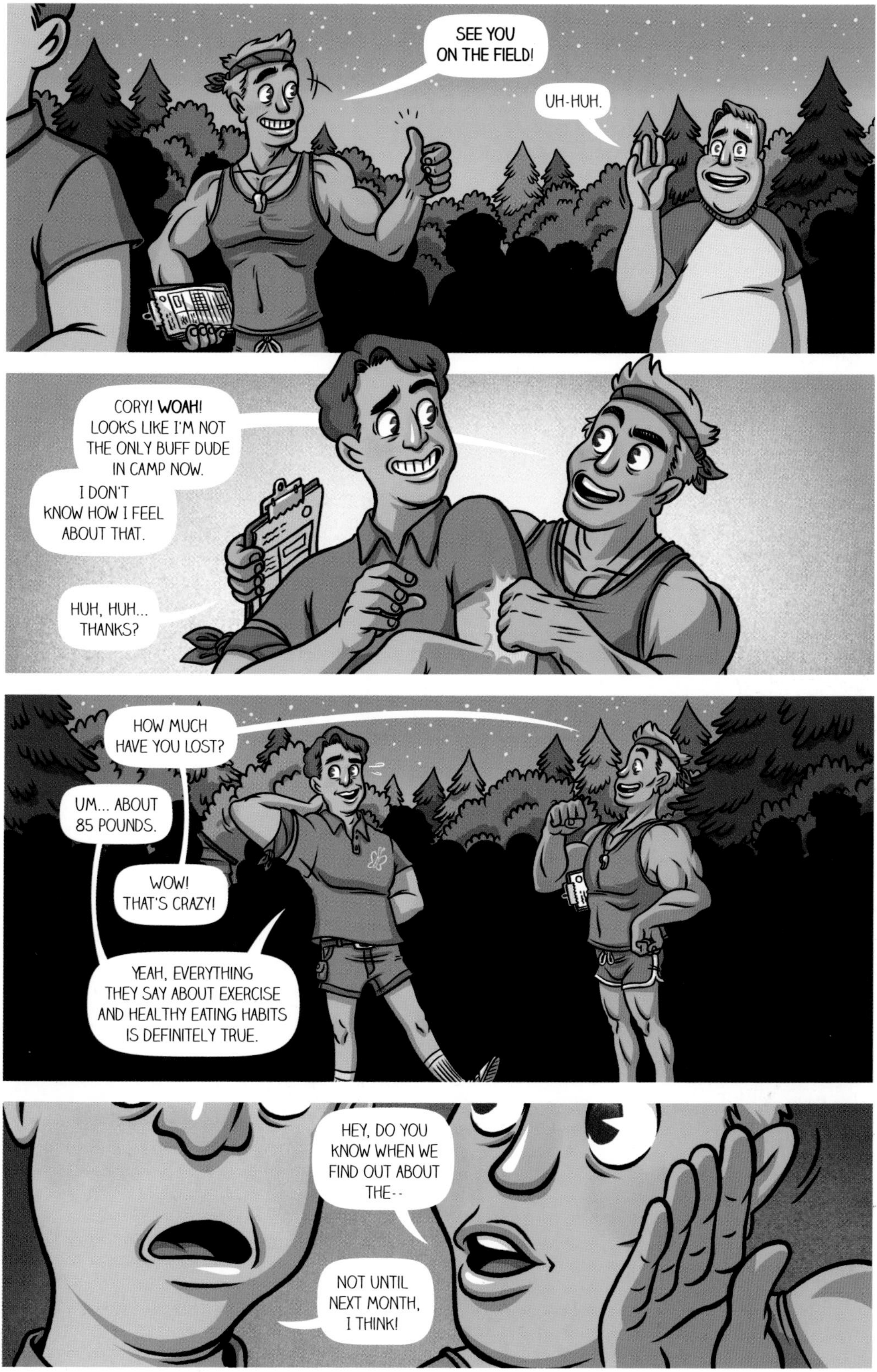
SEE YOU ON THE FIELD!
UH-HUH.
CORY! WOAH! LOOKS LIKE I'M NOT THE ONLY BUFF DUDE IN CAMP NOW.
I DON'T KNOW HOW I FEEL ABOUT THAT.
HUH, HUH... THANKS?
HOW MUCH HAVE YOU LOST?
UM... ABOUT 85 POUNDS.
WOW! THAT'S CRAZY!
YEAH, EVERYTHING THEY SAY ABOUT EXERCISE AND HEALTHY EATING HABITS IS DEFINITELY TRUE.
HEY, DO YOU KNOW WHEN WE FIND OUT ABOUT THE--
NOT UNTIL NEXT MONTH, I THINK!

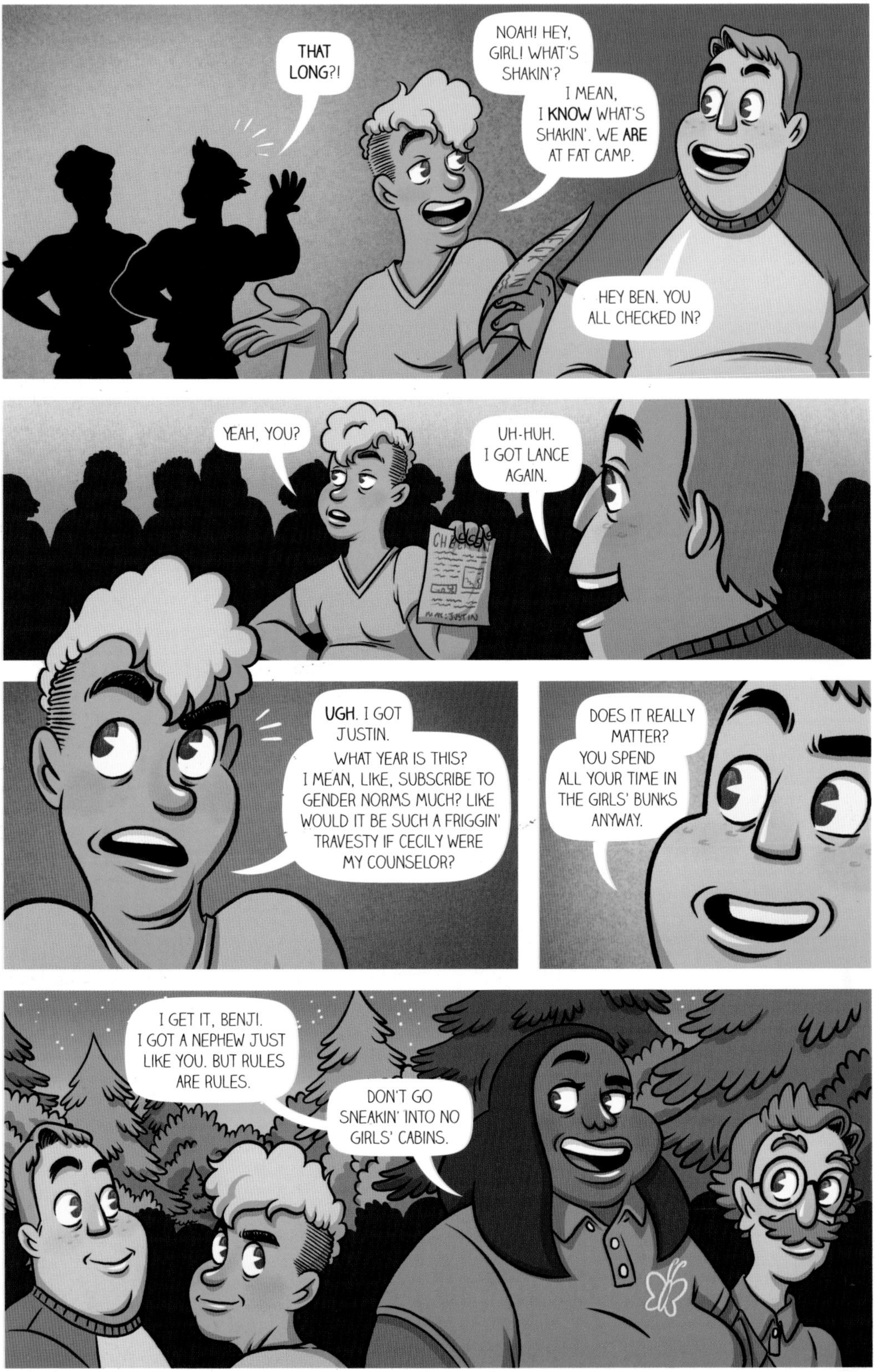
THAT LONG?!
NOAH! HEY, GIRL! WHAT'S SHAKIN'?
I MEAN, I KNOW WHAT'S SHAKIN'. WE ARE AT FAT CAMP.
HEY BEN. YOU ALL CHECKED IN?
YEAH, YOU?
UH-HUH. I GOT LANCE AGAIN.
UGH. I GOT JUSTIN.
WHAT YEAR IS THIS? I MEAN, LIKE, SUBSCRIBE TO GENDER NORMS MUCH? LIKE WOULD IT BE SUCH A FRIGGIN' TRAVESTY IF CECILY WERE MY COUNSELOR?
DOES IT REALLY MATTER?
YOU SPEND ALL YOUR TIME IN THE GIRLS' BUNKS ANYWAY.
I GET IT, BENJI. I GOT A NEPHEW JUST LIKE YOU. BUT RULES ARE RULES.
DON'T GO SNEAKIN' INTO NO GIRLS' CABINS.

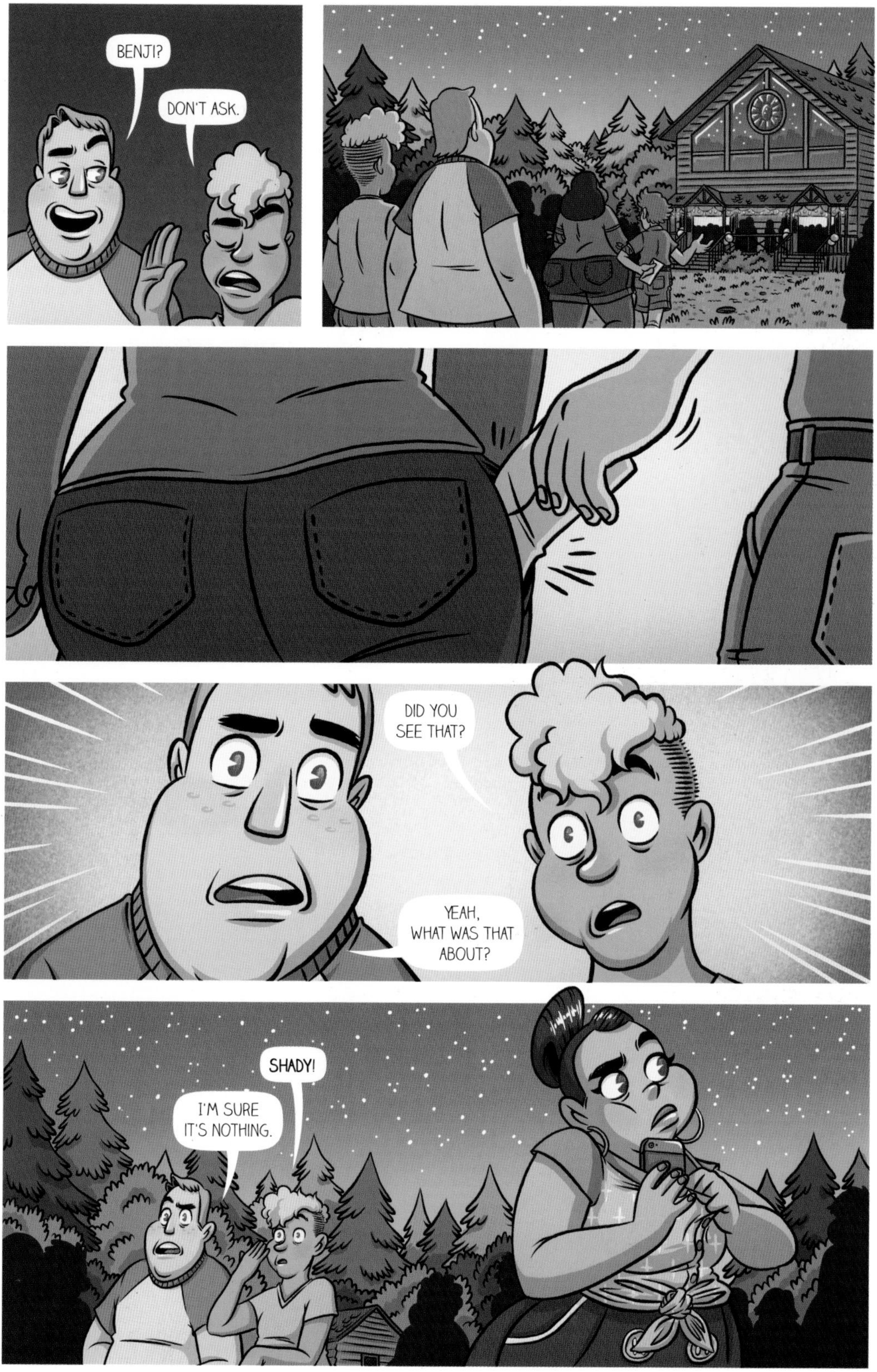
BENJI?
DON'T ASK.
DID YOU SEE THAT?
YEAH, WHAT WAS THAT ABOUT?
I'M SURE IT'S NOTHING.
SHADY!

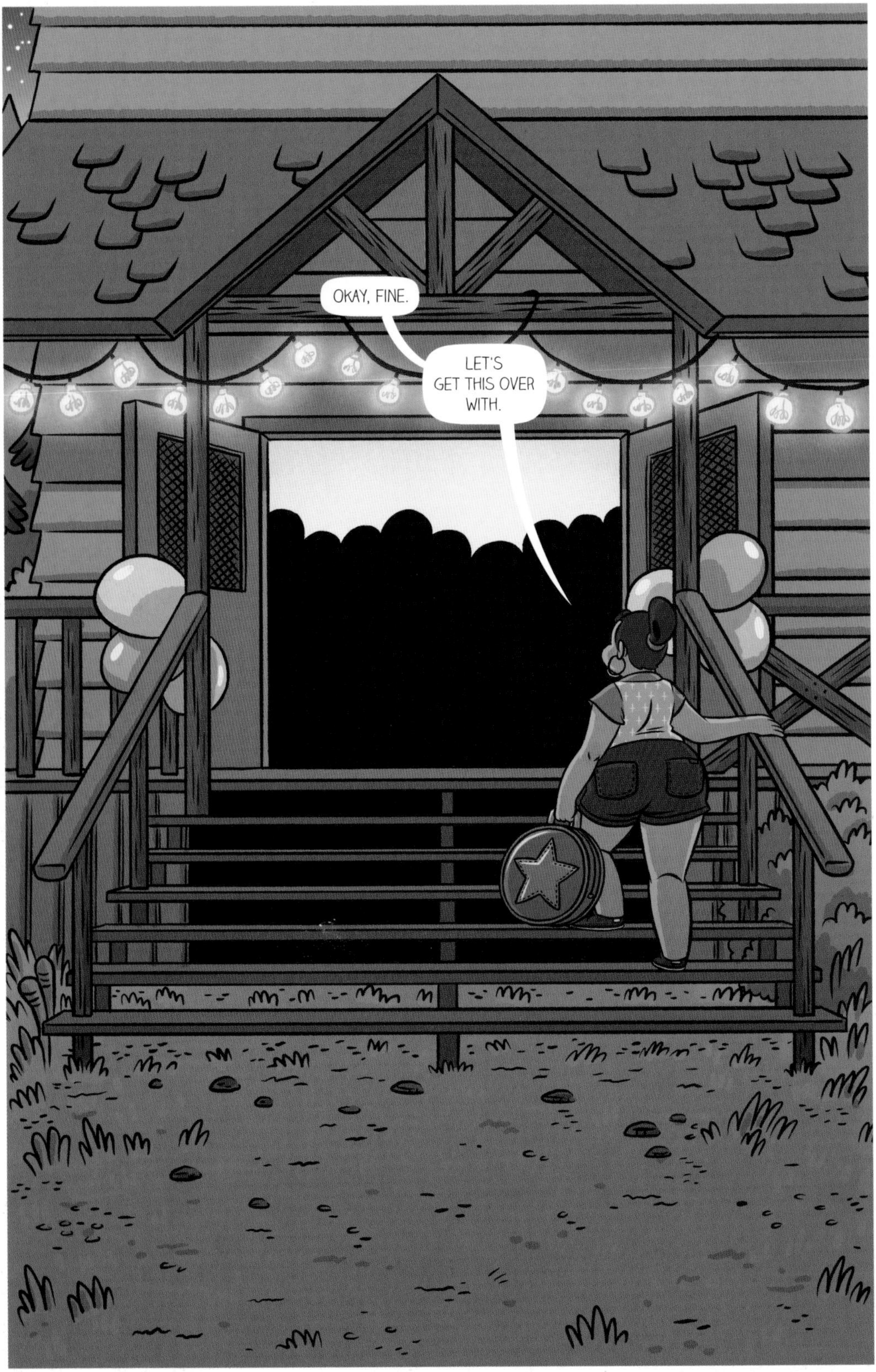
OKAY, FINE.
LET'S GET THIS OVER WITH.

CHAPTER TWO

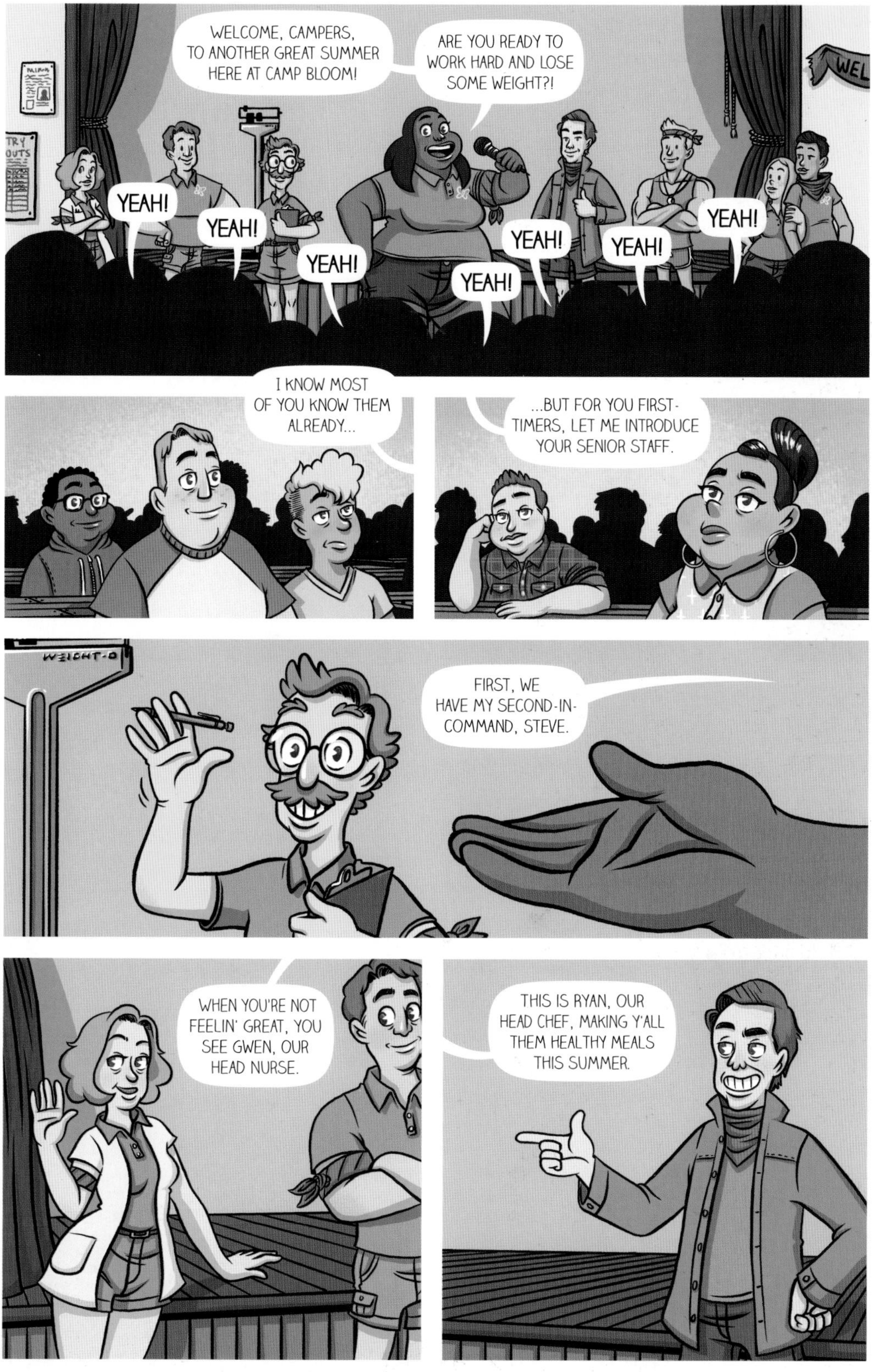

TRY OUTS
WEL
WELCOME, CAMPERS, TO ANOTHER GREAT SUMMER HERE AT CAMP BLOOM!
ARE YOU READY TO WORK HARD AND LOSE SOME WEIGHT?!
YEAH!
YEAH!
YEAH!
YEAH!
YEAH!
YEAH!
YEAH!
I KNOW MOST OF YOU KNOW THEM ALREADY...
...BUT FOR YOU FIRST-TIMERS, LET ME INTRODUCE YOUR SENIOR STAFF.
WEIGHT-O
FIRST, WE HAVE MY SECOND-IN-COMMAND, STEVE.
WHEN YOU'RE NOT FEELIN' GREAT, YOU SEE GWEN, OUR HEAD NURSE.
THIS IS RYAN, OUR HEAD CHEF, MAKING Y'ALL THEM HEALTHY MEALS THIS SUMMER.

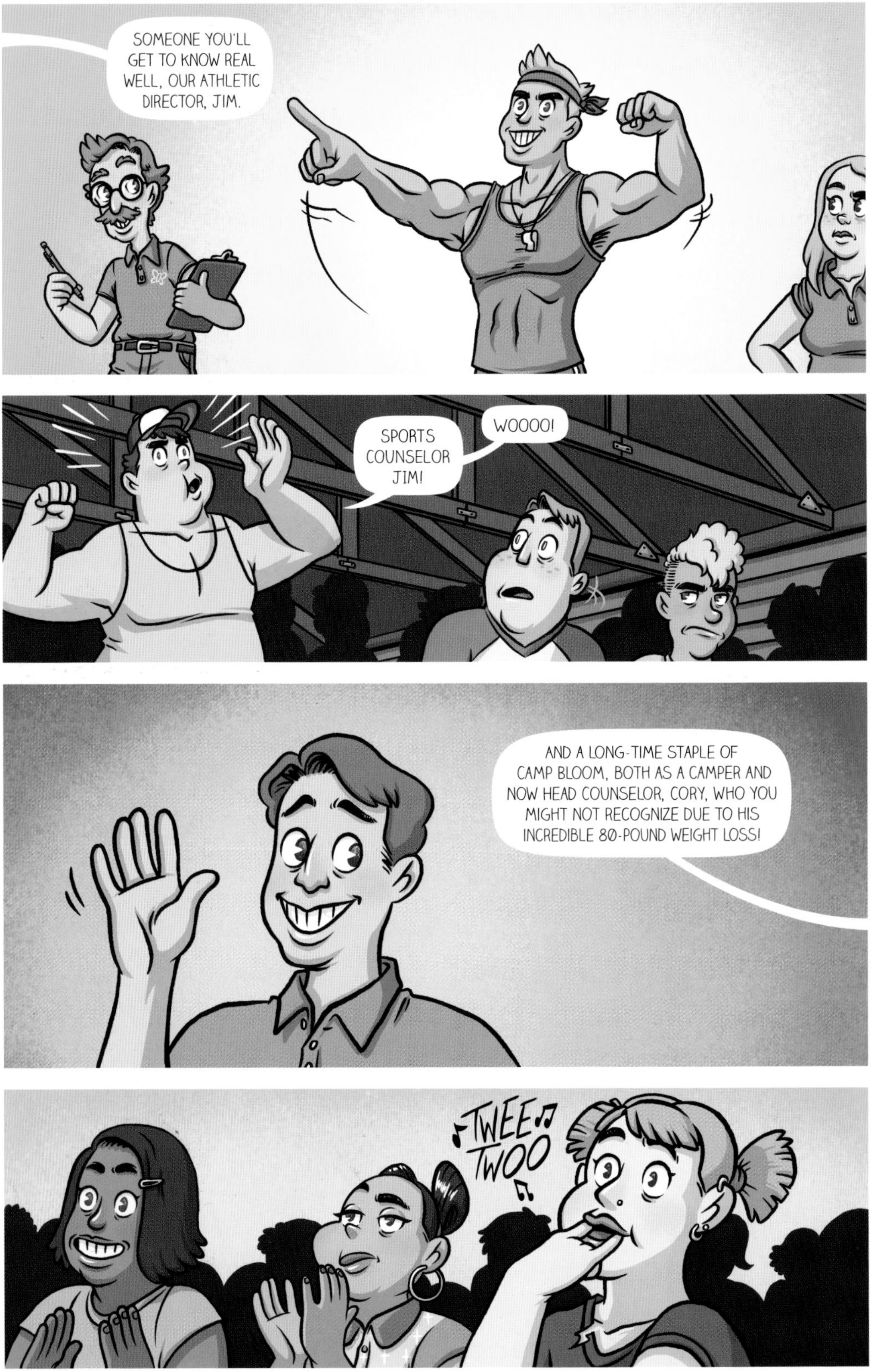
SOMEONE YOU'LL GET TO KNOW REAL WELL, OUR ATHLETIC DIRECTOR, JIM.
SPORTS COUNSELOR JIM!
WOOOO!
AND A LONG-TIME STAPLE OF CAMP BLOOM, BOTH AS A CAMPER AND NOW HEAD COUNSELOR, CORY, WHO YOU MIGHT NOT RECOGNIZE DUE TO HIS INCREDIBLE 80-POUND WEIGHT LOSS!
TWEE TWOO

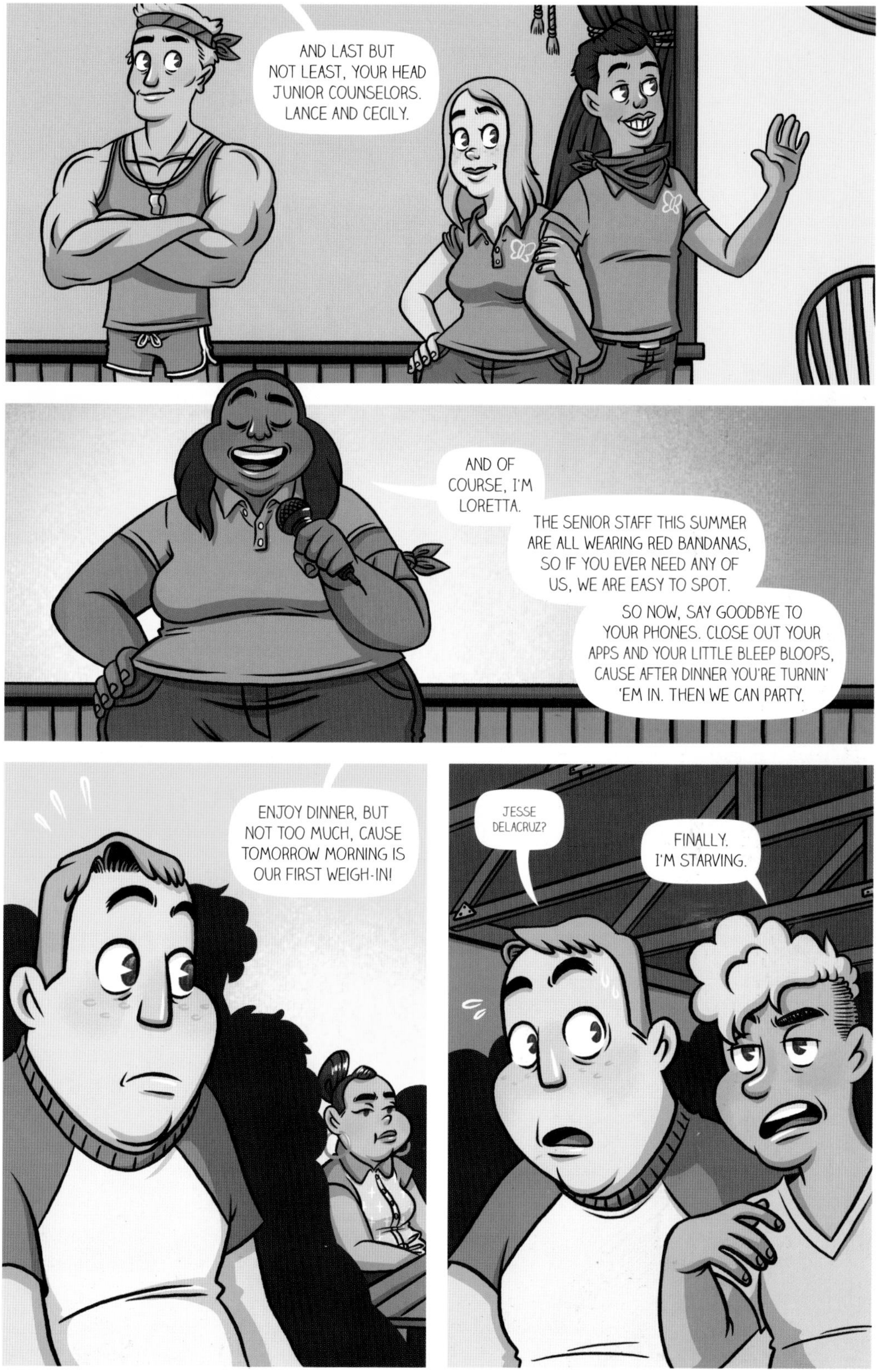
AND LAST BUT NOT LEAST, YOUR HEAD JUNIOR COUNSELORS. LANCE AND CECILY.
AND OF COURSE, I'M LORETTA.
THE SENIOR STAFF THIS SUMMER ARE ALL WEARING RED BANDANAS, SO IF YOU EVER NEED ANY OF US, WE ARE EASY TO SPOT.
SO NOW, SAY GOODBYE TO YOUR PHONES. CLOSE OUT YOUR APPS AND YOUR LITTLE BLEEP BLOOPS, CAUSE AFTER DINNER YOU'RE TURNIN' 'EM IN. THEN WE CAN PARTY.
ENJOY DINNER, BUT NOT TOO MUCH, CAUSE TOMORROW MORNING IS OUR FIRST WEIGH-IN!
JESSE DELACRUZ?
FINALLY. I'M STARVING.

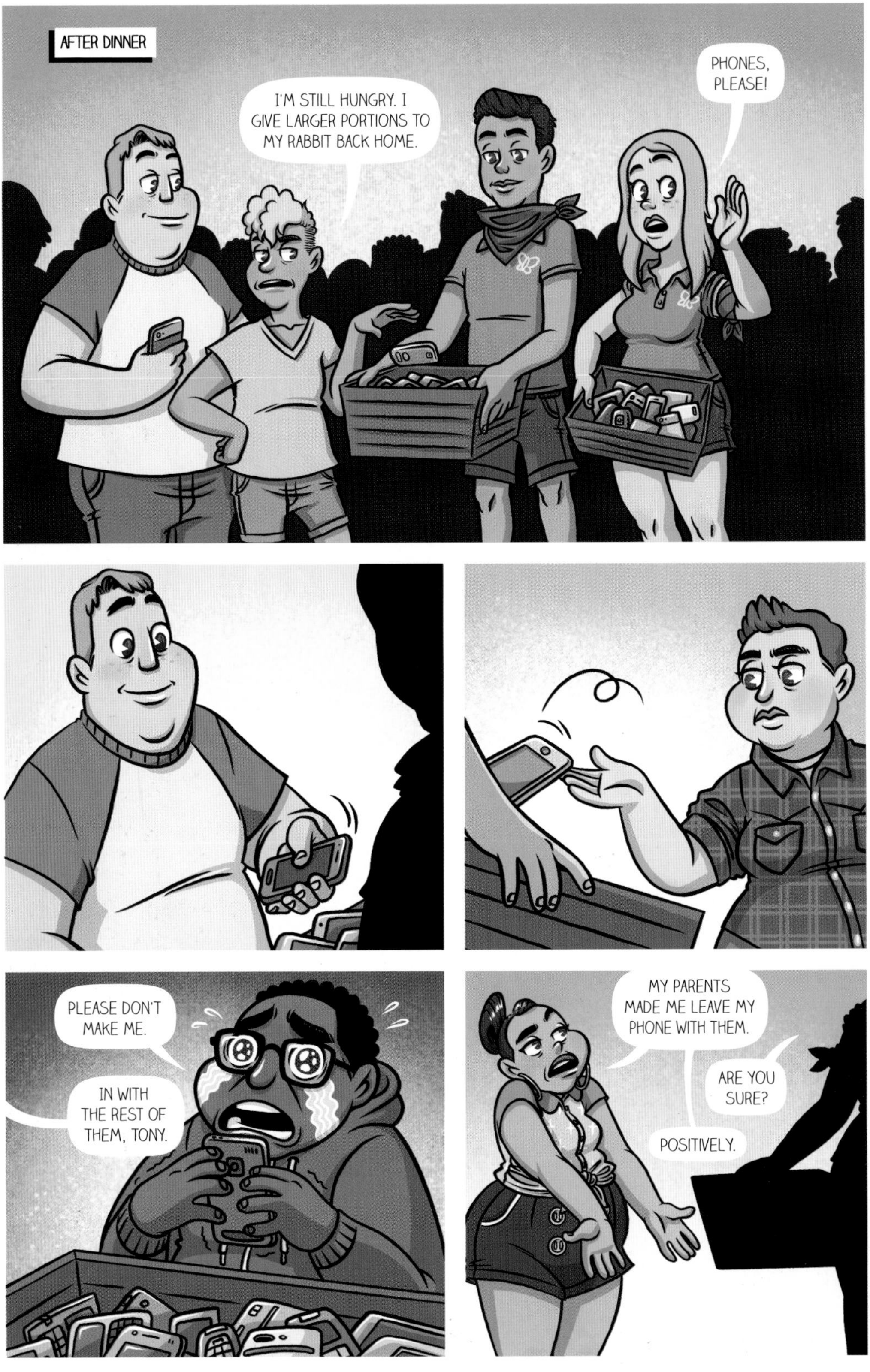
AFTER DINNER
I'M STILL HUNGRY. I GIVE LARGER PORTIONS TO MY RABBIT BACK HOME.
PHONES, PLEASE!
PLEASE DON'T MAKE ME.
IN WITH THE REST OF THEM, TONY.
MY PARENTS MADE ME LEAVE MY PHONE WITH THEM.
ARE YOU SURE?
POSITIVELY.

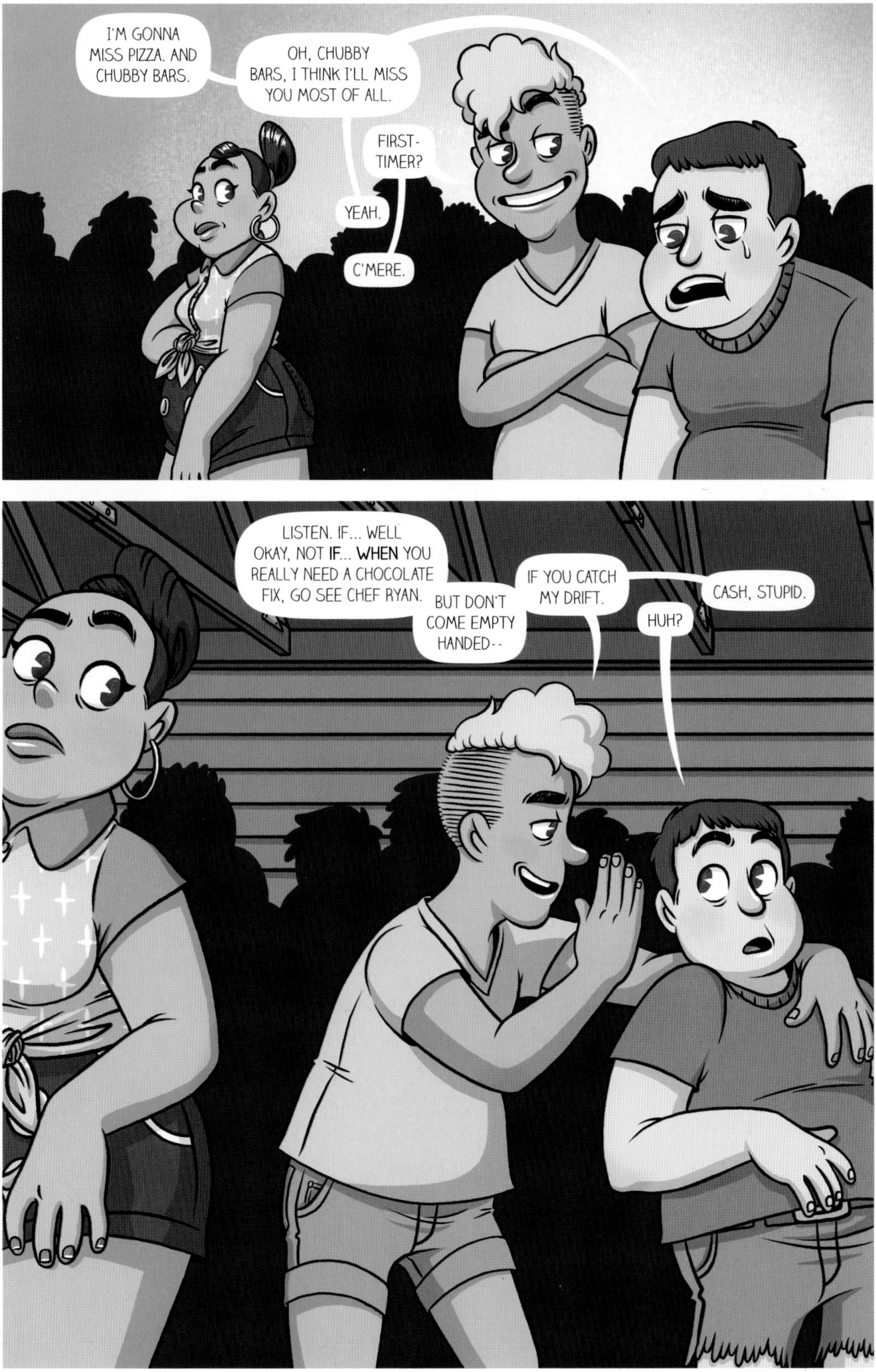
I'M GONNA MISS PIZZA. AND CHUBBY BARS.
OH, CHUBBY BARS, I THINK I'LL MISS YOU MOST OF ALL.
FIRST-TIMER?
YEAH.
C'MERE.
LISTEN. IF... WELL OKAY, NOT IF... WHEN YOU REALLY NEED A CHOCOLATE FIX, GO SEE CHEF RYAN.
BUT DON'T COME EMPTY HANDED--
IF YOU CATCH MY DRIFT.
HUH?
CASH, STUPID.

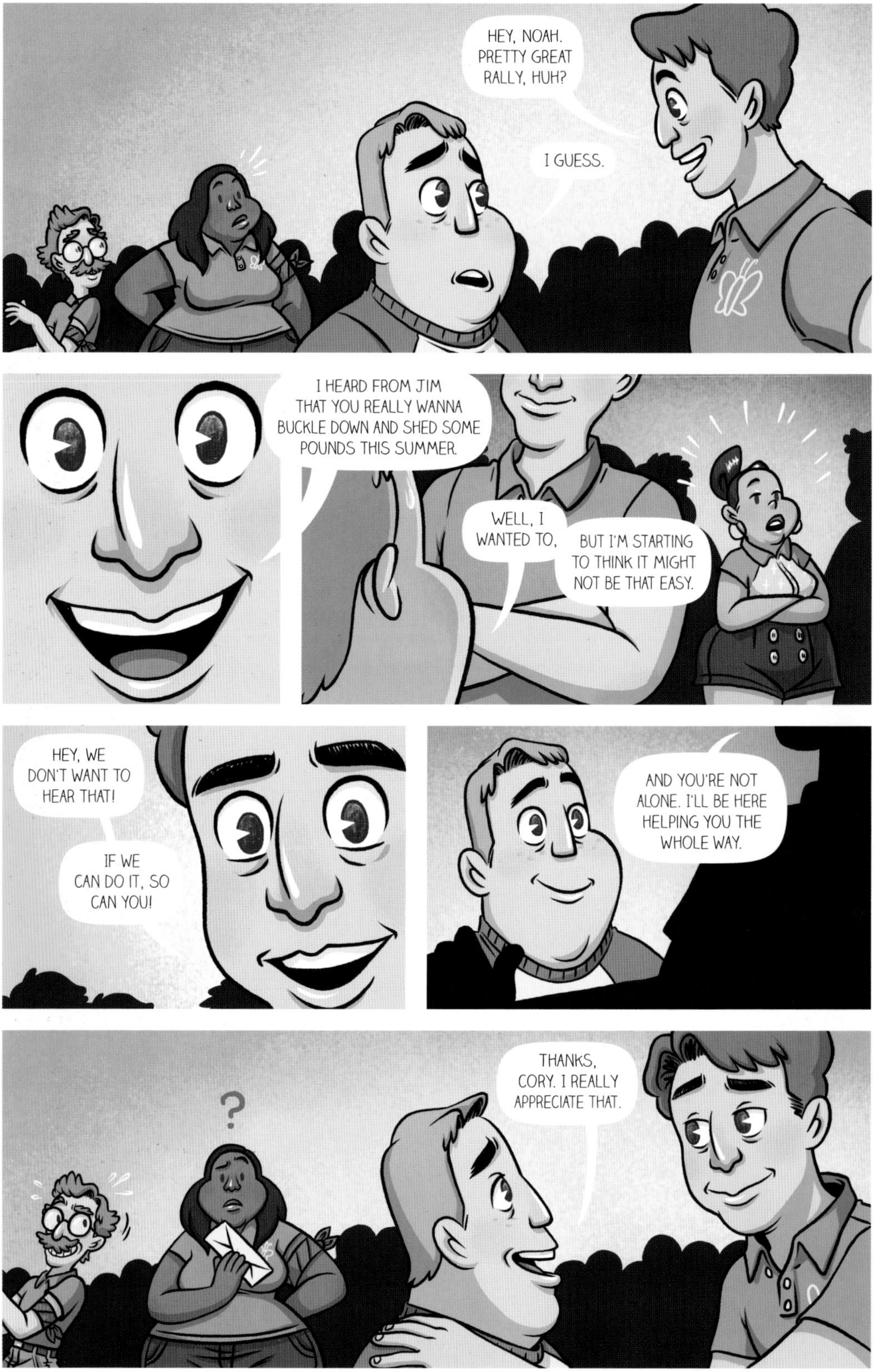
HEY, NOAH. PRETTY GREAT RALLY, HUH?
I GUESS.
I HEARD FROM JIM THAT YOU REALLY WANNA BUCKLE DOWN AND SHED SOME POUNDS THIS SUMMER.
WELL, I WANTED TO,
BUT I'M STARTING TO THINK IT MIGHT NOT BE THAT EASY.
HEY, WE DON'T WANT TO HEAR THAT!
IF WE CAN DO IT, SO CAN YOU!
AND YOU'RE NOT ALONE. I'LL BE HERE HELPING YOU THE WHOLE WAY.
?
THANKS, CORY. I REALLY APPRECIATE THAT.

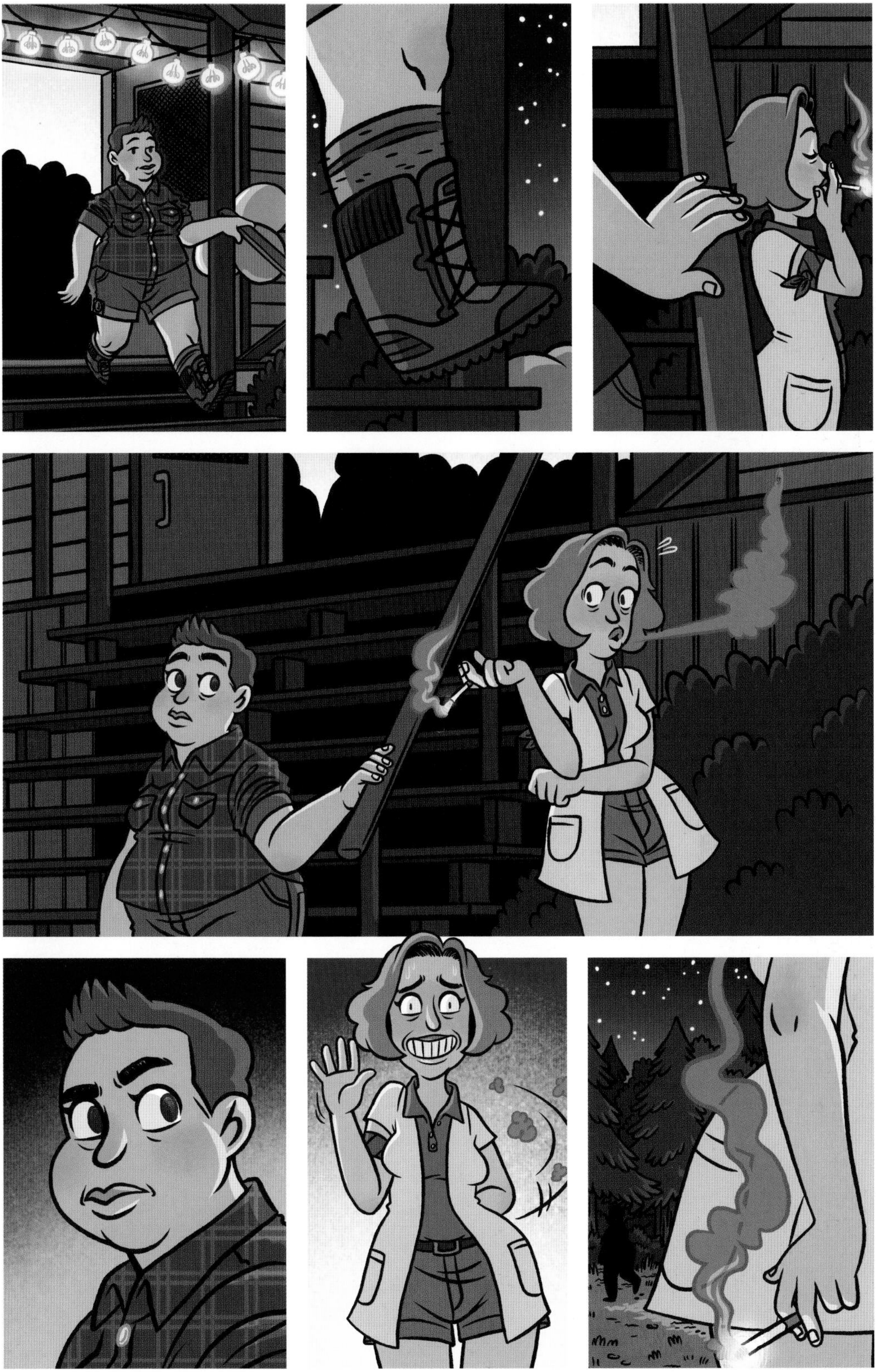

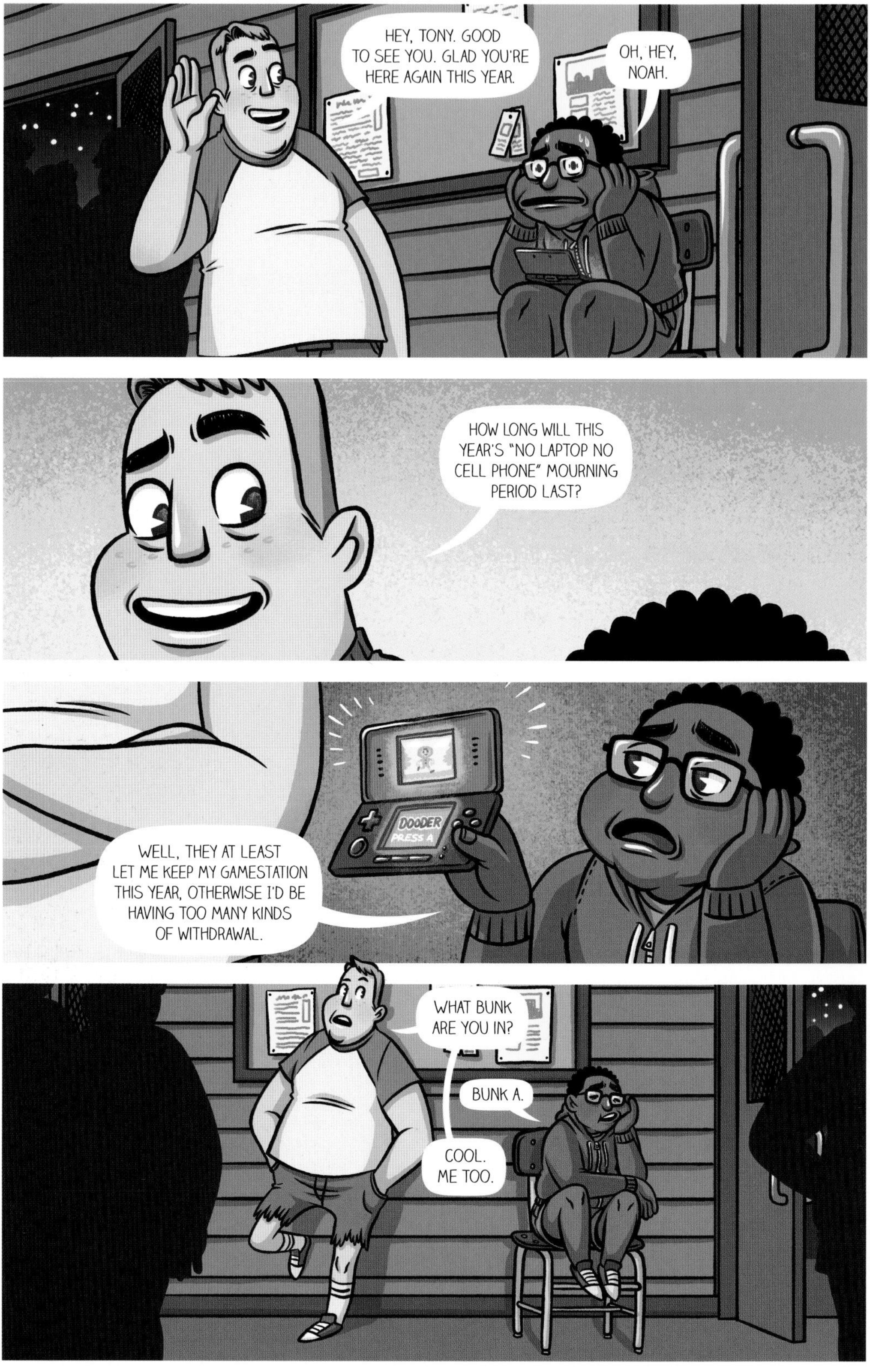
HEY, TONY. GOOD TO SEE YOU. GLAD YOU'RE HERE AGAIN THIS YEAR.
OH, HEY, NOAH.
HOW LONG WILL THIS YEAR'S "NO LAPTOP NO CELL PHONE" MOURNING PERIOD LAST?
DOODER
PRESS A
WELL, THEY AT LEAST LET ME KEEP MY GAMESTATION THIS YEAR, OTHERWISE I'D BE HAVING TOO MANY KINDS OF WITHDRAWAL.
WHAT BUNK ARE YOU IN?
BUNK A.
COOL. ME TOO.

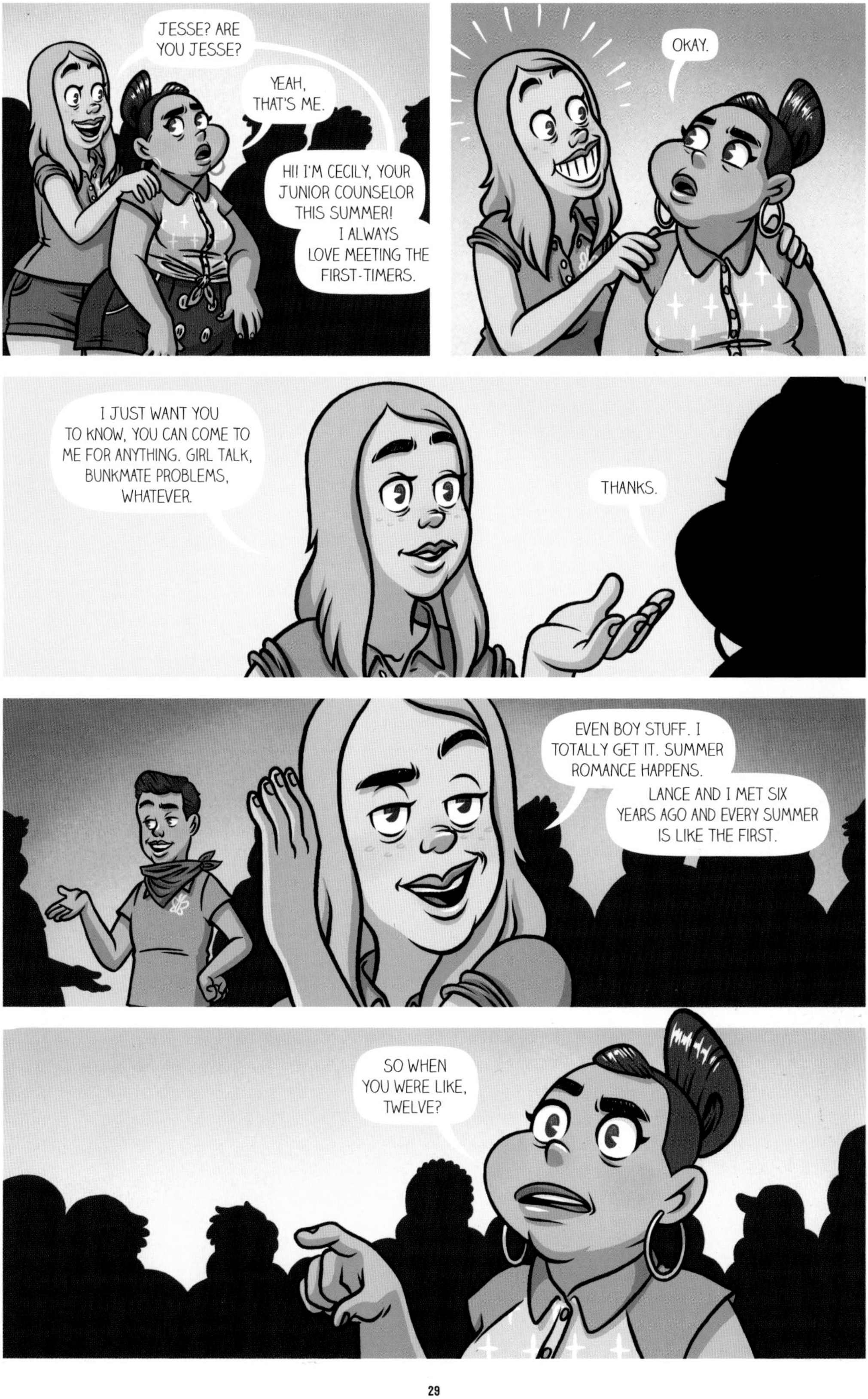
JESSE? ARE YOU JESSE?
YEAH, THAT'S ME.
HI! I'M CECILY, YOUR JUNIOR COUNSELOR THIS SUMMER!
I ALWAYS LOVE MEETING THE FIRST-TIMERS.
OKAY.
I JUST WANT YOU TO KNOW, YOU CAN COME TO ME FOR ANYTHING. GIRL TALK, BUNKMATE PROBLEMS, WHATEVER.
THANKS.
EVEN BOY STUFF. I TOTALLY GET IT. SUMMER ROMANCE HAPPENS.
LANCE AND I MET SIX YEARS AGO AND EVERY SUMMER IS LIKE THE FIRST.
SO WHEN YOU WERE LIKE, TWELVE?

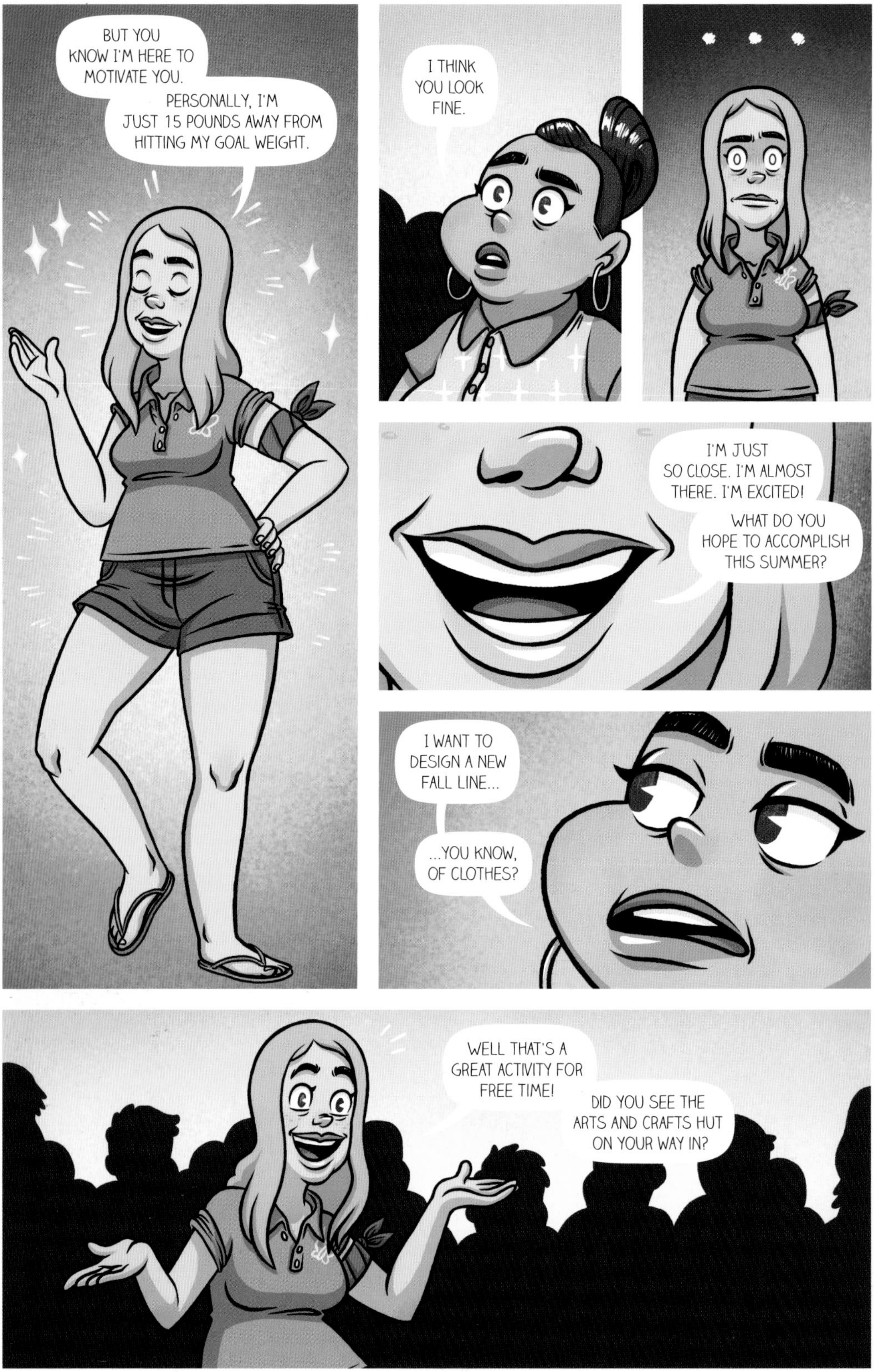
BUT YOU KNOW I'M HERE TO MOTIVATE YOU.
PERSONALLY, I'M JUST 15 POUNDS AWAY FROM HITTING MY GOAL WEIGHT.
I THINK YOU LOOK FINE.
I'M JUST SO CLOSE. I'M ALMOST THERE. I'M EXCITED!
WHAT DO YOU HOPE TO ACCOMPLISH THIS SUMMER?
I WANT TO DESIGN A NEW FALL LINE...
...YOU KNOW, OF CLOTHES?
WELL THAT'S A GREAT ACTIVITY FOR FREE TIME!
DID YOU SEE THE ARTS AND CRAFTS HUT ON YOUR WAY IN?

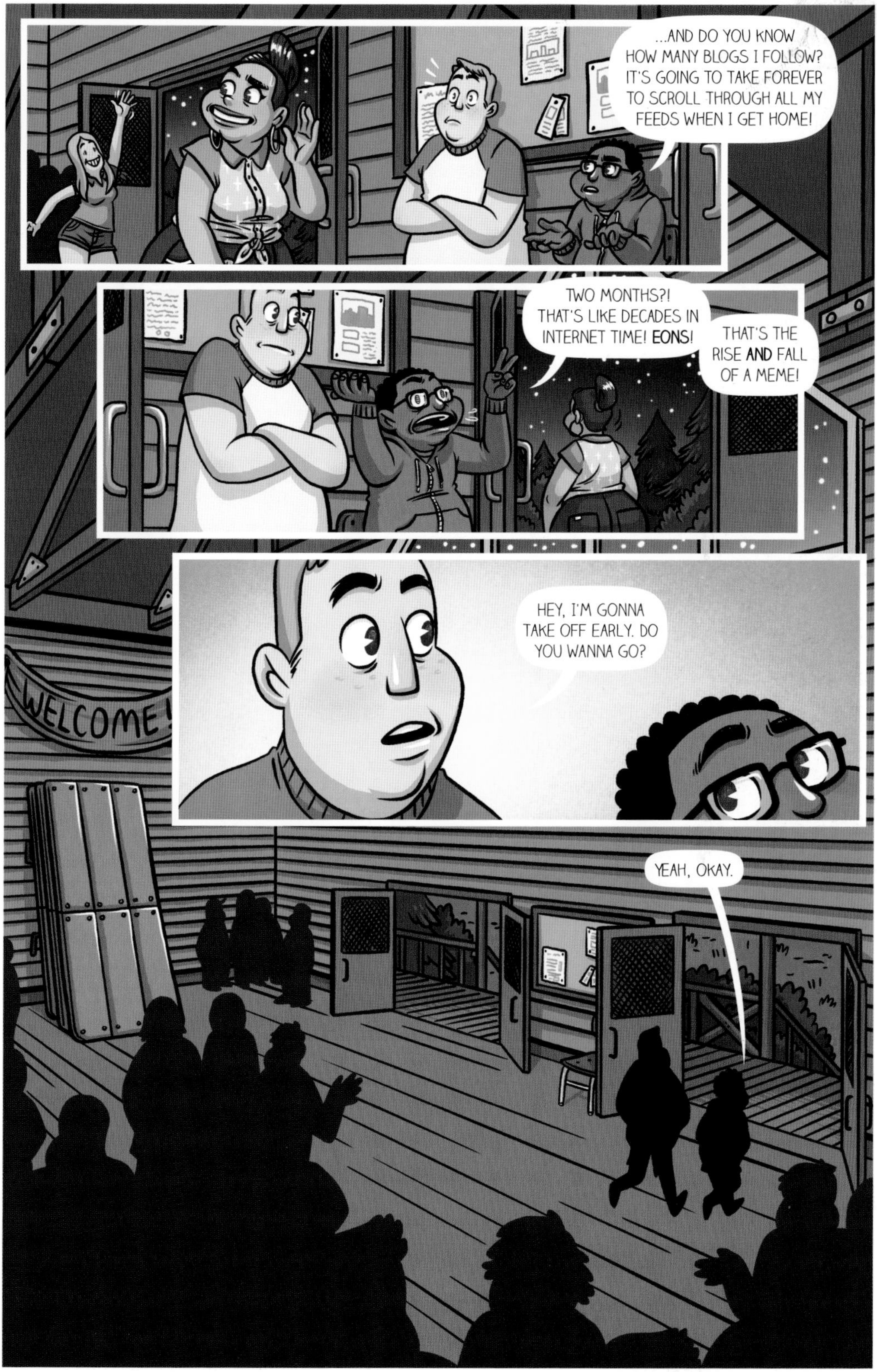
...AND DO YOU KNOW HOW MANY BLOGS I FOLLOW? IT'S GOING TO TAKE FOREVER TO SCROLL THROUGH ALL MY FEEDS WHEN I GET HOME!
TWO MONTHS?! THAT'S LIKE DECADES IN INTERNET TIME! **EONS**!
THAT'S THE RISE **AND** FALL OF A MEME!
HEY, I'M GONNA TAKE OFF EARLY. DO YOU WANNA GO?
WELCOME!
YEAH, OKAY.

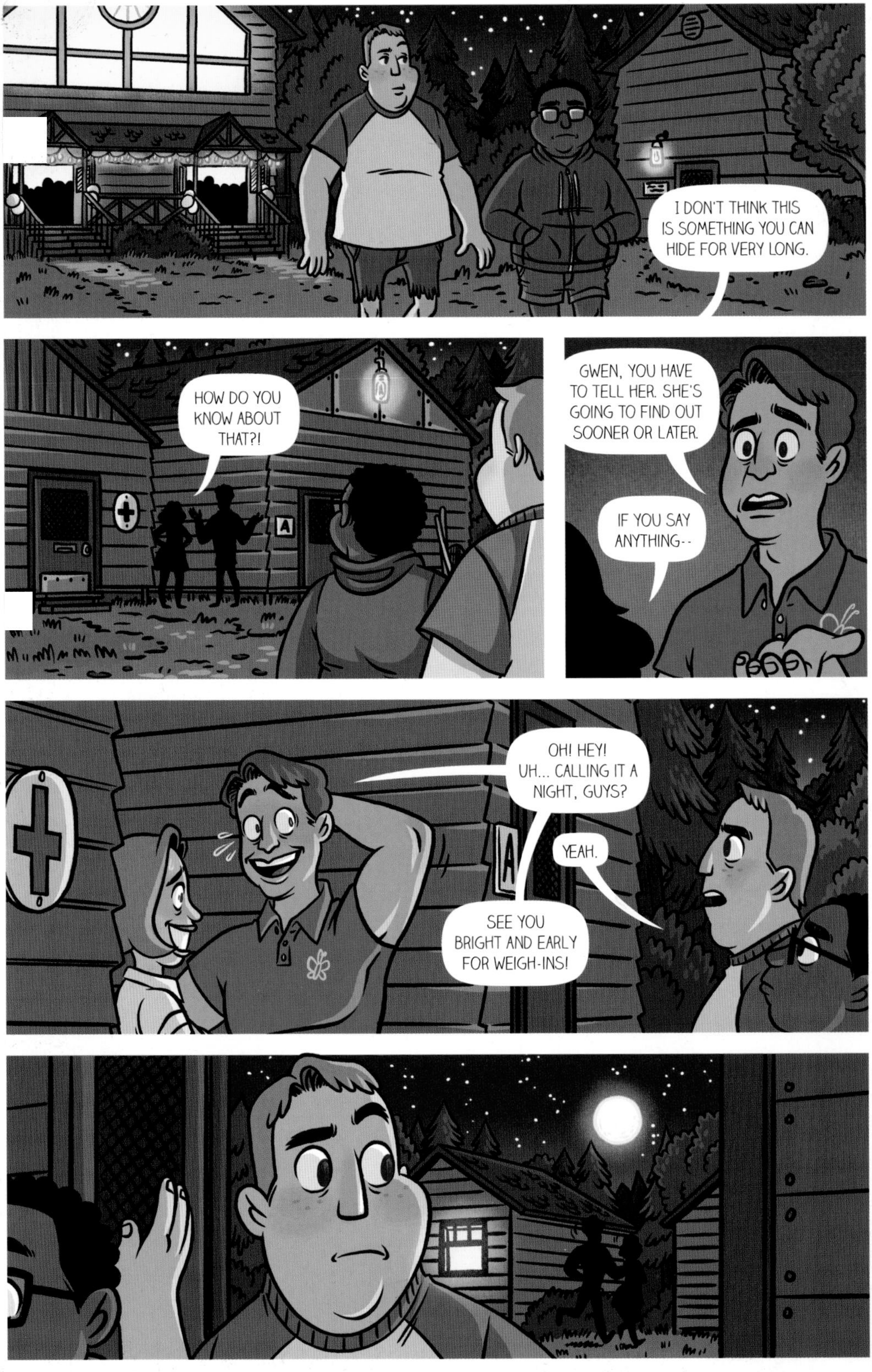

I DON'T THINK THIS IS SOMETHING YOU CAN HIDE FOR VERY LONG.
HOW DO YOU KNOW ABOUT THAT?!
GWEN, YOU HAVE TO TELL HER. SHE'S GOING TO FIND OUT SOONER OR LATER.
IF YOU SAY ANYTHING--
OH! HEY! UH... CALLING IT A NIGHT, GUYS?
YEAH.
SEE YOU BRIGHT AND EARLY FOR WEIGH-INS!

CHAPTER THREE

WEEK ONE.

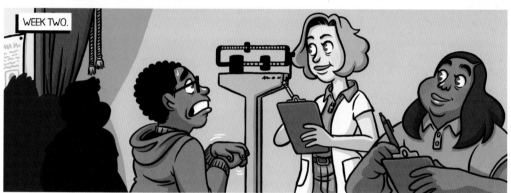

WEEK TWO.

WEEK THREE.

WEEK FOUR.

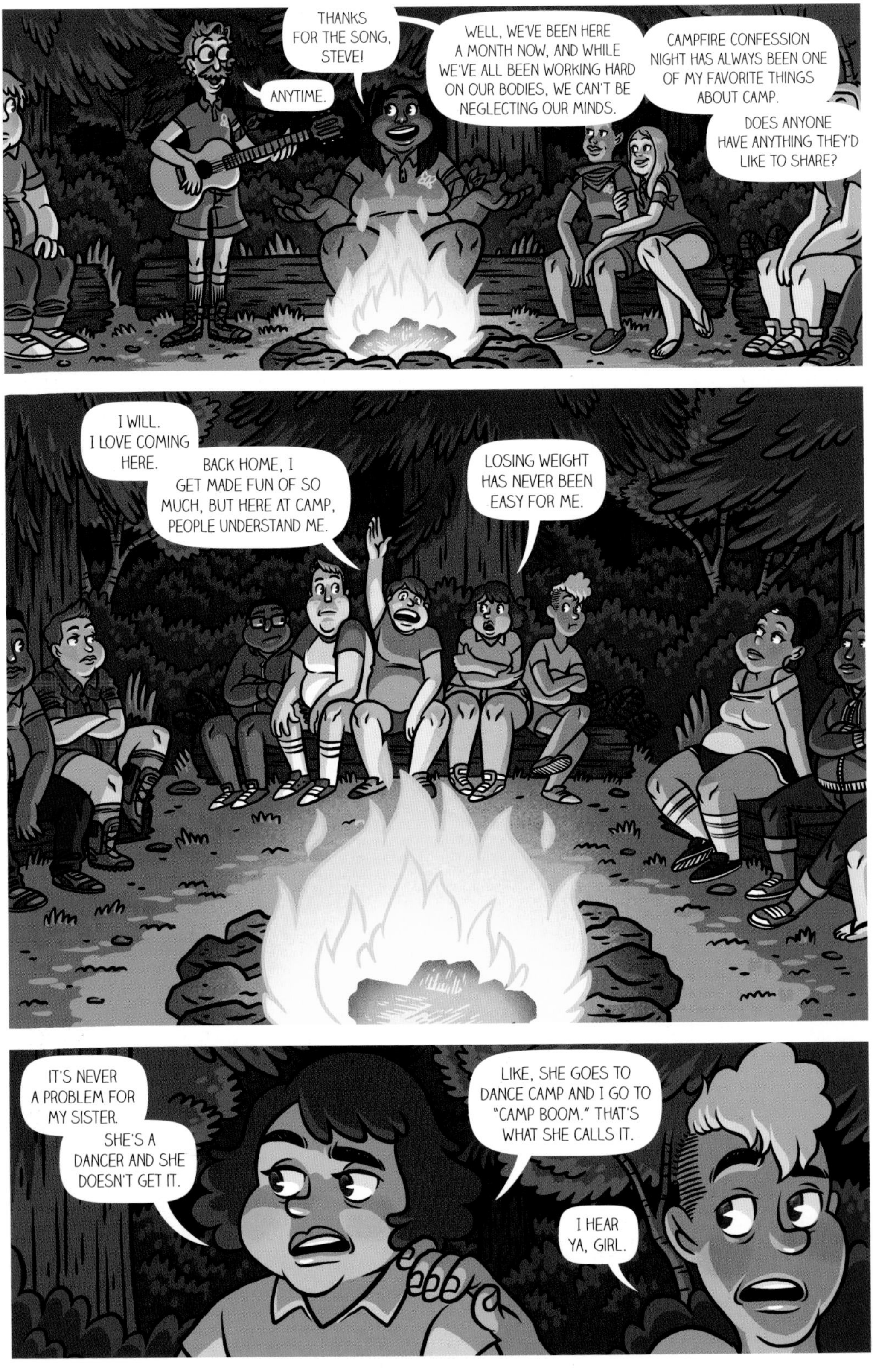
THANKS FOR THE SONG, STEVE!
ANYTIME.
WELL, WE'VE BEEN HERE A MONTH NOW, AND WHILE WE'VE ALL BEEN WORKING HARD ON OUR BODIES, WE CAN'T BE NEGLECTING OUR MINDS.
CAMPFIRE CONFESSION NIGHT HAS ALWAYS BEEN ONE OF MY FAVORITE THINGS ABOUT CAMP.
DOES ANYONE HAVE ANYTHING THEY'D LIKE TO SHARE?
I WILL. I LOVE COMING HERE.
BACK HOME, I GET MADE FUN OF SO MUCH, BUT HERE AT CAMP, PEOPLE UNDERSTAND ME.
LOSING WEIGHT HAS NEVER BEEN EASY FOR ME.
IT'S NEVER A PROBLEM FOR MY SISTER.
SHE'S A DANCER AND SHE DOESN'T GET IT.
LIKE, SHE GOES TO DANCE CAMP AND I GO TO "CAMP BOOM." THAT'S WHAT SHE CALLS IT.
I HEAR YA, GIRL.

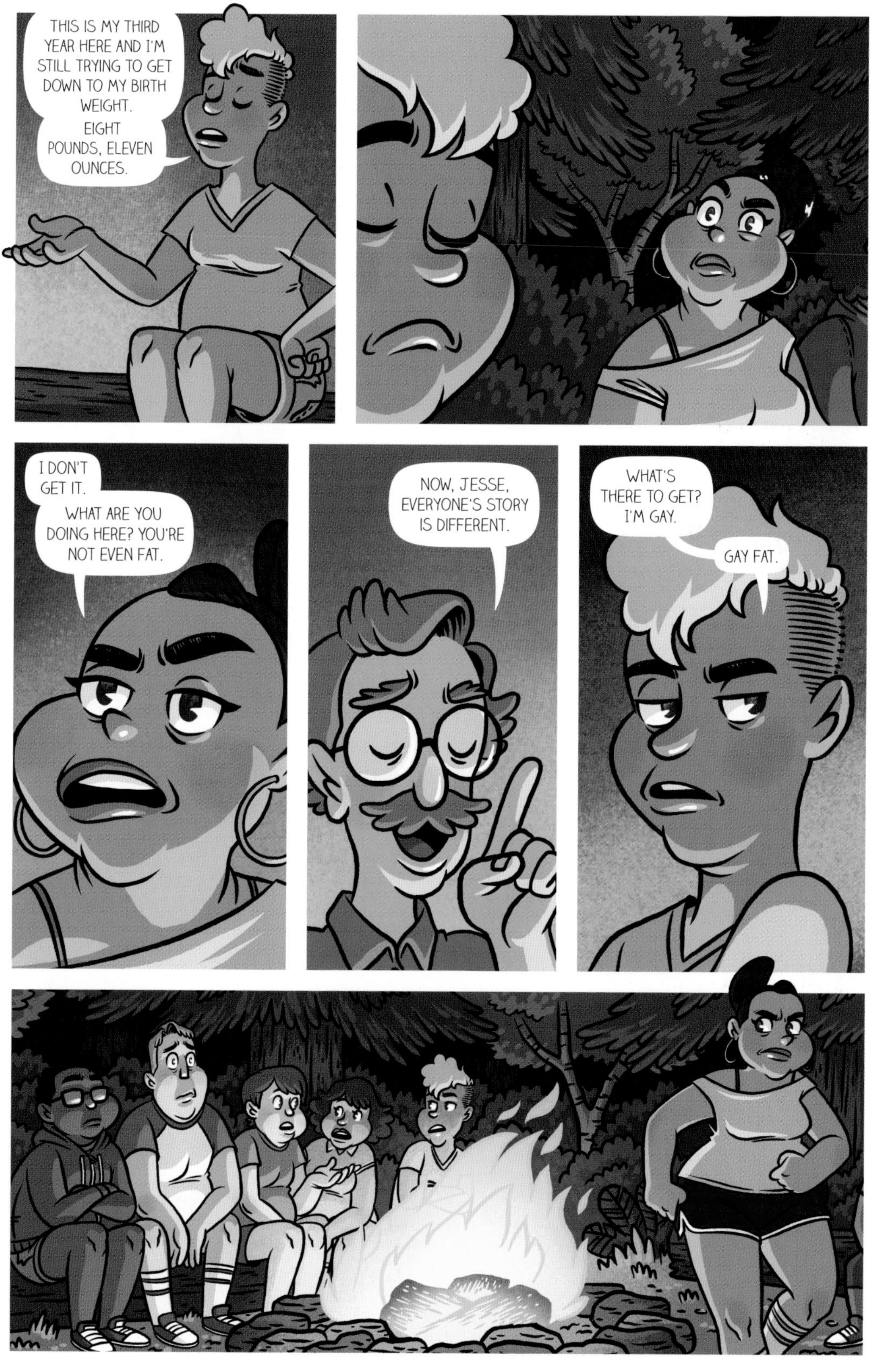
THIS IS MY THIRD YEAR HERE AND I'M STILL TRYING TO GET DOWN TO MY BIRTH WEIGHT.
EIGHT POUNDS, ELEVEN OUNCES.
I DON'T GET IT.
WHAT ARE YOU DOING HERE? YOU'RE NOT EVEN FAT.
NOW, JESSE, EVERYONE'S STORY IS DIFFERENT.
WHAT'S THERE TO GET? I'M GAY.
GAY FAT.

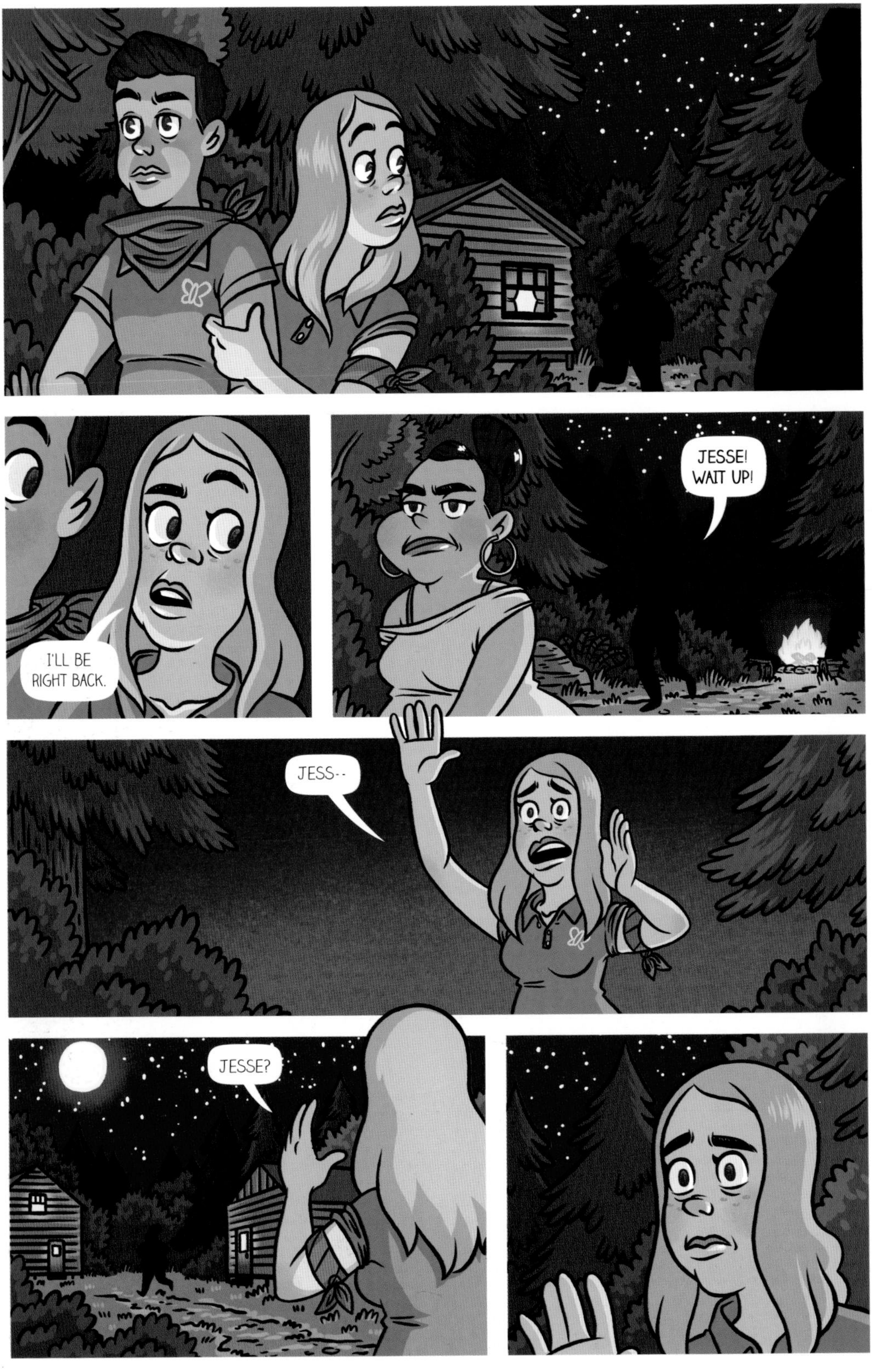
I'LL BE RIGHT BACK.
JESSE! WAIT UP!
JESS--
JESSE?

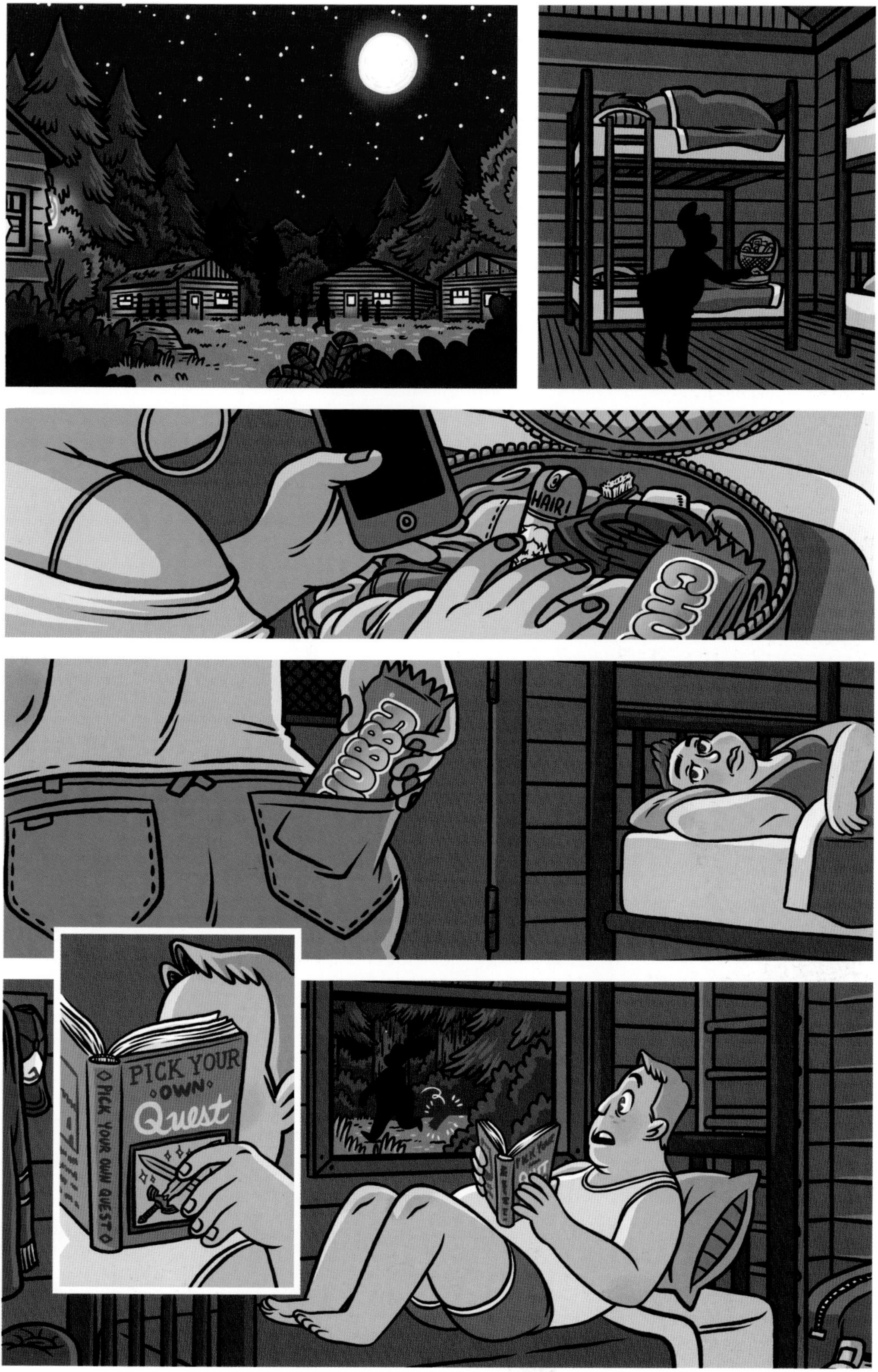
HAIR!
PICK YOUR OWN Quest
PICK YOUR OWN QUEST

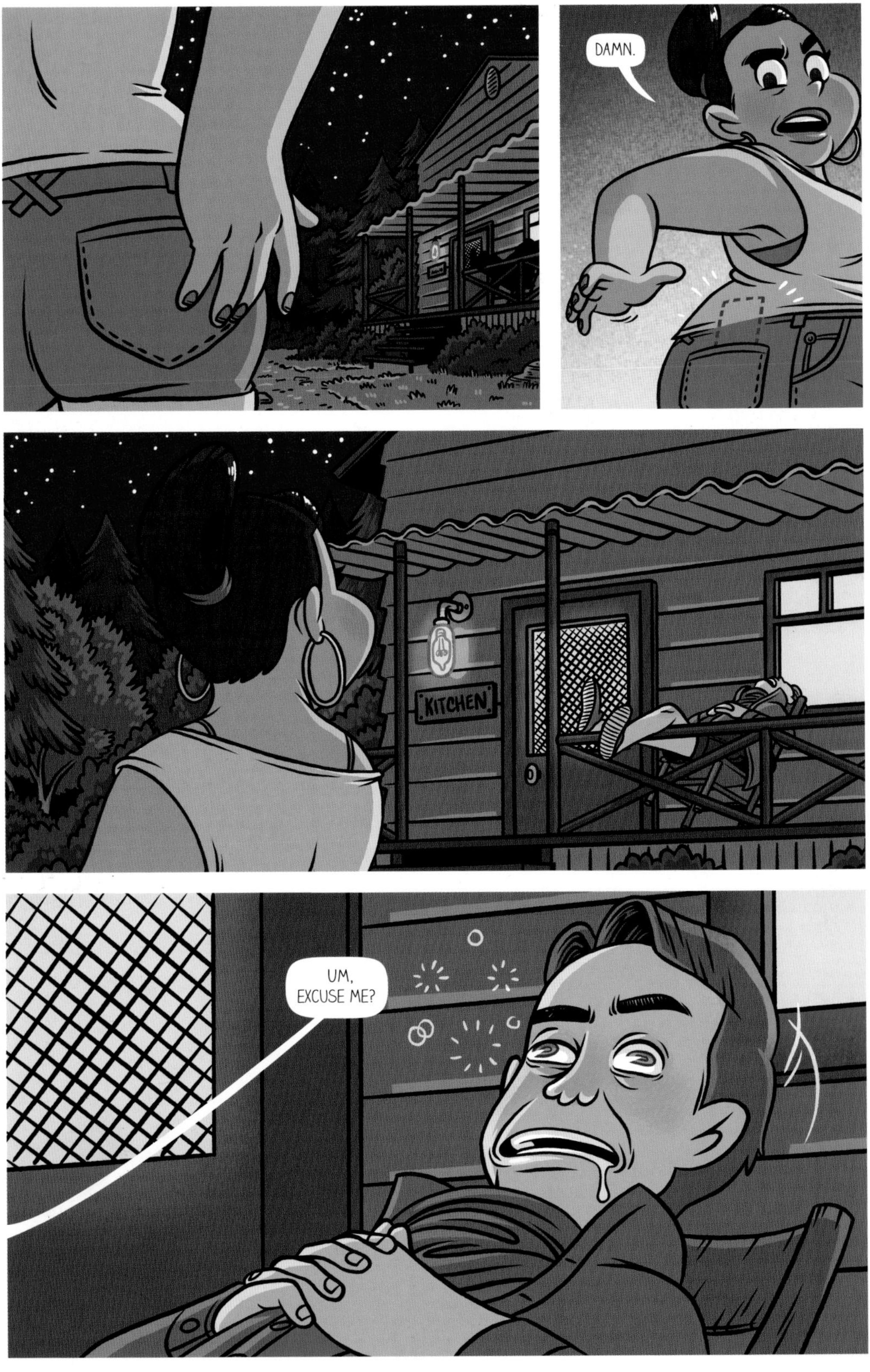
DAMN.
KITCHEN
UM, EXCUSE ME?

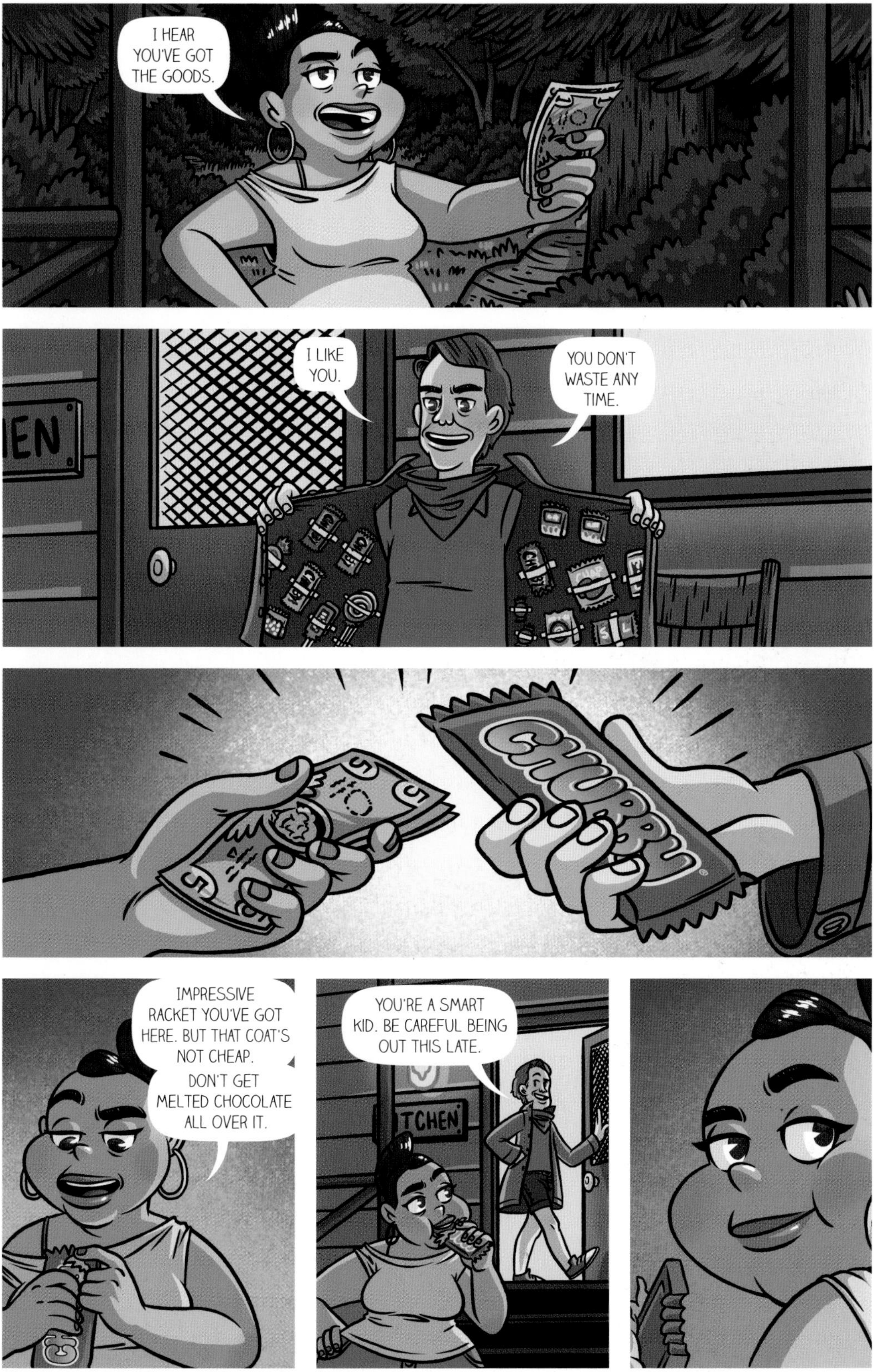
I HEAR YOU'VE GOT THE GOODS.
I LIKE YOU.
YOU DON'T WASTE ANY TIME.
CHUBBY
IMPRESSIVE RACKET YOU'VE GOT HERE. BUT THAT COAT'S NOT CHEAP.
DON'T GET MELTED CHOCOLATE ALL OVER IT.
YOU'RE A SMART KID. BE CAREFUL BEING OUT THIS LATE.
TCHEN

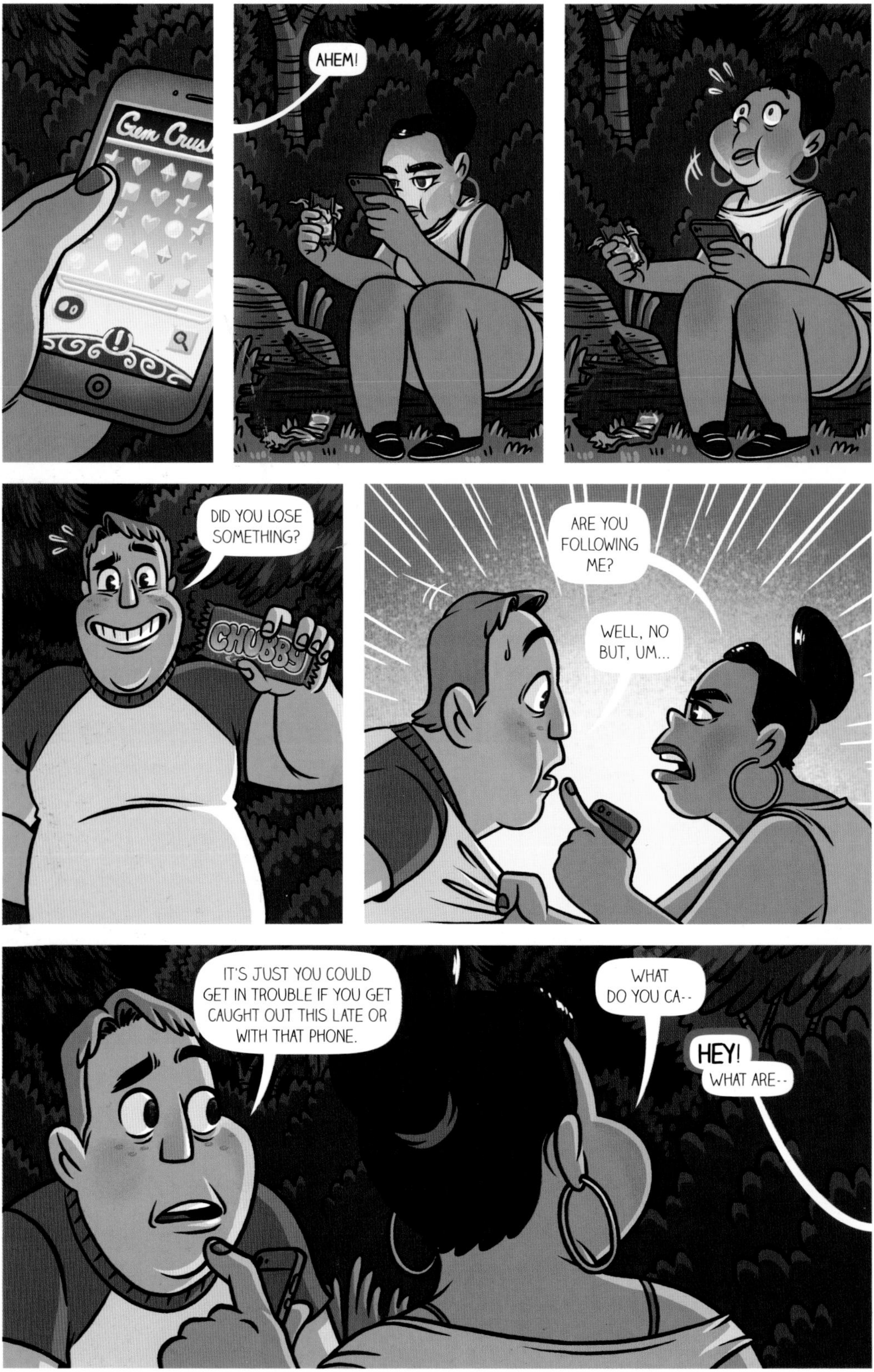
Gem Crush
AHEM!
DID YOU LOSE SOMETHING?
CHUBBY
ARE YOU FOLLOWING ME?
WELL, NO BUT, UM...
IT'S JUST YOU COULD GET IN TROUBLE IF YOU GET CAUGHT OUT THIS LATE OR WITH THAT PHONE.
WHAT DO YOU CA--
HEY!
WHAT ARE--

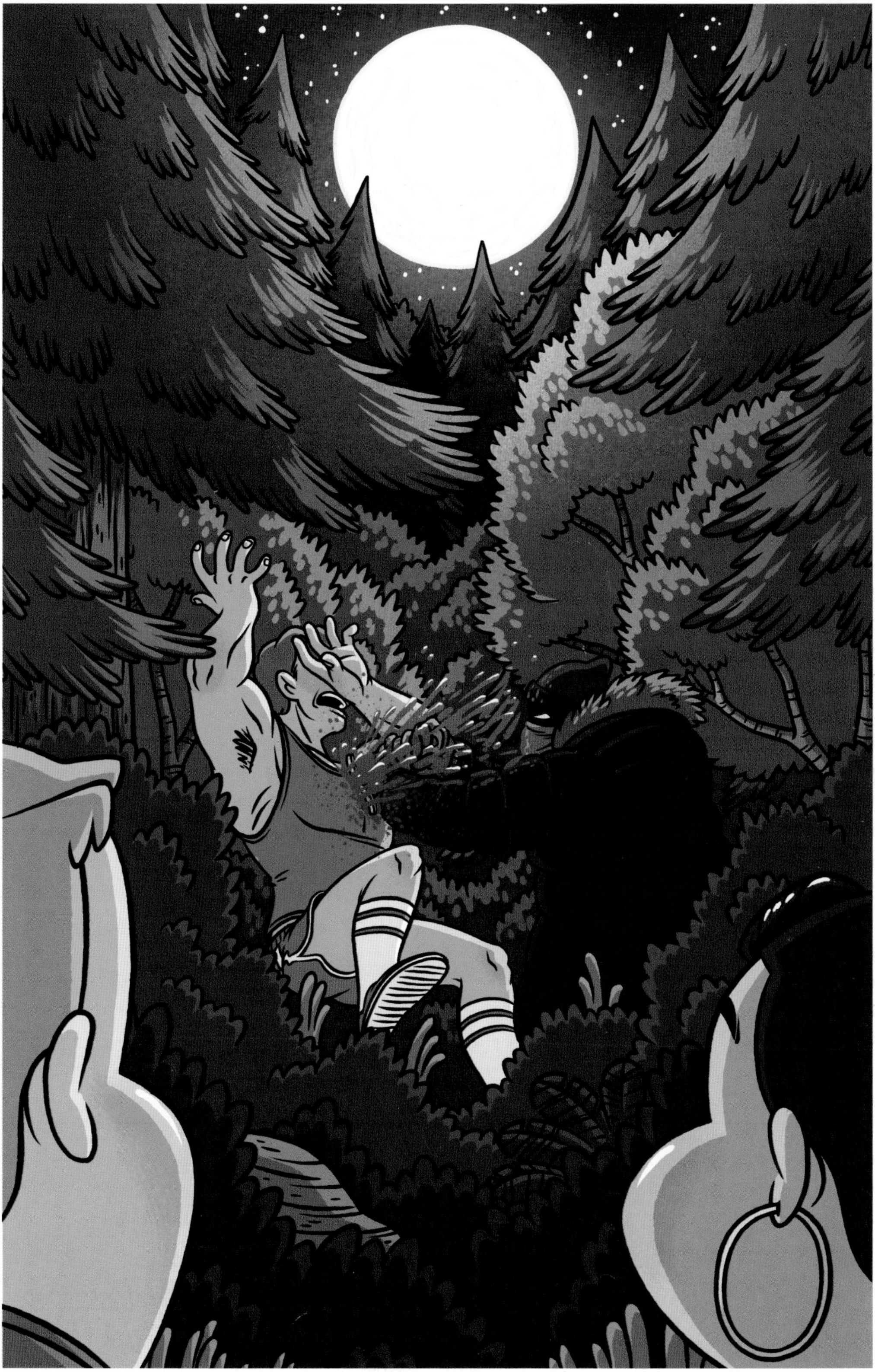

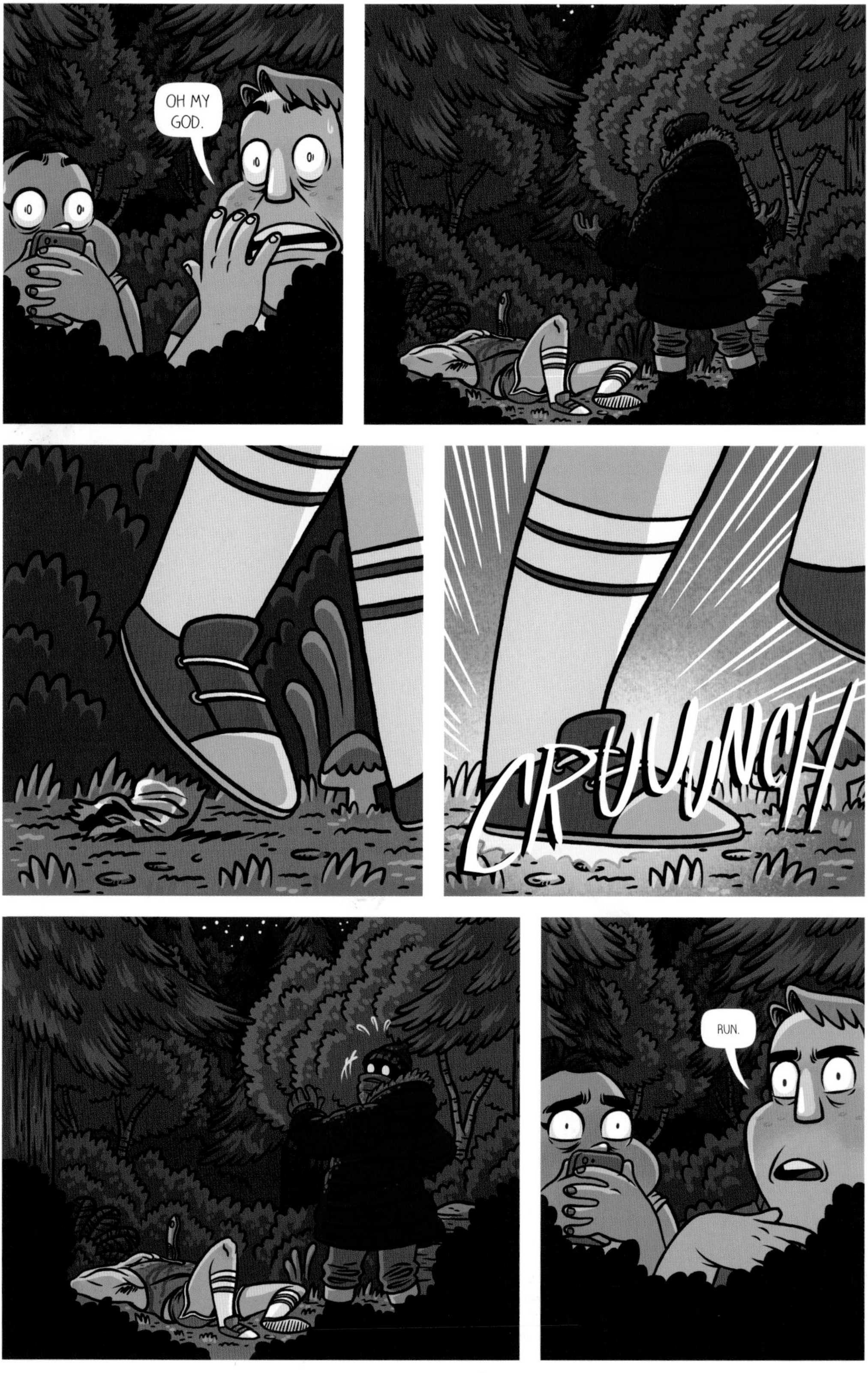
OH MY GOD.
CRUUUNCH
RUN.

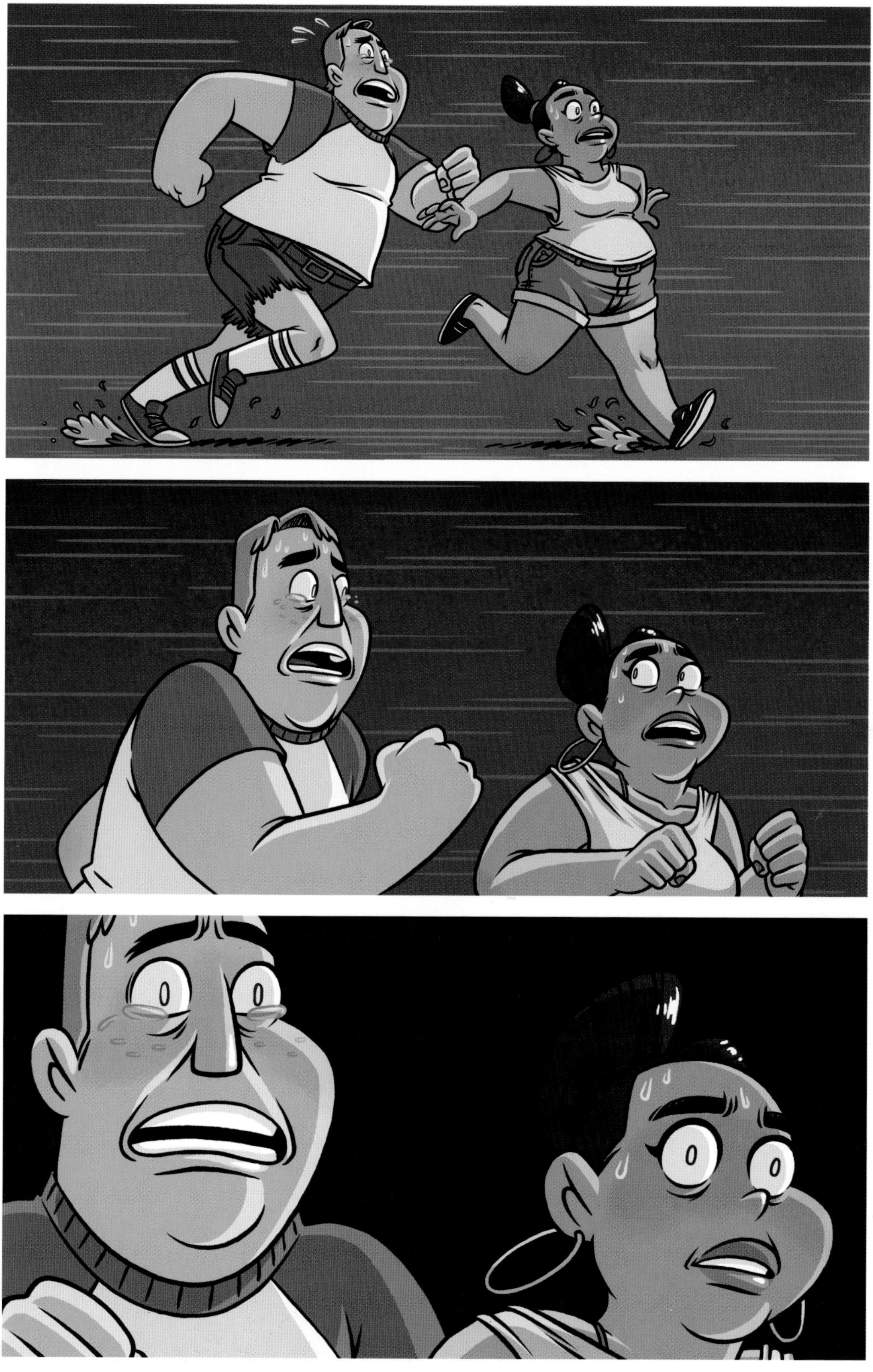

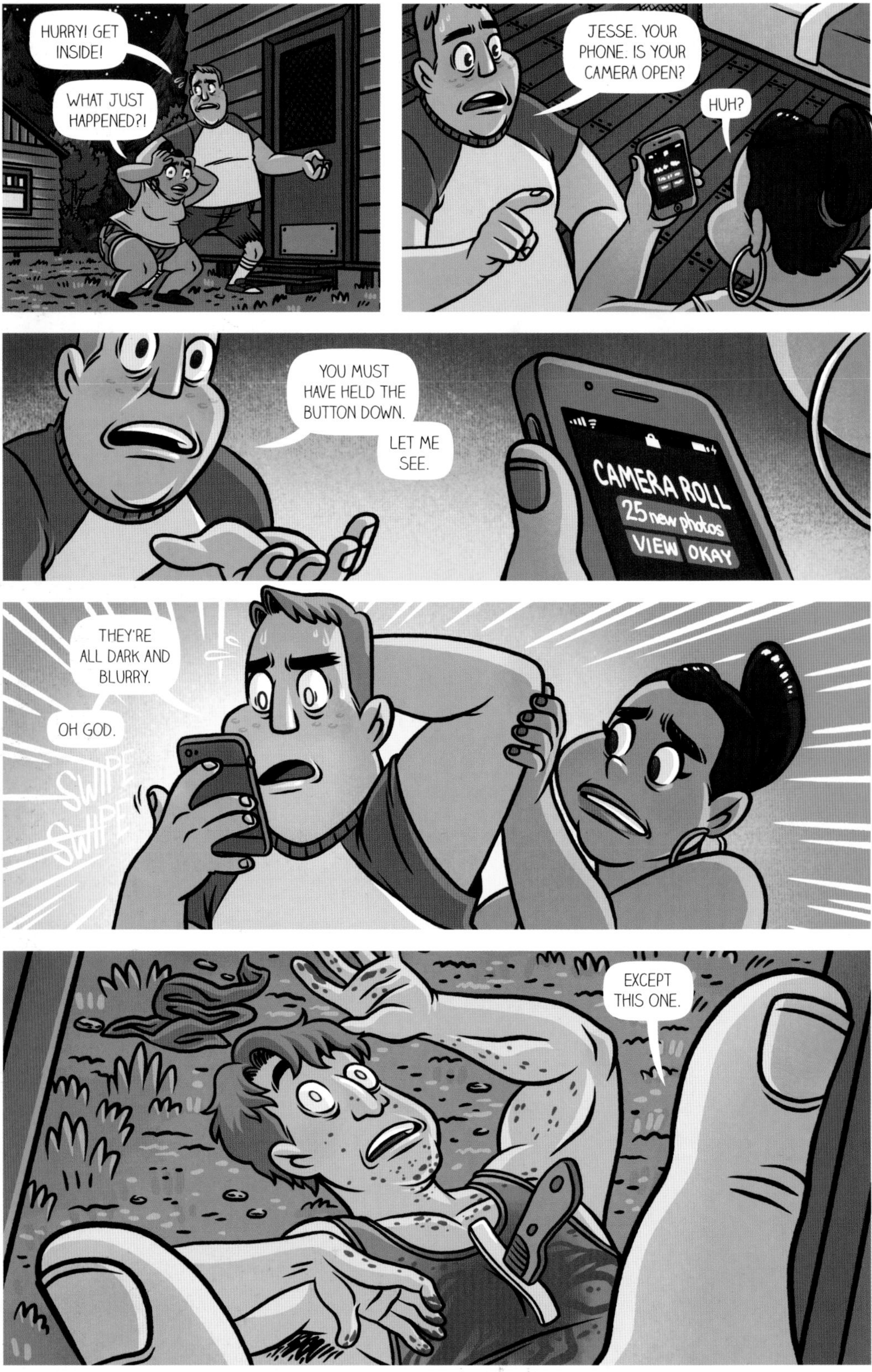
HURRY! GET INSIDE!
WHAT JUST HAPPENED?!
JESSE. YOUR PHONE. IS YOUR CAMERA OPEN?
HUH?
YOU MUST HAVE HELD THE BUTTON DOWN.
LET ME SEE.
CAMERA ROLL
25 new photos
VIEW
OKAY
THEY'RE ALL DARK AND BLURRY.
OH GOD.
SWIPE
SWIPE
EXCEPT THIS ONE.

CHAPTER FOUR

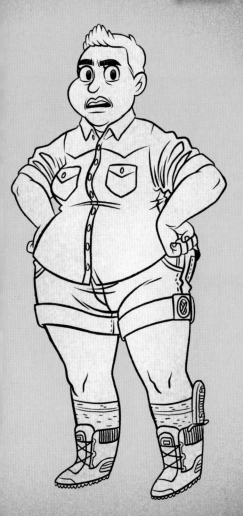

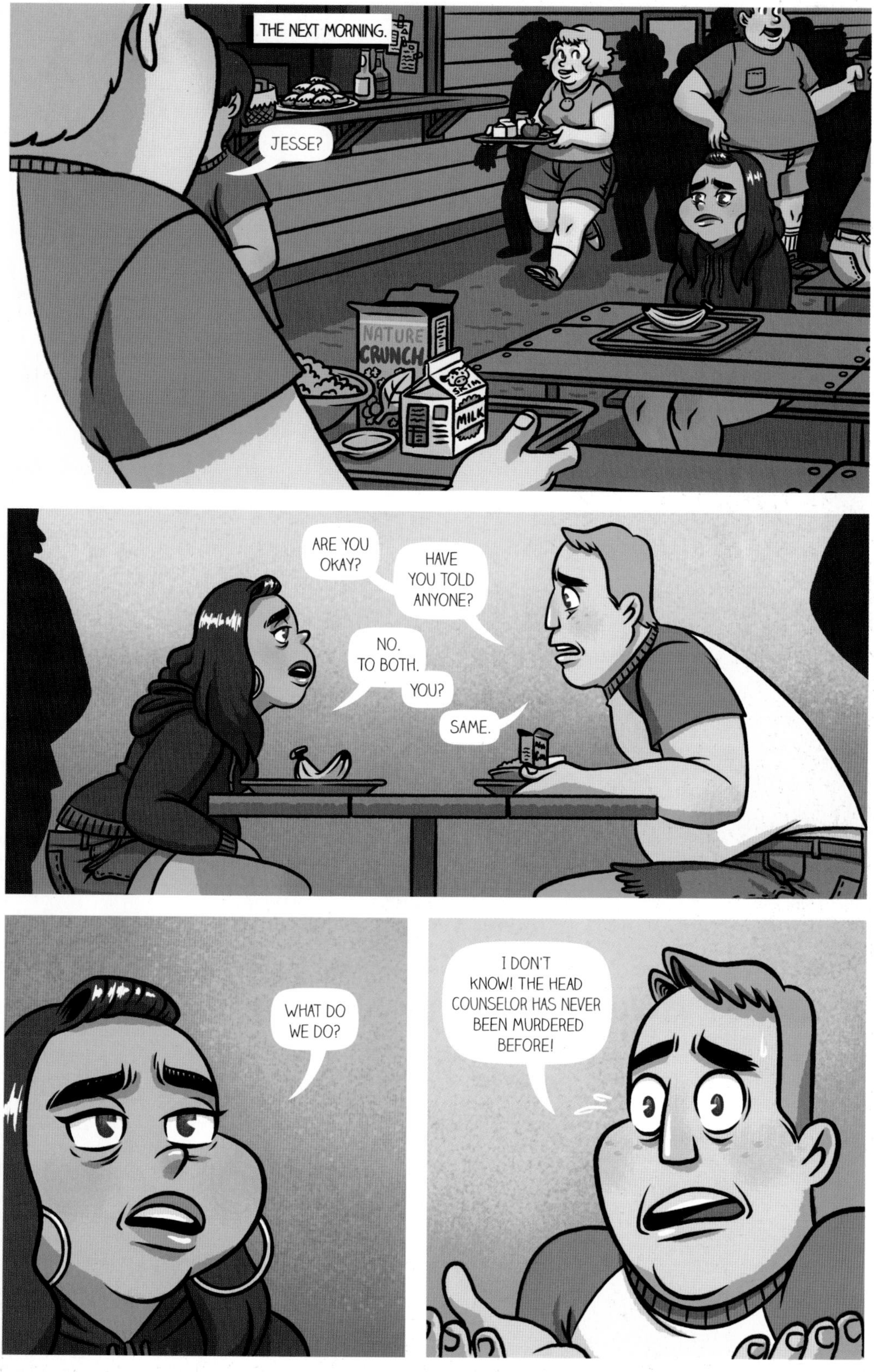
THE NEXT MORNING.
JESSE?
NATURE CRUNCH
SKIM MILK
ARE YOU OKAY?
HAVE YOU TOLD ANYONE?
NO. TO BOTH.
YOU?
SAME.
WHAT DO WE DO?
I DON'T KNOW! THE HEAD COUNSELOR HAS NEVER BEEN MURDERED BEFORE!

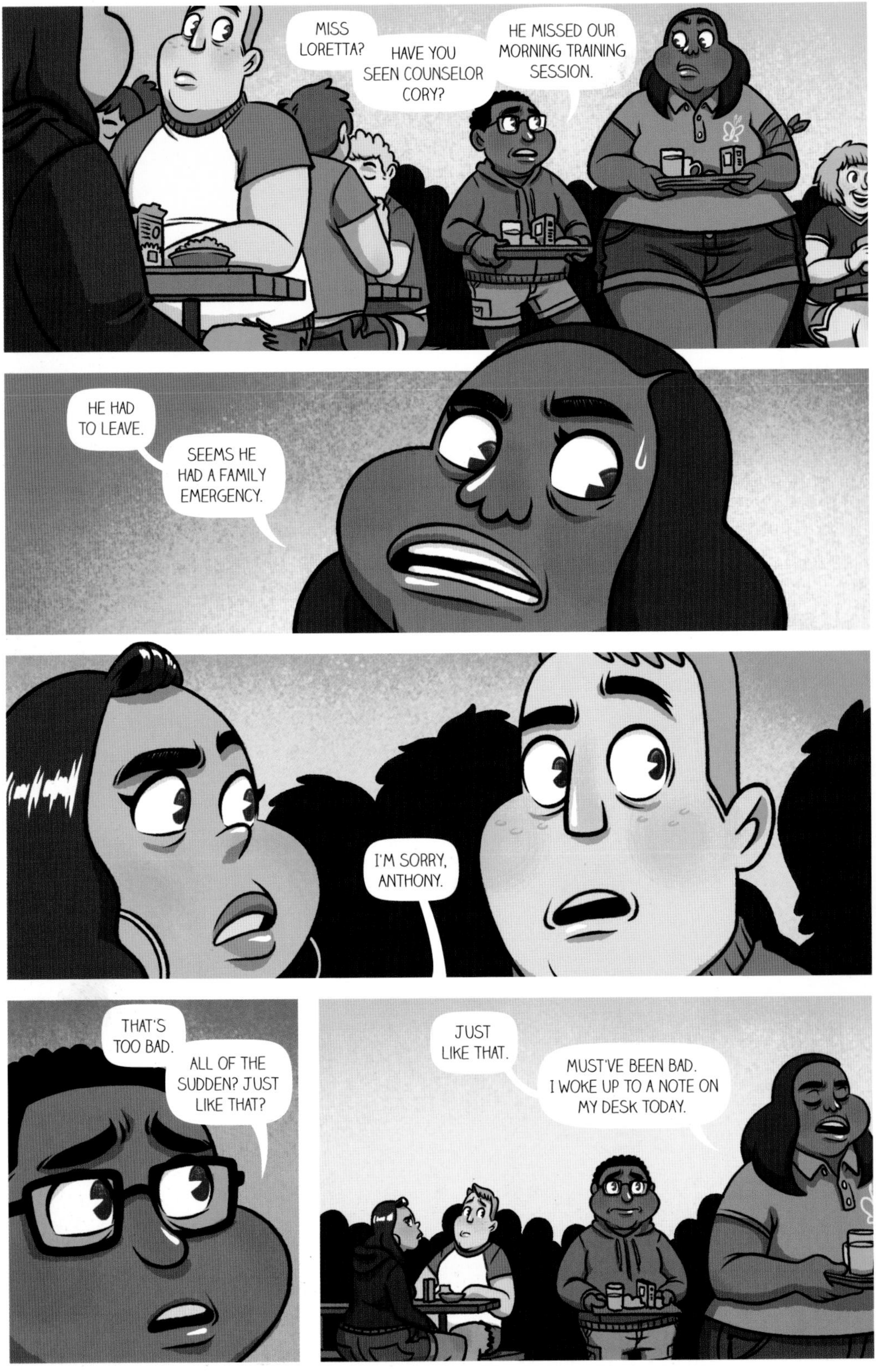
MISS LORETTA?
HAVE YOU SEEN COUNSELOR CORY?
HE MISSED OUR MORNING TRAINING SESSION.
HE HAD TO LEAVE.
SEEMS HE HAD A FAMILY EMERGENCY.
I'M SORRY, ANTHONY.
THAT'S TOO BAD.
ALL OF THE SUDDEN? JUST LIKE THAT?
JUST LIKE THAT.
MUST'VE BEEN BAD. I WOKE UP TO A NOTE ON MY DESK TODAY.

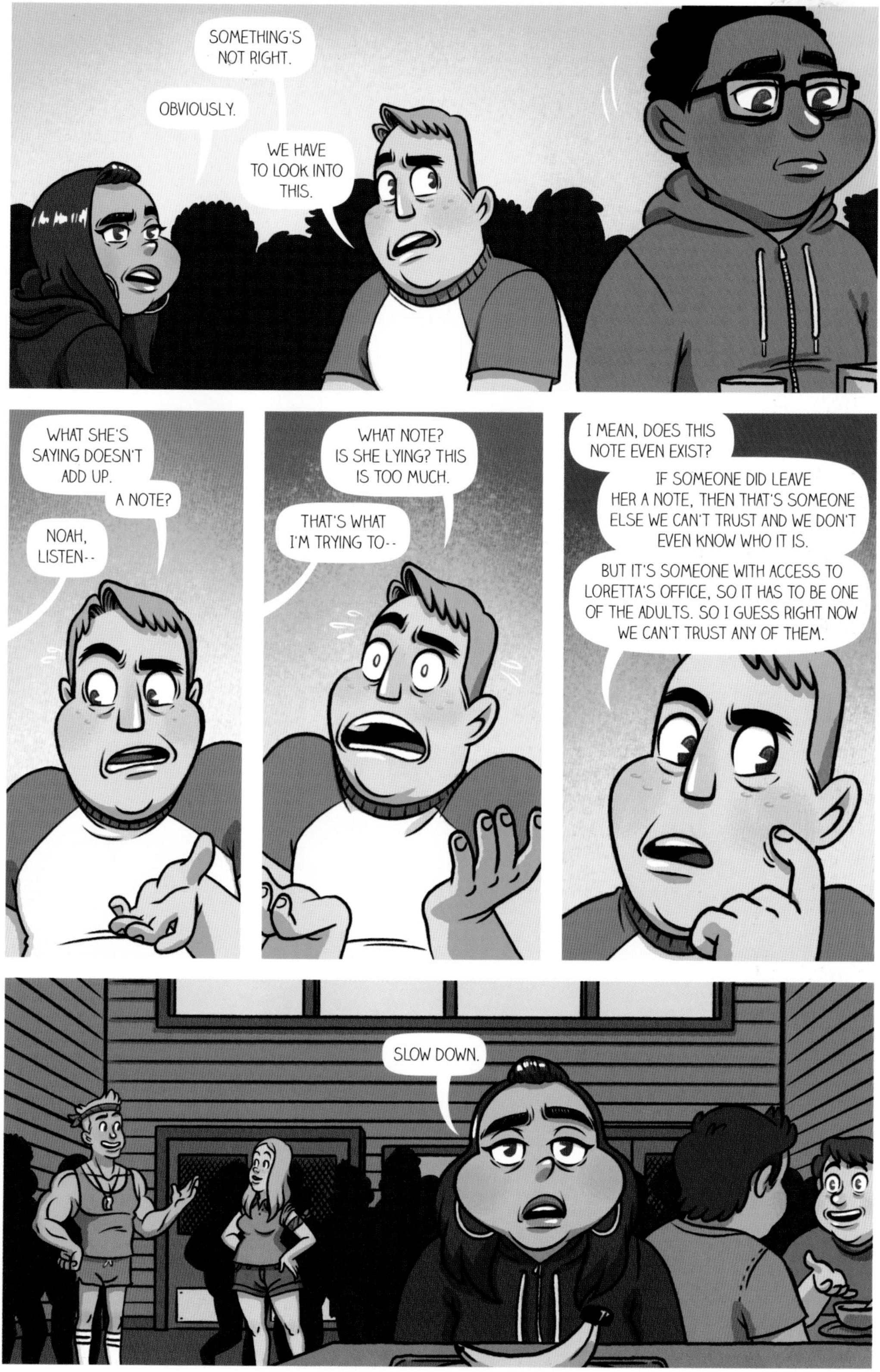
SOMETHING'S NOT RIGHT.
OBVIOUSLY.
WE HAVE TO LOOK INTO THIS.
WHAT SHE'S SAYING DOESN'T ADD UP.
A NOTE?
NOAH, LISTEN--
WHAT NOTE? IS SHE LYING? THIS IS TOO MUCH.
THAT'S WHAT I'M TRYING TO--
I MEAN, DOES THIS NOTE EVEN EXIST?
IF SOMEONE DID LEAVE HER A NOTE, THEN THAT'S SOMEONE ELSE WE CAN'T TRUST AND WE DON'T EVEN KNOW WHO IT IS.
BUT IT'S SOMEONE WITH ACCESS TO LORETTA'S OFFICE, SO IT HAS TO BE ONE OF THE ADULTS. SO I GUESS RIGHT NOW WE CAN'T TRUST ANY OF THEM.
SLOW DOWN.

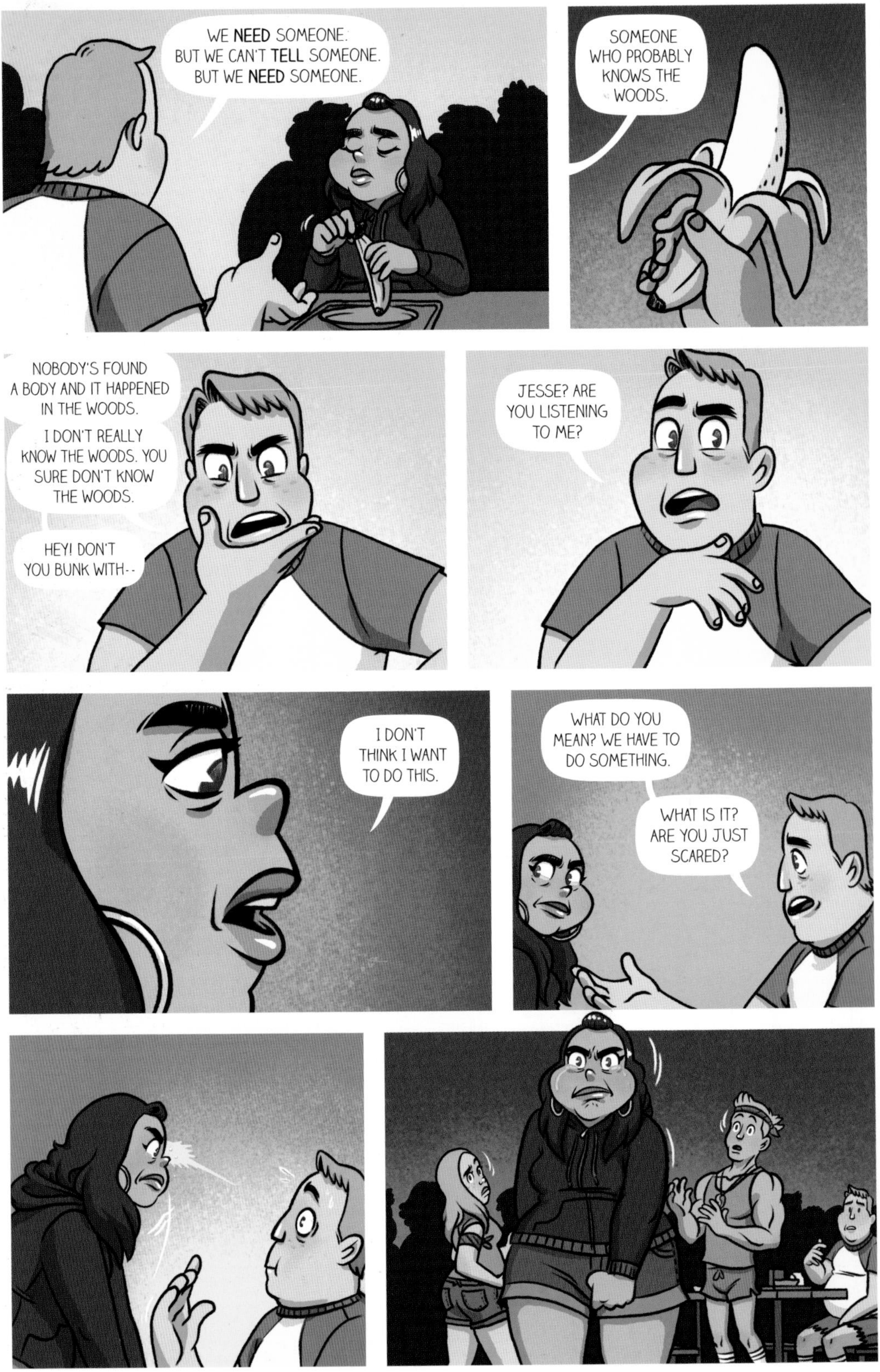

WE **NEED** SOMEONE. BUT WE CAN'T **TELL** SOMEONE. BUT WE **NEED** SOMEONE.
SOMEONE WHO PROBABLY KNOWS THE WOODS.
NOBODY'S FOUND A BODY AND IT HAPPENED IN THE WOODS.
I DON'T REALLY KNOW THE WOODS. YOU SURE DON'T KNOW THE WOODS.
HEY! DON'T YOU BUNK WITH--
JESSE? ARE YOU LISTENING TO ME?
I DON'T THINK I WANT TO DO THIS.
WHAT DO YOU MEAN? WE HAVE TO DO SOMETHING.
WHAT IS IT? ARE YOU JUST SCARED?

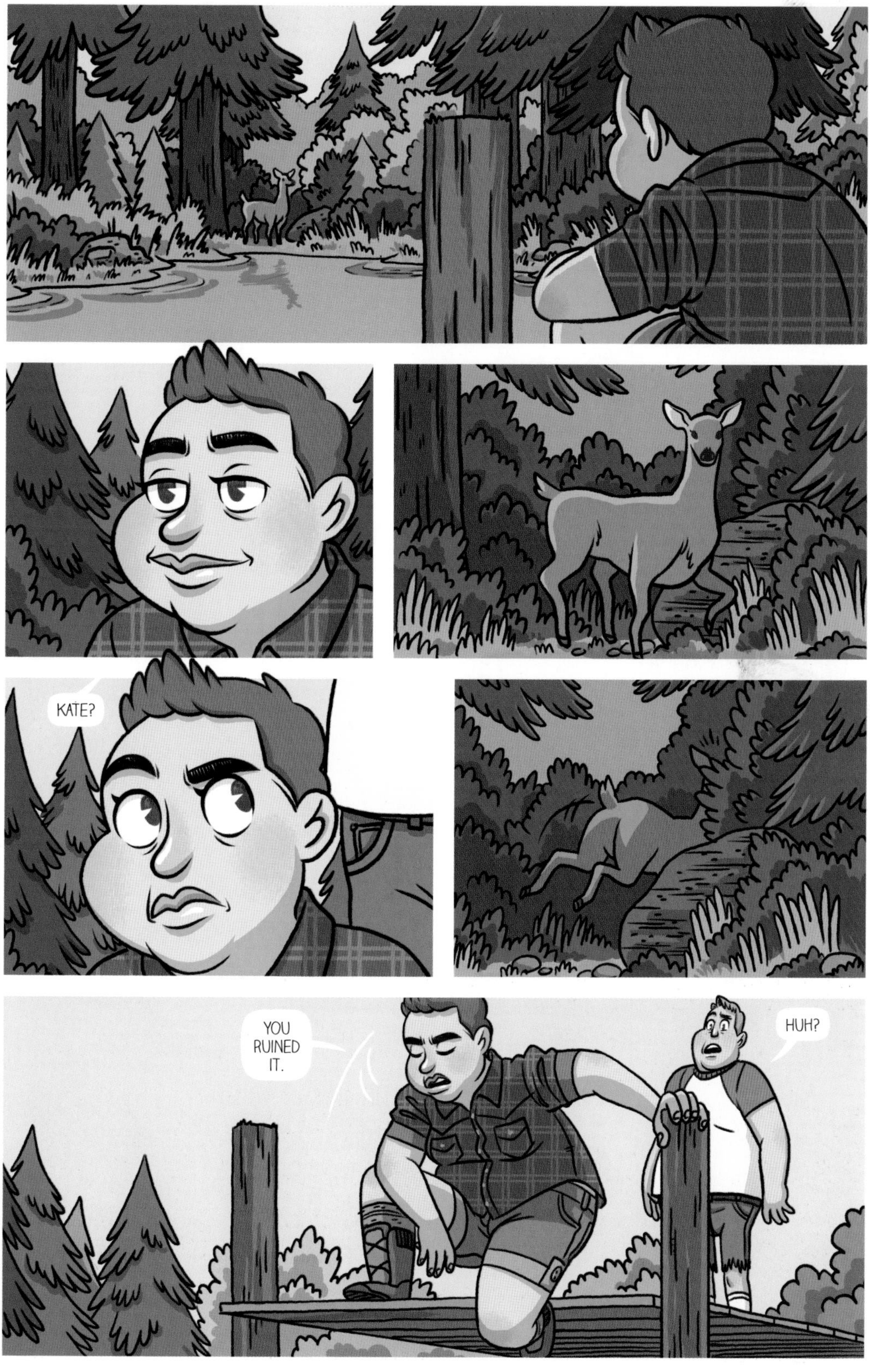
KATE?
YOU RUINED IT.
HUH?

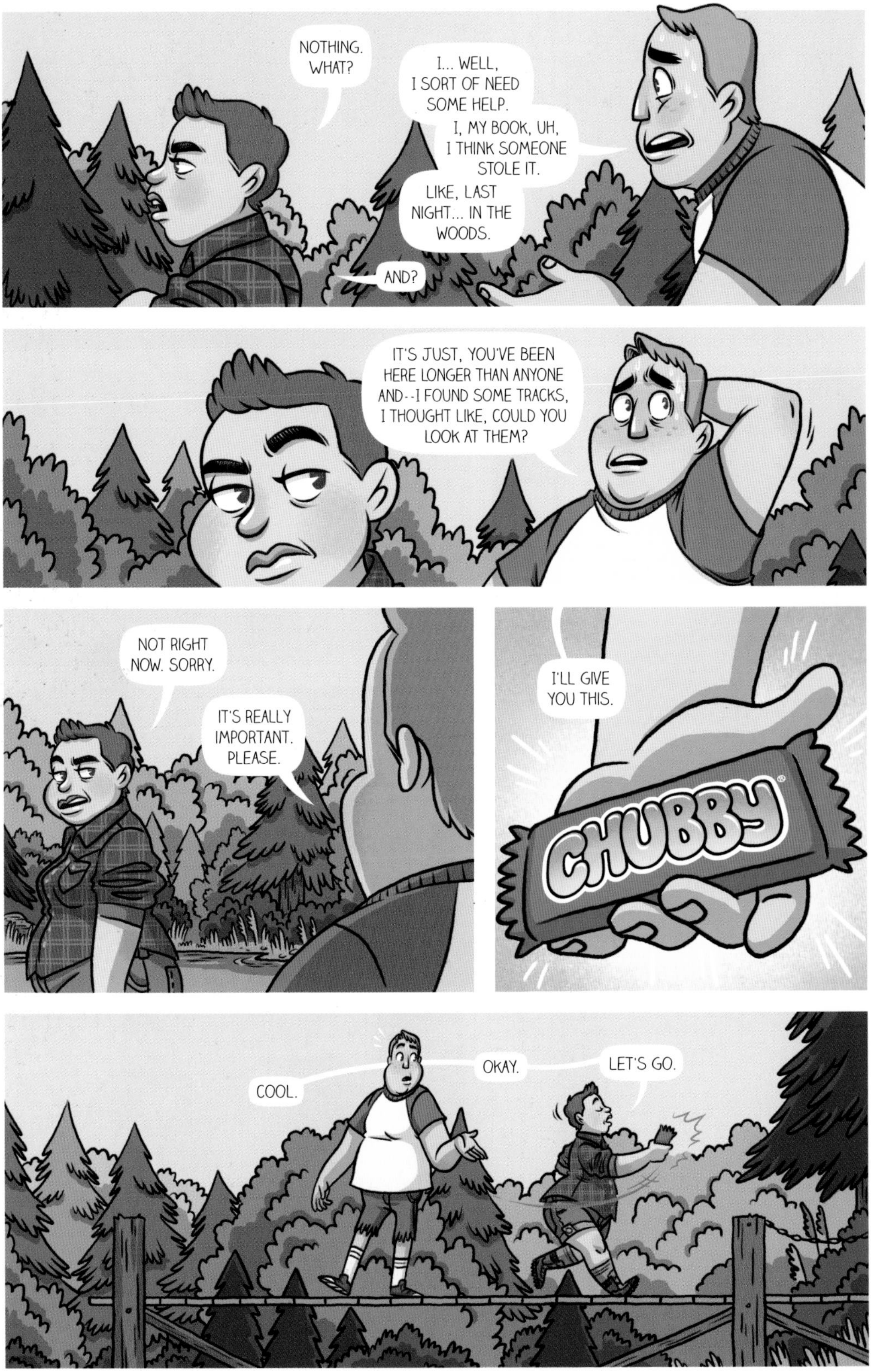
NOTHING. WHAT?
I... WELL, I SORT OF NEED SOME HELP.
I, MY BOOK, UH, I THINK SOMEONE STOLE IT.
LIKE, LAST NIGHT... IN THE WOODS.
AND?
IT'S JUST, YOU'VE BEEN HERE LONGER THAN ANYONE AND--I FOUND SOME TRACKS, I THOUGHT LIKE, COULD YOU LOOK AT THEM?
NOT RIGHT NOW. SORRY.
IT'S REALLY IMPORTANT. PLEASE.
I'LL GIVE YOU THIS.
CHUBBY
COOL.
OKAY.
LET'S GO.

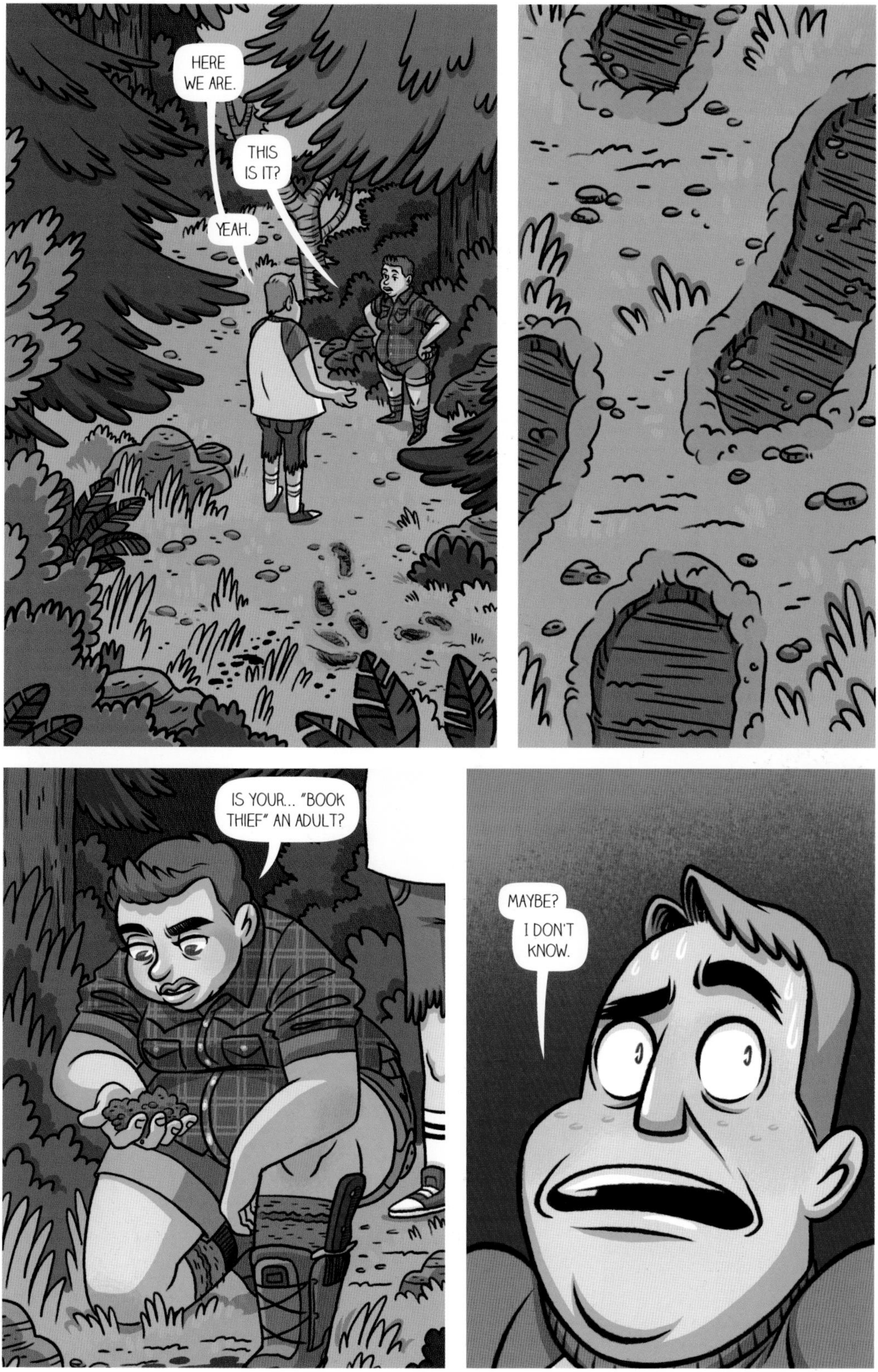
HERE WE ARE.
THIS IS IT?
YEAH.
IS YOUR... "BOOK THIEF" AN ADULT?
MAYBE?
I DON'T KNOW.

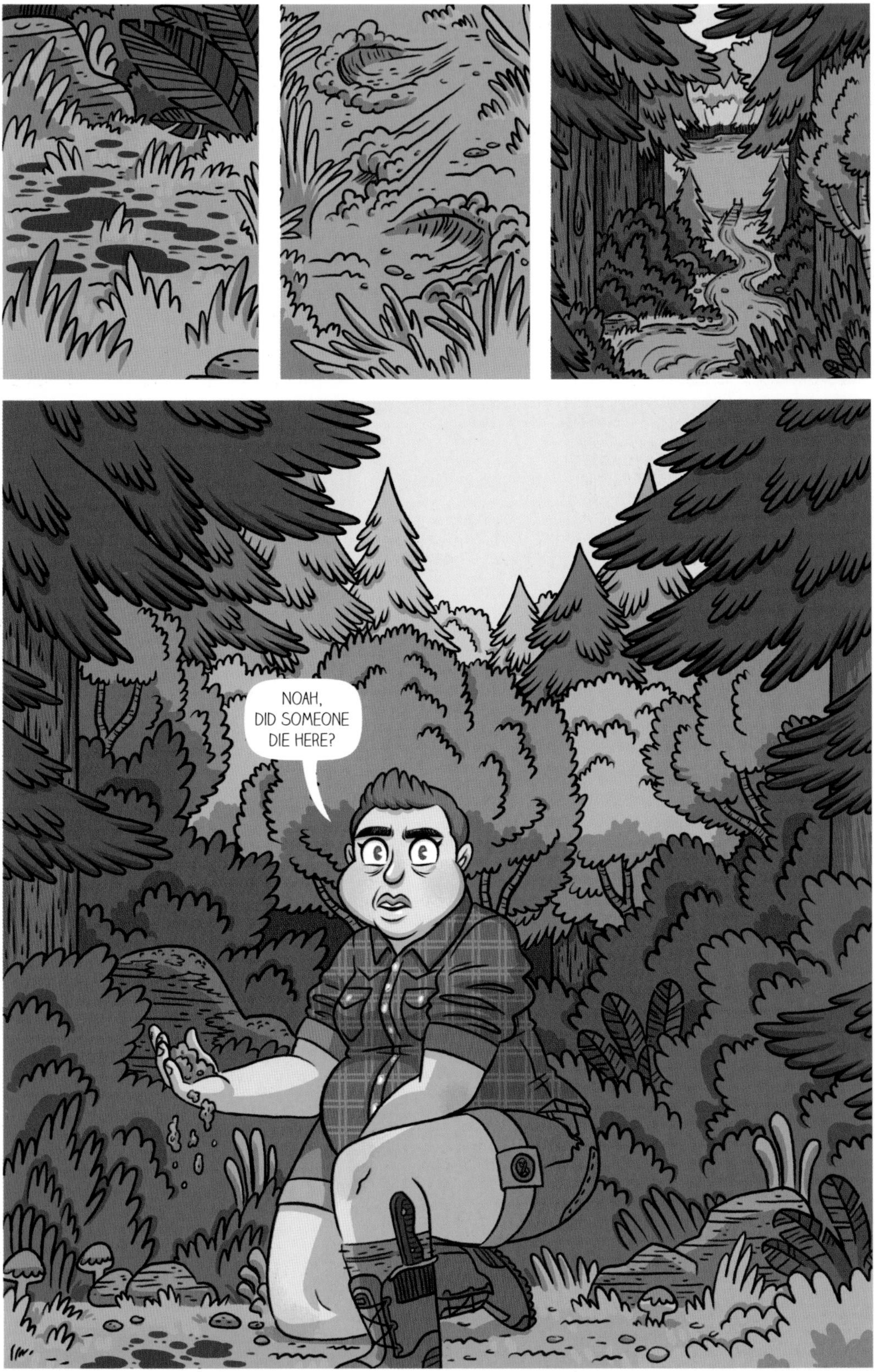
NOAH,
DID SOMEONE
DIE HERE?

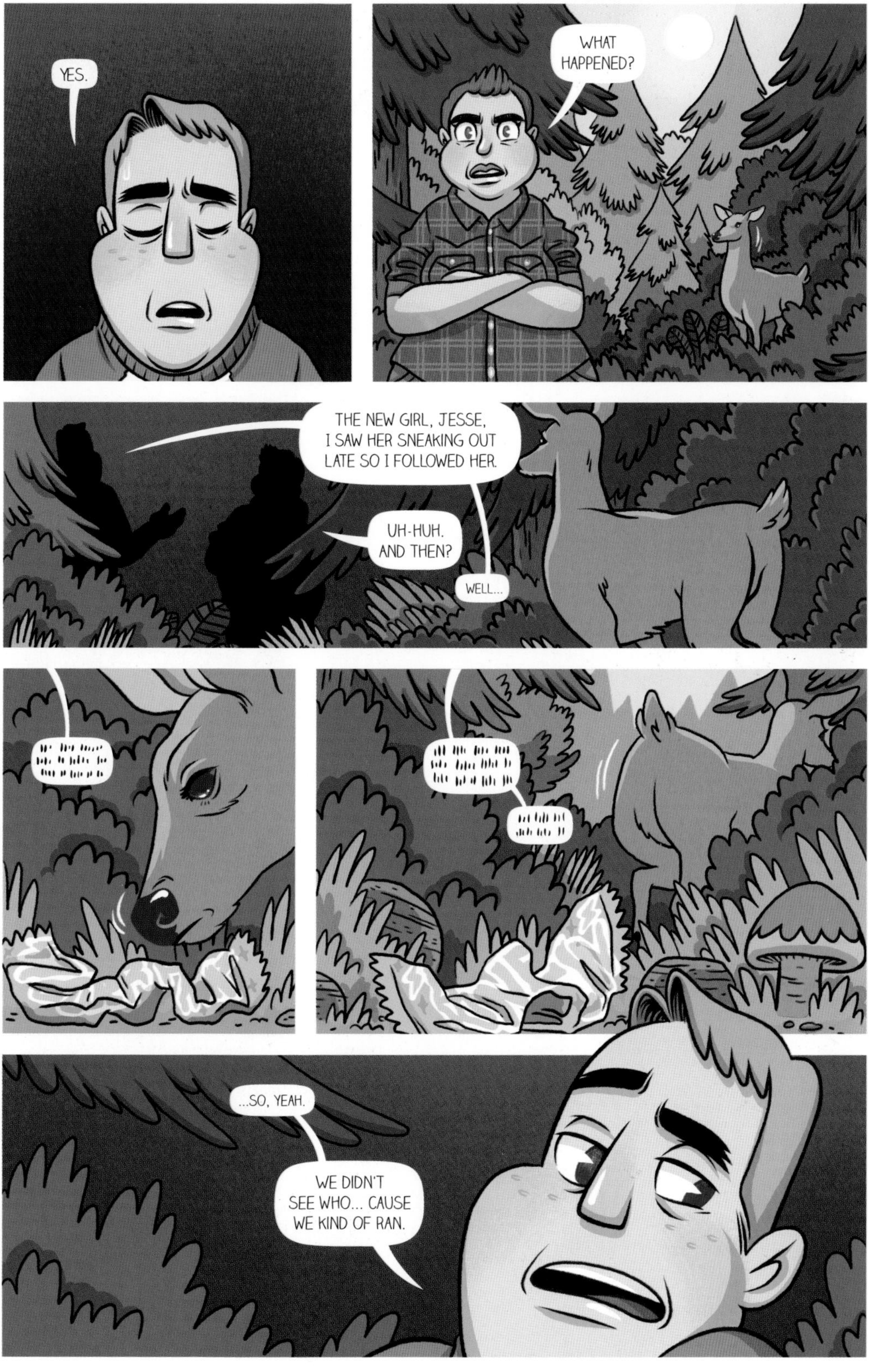

YES.
WHAT HAPPENED?
THE NEW GIRL, JESSE, I SAW HER SNEAKING OUT LATE SO I FOLLOWED HER.
UH-HUH. AND THEN?
WELL...
...SO, YEAH.
WE DIDN'T SEE WHO... CAUSE WE KIND OF RAN.

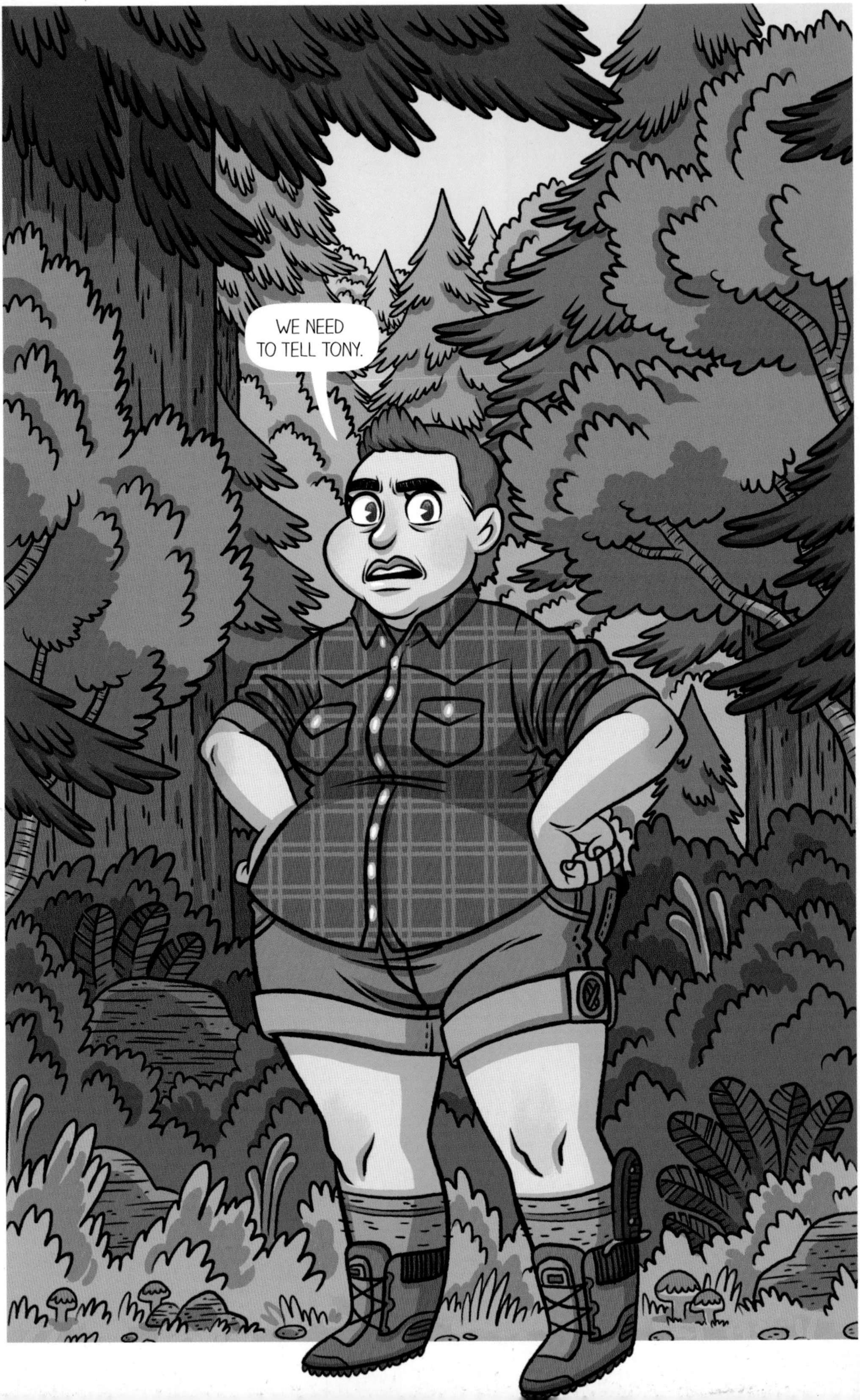
WE NEED TO TELL TONY.

CHAPTER FIVE

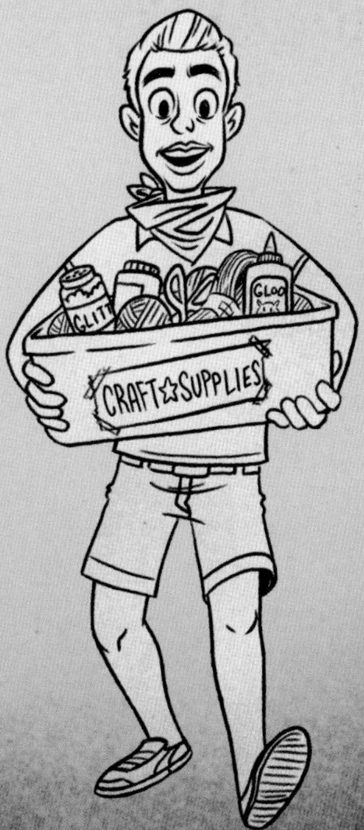
CRAFT☆SUPPLIES

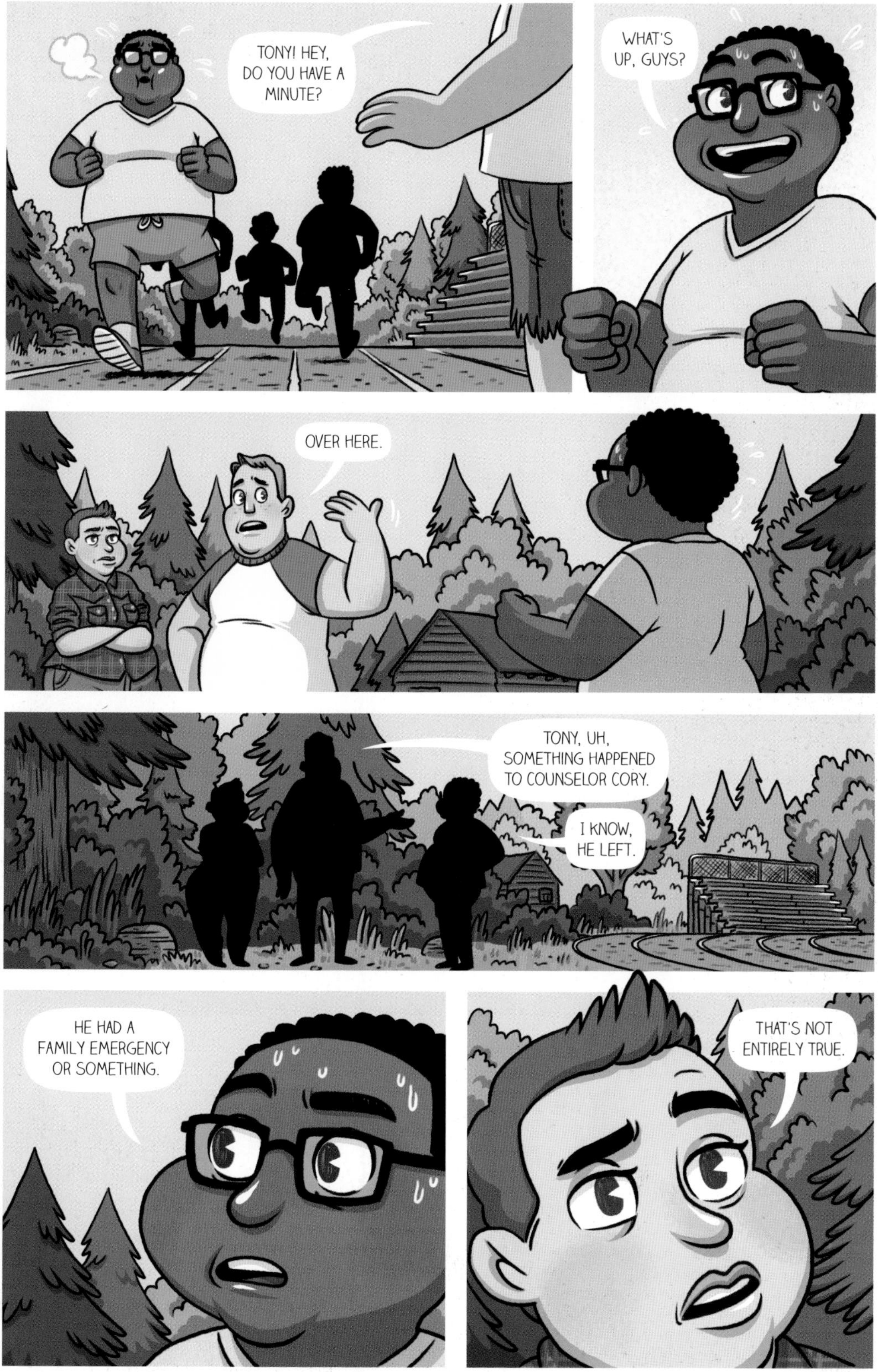
TONY! HEY, DO YOU HAVE A MINUTE?
WHAT'S UP, GUYS?
OVER HERE.
TONY, UH, SOMETHING HAPPENED TO COUNSELOR CORY.
I KNOW, HE LEFT.
HE HAD A FAMILY EMERGENCY OR SOMETHING.
THAT'S NOT ENTIRELY TRUE.

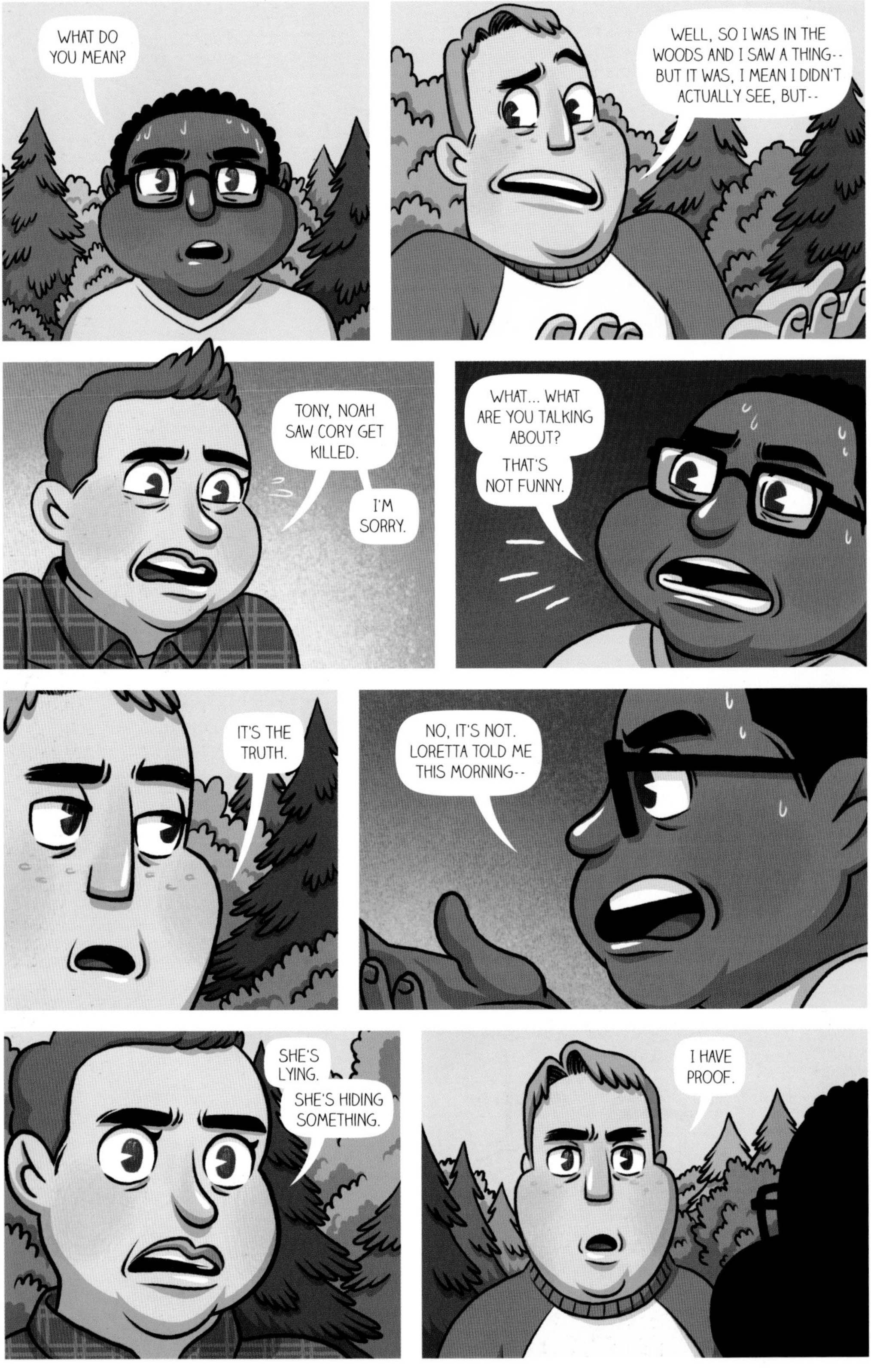
WHAT DO YOU MEAN?
WELL, SO I WAS IN THE WOODS AND I SAW A THING-- BUT IT WAS, I MEAN I DIDN'T ACTUALLY SEE, BUT--
TONY, NOAH SAW CORY GET KILLED.
I'M SORRY.
WHAT... WHAT ARE YOU TALKING ABOUT?
THAT'S NOT FUNNY.
IT'S THE TRUTH.
NO, IT'S NOT. LORETTA TOLD ME THIS MORNING--
SHE'S LYING.
SHE'S HIDING SOMETHING.
I HAVE PROOF.

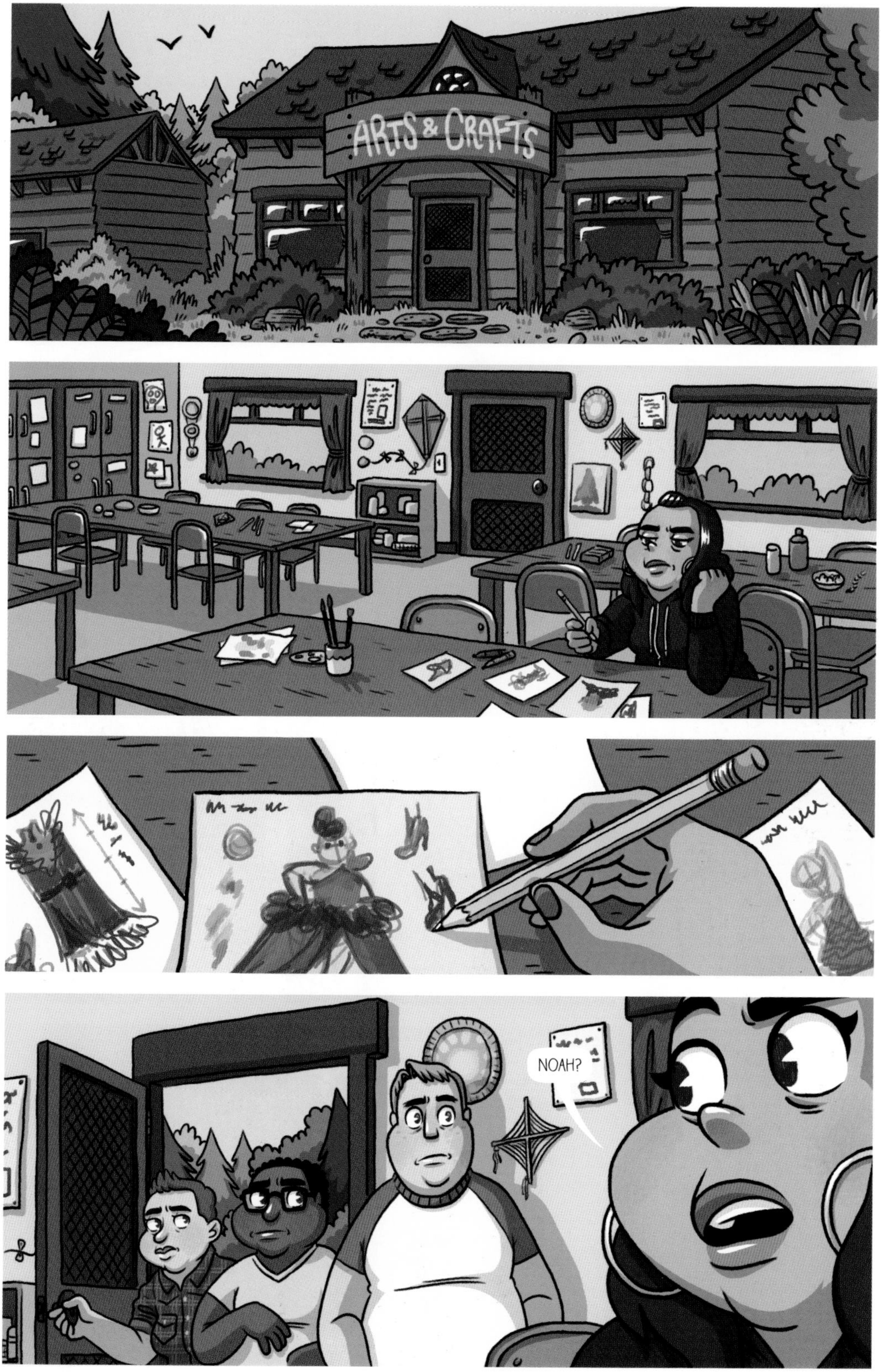
ARTS & CRAFTS
NOAH?

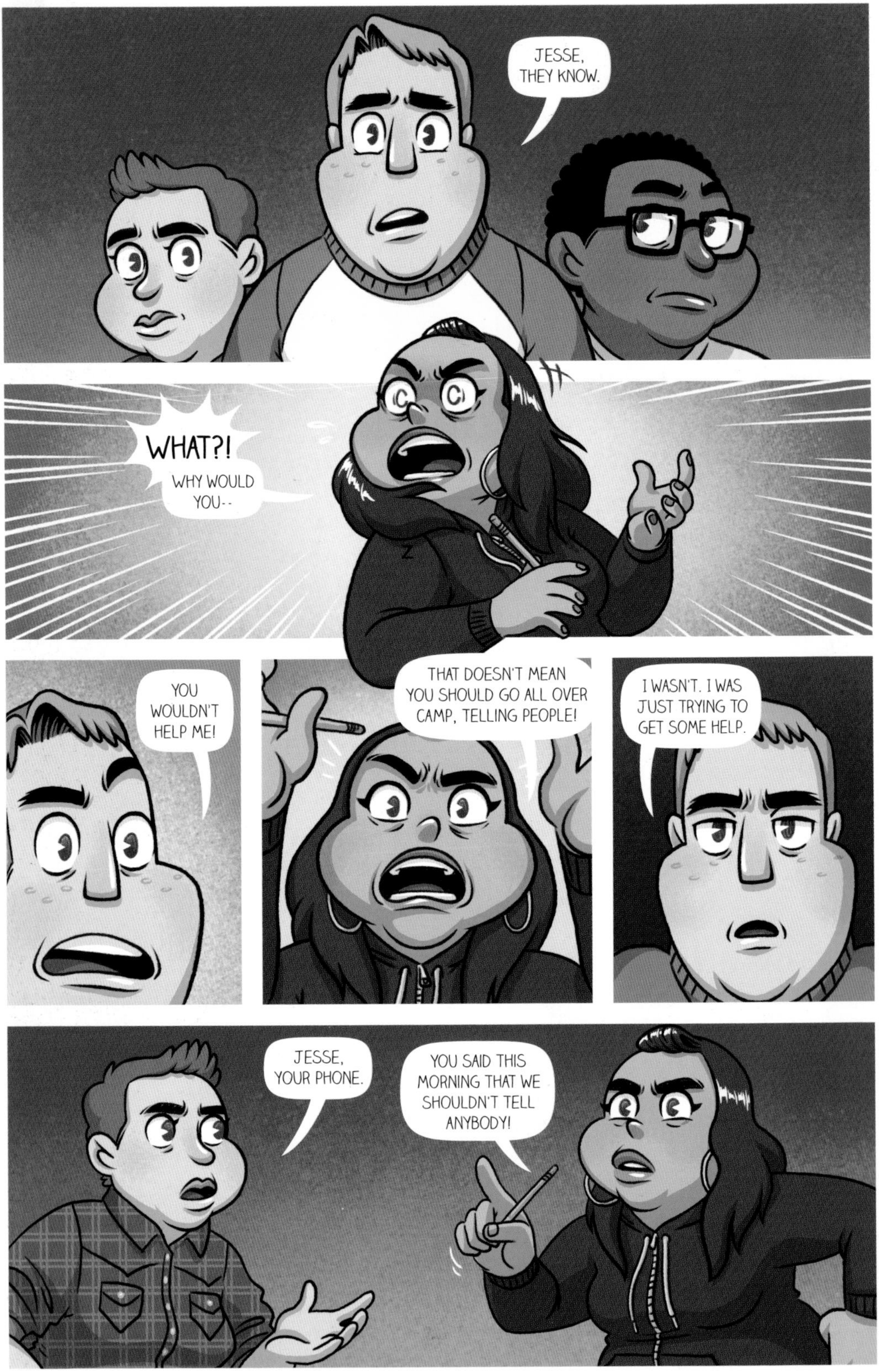
JESSE, THEY KNOW.
WHAT?!
WHY WOULD YOU--
YOU WOULDN'T HELP ME!
THAT DOESN'T MEAN YOU SHOULD GO ALL OVER CAMP, TELLING PEOPLE!
I WASN'T. I WAS JUST TRYING TO GET SOME HELP.
JESSE, YOUR PHONE.
YOU SAID THIS MORNING THAT WE SHOULDN'T TELL ANYBODY!

I TRUST KATE, AND TONY HAD TO KNOW.
WHY?
JESSE, I NEED TO SEE YOUR PHONE.
SWIPE SWIPE
SWIPE SWIPE

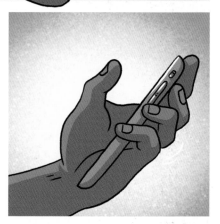

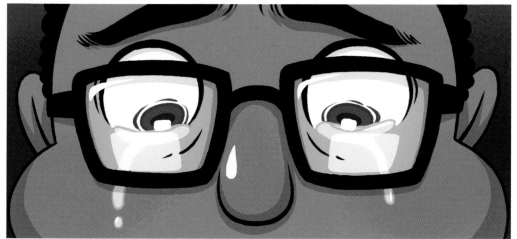

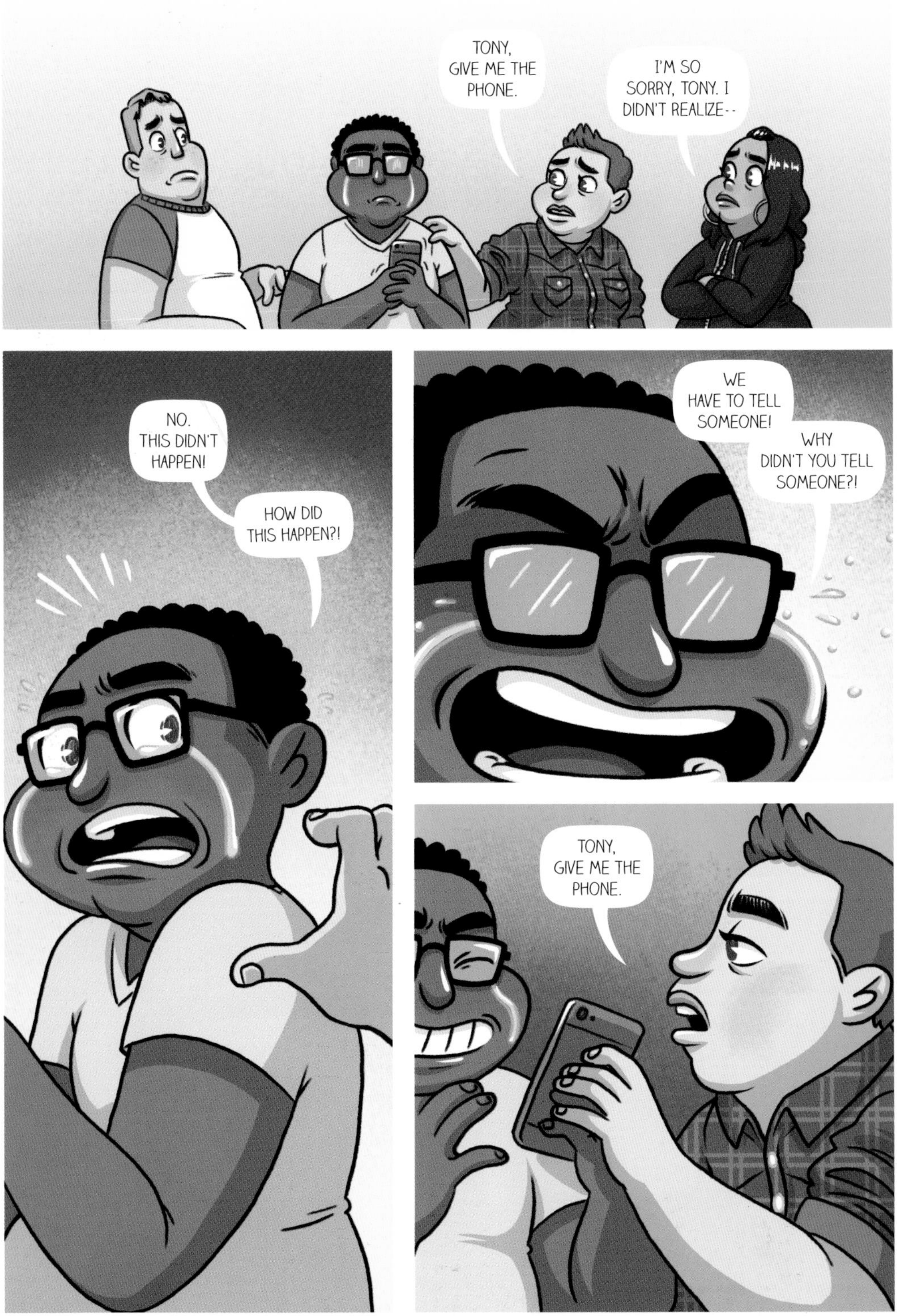
TONY, GIVE ME THE PHONE.
I'M SO SORRY, TONY. I DIDN'T REALIZE--
NO. THIS DIDN'T HAPPEN!
HOW DID THIS HAPPEN?!
WE HAVE TO TELL SOMEONE!
WHY DIDN'T YOU TELL SOMEONE?!
TONY, GIVE ME THE PHONE.

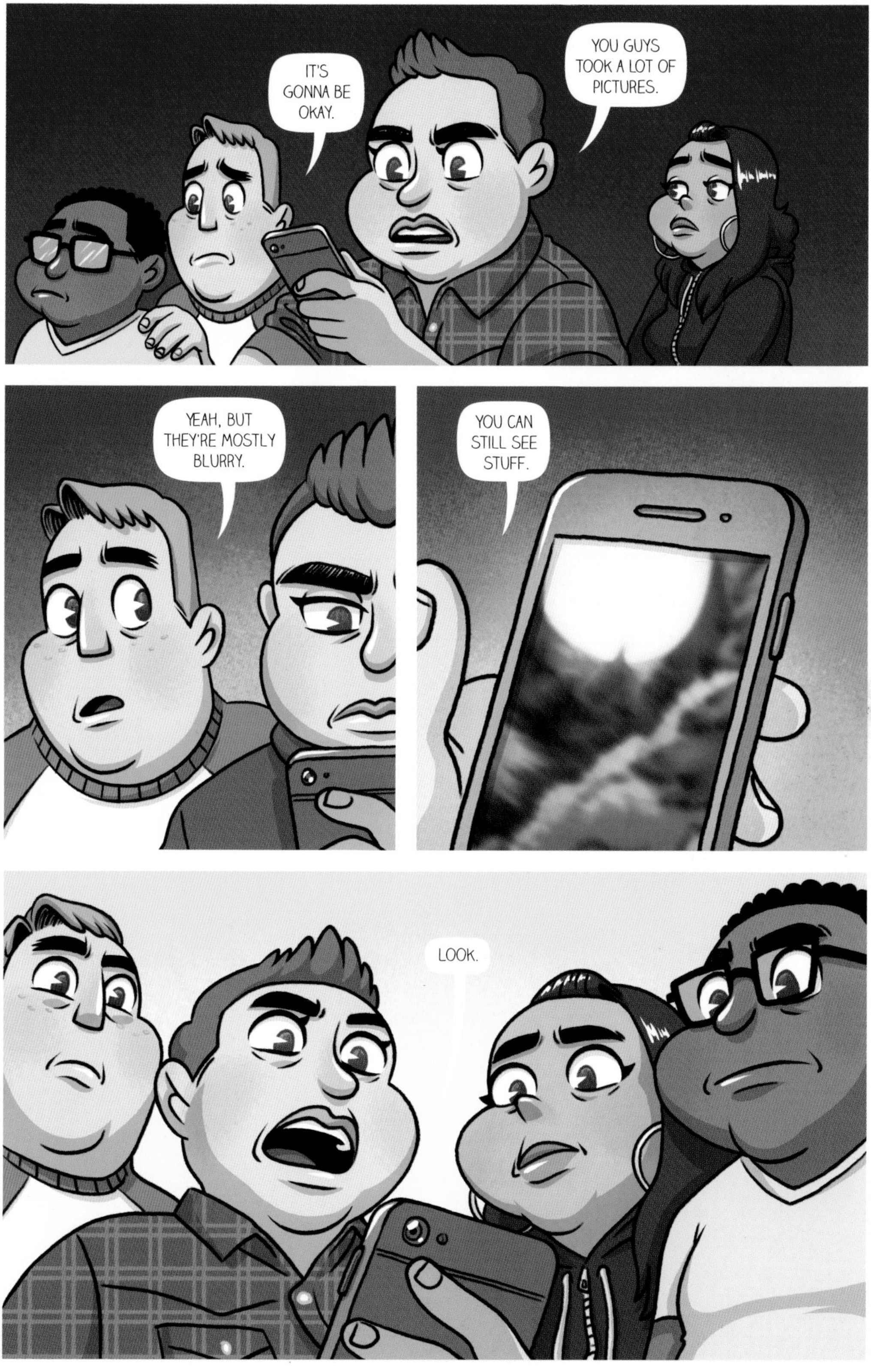
IT'S GONNA BE OKAY.
YOU GUYS TOOK A LOT OF PICTURES.
YEAH, BUT THEY'RE MOSTLY BLURRY.
YOU CAN STILL SEE STUFF.
LOOK.

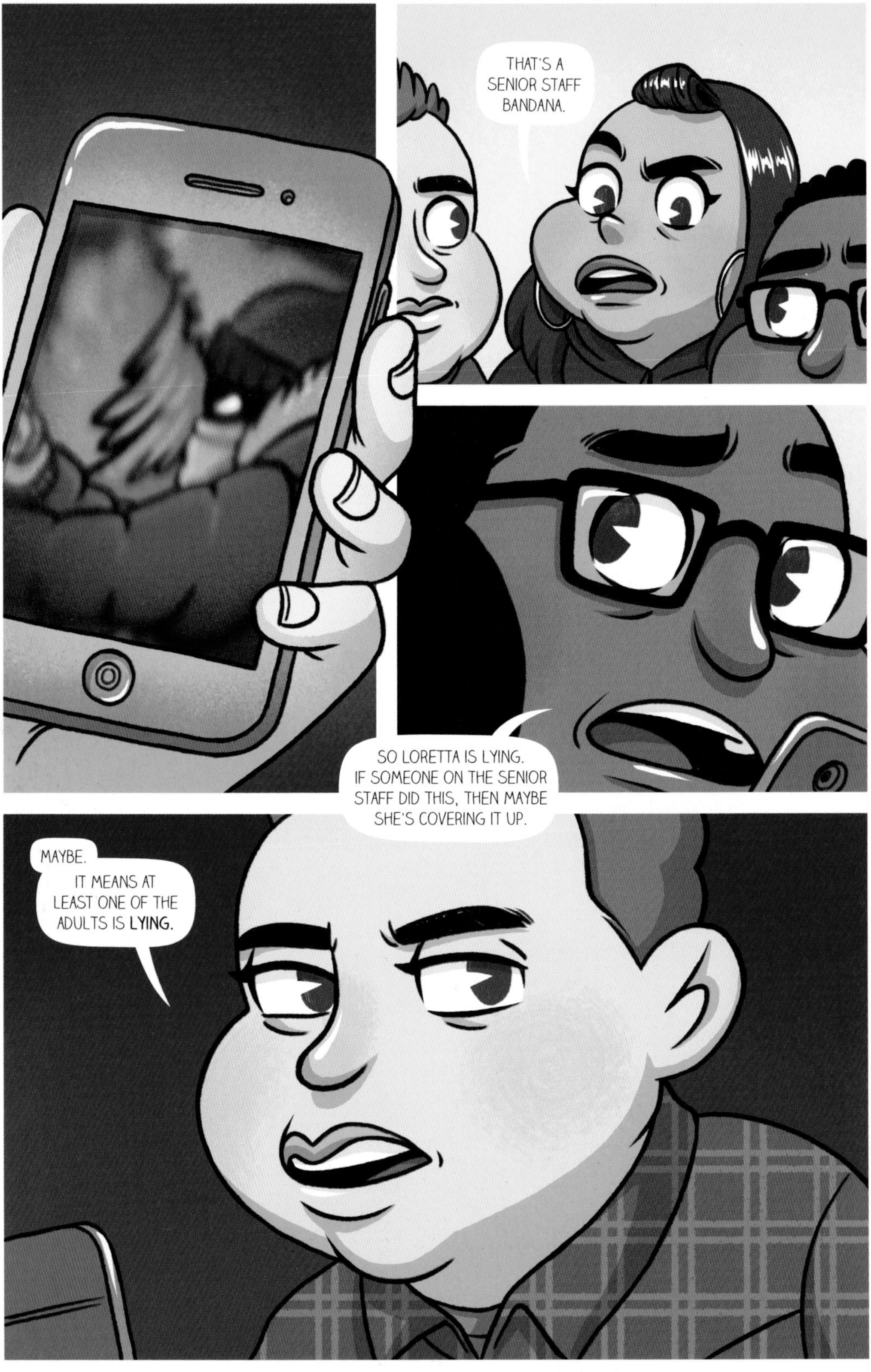
THAT'S A SENIOR STAFF BANDANA.
SO LORETTA IS LYING. IF SOMEONE ON THE SENIOR STAFF DID THIS, THEN MAYBE SHE'S COVERING IT UP.
MAYBE.
IT MEANS AT LEAST ONE OF THE ADULTS IS LYING.

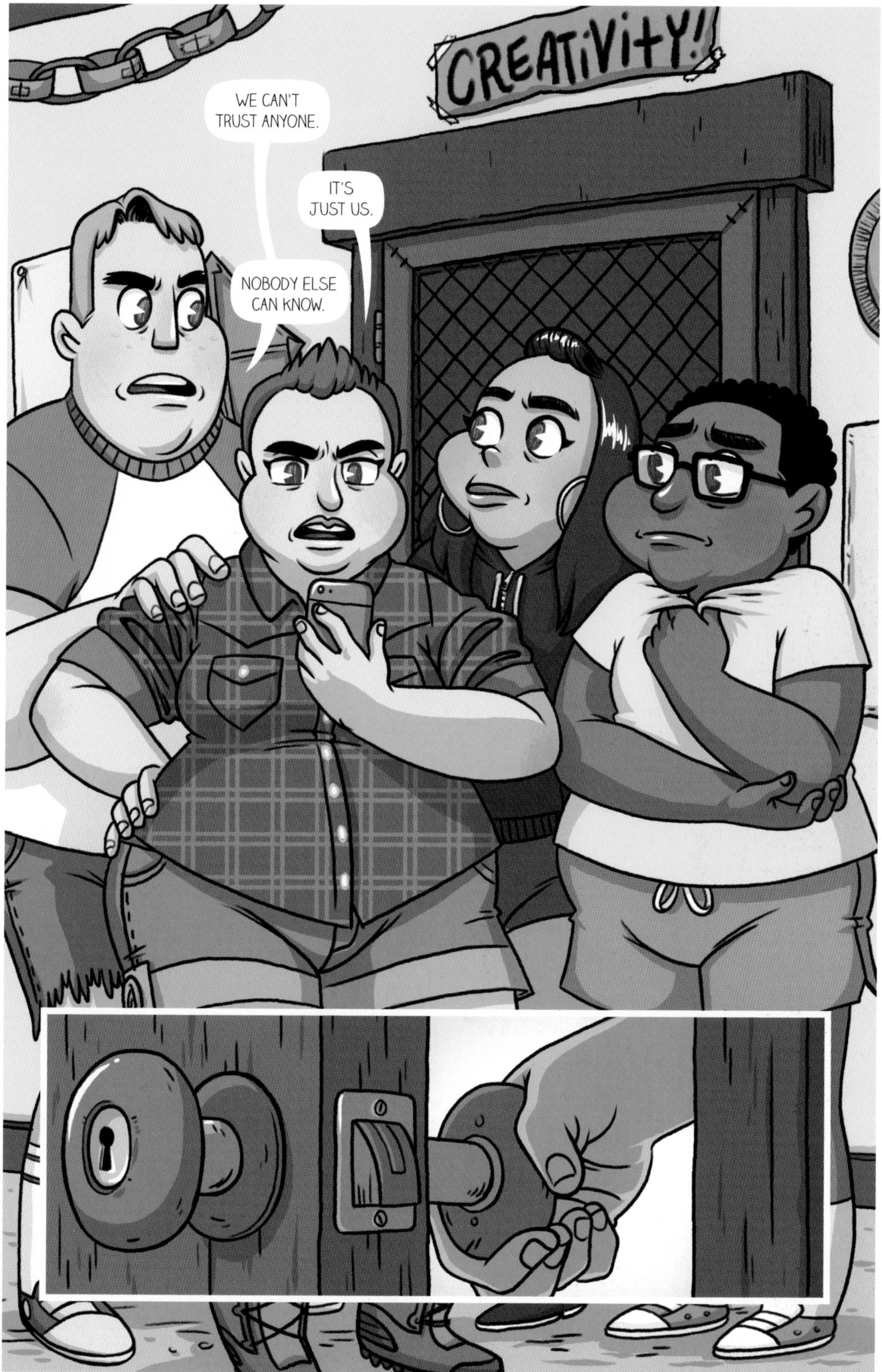
CREATiVity!
WE CAN'T TRUST ANYONE.
IT'S JUST US.
NOBODY ELSE CAN KNOW.

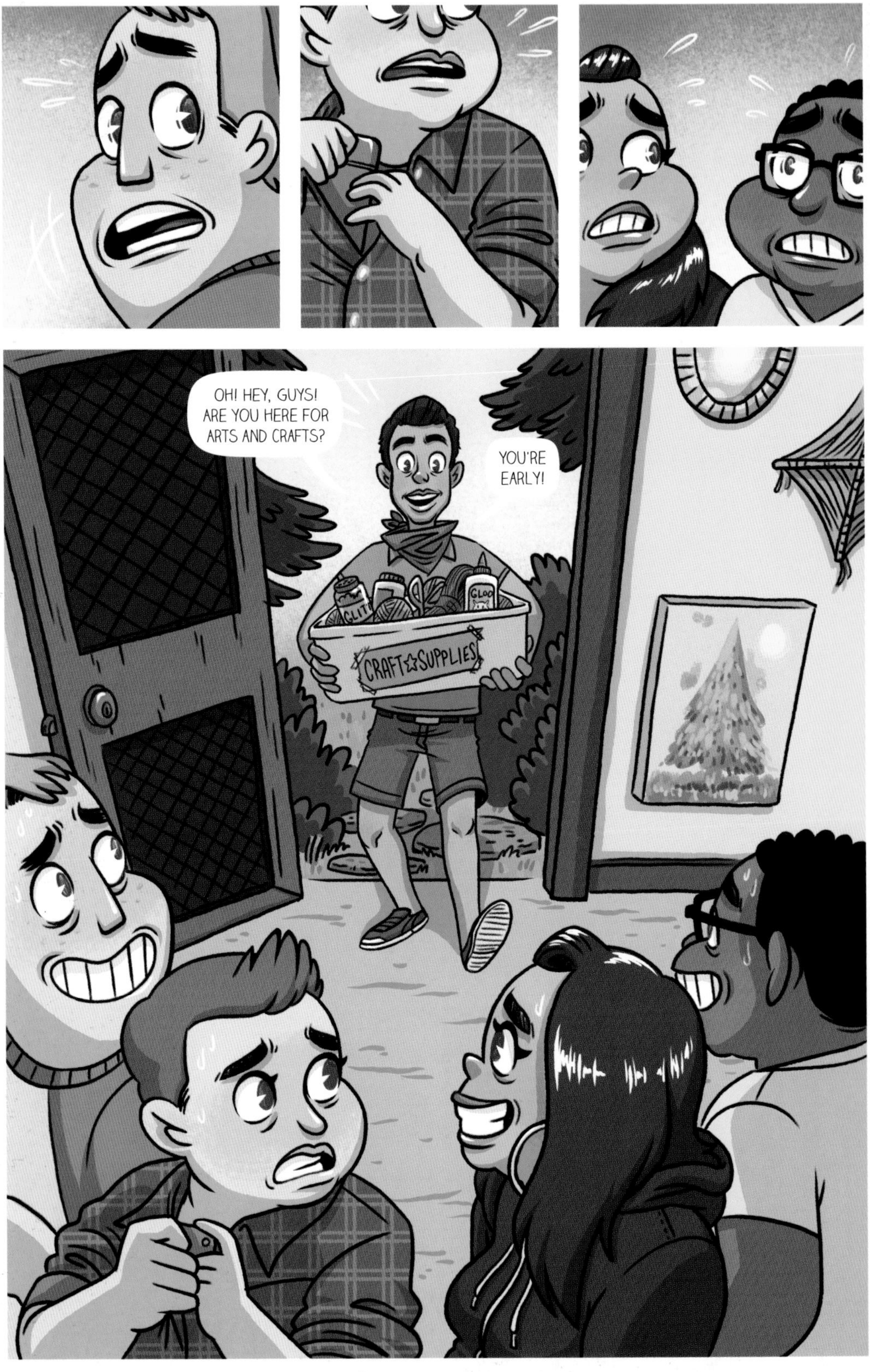
OH! HEY, GUYS! ARE YOU HERE FOR ARTS AND CRAFTS?
YOU'RE EARLY!
GLITT
GLOO
CRAFT☆SUPPLIES

CHAPTER SIX

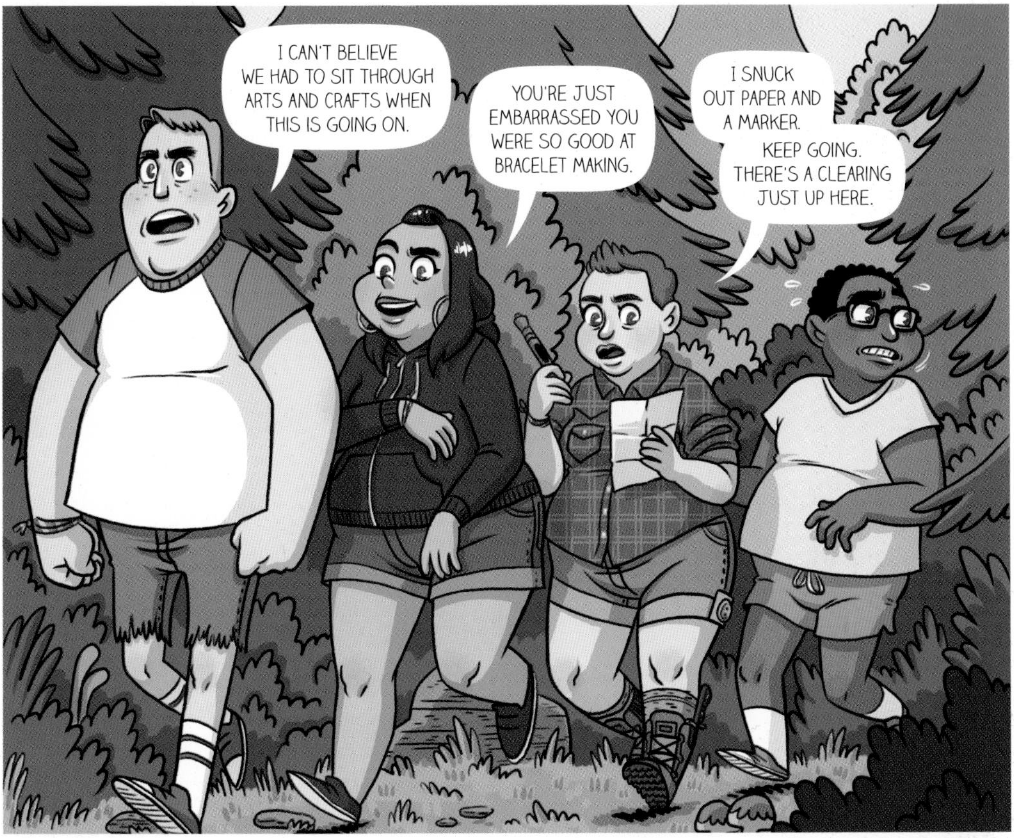
I CAN'T BELIEVE WE HAD TO SIT THROUGH ARTS AND CRAFTS WHEN THIS IS GOING ON.
YOU'RE JUST EMBARRASSED YOU WERE SO GOOD AT BRACELET MAKING.
I SNUCK OUT PAPER AND A MARKER.
KEEP GOING. THERE'S A CLEARING JUST UP HERE.

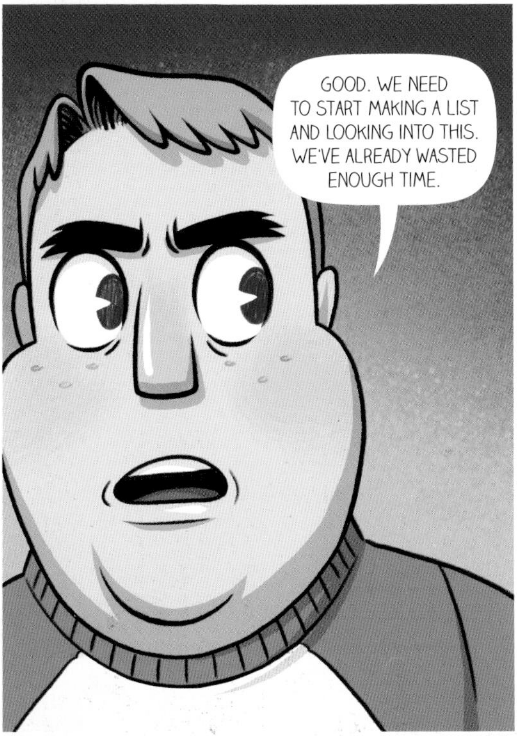
GOOD. WE NEED TO START MAKING A LIST AND LOOKING INTO THIS. WE'VE ALREADY WASTED ENOUGH TIME.

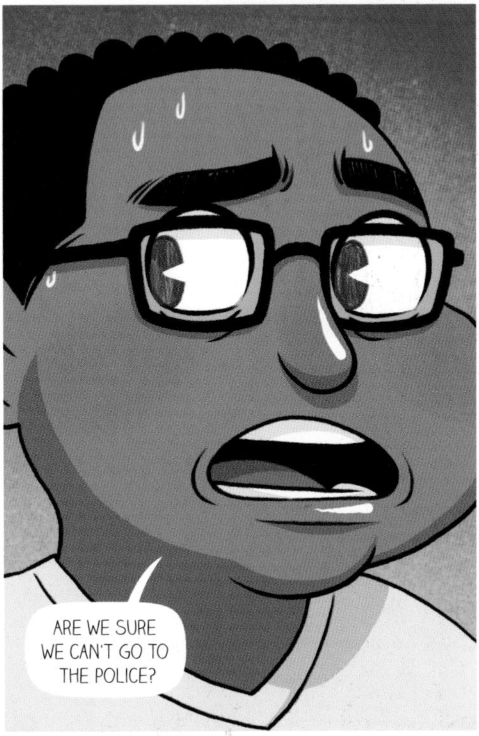
ARE WE SURE WE CAN'T GO TO THE POLICE?

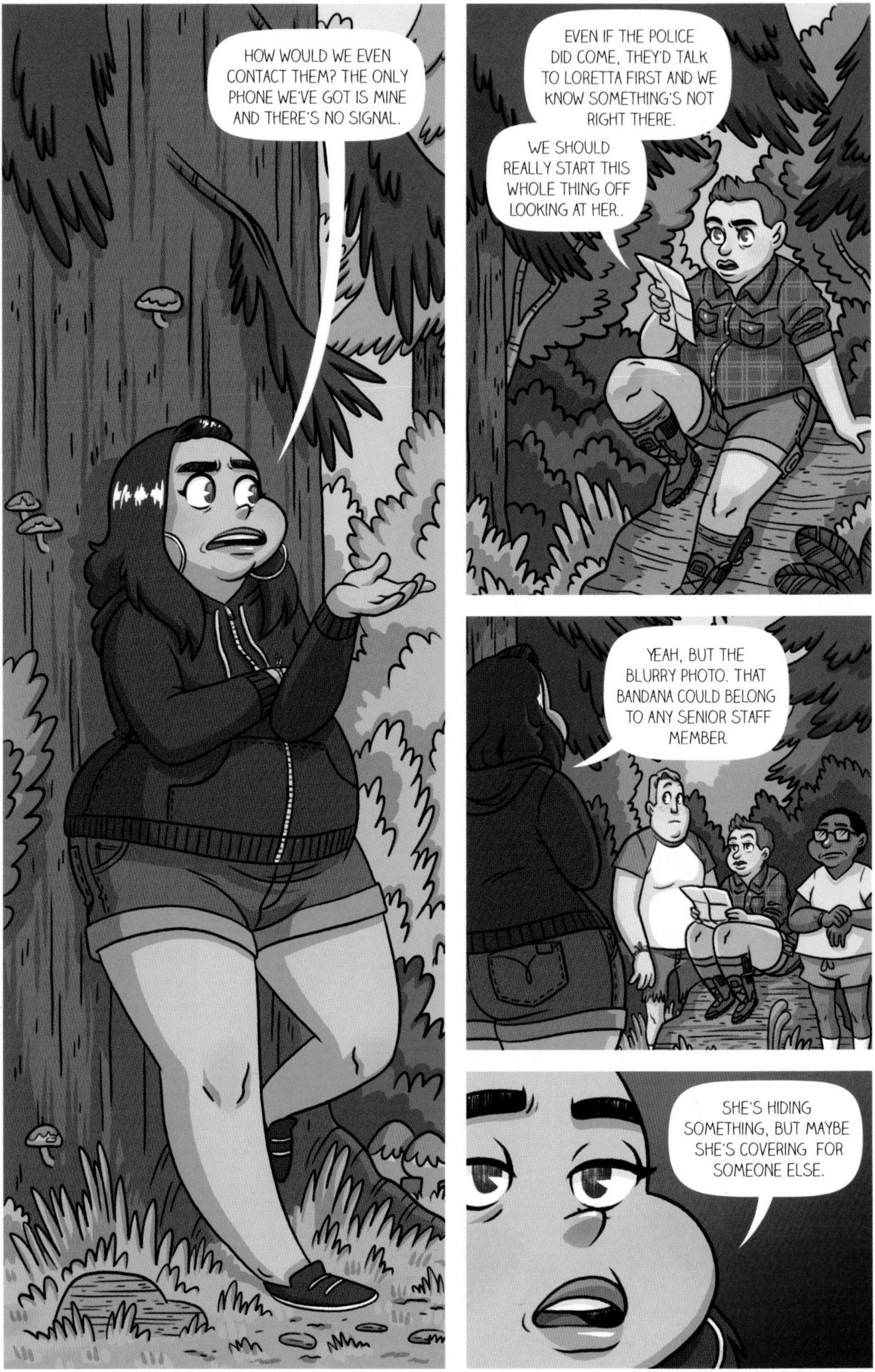
HOW WOULD WE EVEN CONTACT THEM? THE ONLY PHONE WE'VE GOT IS MINE AND THERE'S NO SIGNAL.
EVEN IF THE POLICE DID COME, THEY'D TALK TO LORETTA FIRST AND WE KNOW SOMETHING'S NOT RIGHT THERE.
WE SHOULD REALLY START THIS WHOLE THING OFF LOOKING AT HER..
YEAH, BUT THE BLURRY PHOTO. THAT BANDANA COULD BELONG TO ANY SENIOR STAFF MEMBER.
SHE'S HIDING SOMETHING, BUT MAYBE SHE'S COVERING FOR SOMEONE ELSE.

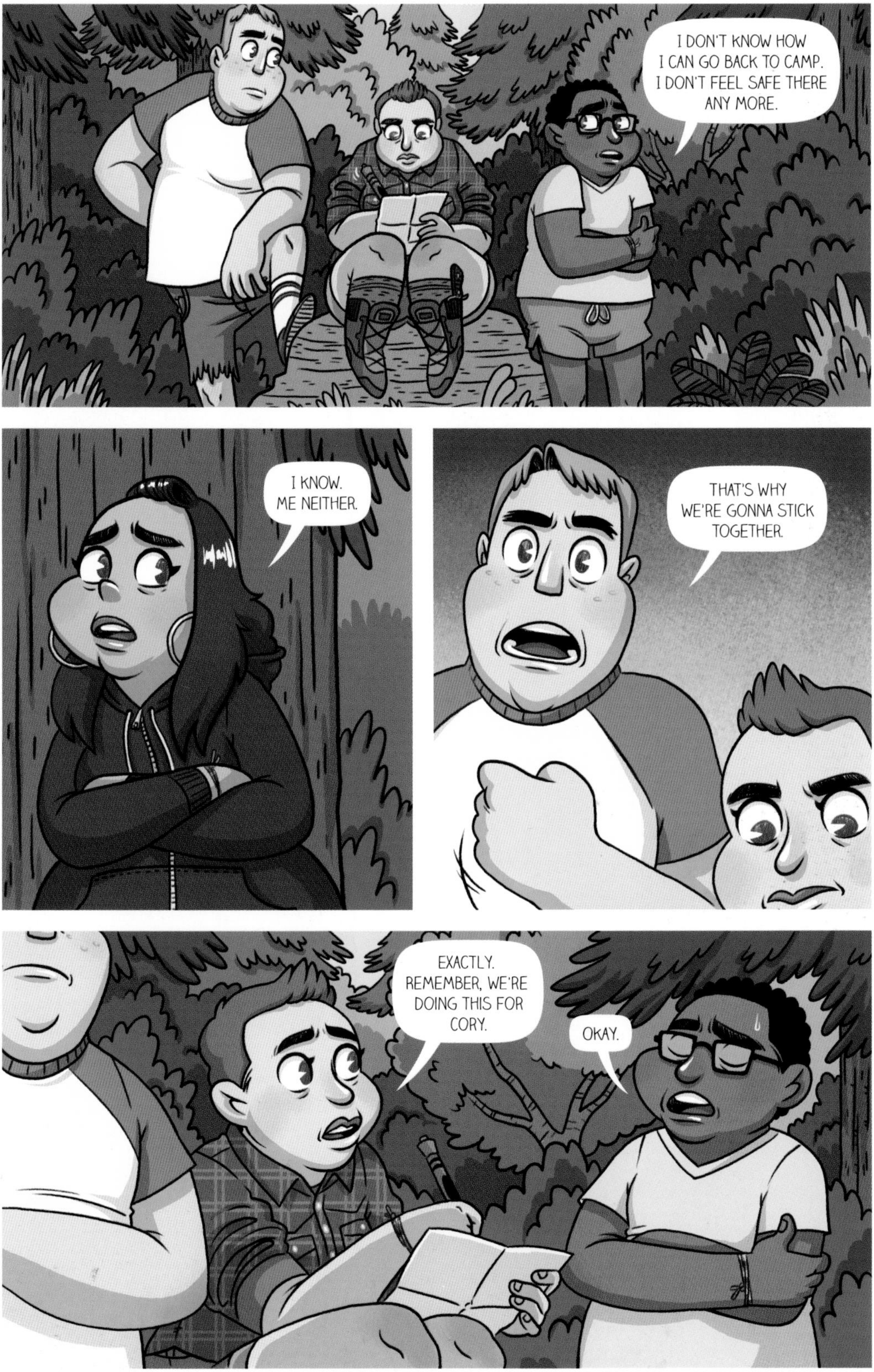
I DON'T KNOW HOW I CAN GO BACK TO CAMP. I DON'T FEEL SAFE THERE ANY MORE.
I KNOW. ME NEITHER.
THAT'S WHY WE'RE GONNA STICK TOGETHER.
EXACTLY. REMEMBER, WE'RE DOING THIS FOR CORY.
OKAY.

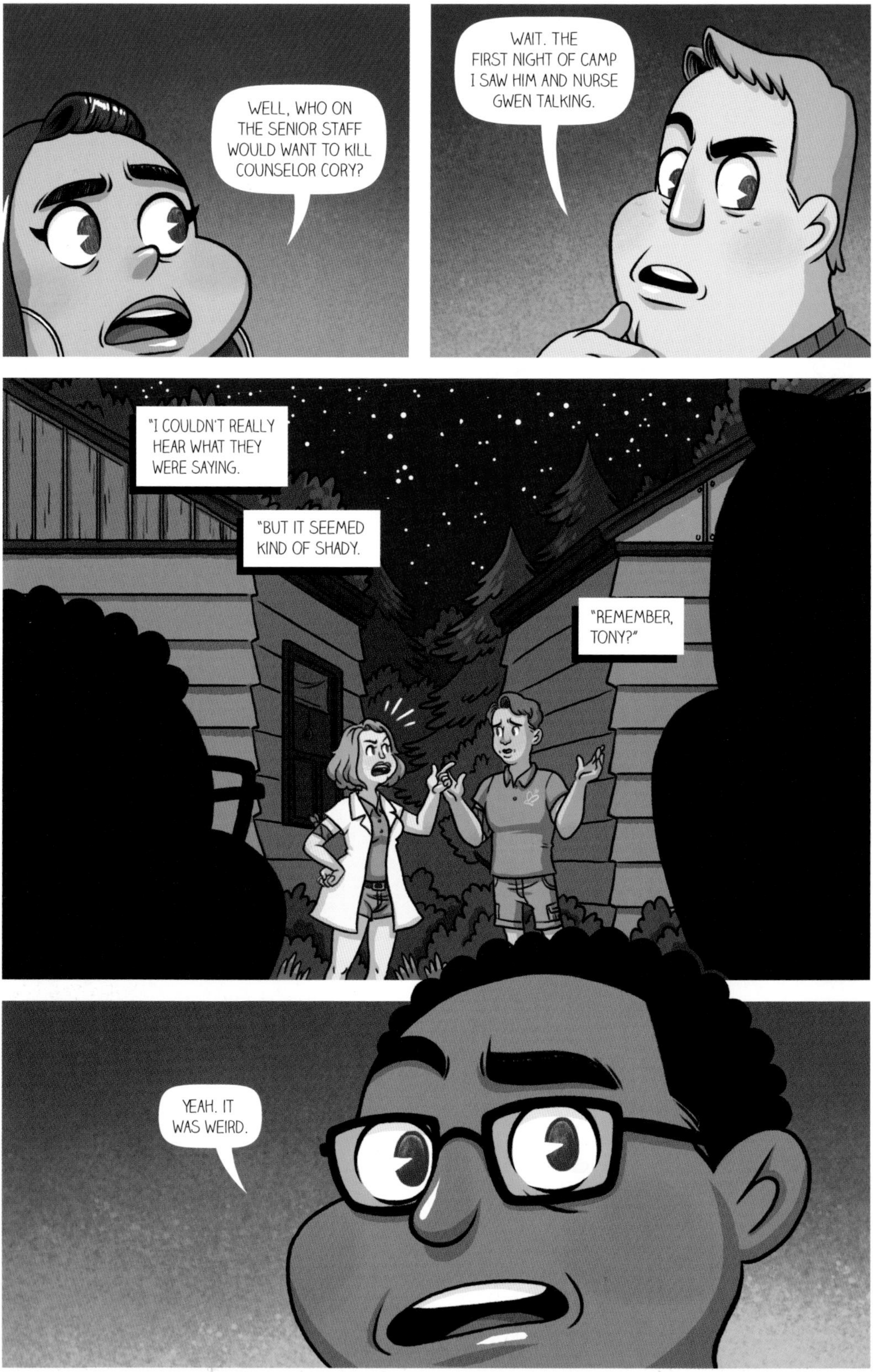
WELL, WHO ON THE SENIOR STAFF WOULD WANT TO KILL COUNSELOR CORY?
WAIT. THE FIRST NIGHT OF CAMP I SAW HIM AND NURSE GWEN TALKING.
"I COULDN'T REALLY HEAR WHAT THEY WERE SAYING.
"BUT IT SEEMED KIND OF SHADY.
"REMEMBER, TONY?"
YEAH. IT WAS WEIRD.

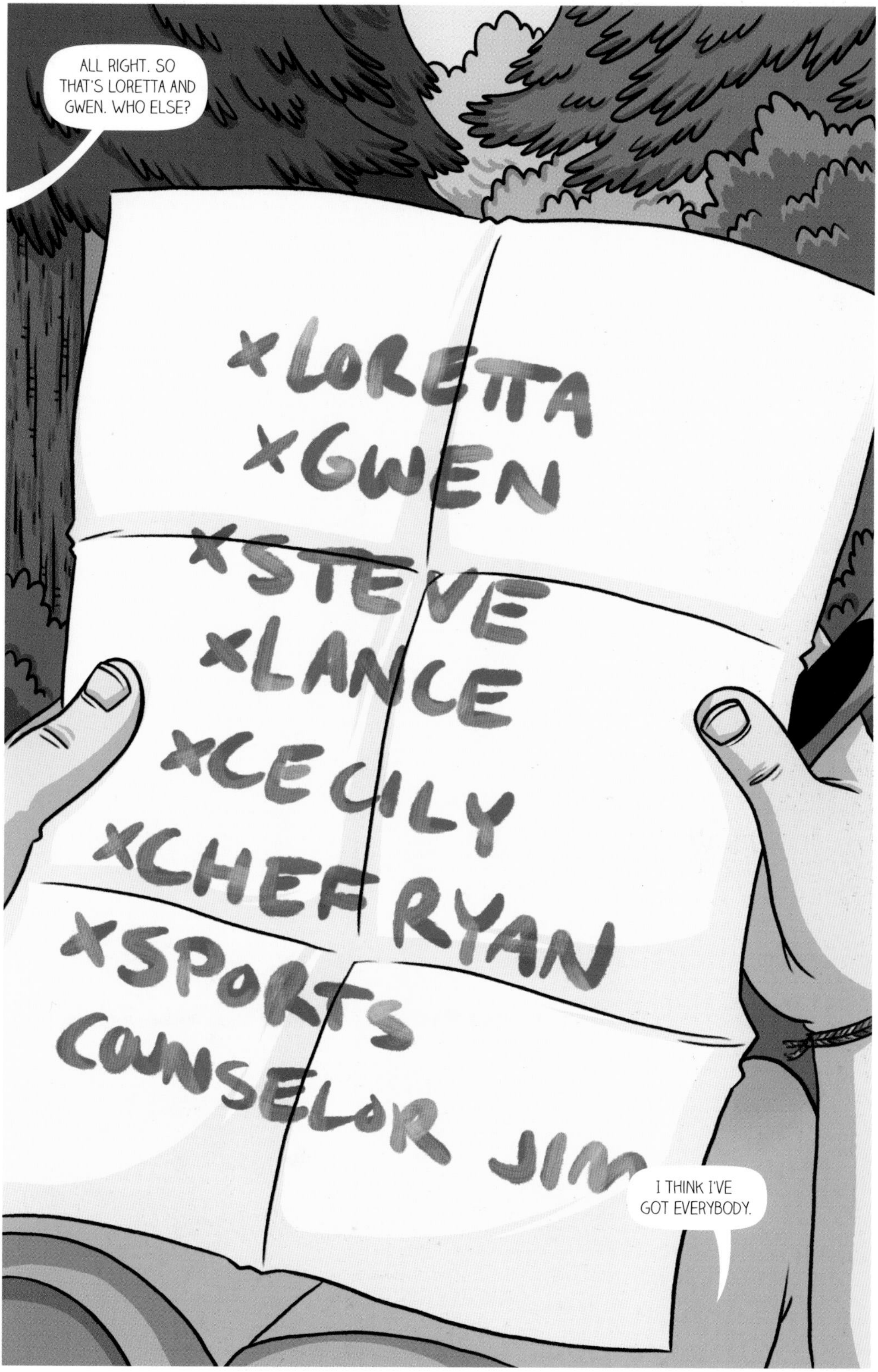

ALL RIGHT. SO THAT'S LORETTA AND GWEN. WHO ELSE?
xLORETTA
xGWEN
xSTEVE
xLANCE
xCECILY
xCHEF RYAN
xSPORTS COUNSELOR JIM
I THINK I'VE GOT EVERYBODY.

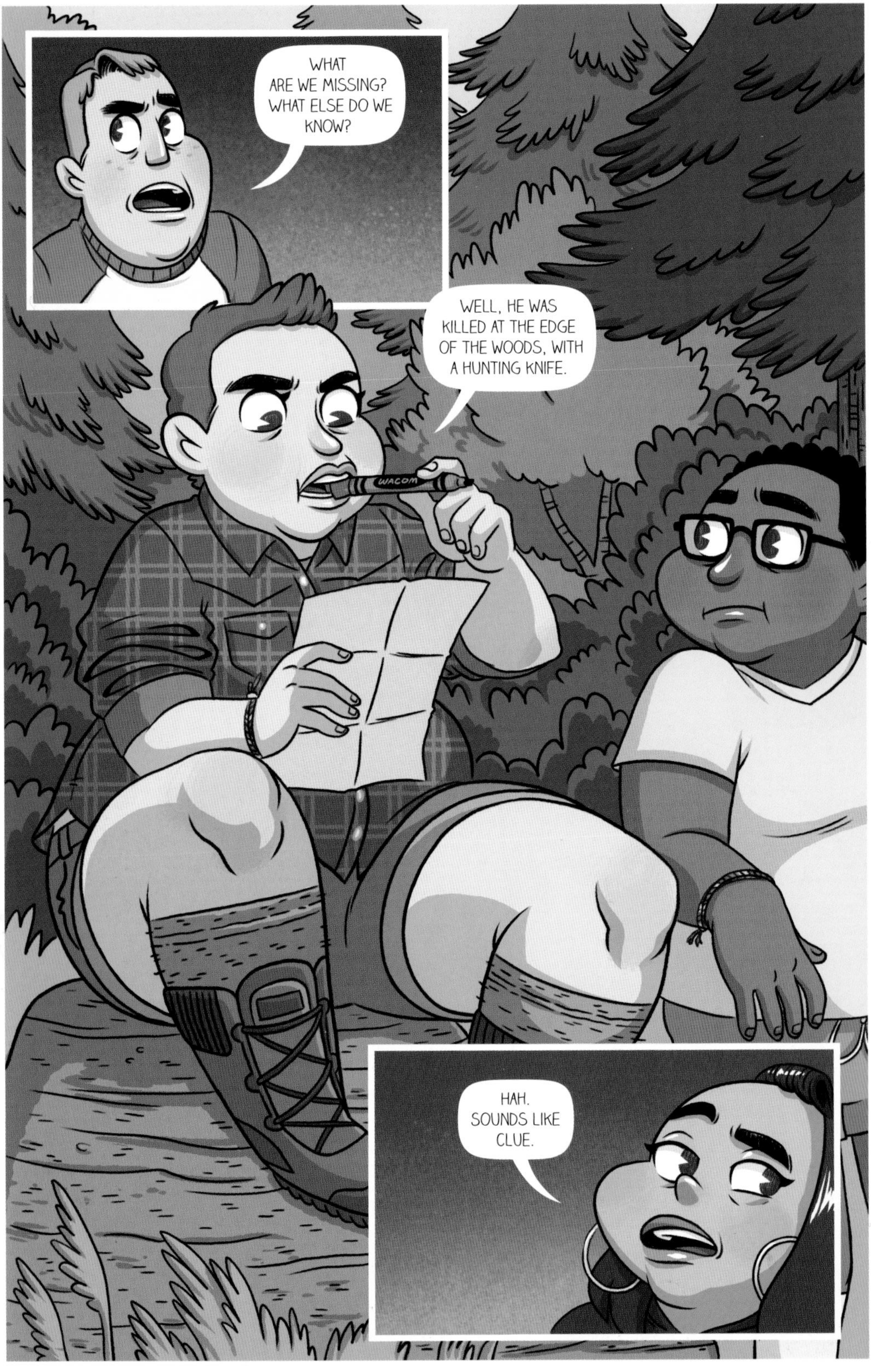
WHAT ARE WE MISSING? WHAT ELSE DO WE KNOW?
WELL, HE WAS KILLED AT THE EDGE OF THE WOODS, WITH A HUNTING KNIFE.
WACOM
HAH. SOUNDS LIKE CLUE.

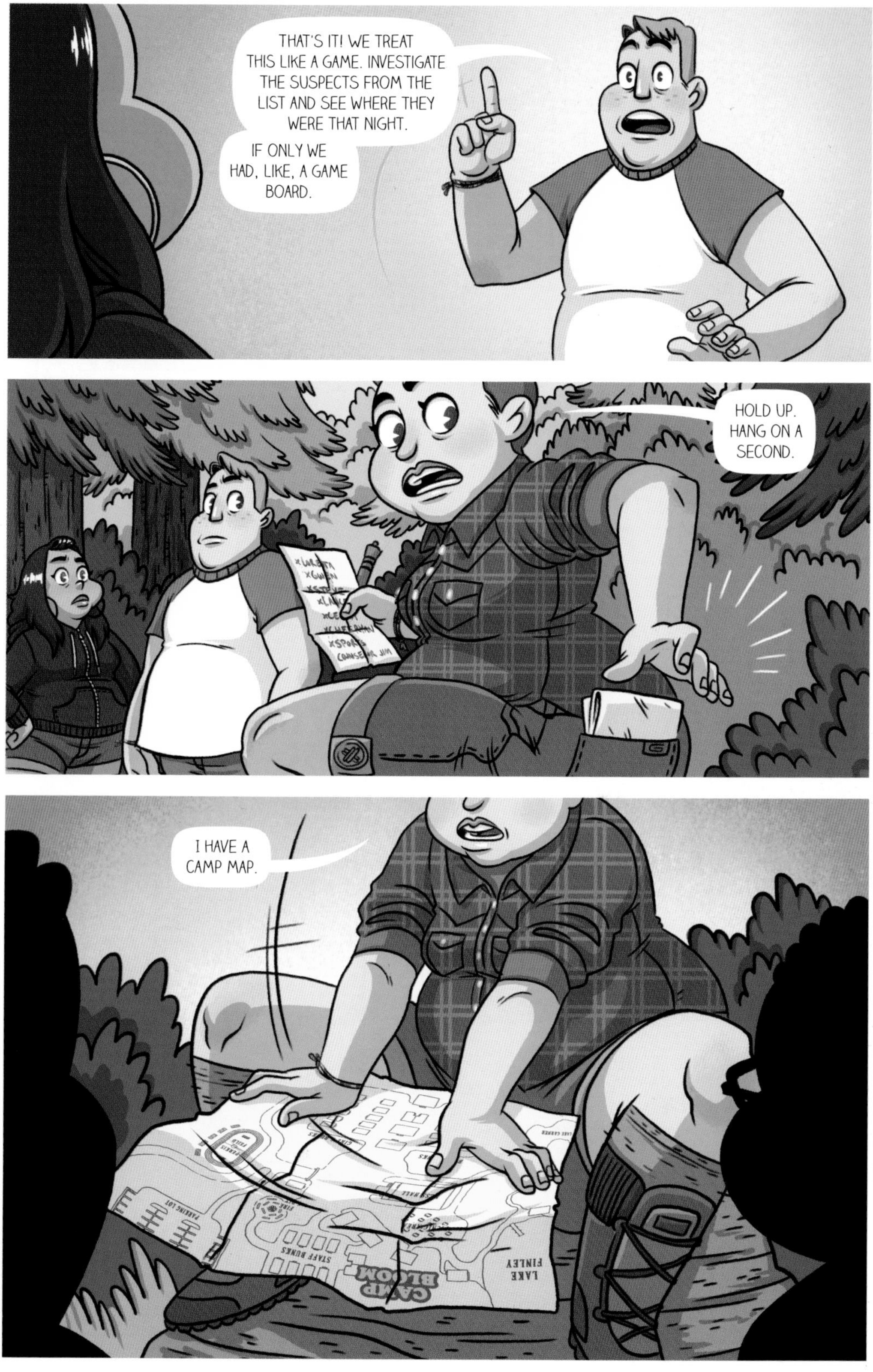
THAT'S IT! WE TREAT THIS LIKE A GAME. INVESTIGATE THE SUSPECTS FROM THE LIST AND SEE WHERE THEY WERE THAT NIGHT.
IF ONLY WE HAD, LIKE, A GAME BOARD.
HOLD UP. HANG ON A SECOND.
I HAVE A CAMP MAP.
PARKING LOT
STAFF BUNKS
LAKE FINLEY
CAMP BLOOM

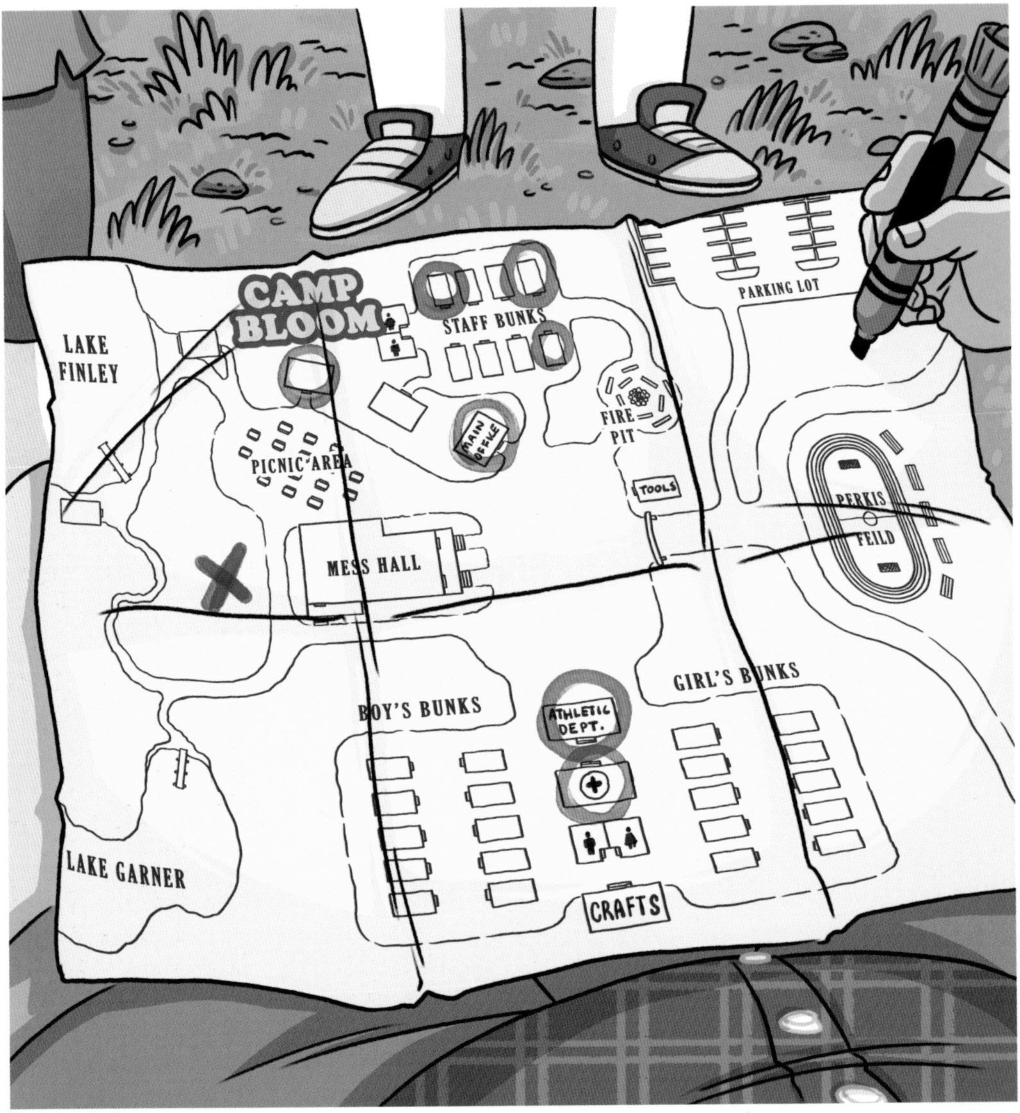
CAMP BLOOM
LAKE FINLEY
STAFF BUNKS
PARKING LOT
FIRE PIT
MAIN OFFICE
PICNIC AREA
TOOLS
PERKIS FEILD
MESS HALL
GIRL'S BUNKS
BOY'S BUNKS
ATHLETIC DEPT.
LAKE GARNER
CRAFTS

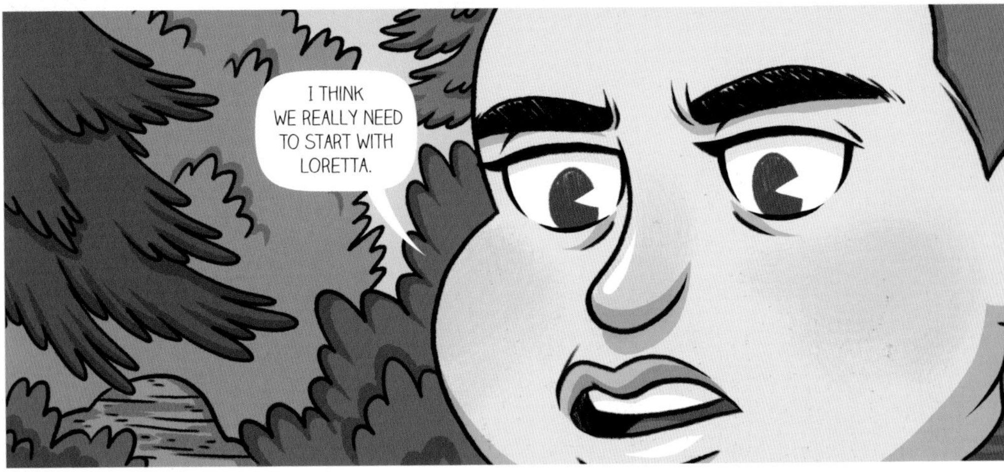
I THINK WE REALLY NEED TO START WITH LORETTA.

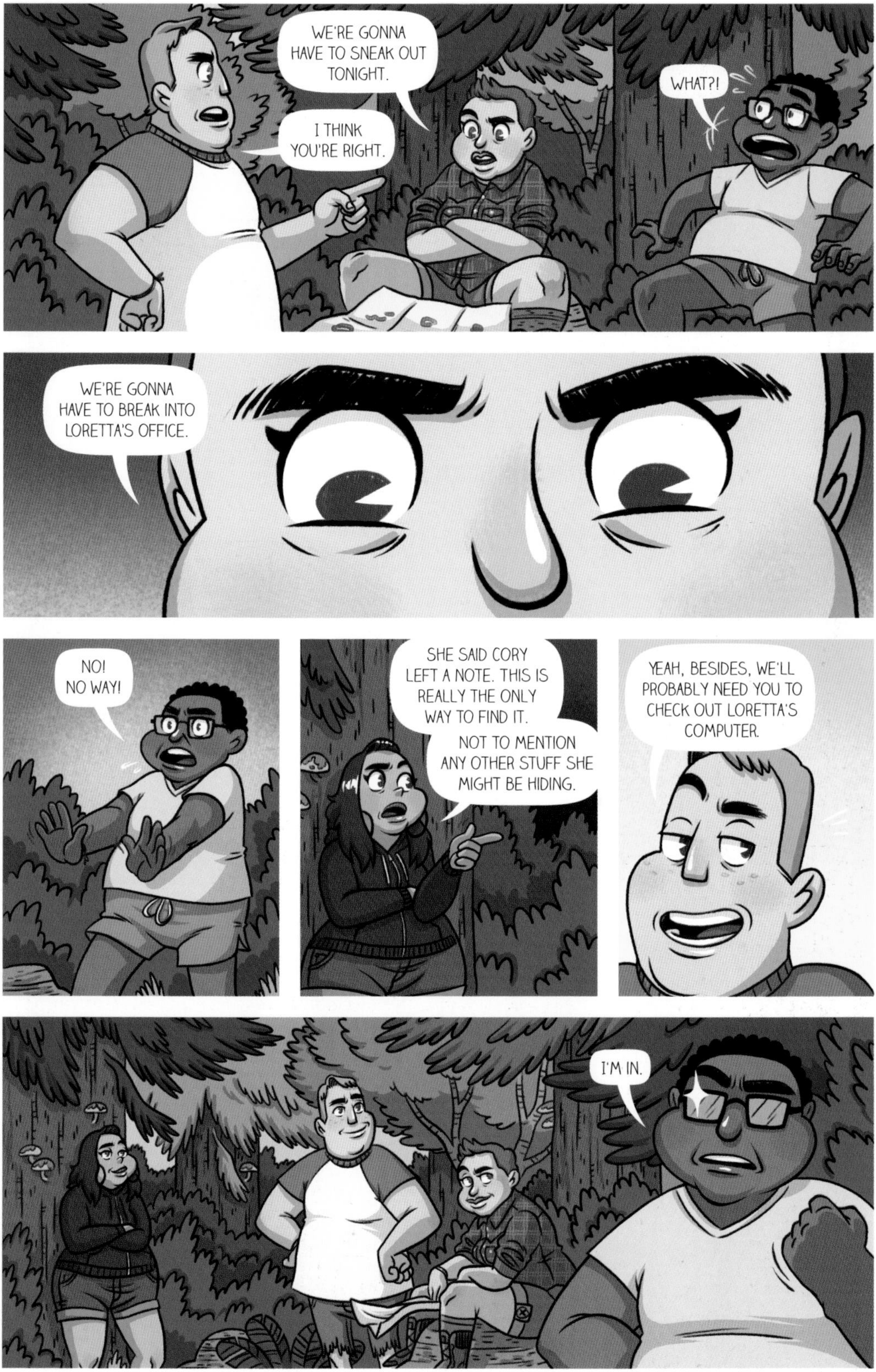
WE'RE GONNA HAVE TO SNEAK OUT TONIGHT.
I THINK YOU'RE RIGHT.
WHAT?!
WE'RE GONNA HAVE TO BREAK INTO LORETTA'S OFFICE.
NO! NO WAY!
SHE SAID CORY LEFT A NOTE. THIS IS REALLY THE ONLY WAY TO FIND IT.
NOT TO MENTION ANY OTHER STUFF SHE MIGHT BE HIDING.
YEAH, BESIDES, WE'LL PROBABLY NEED YOU TO CHECK OUT LORETTA'S COMPUTER.
I'M IN.

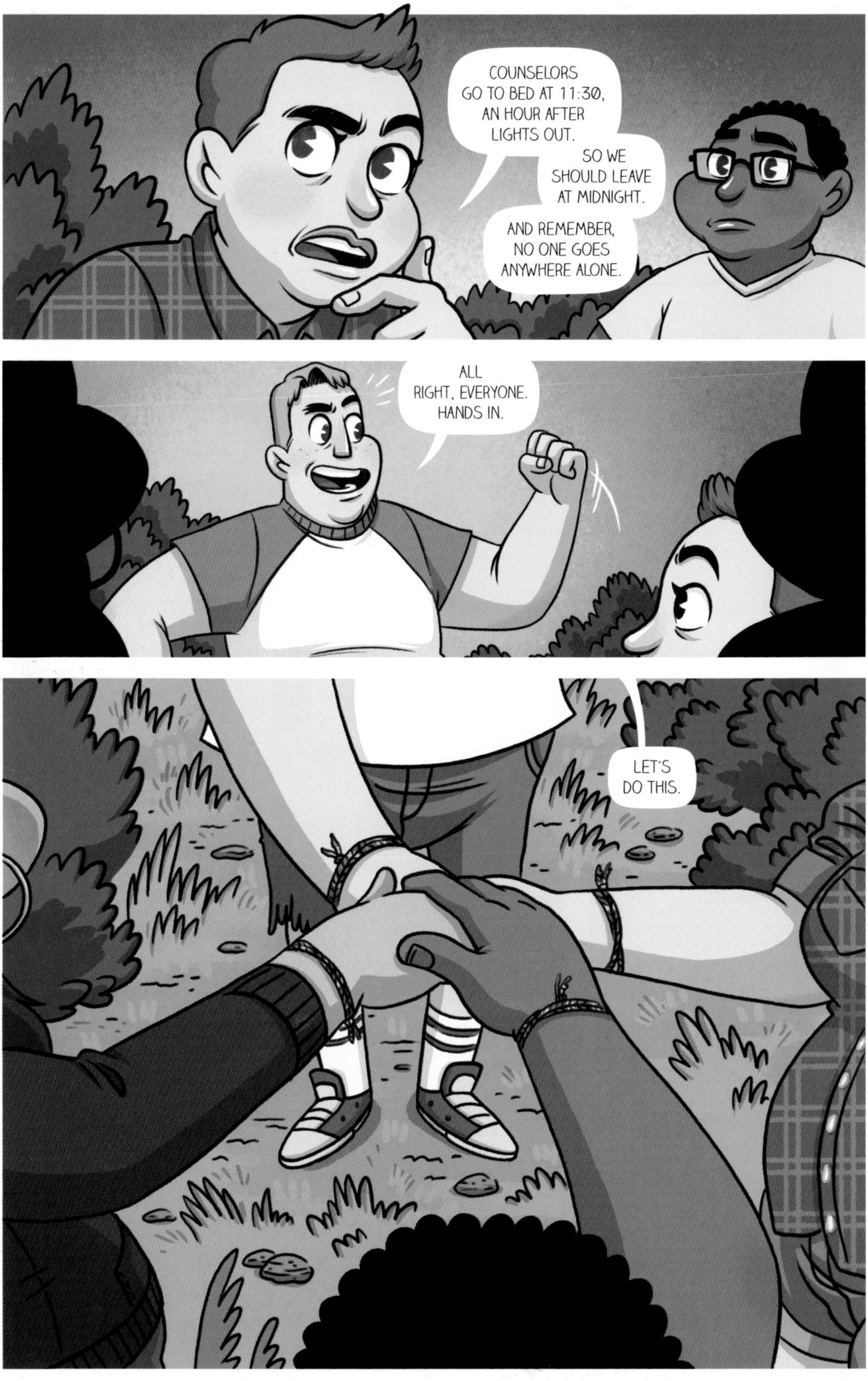
COUNSELORS GO TO BED AT 11:30, AN HOUR AFTER LIGHTS OUT.
SO WE SHOULD LEAVE AT MIDNIGHT.
AND REMEMBER, NO ONE GOES ANYWHERE ALONE.
ALL RIGHT, EVERYONE. HANDS IN.
LET'S DO THIS.

CHAPTER SEVEN

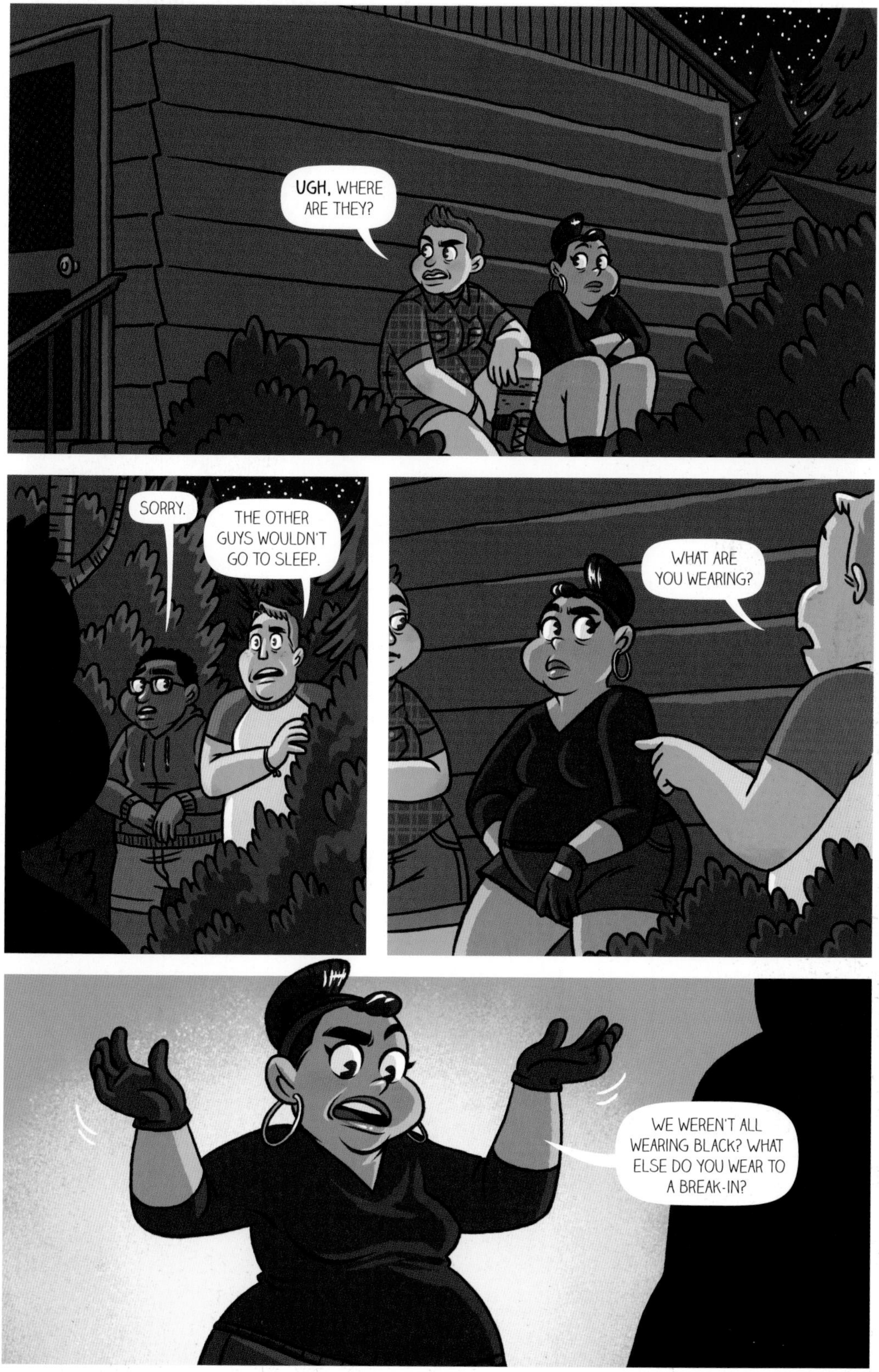
UGH, WHERE ARE THEY?
SORRY.
THE OTHER GUYS WOULDN'T GO TO SLEEP.
WHAT ARE YOU WEARING?
WE WEREN'T ALL WEARING BLACK? WHAT ELSE DO YOU WEAR TO A BREAK-IN?

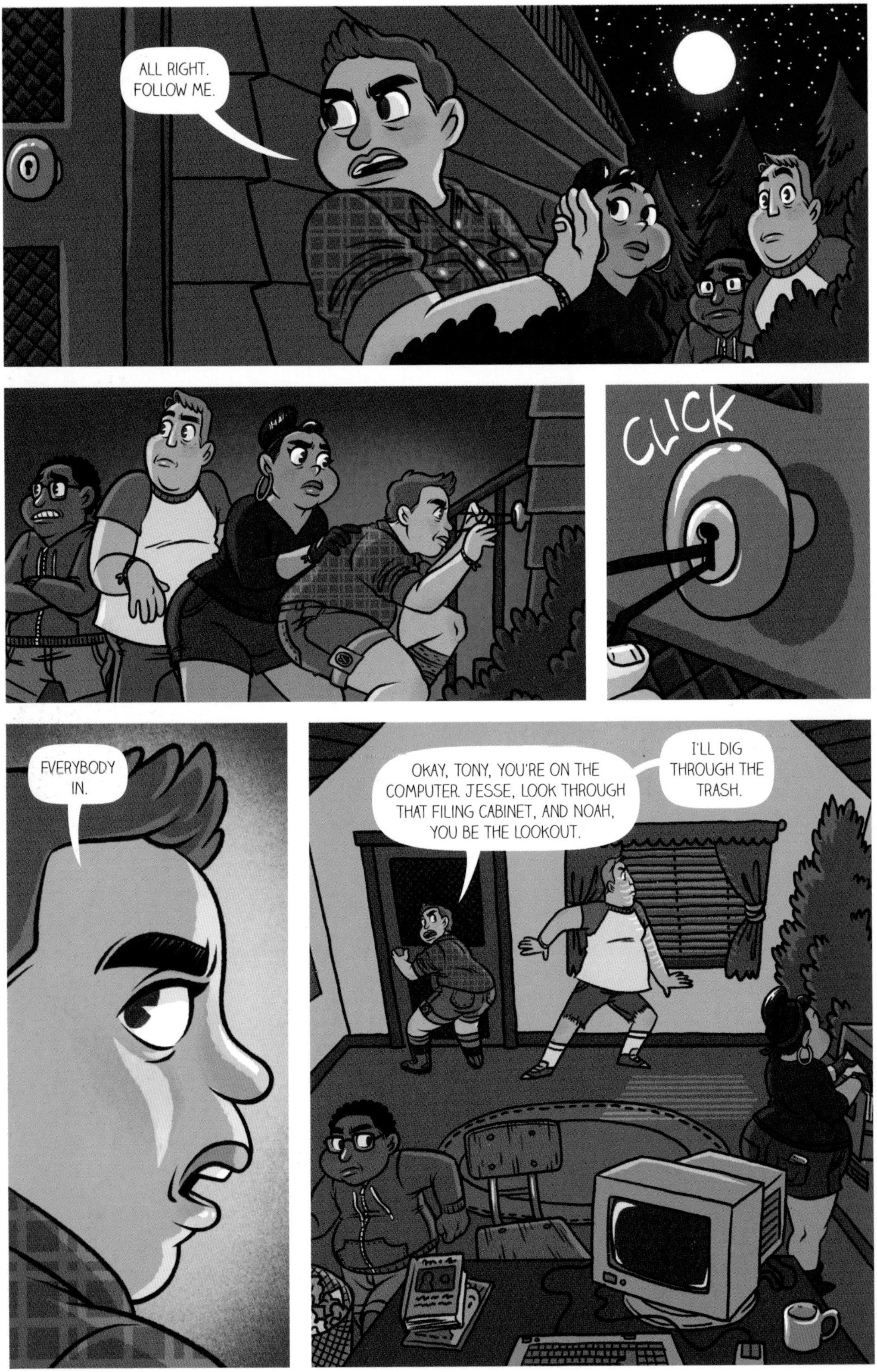
ALL RIGHT. FOLLOW ME.
CLICK
EVERYBODY IN.
OKAY, TONY, YOU'RE ON THE COMPUTER. JESSE, LOOK THROUGH THAT FILING CABINET, AND NOAH, YOU BE THE LOOKOUT.
I'LL DIG THROUGH THE TRASH.

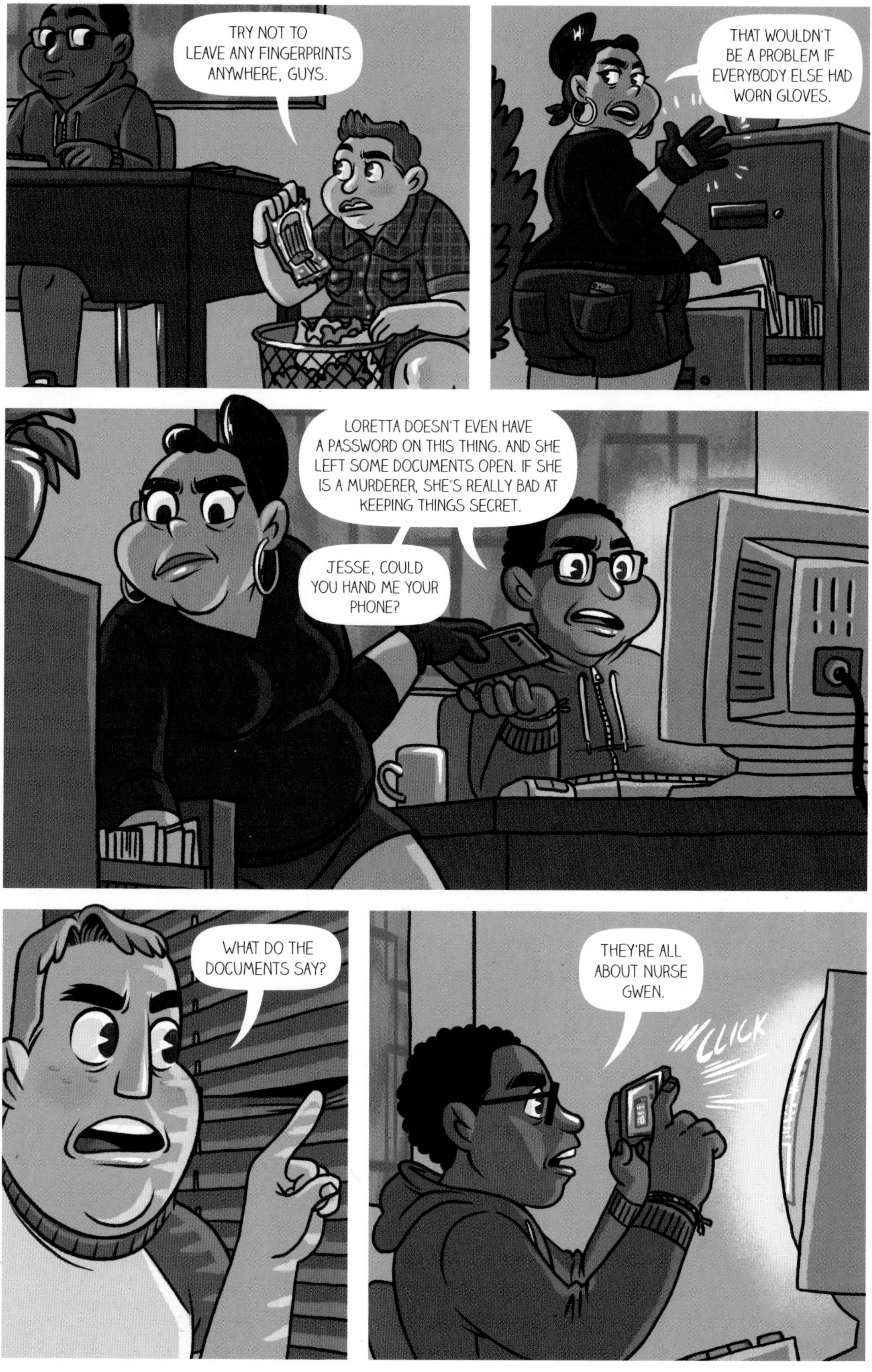
TRY NOT TO LEAVE ANY FINGERPRINTS ANYWHERE, GUYS.
THAT WOULDN'T BE A PROBLEM IF EVERYBODY ELSE HAD WORN GLOVES.
LORETTA DOESN'T EVEN HAVE A PASSWORD ON THIS THING. AND SHE LEFT SOME DOCUMENTS OPEN. IF SHE IS A MURDERER, SHE'S REALLY BAD AT KEEPING THINGS SECRET.
JESSE, COULD YOU HAND ME YOUR PHONE?
WHAT DO THE DOCUMENTS SAY?
THEY'RE ALL ABOUT NURSE GWEN.
CLICK

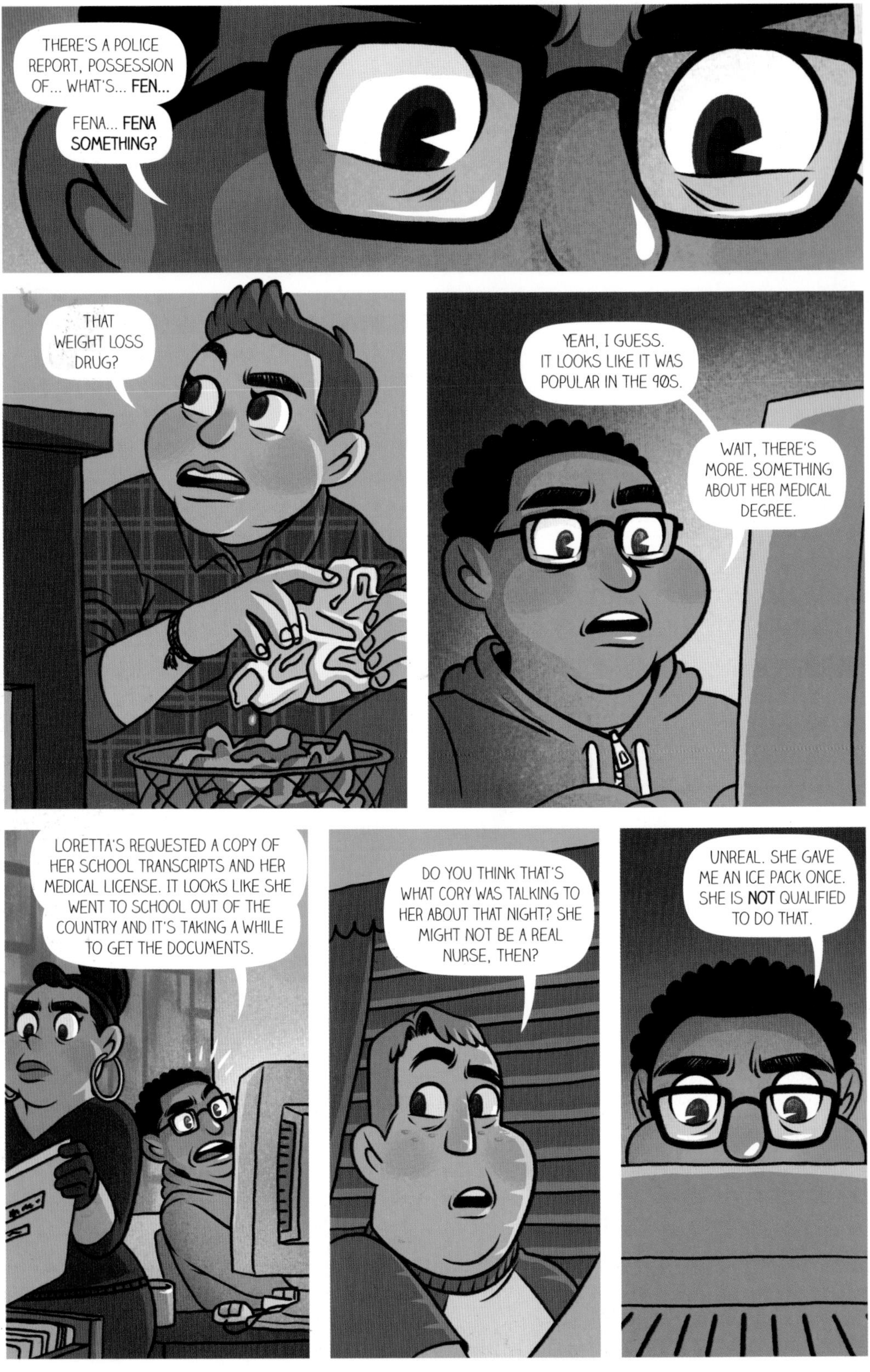
THERE'S A POLICE REPORT, POSSESSION OF... WHAT'S... **FEN...**
FENA... **FENA SOMETHING?**
THAT WEIGHT LOSS DRUG?
YEAH, I GUESS. IT LOOKS LIKE IT WAS POPULAR IN THE 90S.
WAIT, THERE'S MORE. SOMETHING ABOUT HER MEDICAL DEGREE.
LORETTA'S REQUESTED A COPY OF HER SCHOOL TRANSCRIPTS AND HER MEDICAL LICENSE. IT LOOKS LIKE SHE WENT TO SCHOOL OUT OF THE COUNTRY AND IT'S TAKING A WHILE TO GET THE DOCUMENTS.
DO YOU THINK THAT'S WHAT CORY WAS TALKING TO HER ABOUT THAT NIGHT? SHE MIGHT NOT BE A REAL NURSE, THEN?
UNREAL. SHE GAVE ME AN ICE PACK ONCE. SHE IS **NOT** QUALIFIED TO DO THAT.

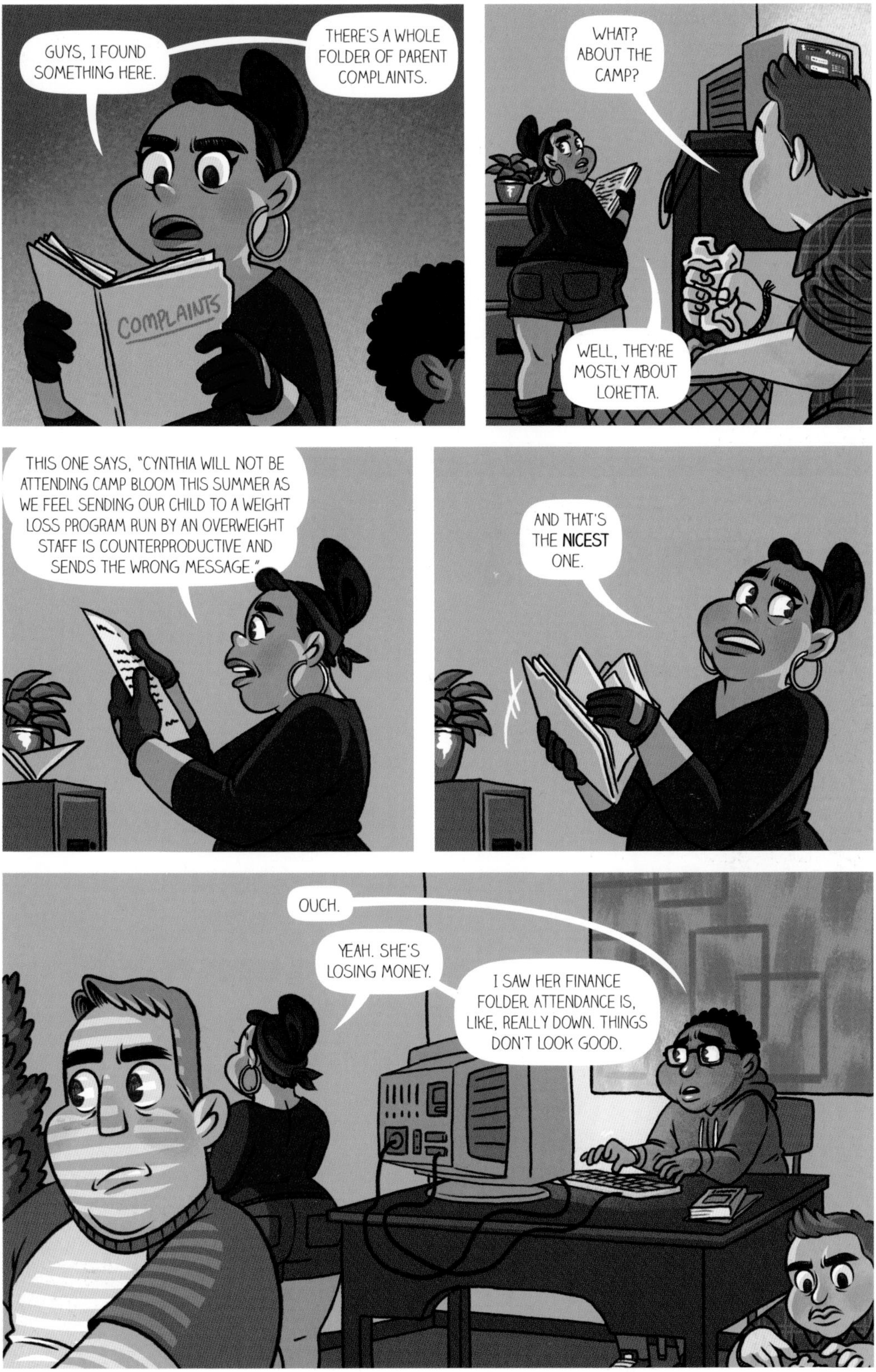
GUYS, I FOUND SOMETHING HERE.
THERE'S A WHOLE FOLDER OF PARENT COMPLAINTS.
COMPLAINTS
WHAT? ABOUT THE CAMP?
WELL, THEY'RE MOSTLY ABOUT LORETTA.
THIS ONE SAYS, "CYNTHIA WILL NOT BE ATTENDING CAMP BLOOM THIS SUMMER AS WE FEEL SENDING OUR CHILD TO A WEIGHT LOSS PROGRAM RUN BY AN OVERWEIGHT STAFF IS COUNTERPRODUCTIVE AND SENDS THE WRONG MESSAGE."
AND THAT'S THE **NICEST** ONE.
OUCH.
YEAH. SHE'S LOSING MONEY.
I SAW HER FINANCE FOLDER. ATTENDANCE IS, LIKE, REALLY DOWN. THINGS DON'T LOOK GOOD.

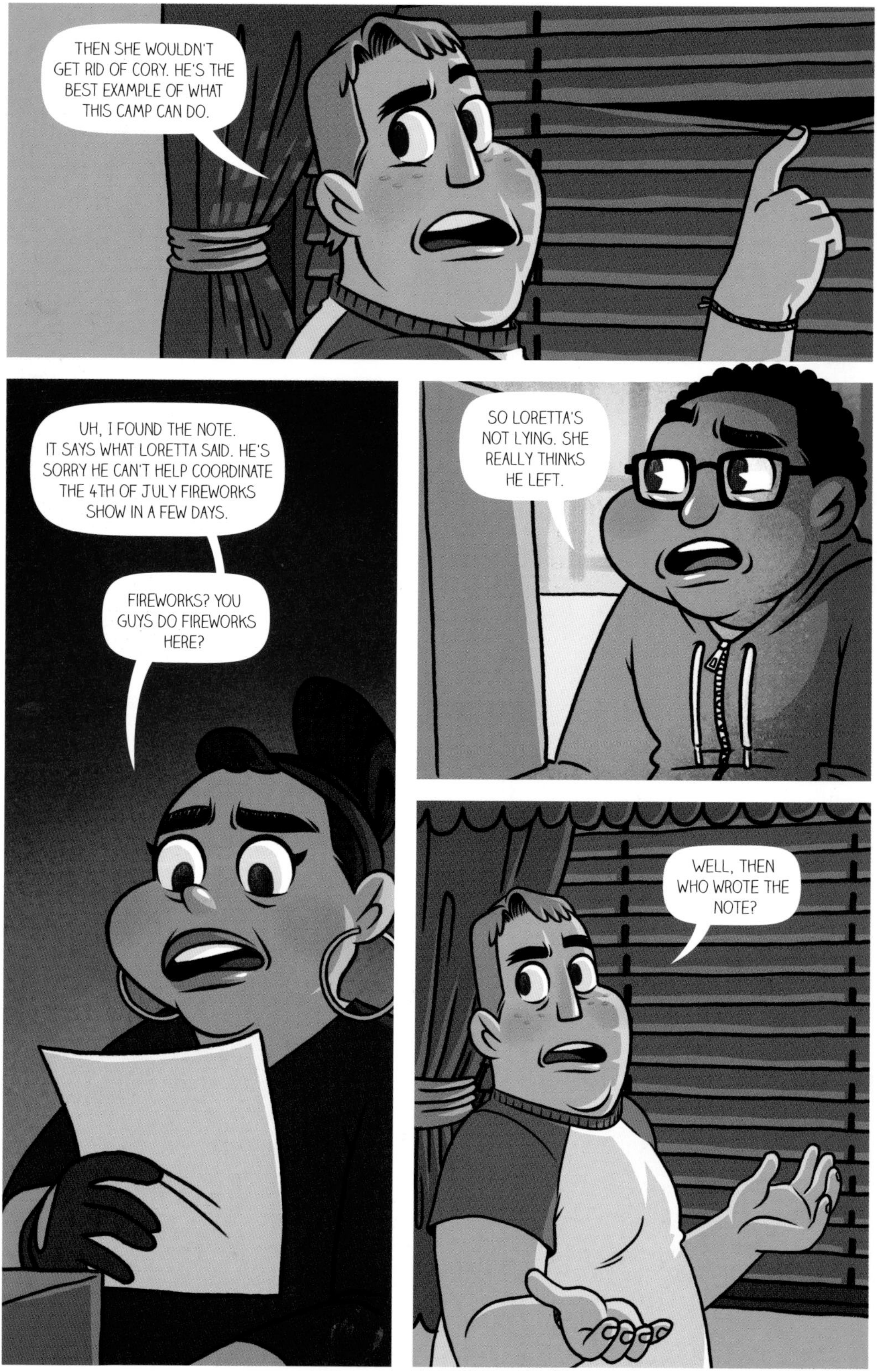
THEN SHE WOULDN'T GET RID OF CORY. HE'S THE BEST EXAMPLE OF WHAT THIS CAMP CAN DO.
UH, I FOUND THE NOTE. IT SAYS WHAT LORETTA SAID. HE'S SORRY HE CAN'T HELP COORDINATE THE 4TH OF JULY FIREWORKS SHOW IN A FEW DAYS.
FIREWORKS? YOU GUYS DO FIREWORKS HERE?
SO LORETTA'S NOT LYING. SHE REALLY THINKS HE LEFT.
WELL, THEN WHO WROTE THE NOTE?

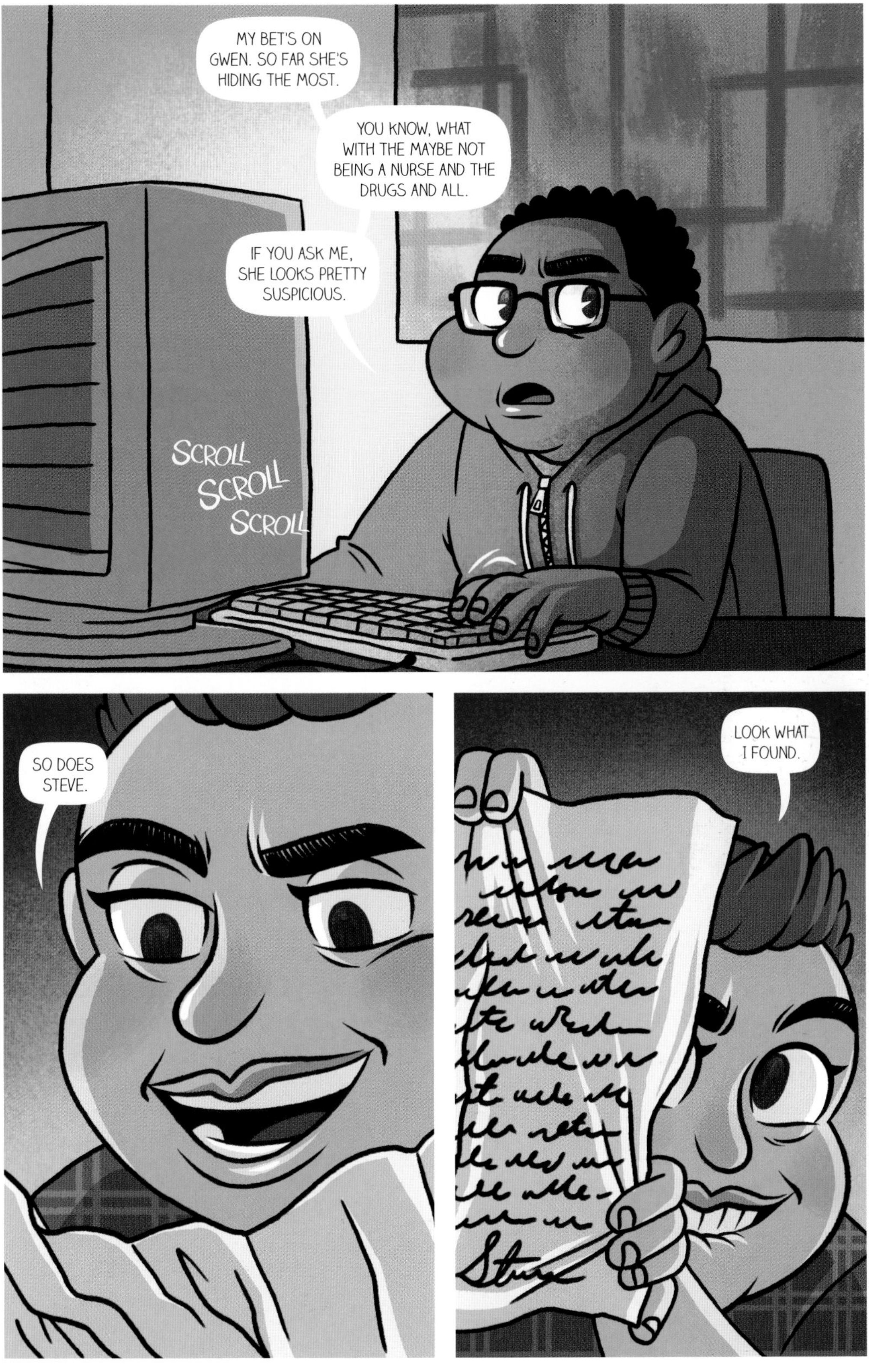
MY BET'S ON GWEN. SO FAR SHE'S HIDING THE MOST.
YOU KNOW, WHAT WITH THE MAYBE NOT BEING A NURSE AND THE DRUGS AND ALL.
IF YOU ASK ME, SHE LOOKS PRETTY SUSPICIOUS.
SCROLL
SCROLL
SCROLL
SO DOES STEVE.
LOOK WHAT I FOUND.

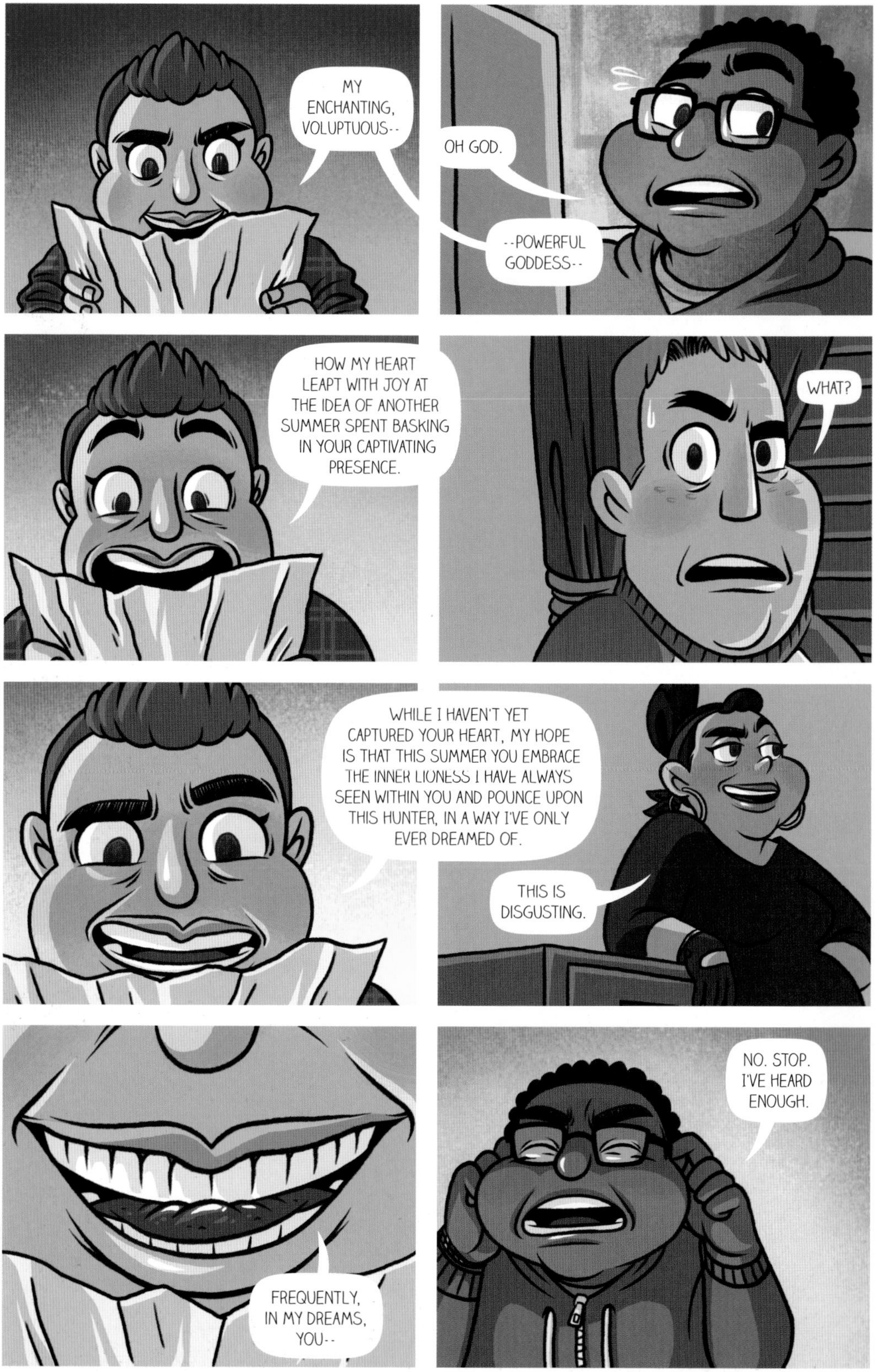
MY ENCHANTING, VOLUPTUOUS--
OH GOD.
--POWERFUL GODDESS--
HOW MY HEART LEAPT WITH JOY AT THE IDEA OF ANOTHER SUMMER SPENT BASKING IN YOUR CAPTIVATING PRESENCE.
WHAT?
WHILE I HAVEN'T YET CAPTURED YOUR HEART, MY HOPE IS THAT THIS SUMMER YOU EMBRACE THE INNER LIONESS I HAVE ALWAYS SEEN WITHIN YOU AND POUNCE UPON THIS HUNTER, IN A WAY I'VE ONLY EVER DREAMED OF.
THIS IS DISGUSTING.
FREQUENTLY, IN MY DREAMS, YOU--
NO. STOP. I'VE HEARD ENOUGH.

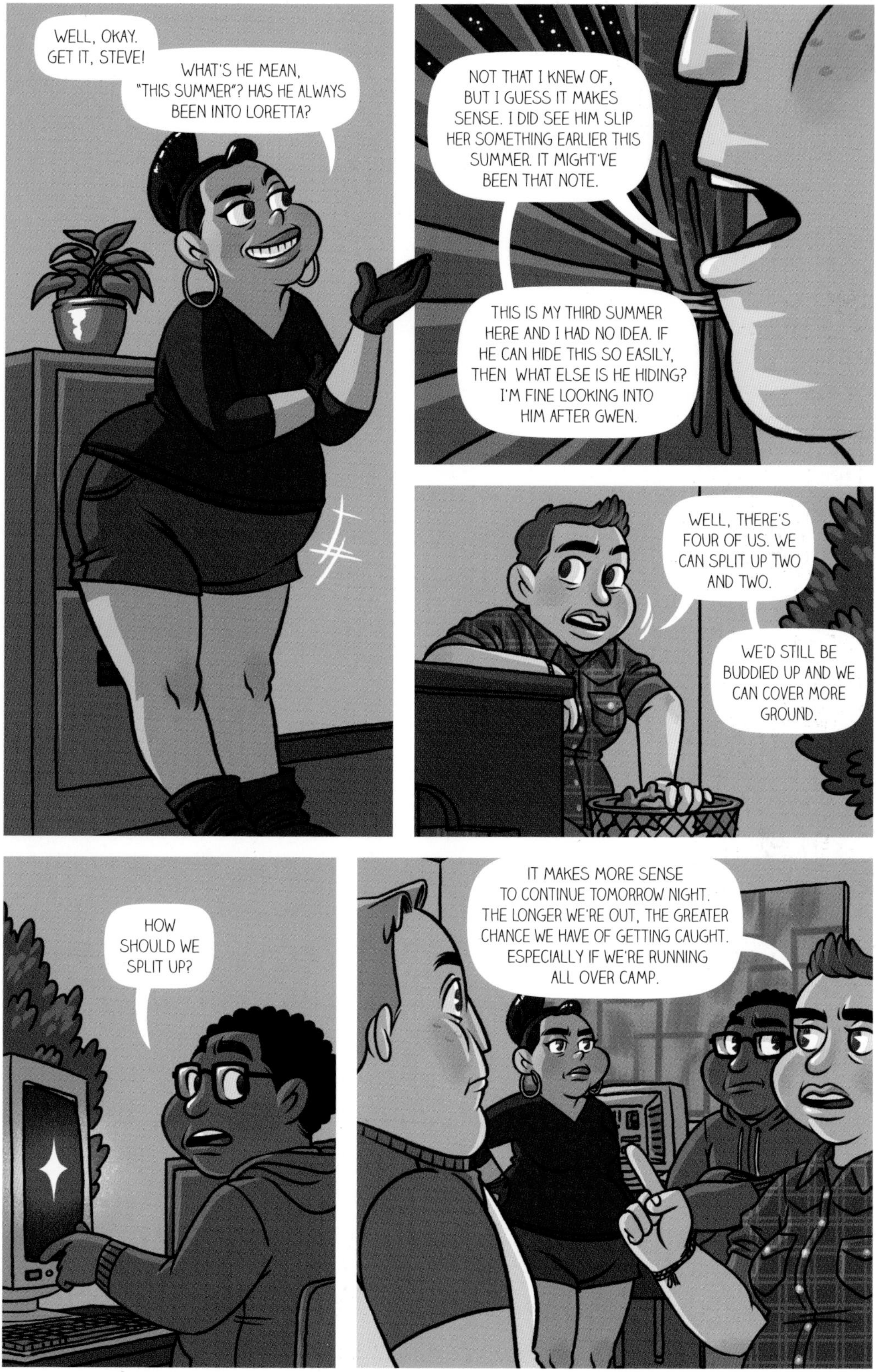
WELL, OKAY. GET IT, STEVE!
WHAT'S HE MEAN, "THIS SUMMER"? HAS HE ALWAYS BEEN INTO LORETTA?
NOT THAT I KNEW OF, BUT I GUESS IT MAKES SENSE. I DID SEE HIM SLIP HER SOMETHING EARLIER THIS SUMMER. IT MIGHT'VE BEEN THAT NOTE.
THIS IS MY THIRD SUMMER HERE AND I HAD NO IDEA. IF HE CAN HIDE THIS SO EASILY, THEN WHAT ELSE IS HE HIDING? I'M FINE LOOKING INTO HIM AFTER GWEN.
WELL, THERE'S FOUR OF US. WE CAN SPLIT UP TWO AND TWO.
WE'D STILL BE BUDDIED UP AND WE CAN COVER MORE GROUND.
HOW SHOULD WE SPLIT UP?
IT MAKES MORE SENSE TO CONTINUE TOMORROW NIGHT. THE LONGER WE'RE OUT, THE GREATER CHANCE WE HAVE OF GETTING CAUGHT. ESPECIALLY IF WE'RE RUNNING ALL OVER CAMP.

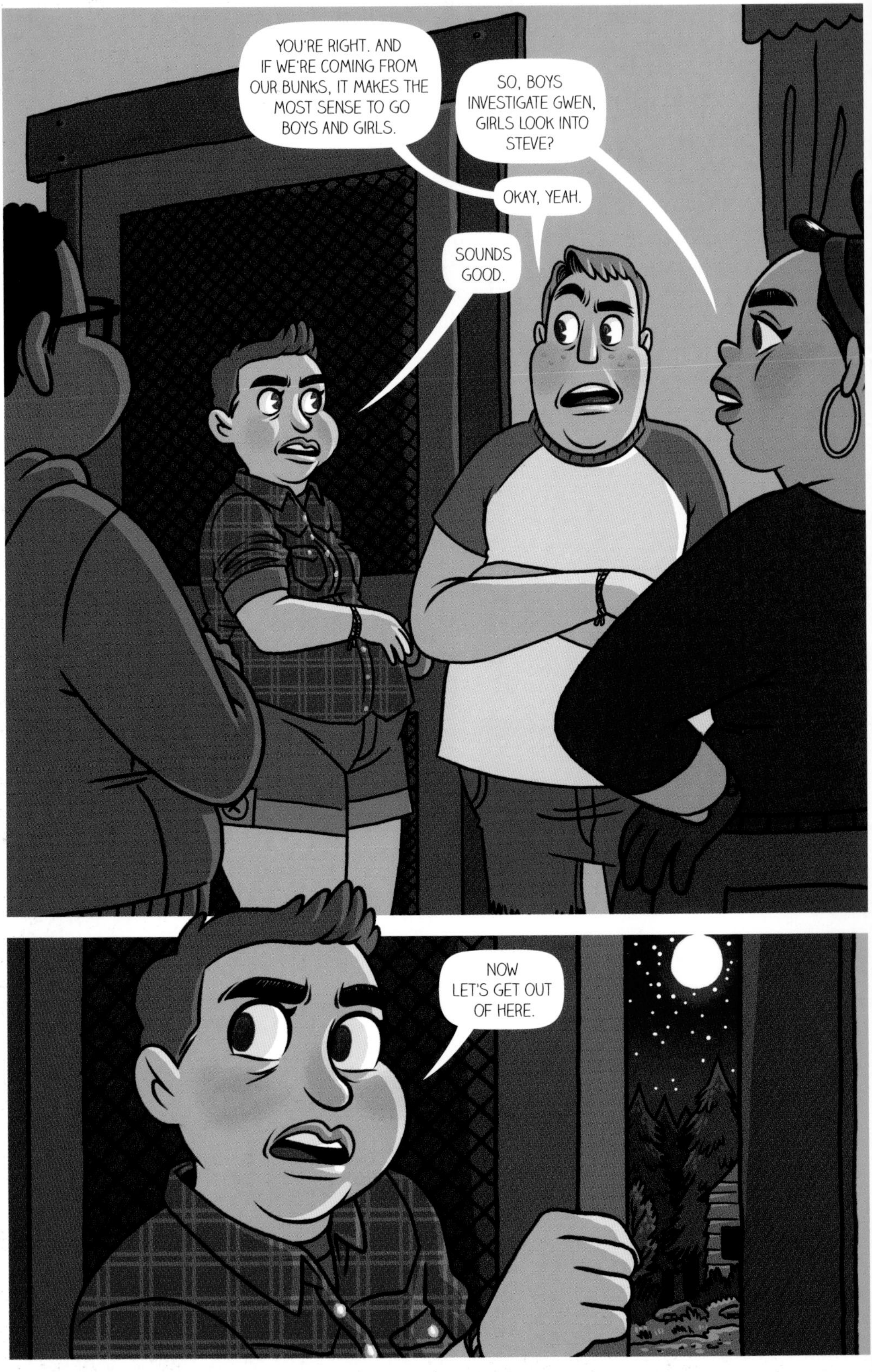
YOU'RE RIGHT. AND IF WE'RE COMING FROM OUR BUNKS, IT MAKES THE MOST SENSE TO GO BOYS AND GIRLS.
SO, BOYS INVESTIGATE GWEN, GIRLS LOOK INTO STEVE?
OKAY, YEAH.
SOUNDS GOOD.
NOW LET'S GET OUT OF HERE.

CHAPTER EIGHT

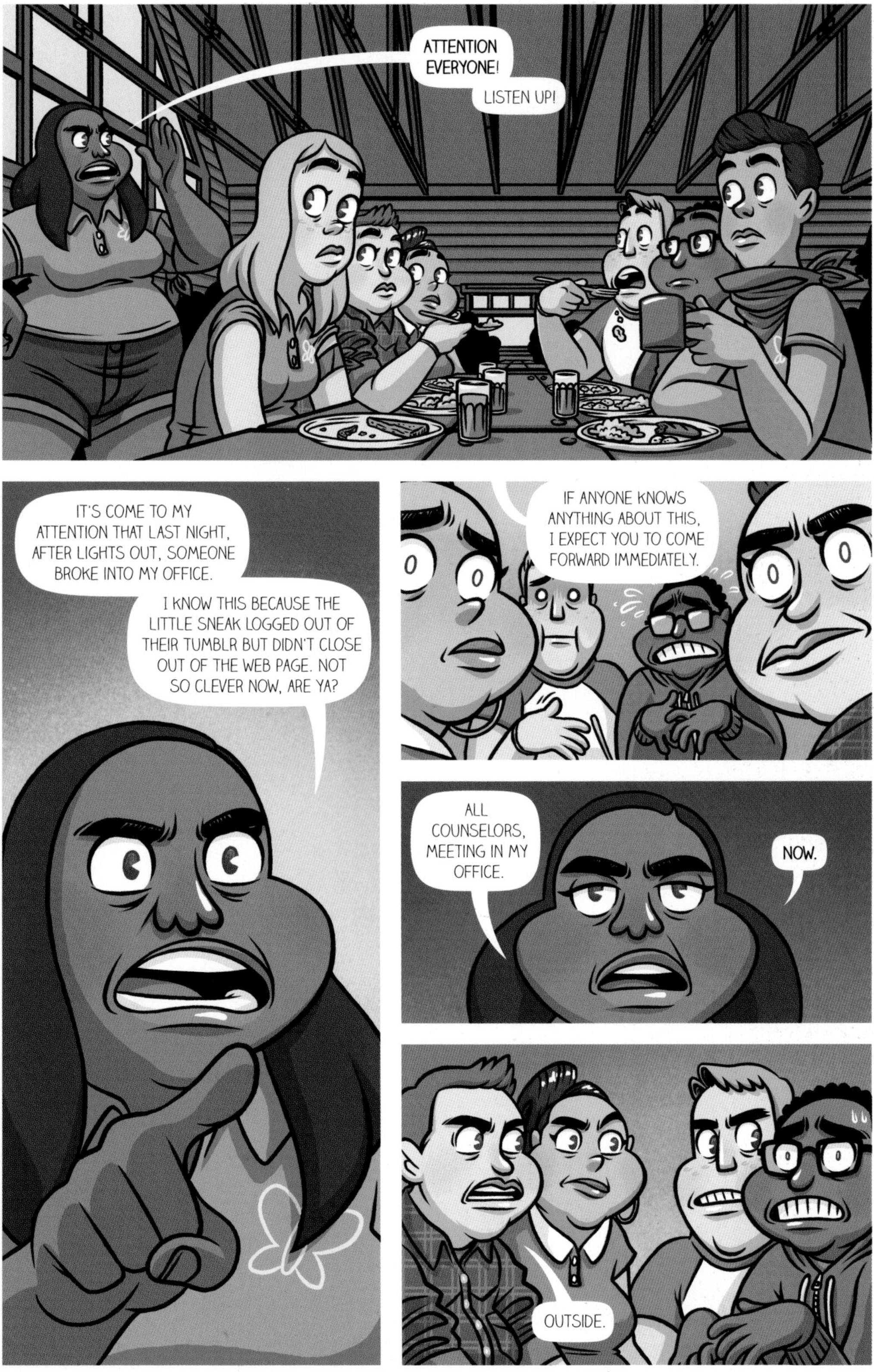
ATTENTION EVERYONE!
LISTEN UP!
IT'S COME TO MY ATTENTION THAT LAST NIGHT, AFTER LIGHTS OUT, SOMEONE BROKE INTO MY OFFICE.
I KNOW THIS BECAUSE THE LITTLE SNEAK LOGGED OUT OF THEIR TUMBLR BUT DIDN'T CLOSE OUT OF THE WEB PAGE. NOT SO CLEVER NOW, ARE YA?
IF ANYONE KNOWS ANYTHING ABOUT THIS, I EXPECT YOU TO COME FORWARD IMMEDIATELY.
ALL COUNSELORS, MEETING IN MY OFFICE.
NOW.
OUTSIDE.

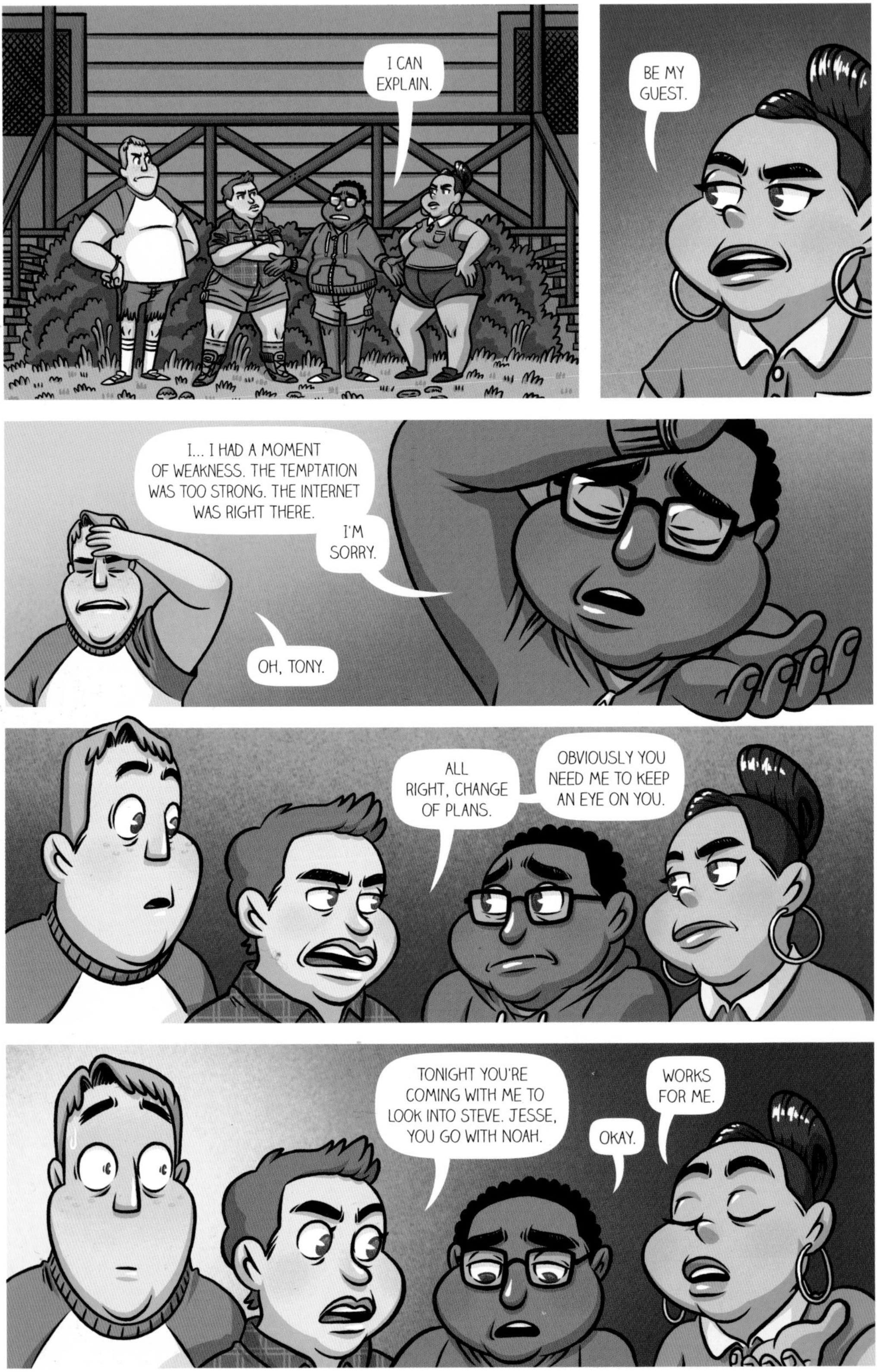
I CAN EXPLAIN.
BE MY GUEST.
I... I HAD A MOMENT OF WEAKNESS. THE TEMPTATION WAS TOO STRONG. THE INTERNET WAS RIGHT THERE.
I'M SORRY.
OH, TONY.
ALL RIGHT, CHANGE OF PLANS.
OBVIOUSLY YOU NEED ME TO KEEP AN EYE ON YOU.
TONIGHT YOU'RE COMING WITH ME TO LOOK INTO STEVE. JESSE, YOU GO WITH NOAH.
OKAY.
WORKS FOR ME.

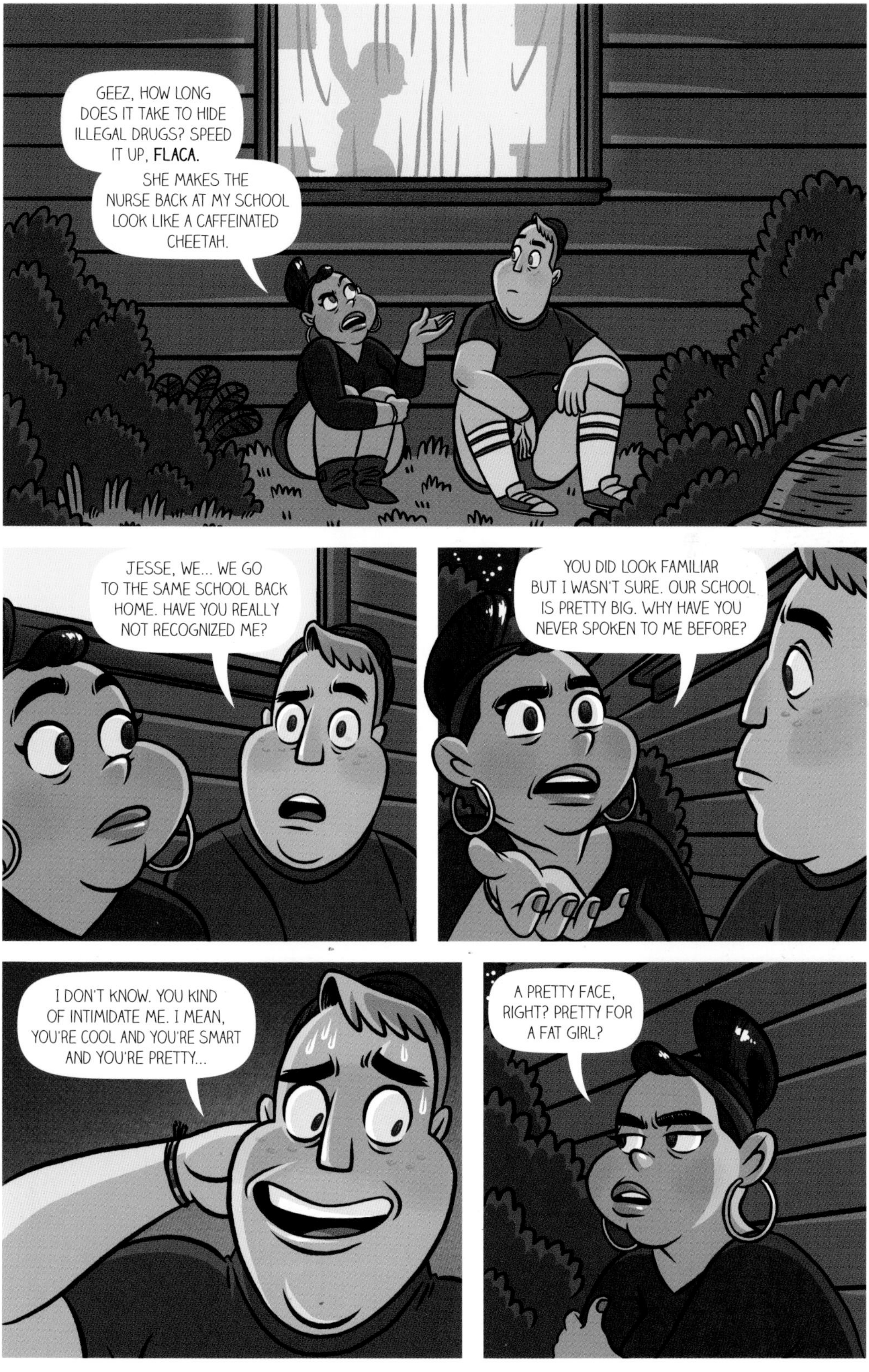
GEEZ, HOW LONG DOES IT TAKE TO HIDE ILLEGAL DRUGS? SPEED IT UP, **FLACA.**
SHE MAKES THE NURSE BACK AT MY SCHOOL LOOK LIKE A CAFFEINATED CHEETAH.
JESSE, WE... WE GO TO THE SAME SCHOOL BACK HOME. HAVE YOU REALLY NOT RECOGNIZED ME?
YOU DID LOOK FAMILIAR BUT I WASN'T SURE. OUR SCHOOL IS PRETTY BIG. WHY HAVE YOU NEVER SPOKEN TO ME BEFORE?
I DON'T KNOW. YOU KIND OF INTIMIDATE ME. I MEAN, YOU'RE COOL AND YOU'RE SMART AND YOU'RE PRETTY...
A PRETTY FACE, RIGHT? PRETTY FOR A FAT GIRL?

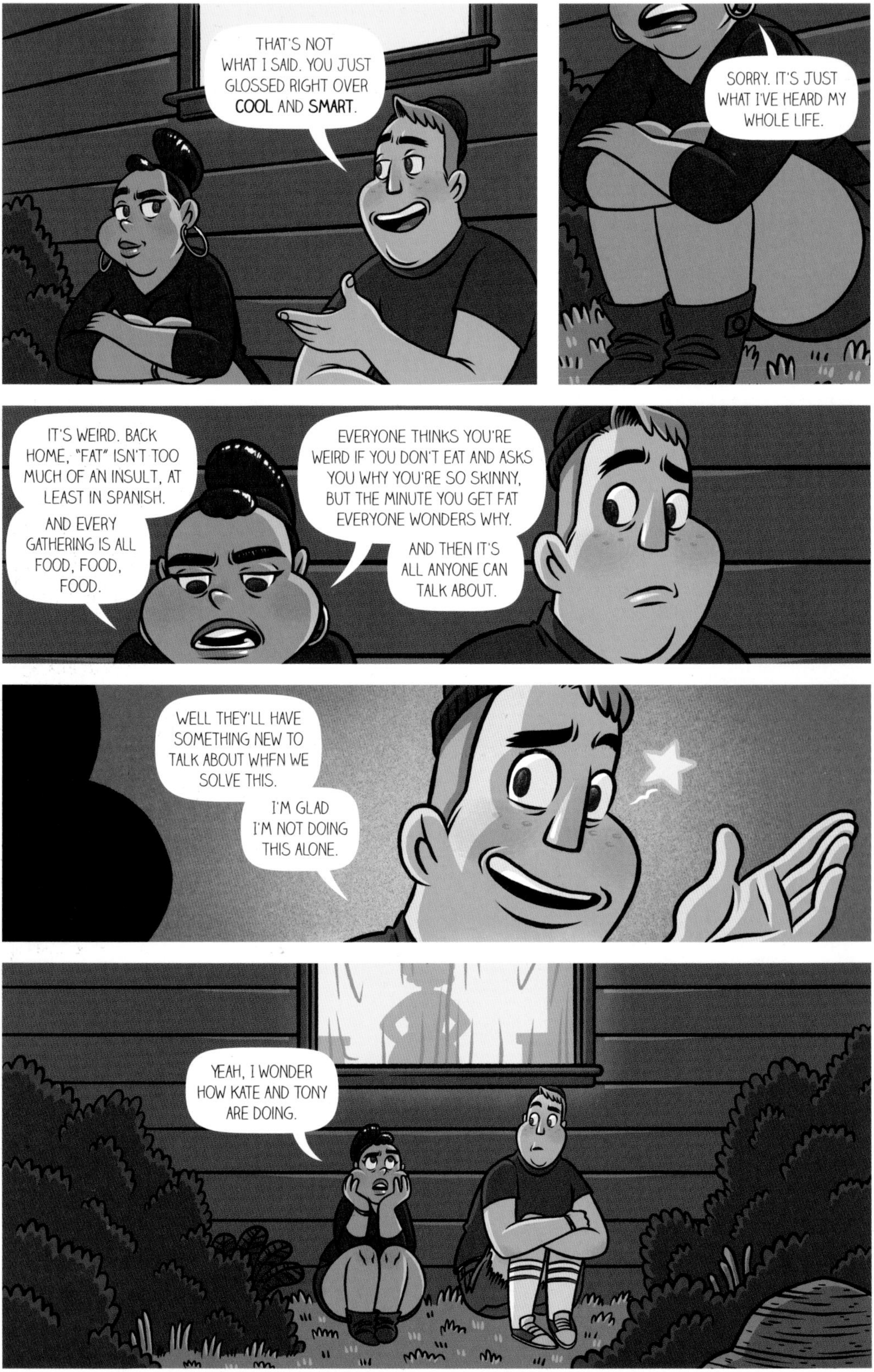
THAT'S NOT WHAT I SAID. YOU JUST GLOSSED RIGHT OVER **COOL** AND **SMART**.
SORRY. IT'S JUST WHAT I'VE HEARD MY WHOLE LIFE.
IT'S WEIRD. BACK HOME, "FAT" ISN'T TOO MUCH OF AN INSULT, AT LEAST IN SPANISH.
AND EVERY GATHERING IS ALL FOOD, FOOD, FOOD.
EVERYONE THINKS YOU'RE WEIRD IF YOU DON'T EAT AND ASKS YOU WHY YOU'RE SO SKINNY, BUT THE MINUTE YOU GET FAT EVERYONE WONDERS WHY.
AND THEN IT'S ALL ANYONE CAN TALK ABOUT.
WELL THEY'LL HAVE SOMETHING NEW TO TALK ABOUT WHFN WE SOLVE THIS.
I'M GLAD I'M NOT DOING THIS ALONE.
YEAH, I WONDER HOW KATE AND TONY ARE DOING.

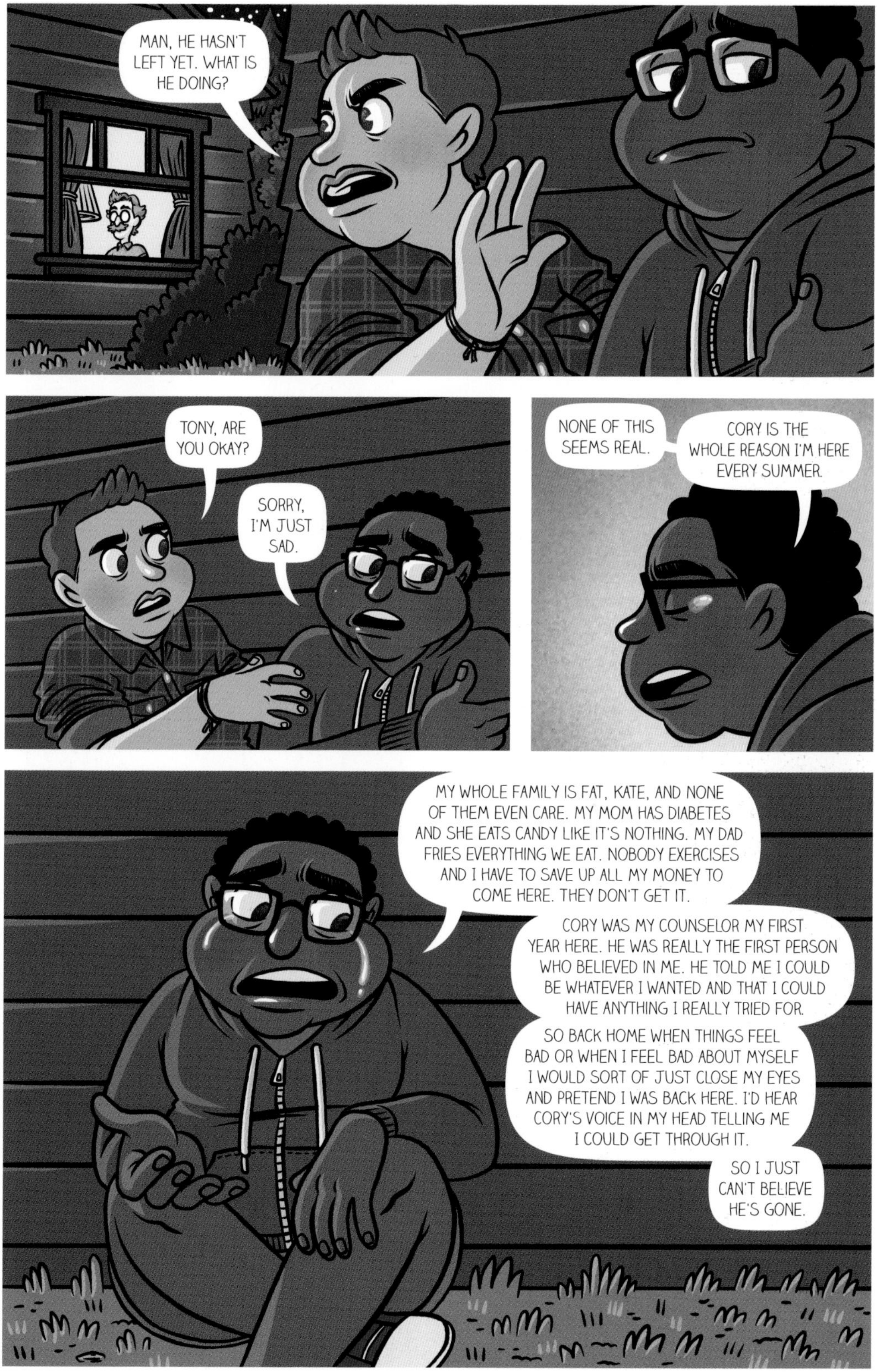
MAN, HE HASN'T LEFT YET. WHAT IS HE DOING?
TONY, ARE YOU OKAY?
SORRY, I'M JUST SAD.
NONE OF THIS SEEMS REAL.
CORY IS THE WHOLE REASON I'M HERE EVERY SUMMER.
MY WHOLE FAMILY IS FAT, KATE, AND NONE OF THEM EVEN CARE. MY MOM HAS DIABETES AND SHE EATS CANDY LIKE IT'S NOTHING. MY DAD FRIES EVERYTHING WE EAT. NOBODY EXERCISES AND I HAVE TO SAVE UP ALL MY MONEY TO COME HERE. THEY DON'T GET IT.
CORY WAS MY COUNSELOR MY FIRST YEAR HERE. HE WAS REALLY THE FIRST PERSON WHO BELIEVED IN ME. HE TOLD ME I COULD BE WHATEVER I WANTED AND THAT I COULD HAVE ANYTHING I REALLY TRIED FOR.
SO BACK HOME WHEN THINGS FEEL BAD OR WHEN I FEEL BAD ABOUT MYSELF I WOULD SORT OF JUST CLOSE MY EYES AND PRETEND I WAS BACK HERE. I'D HEAR CORY'S VOICE IN MY HEAD TELLING ME I COULD GET THROUGH IT.
SO I JUST CAN'T BELIEVE HE'S GONE.

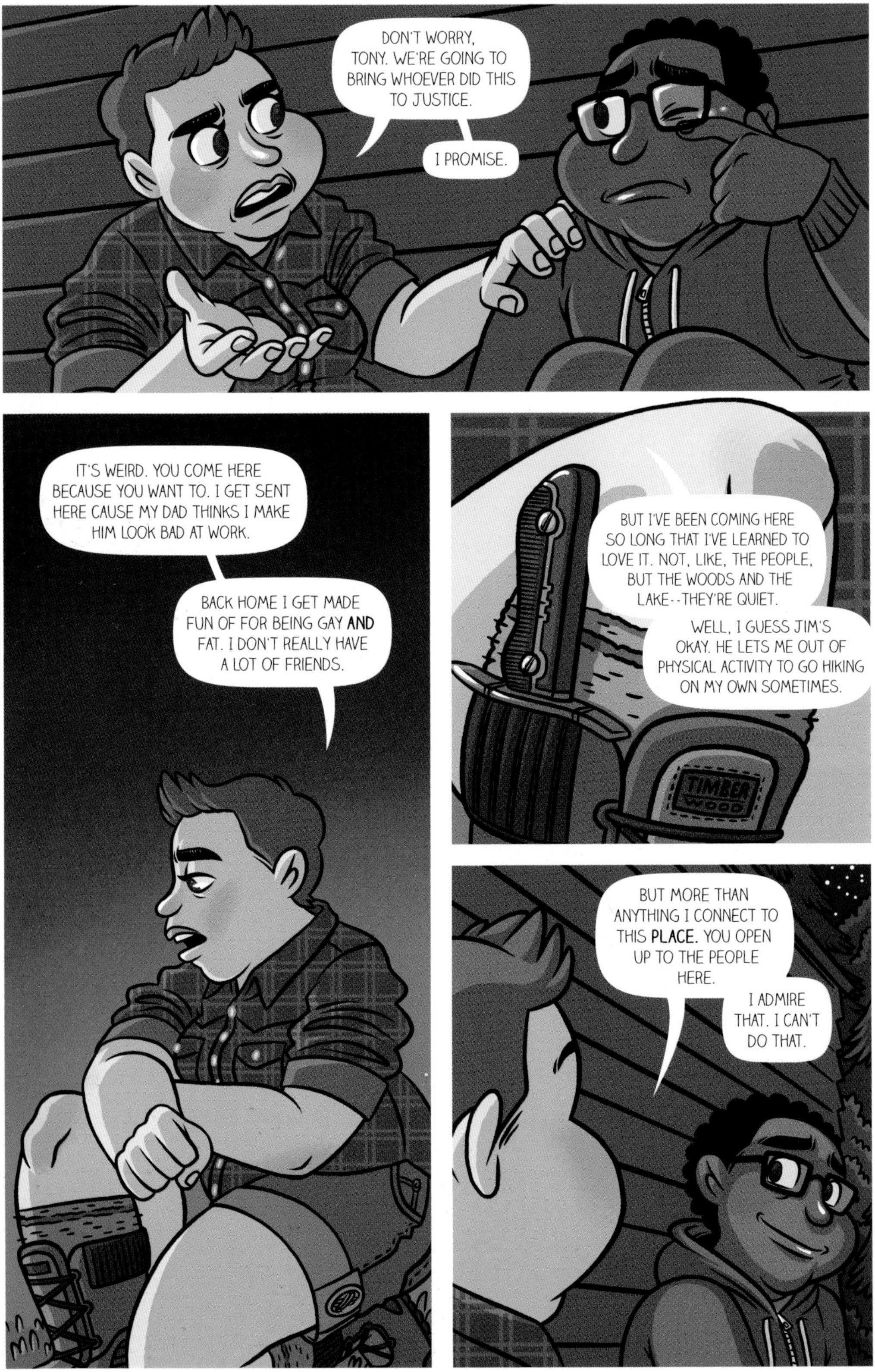
DON'T WORRY, TONY. WE'RE GOING TO BRING WHOEVER DID THIS TO JUSTICE.
I PROMISE.
IT'S WEIRD. YOU COME HERE BECAUSE YOU WANT TO. I GET SENT HERE CAUSE MY DAD THINKS I MAKE HIM LOOK BAD AT WORK.
BACK HOME I GET MADE FUN OF FOR BEING GAY AND FAT. I DON'T REALLY HAVE A LOT OF FRIENDS.
BUT I'VE BEEN COMING HERE SO LONG THAT I'VE LEARNED TO LOVE IT. NOT, LIKE, THE PEOPLE, BUT THE WOODS AND THE LAKE--THEY'RE QUIET.
WELL, I GUESS JIM'S OKAY. HE LETS ME OUT OF PHYSICAL ACTIVITY TO GO HIKING ON MY OWN SOMETIMES.
TIMBER WOOD
BUT MORE THAN ANYTHING I CONNECT TO THIS PLACE. YOU OPEN UP TO THE PEOPLE HERE.
I ADMIRE THAT. I CAN'T DO THAT.

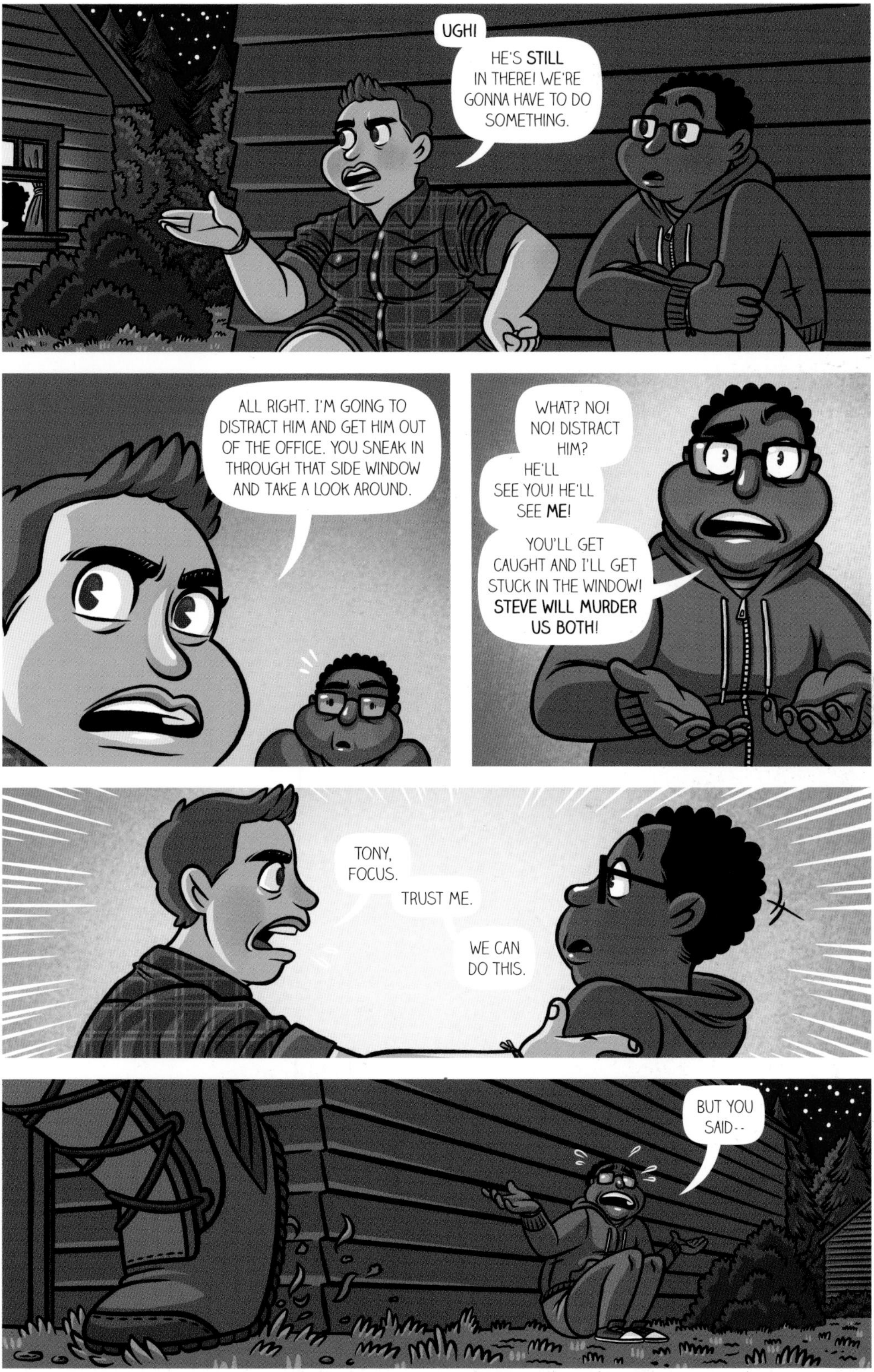
UGH!
HE'S STILL IN THERE! WE'RE GONNA HAVE TO DO SOMETHING.
ALL RIGHT. I'M GOING TO DISTRACT HIM AND GET HIM OUT OF THE OFFICE. YOU SNEAK IN THROUGH THAT SIDE WINDOW AND TAKE A LOOK AROUND.
WHAT? NO! NO! DISTRACT HIM?
HE'LL SEE YOU! HE'LL SEE ME!
YOU'LL GET CAUGHT AND I'LL GET STUCK IN THE WINDOW! STEVE WILL MURDER US BOTH!
TONY, FOCUS.
TRUST ME.
WE CAN DO THIS.
BUT YOU SAID--

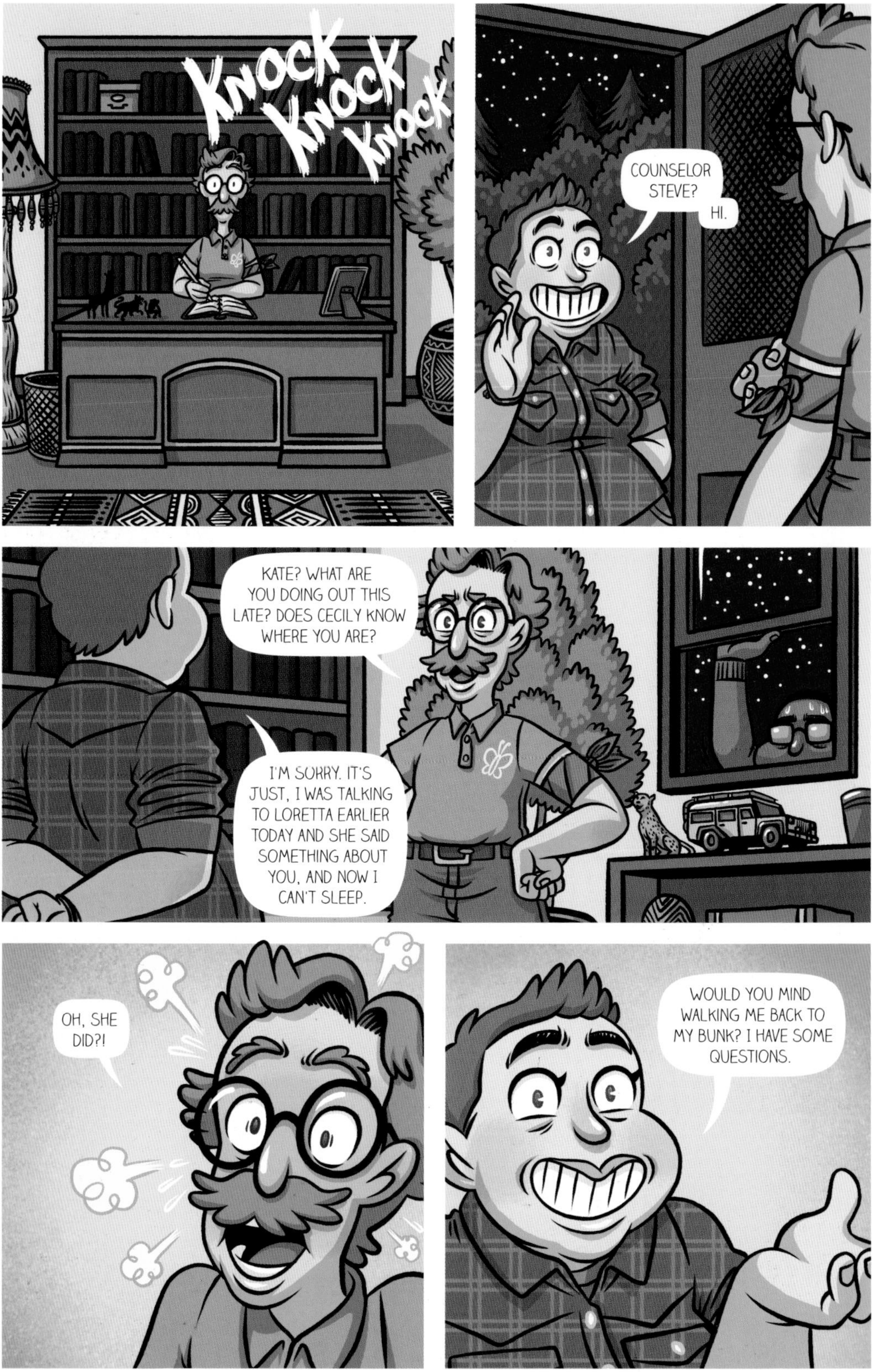
KNOCK KNOCK KNOCK
COUNSELOR STEVE?
HI.
KATE? WHAT ARE YOU DOING OUT THIS LATE? DOES CECILY KNOW WHERE YOU ARE?
I'M SORRY. IT'S JUST, I WAS TALKING TO LORETTA EARLIER TODAY AND SHE SAID SOMETHING ABOUT YOU, AND NOW I CAN'T SLEEP.
OH, SHE DID?!
WOULD YOU MIND WALKING ME BACK TO MY BUNK? I HAVE SOME QUESTIONS.

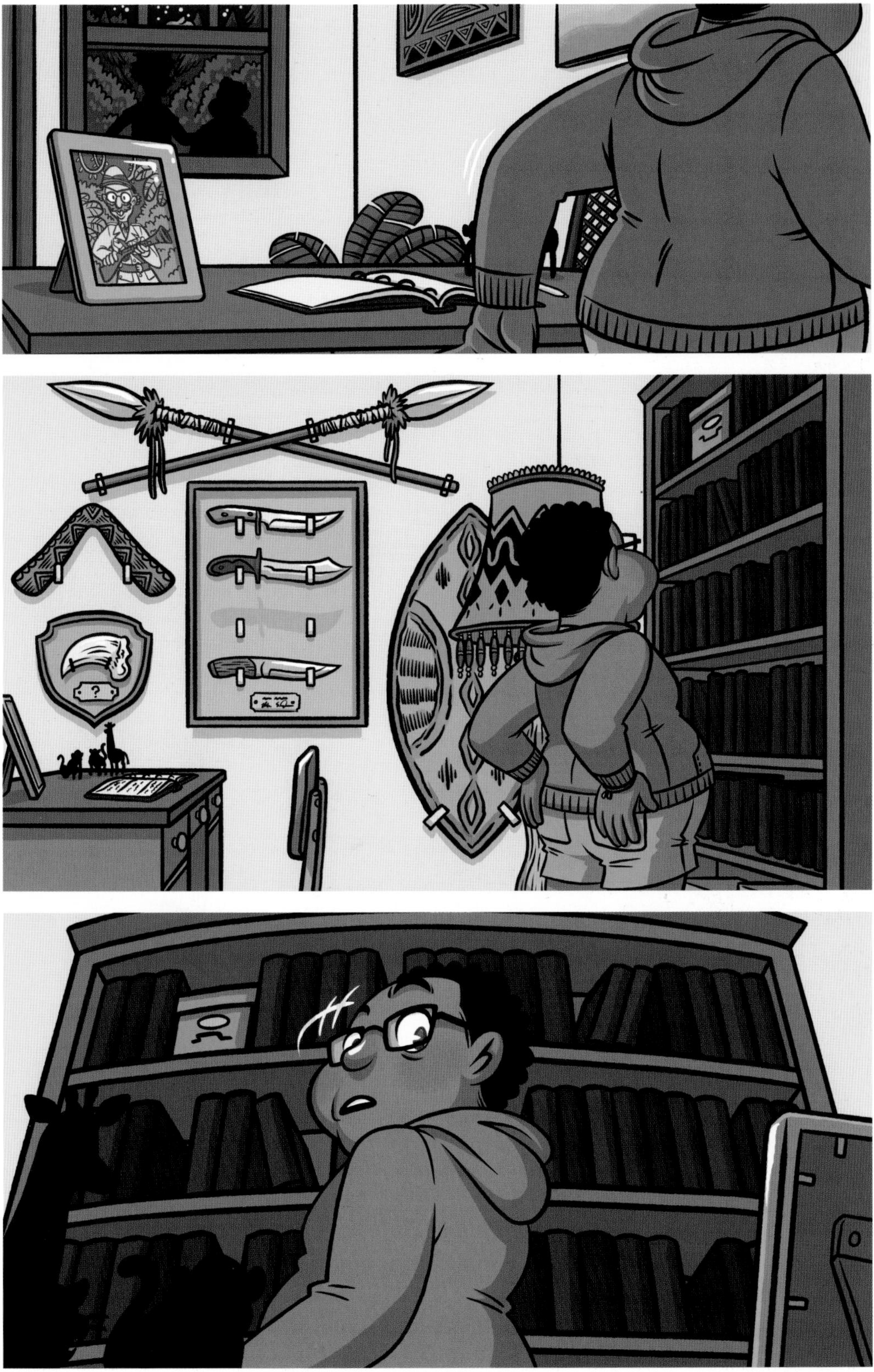
?

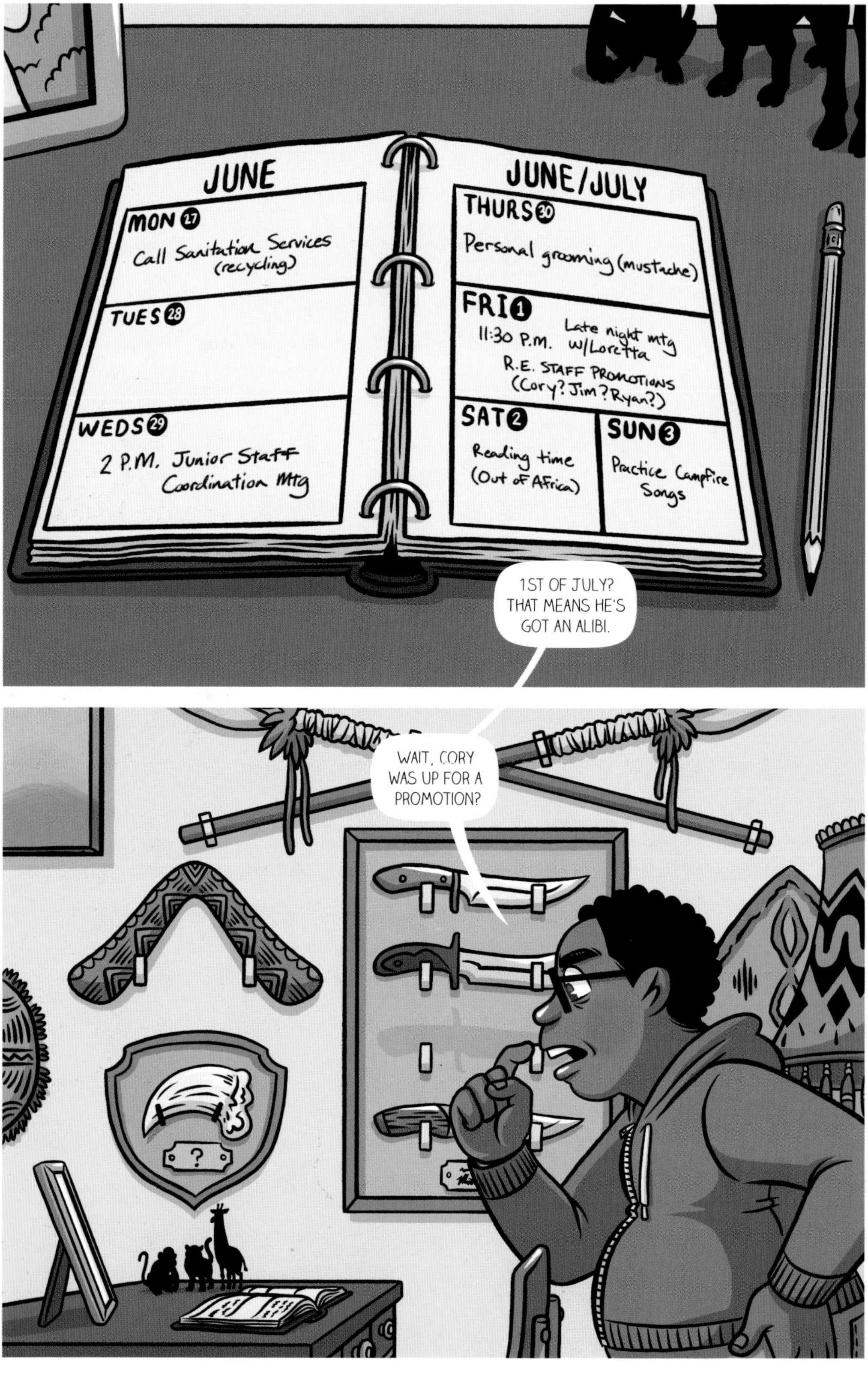
JUNE
MON 27
Call Sanitation Services (recycling)
TUES 28
WEDS 29
2 P.M. Junior Staff Coordination Mtg
JUNE/JULY
THURS 30
Personal grooming (mustache)
FRI 1
11:30 P.M. Late night mtg w/Loretta
R.E. STAFF PROMOTIONS (Cory? Jim? Ryan?)
SAT 2
Reading time (Out of Africa)
SUN 3
Practice Campfire Songs
1ST OF JULY? THAT MEANS HE'S GOT AN ALIBI.
WAIT, CORY WAS UP FOR A PROMOTION?

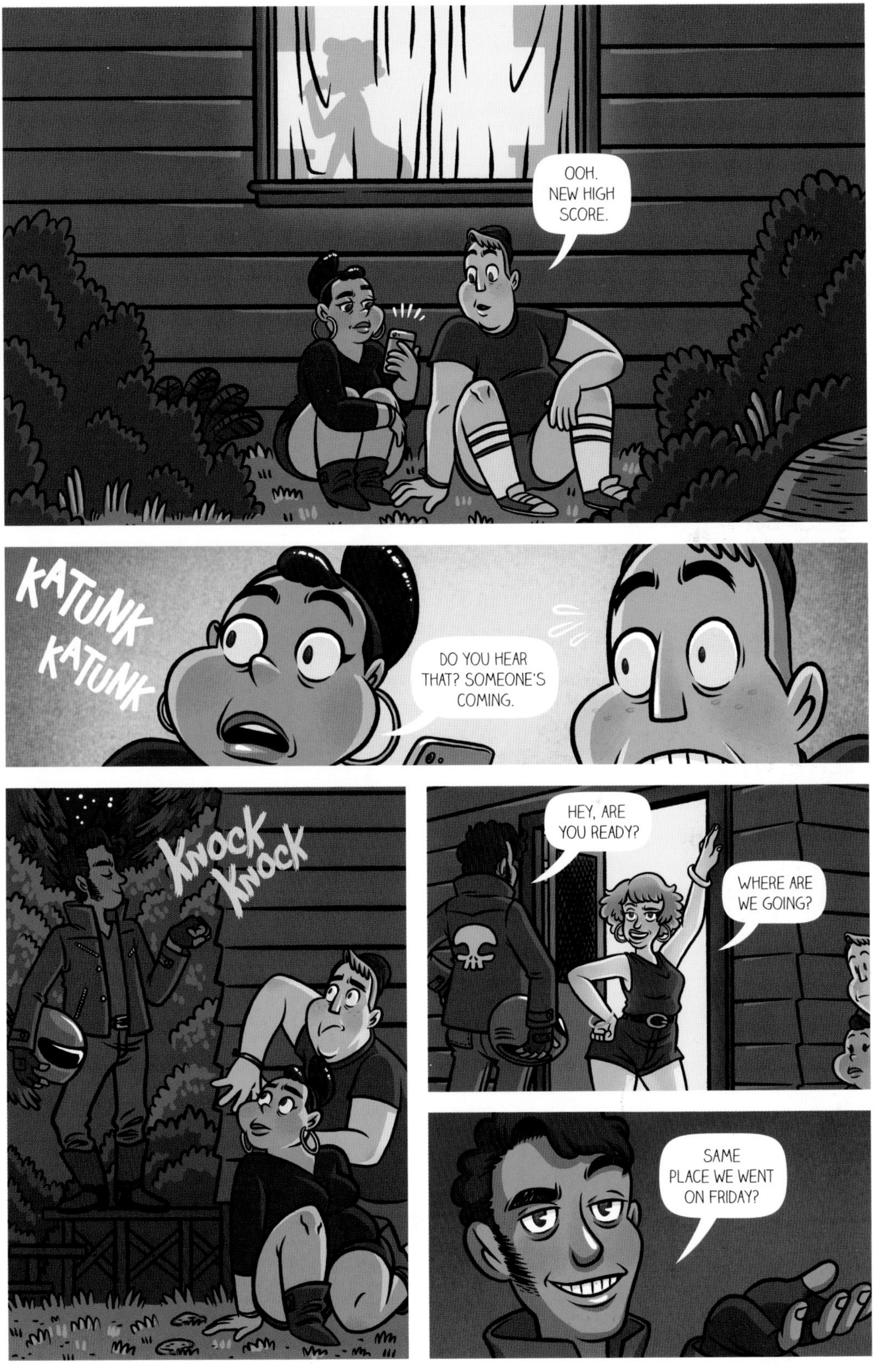
OOH.
NEW HIGH
SCORE.
KATUNK
KATUNK
DO YOU HEAR
THAT? SOMEONE'S
COMING.
KNOCK
KNOCK
HEY, ARE
YOU READY?
WHERE ARE
WE GOING?
SAME
PLACE WE WENT
ON FRIDAY?

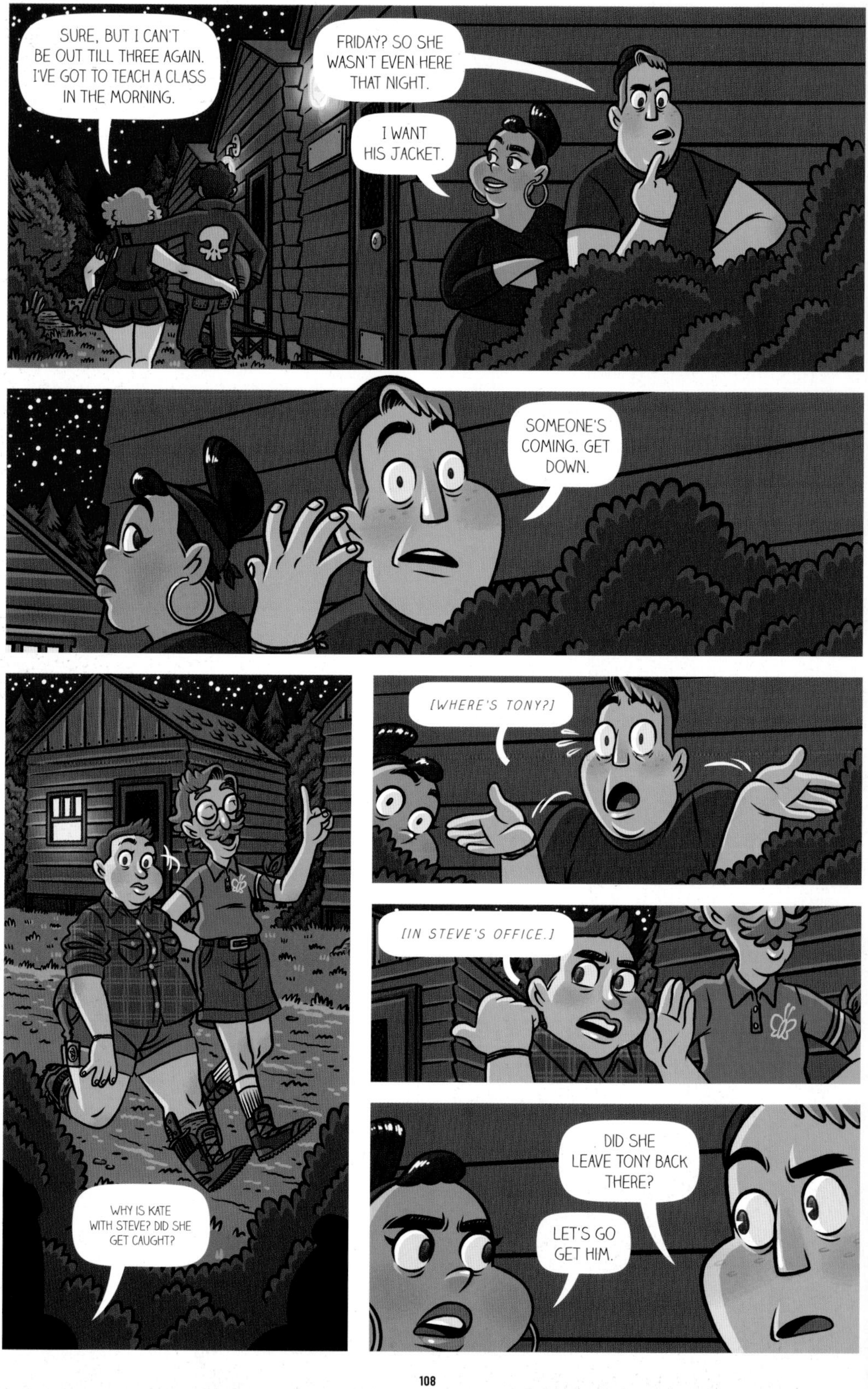
SURE, BUT I CAN'T BE OUT TILL THREE AGAIN. I'VE GOT TO TEACH A CLASS IN THE MORNING.
FRIDAY? SO SHE WASN'T EVEN HERE THAT NIGHT.
I WANT HIS JACKET.
SOMEONE'S COMING. GET DOWN.
WHY IS KATE WITH STEVE? DID SHE GET CAUGHT?
[WHERE'S TONY?]
[IN STEVE'S OFFICE.]
DID SHE LEAVE TONY BACK THERE?
LET'S GO GET HIM.

CHAPTER NINE

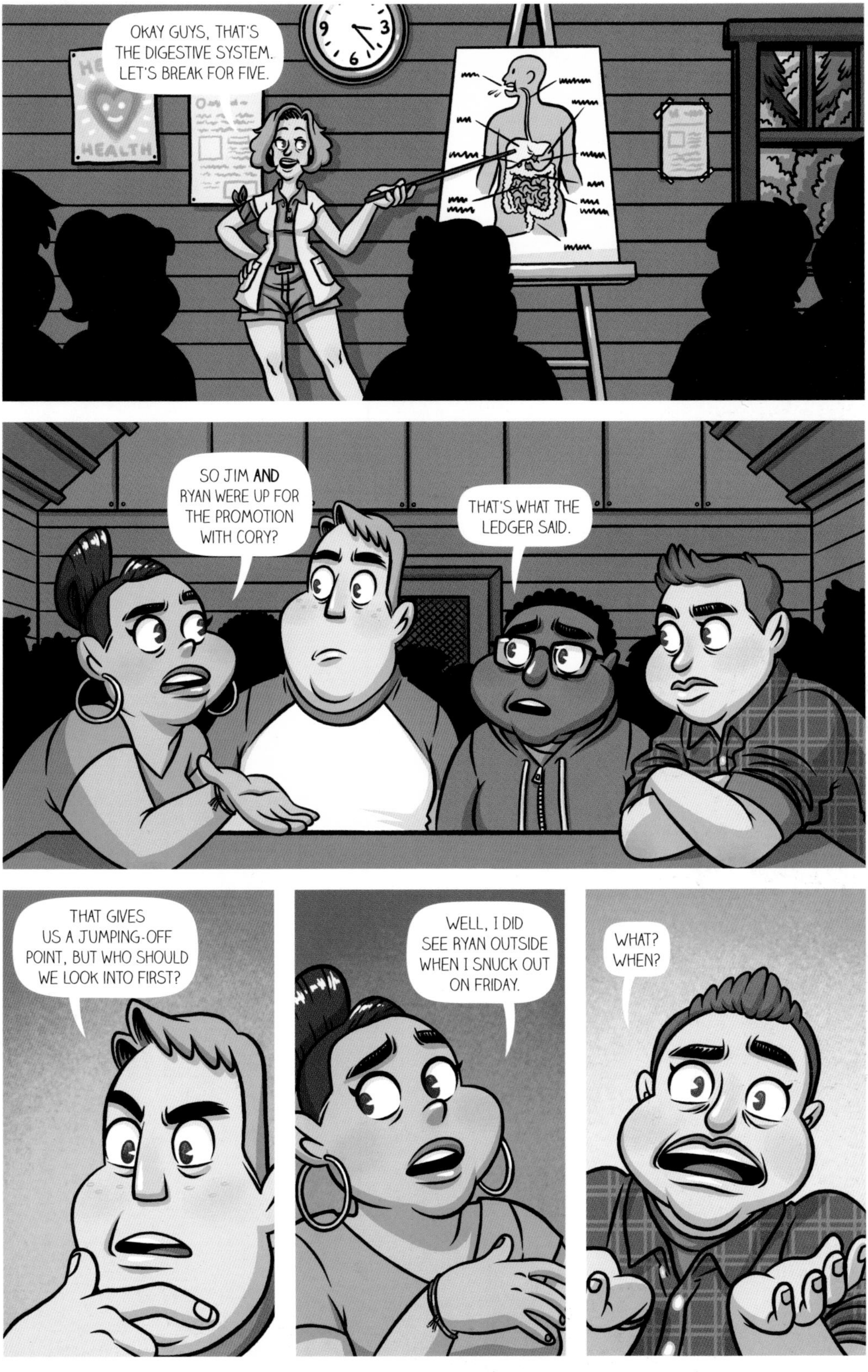

OKAY GUYS, THAT'S THE DIGESTIVE SYSTEM. LET'S BREAK FOR FIVE.
HEALTH
SO JIM **AND** RYAN WERE UP FOR THE PROMOTION WITH CORY?
THAT'S WHAT THE LEDGER SAID.
THAT GIVES US A JUMPING-OFF POINT, BUT WHO SHOULD WE LOOK INTO FIRST?
WELL, I DID SEE RYAN OUTSIDE WHEN I SNUCK OUT ON FRIDAY.
WHAT? WHEN?

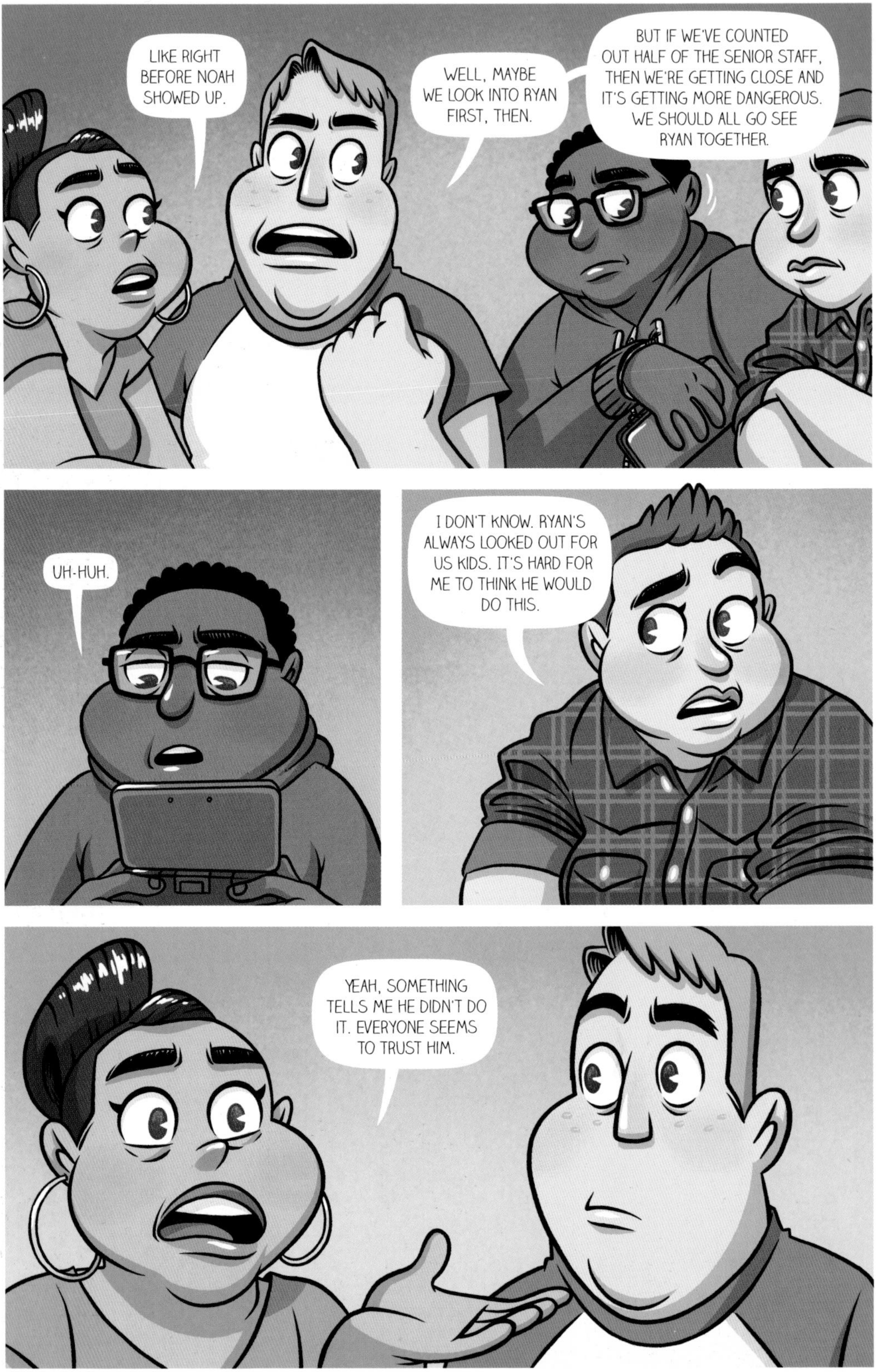
LIKE RIGHT BEFORE NOAH SHOWED UP.
WELL, MAYBE WE LOOK INTO RYAN FIRST, THEN.
BUT IF WE'VE COUNTED OUT HALF OF THE SENIOR STAFF, THEN WE'RE GETTING CLOSE AND IT'S GETTING MORE DANGEROUS. WE SHOULD ALL GO SEE RYAN TOGETHER.
UH-HUH.
I DON'T KNOW. RYAN'S ALWAYS LOOKED OUT FOR US KIDS. IT'S HARD FOR ME TO THINK HE WOULD DO THIS.
YEAH, SOMETHING TELLS ME HE DIDN'T DO IT. EVERYONE SEEMS TO TRUST HIM.

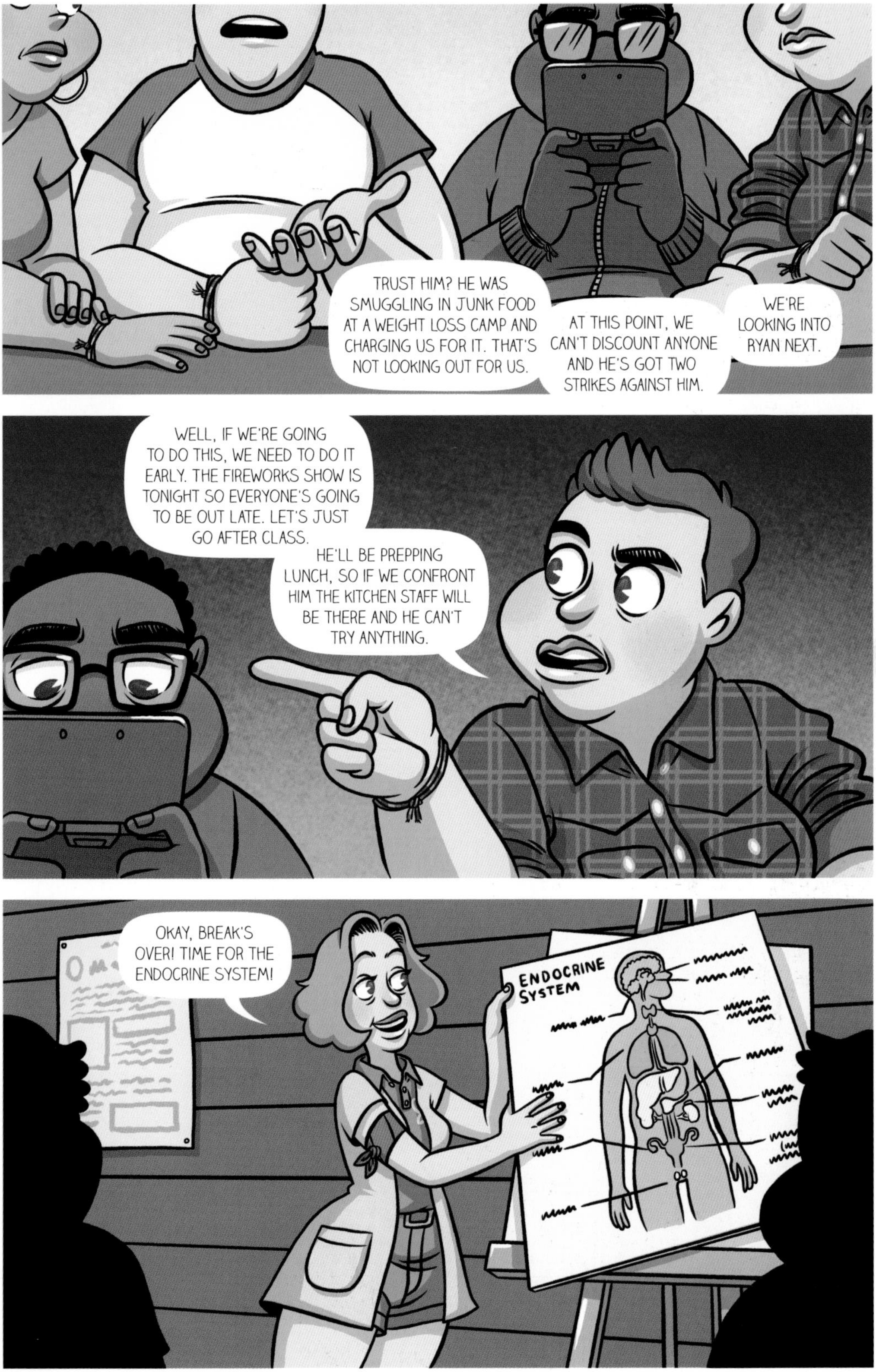
TRUST HIM? HE WAS SMUGGLING IN JUNK FOOD AT A WEIGHT LOSS CAMP AND CHARGING US FOR IT. THAT'S NOT LOOKING OUT FOR US.
AT THIS POINT, WE CAN'T DISCOUNT ANYONE AND HE'S GOT TWO STRIKES AGAINST HIM.
WE'RE LOOKING INTO RYAN NEXT.
WELL, IF WE'RE GOING TO DO THIS, WE NEED TO DO IT EARLY. THE FIREWORKS SHOW IS TONIGHT SO EVERYONE'S GOING TO BE OUT LATE. LET'S JUST GO AFTER CLASS.
HE'LL BE PREPPING LUNCH, SO IF WE CONFRONT HIM THE KITCHEN STAFF WILL BE THERE AND HE CAN'T TRY ANYTHING.
OKAY, BREAK'S OVER! TIME FOR THE ENDOCRINE SYSTEM!
ENDOCRINE SYSTEM

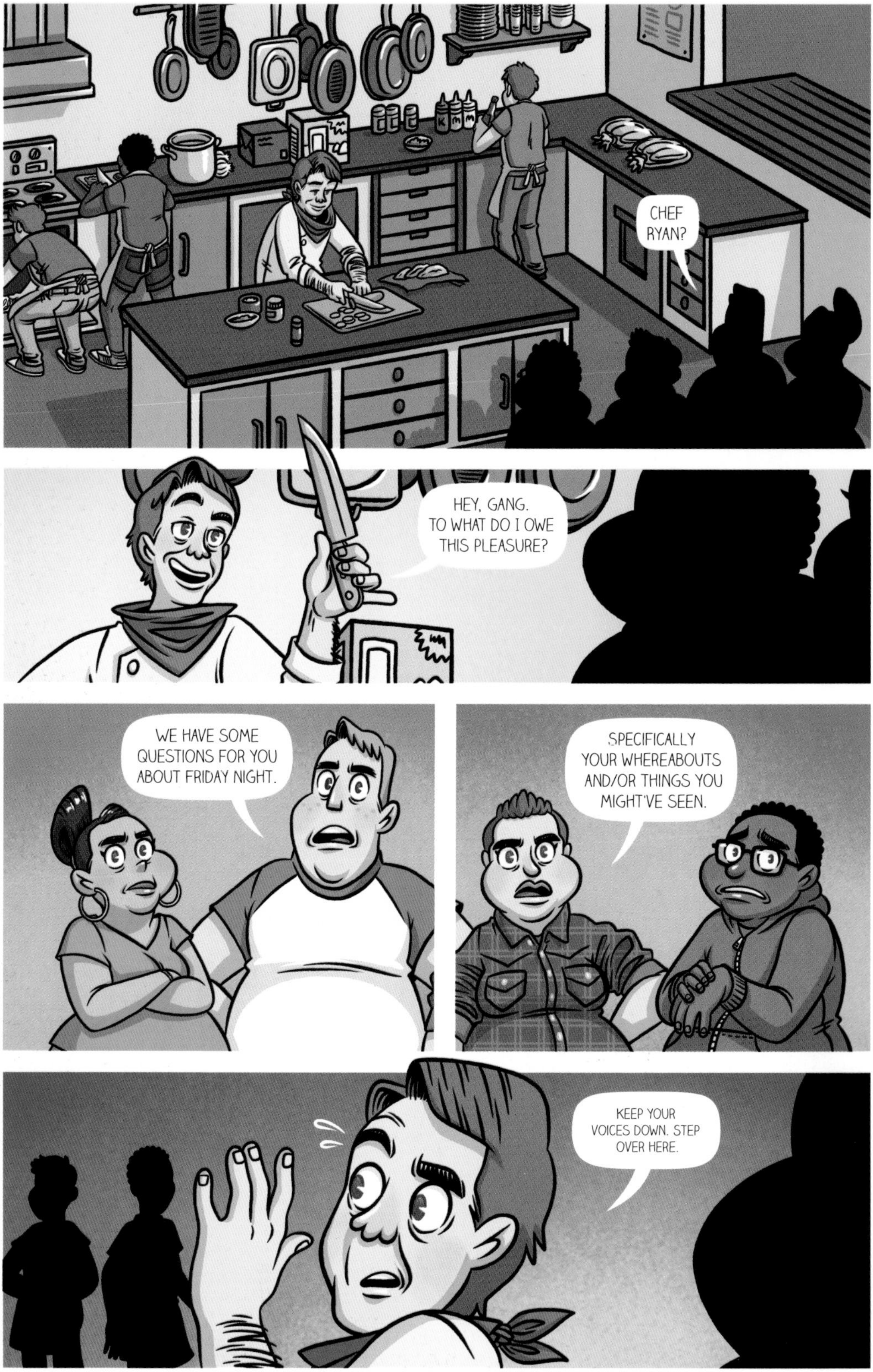
CHEF RYAN?
HEY, GANG. TO WHAT DO I OWE THIS PLEASURE?
WE HAVE SOME QUESTIONS FOR YOU ABOUT FRIDAY NIGHT.
SPECIFICALLY YOUR WHEREABOUTS AND/OR THINGS YOU MIGHT'VE SEEN.
KEEP YOUR VOICES DOWN. STEP OVER HERE.

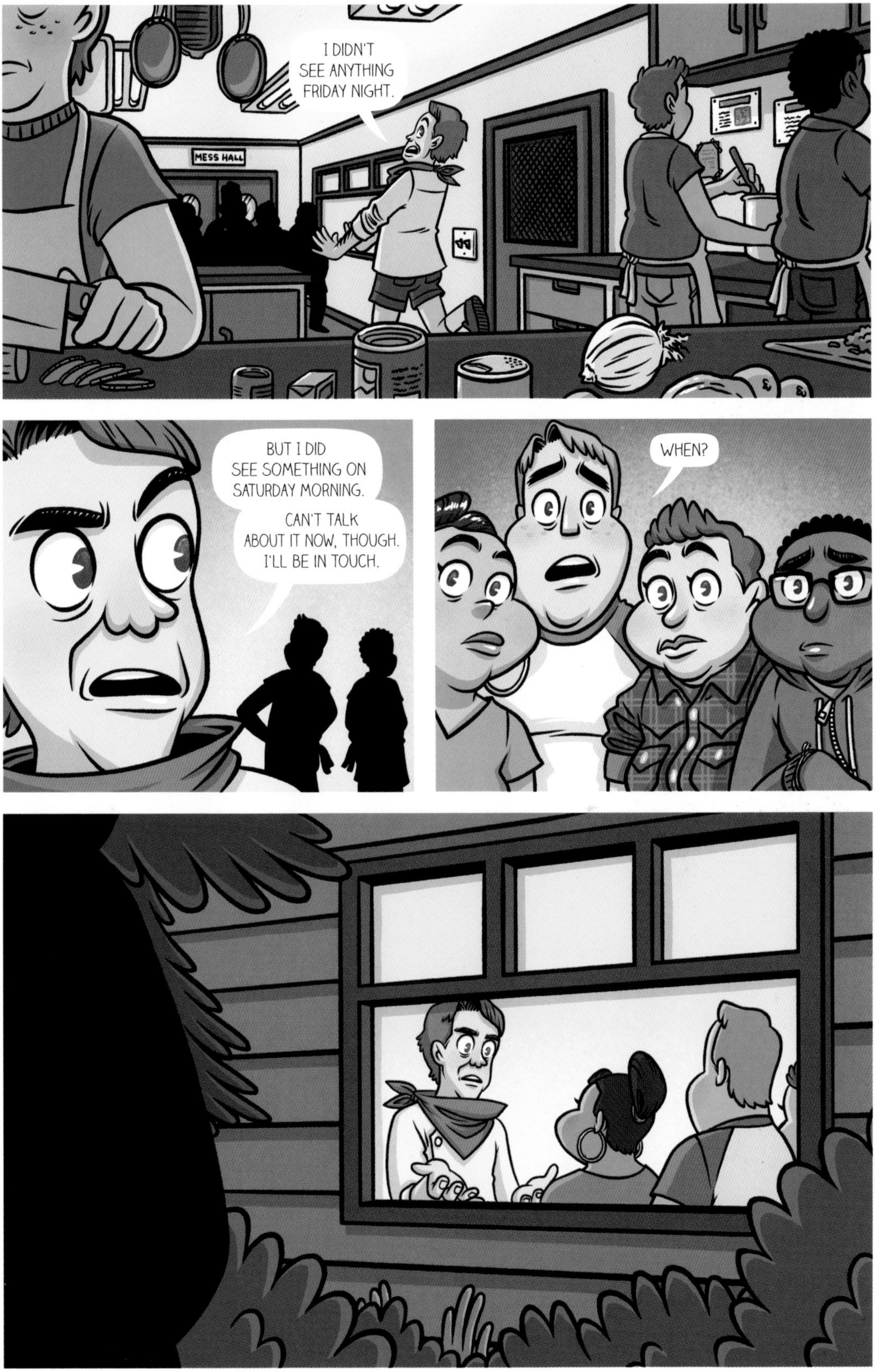
I DIDN'T SEE ANYTHING FRIDAY NIGHT.
MESS HALL
BUT I DID SEE SOMETHING ON SATURDAY MORNING.
CAN'T TALK ABOUT IT NOW, THOUGH. I'LL BE IN TOUCH.
WHEN?

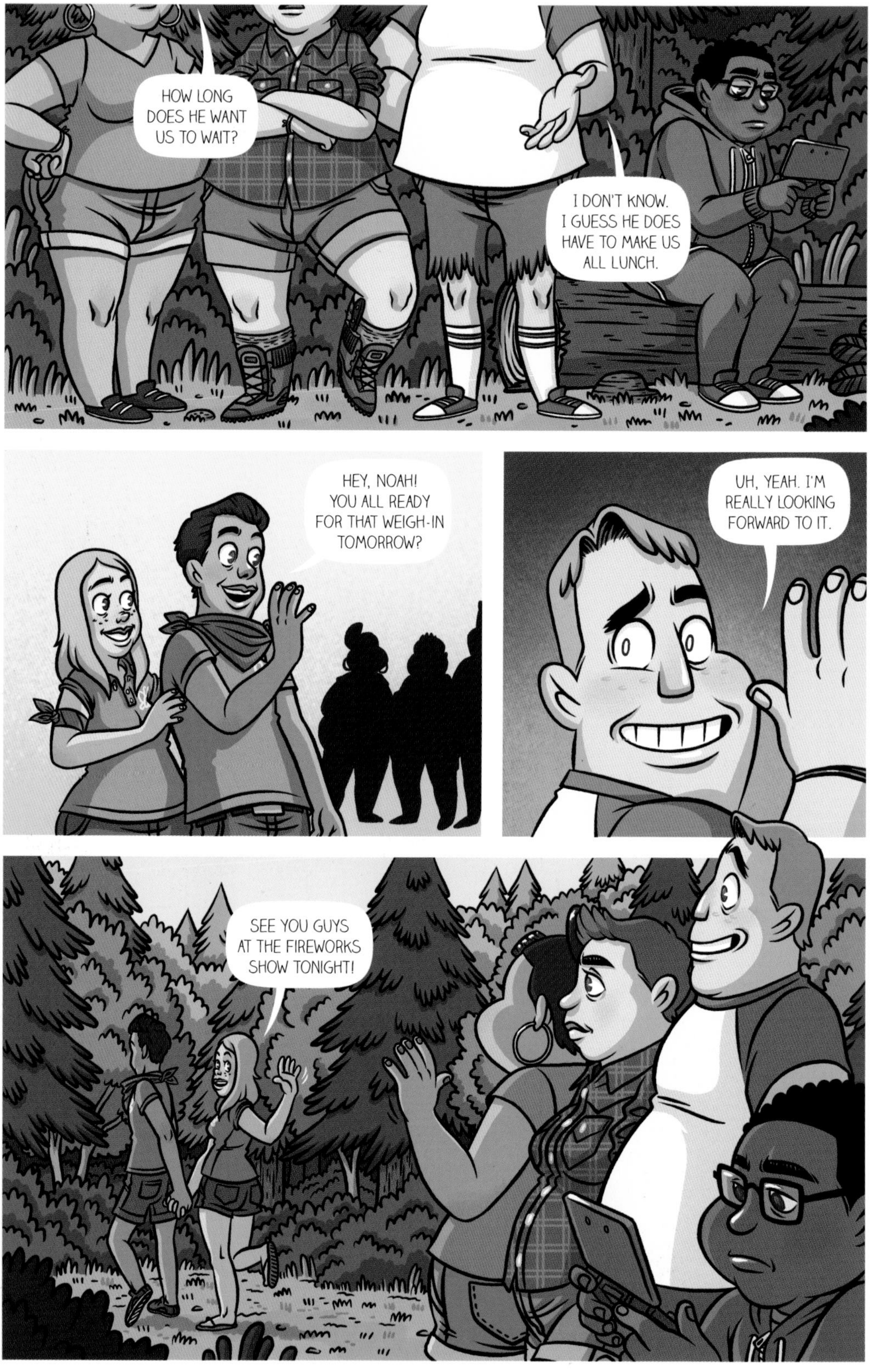
HOW LONG DOES HE WANT US TO WAIT?
I DON'T KNOW. I GUESS HE DOES HAVE TO MAKE US ALL LUNCH.
HEY, NOAH! YOU ALL READY FOR THAT WEIGH-IN TOMORROW?
UH, YEAH. I'M REALLY LOOKING FORWARD TO IT.
SEE YOU GUYS AT THE FIREWORKS SHOW TONIGHT!

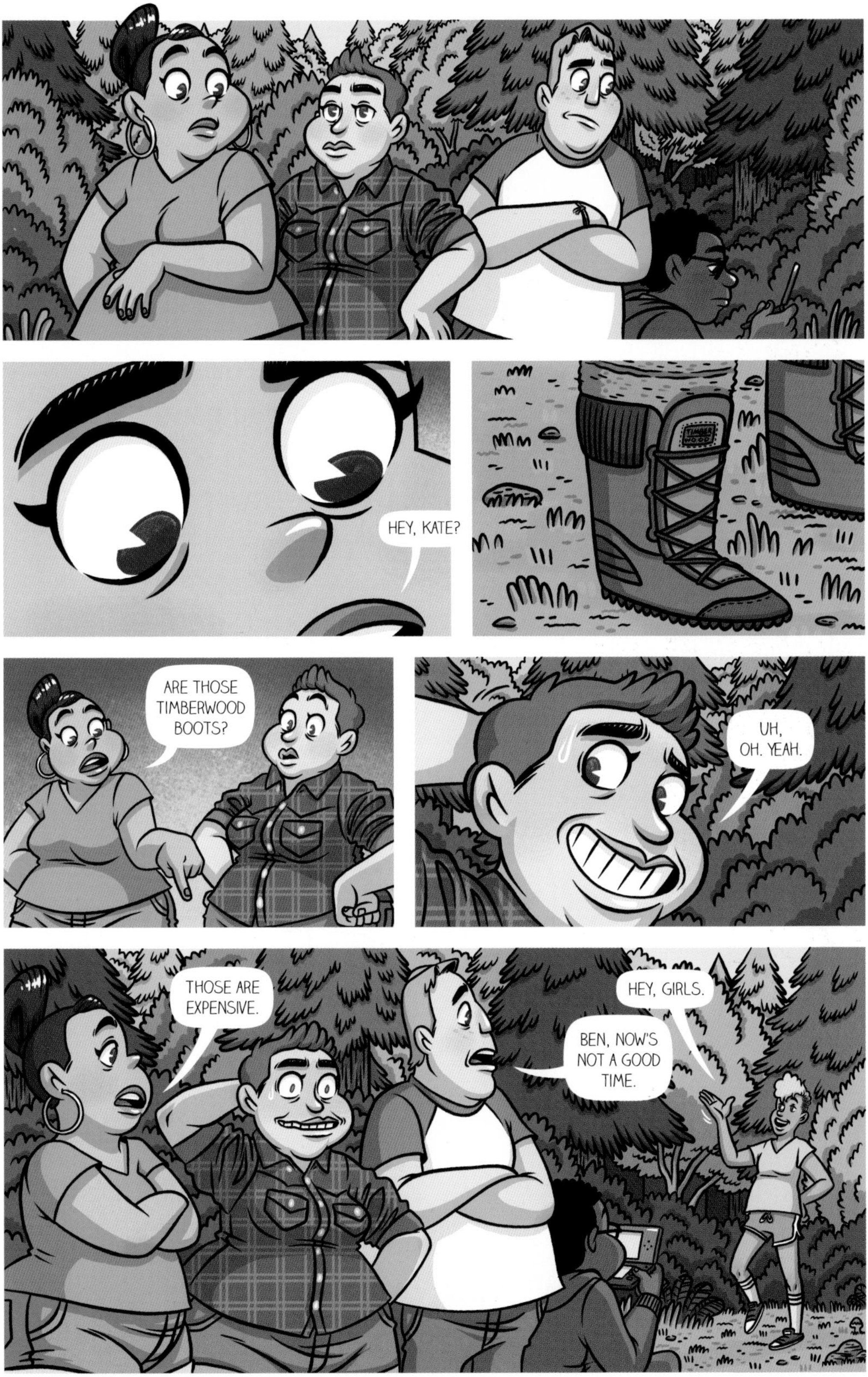
HEY, KATE?
ARE THOSE TIMBERWOOD BOOTS?
UH, OH. YEAH.
THOSE ARE EXPENSIVE.
HEY, GIRLS.
BEN, NOW'S NOT A GOOD TIME.

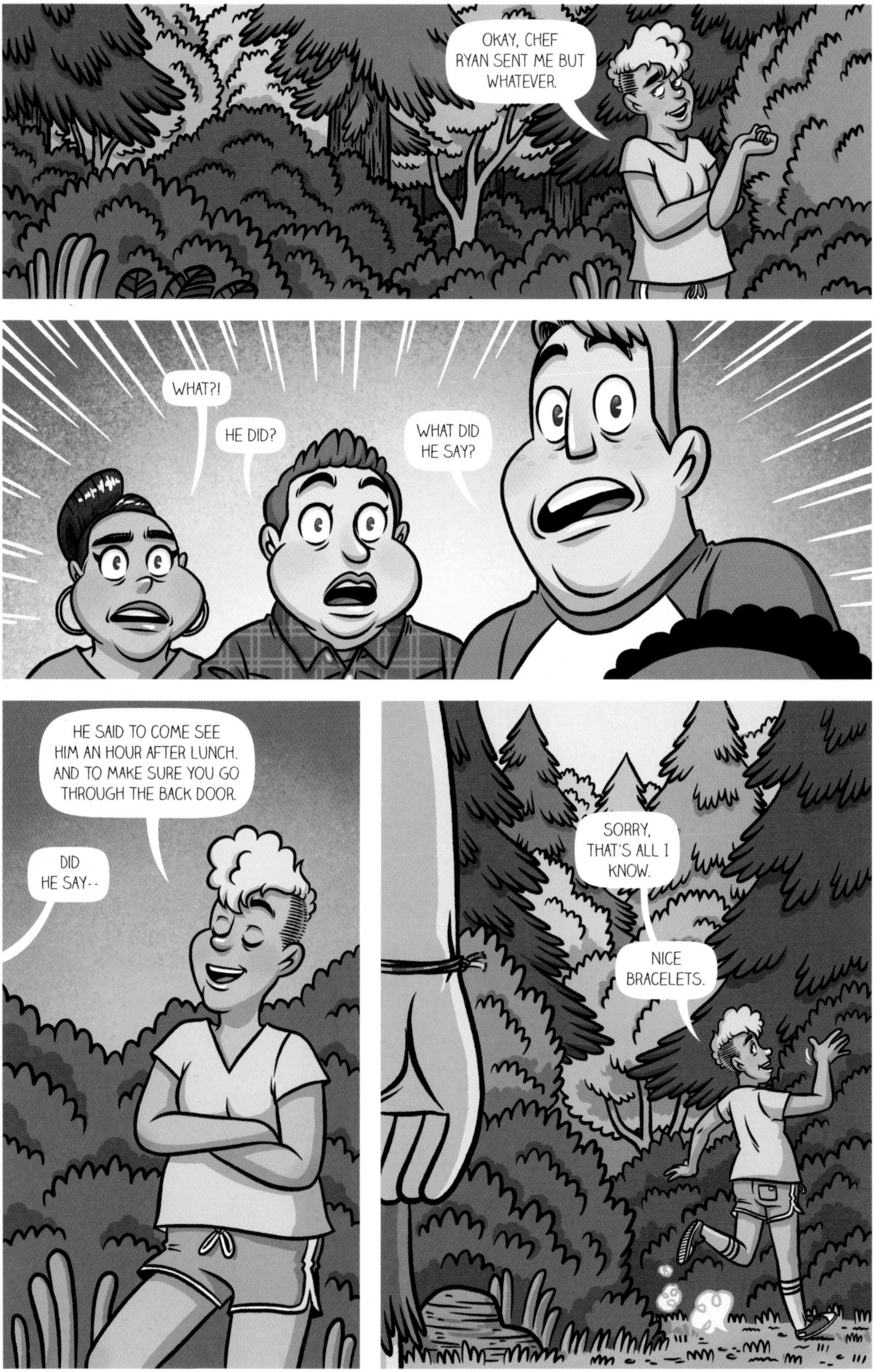
OKAY, CHEF RYAN SENT ME BUT WHATEVER.
WHAT?!
HE DID?
WHAT DID HE SAY?
HE SAID TO COME SEE HIM AN HOUR AFTER LUNCH. AND TO MAKE SURE YOU GO THROUGH THE BACK DOOR.
DID HE SAY--
SORRY, THAT'S ALL I KNOW.
NICE BRACELETS.

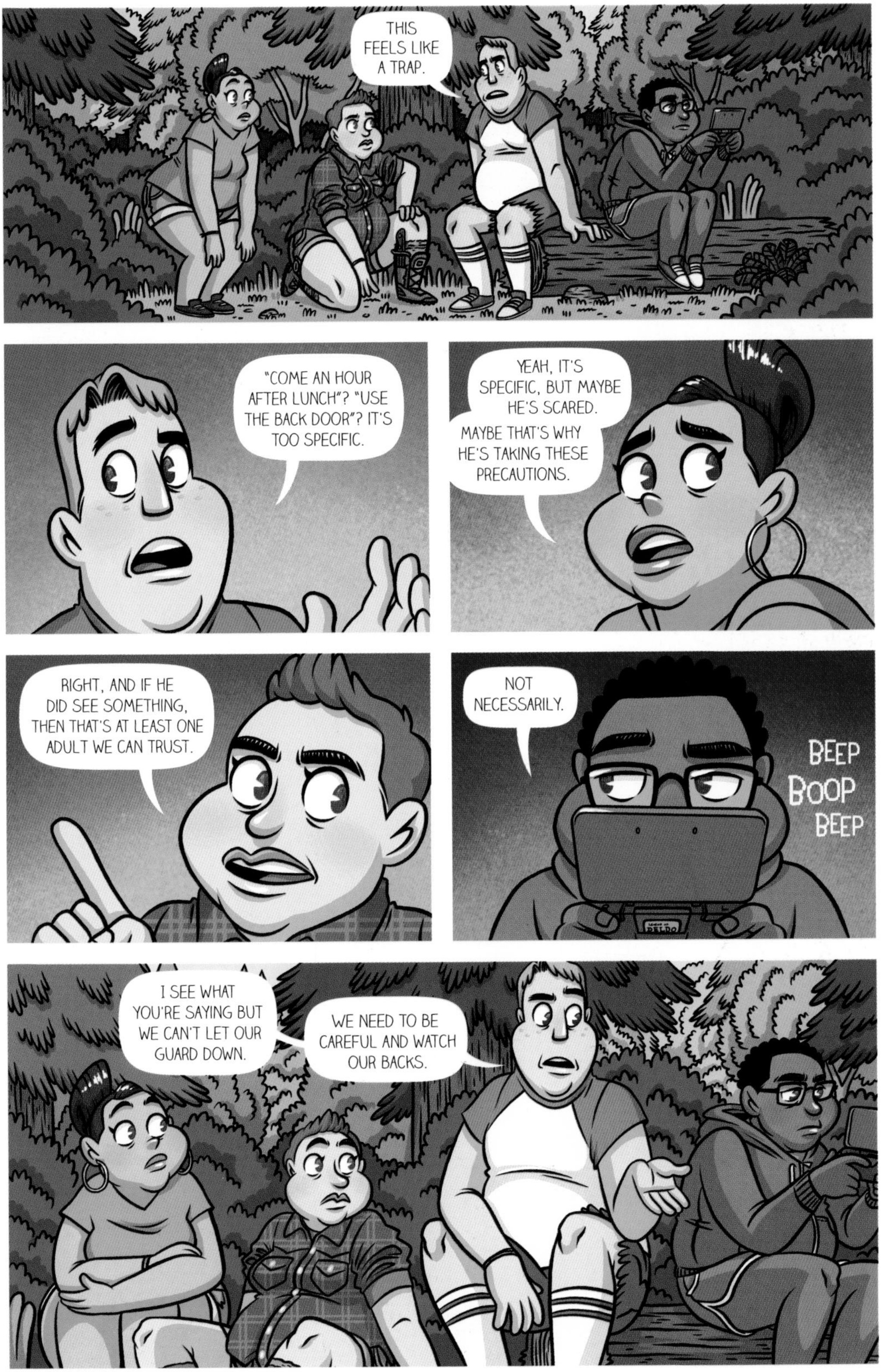
THIS FEELS LIKE A TRAP.
"COME AN HOUR AFTER LUNCH"? "USE THE BACK DOOR"? IT'S TOO SPECIFIC.
YEAH, IT'S SPECIFIC, BUT MAYBE HE'S SCARED.
MAYBE THAT'S WHY HE'S TAKING THESE PRECAUTIONS.
RIGHT, AND IF HE DID SEE SOMETHING, THEN THAT'S AT LEAST ONE ADULT WE CAN TRUST.
NOT NECESSARILY.
BEEP BOOP BEEP
I SEE WHAT YOU'RE SAYING BUT WE CAN'T LET OUR GUARD DOWN.
WE NEED TO BE CAREFUL AND WATCH OUR BACKS.

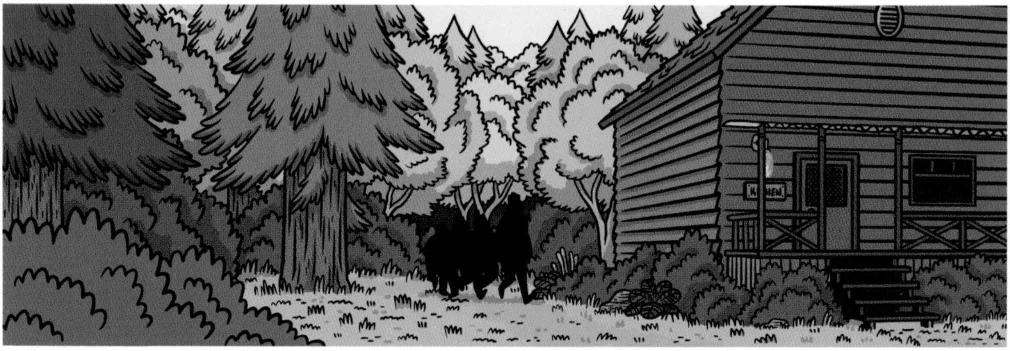

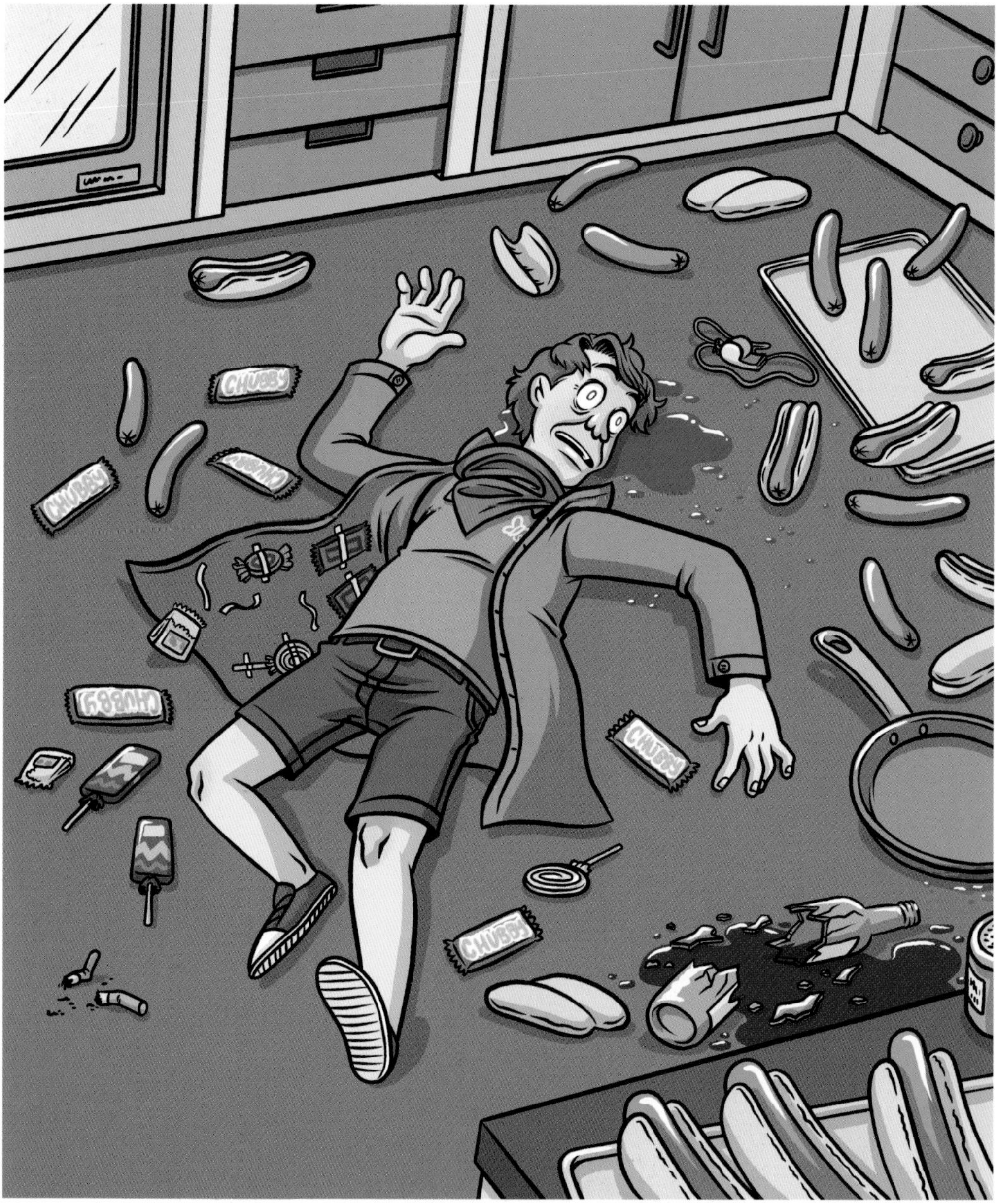
CHUBBY
CHUBBY
CHUBBY
CHUBBY

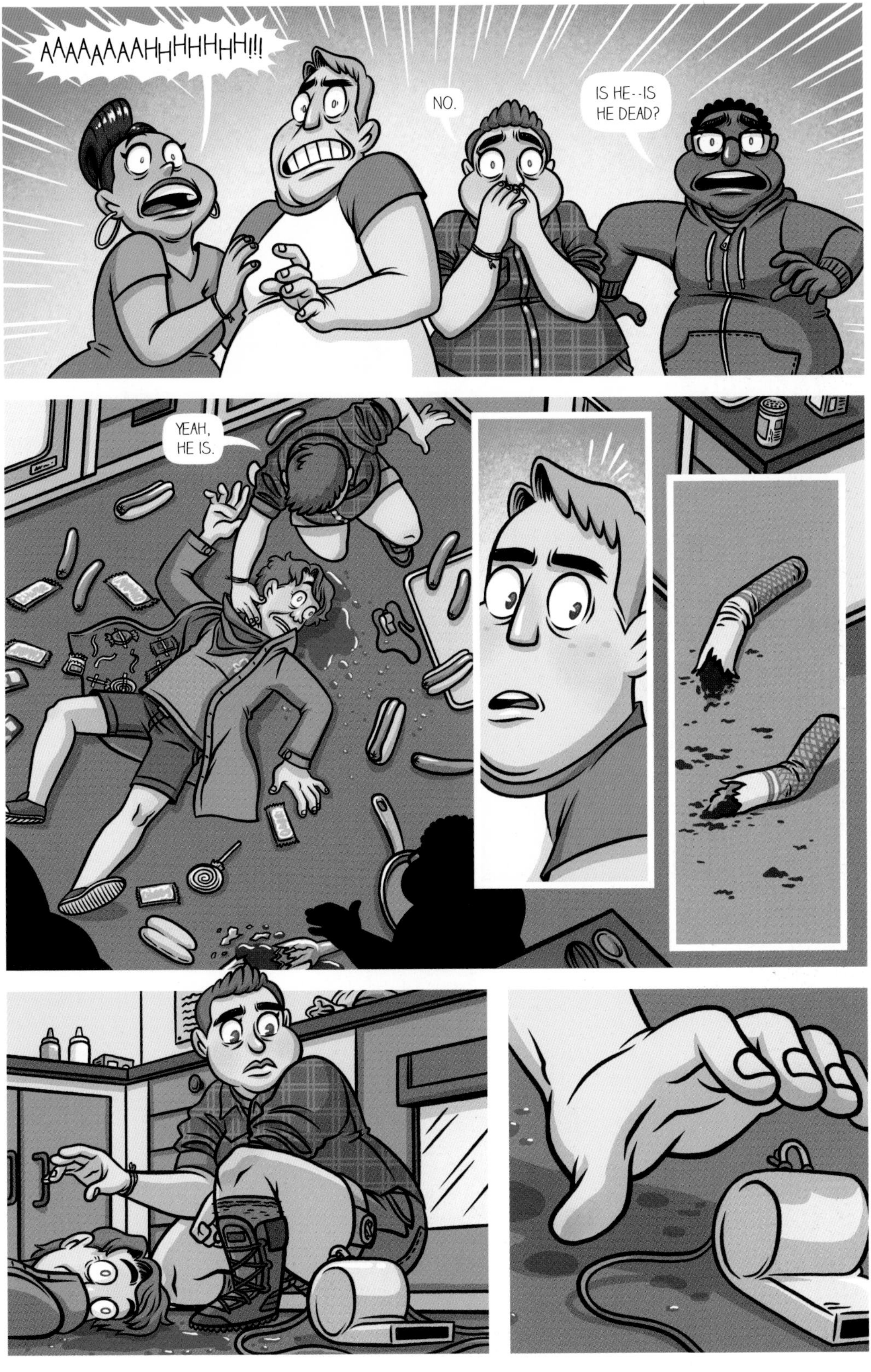
AAAAAAAAHHHHHHH!!!
NO.
IS HE--IS HE DEAD?
YEAH, HE IS.

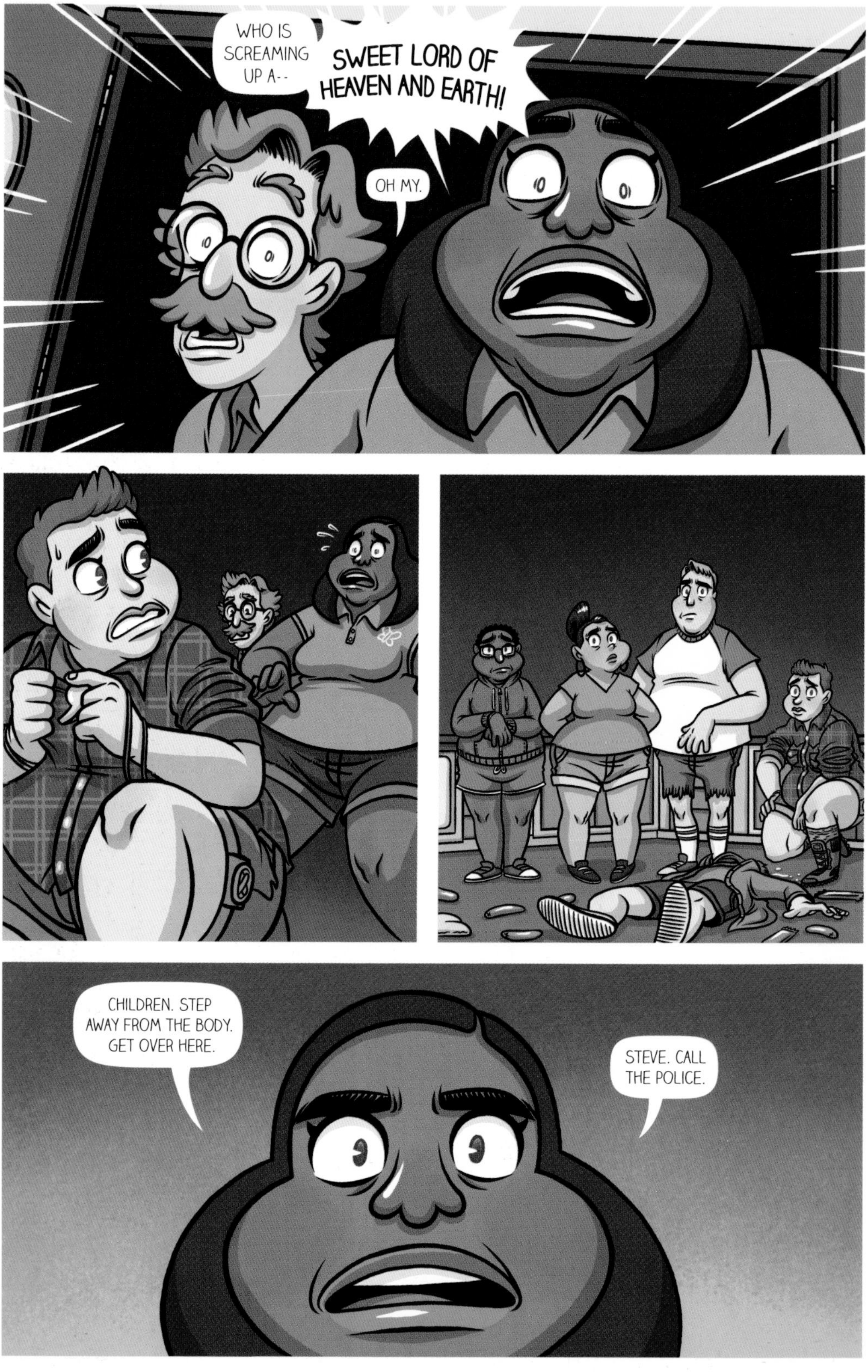
WHO IS SCREAMING UP A--
SWEET LORD OF HEAVEN AND EARTH!
OH MY.
CHILDREN. STEP AWAY FROM THE BODY. GET OVER HERE.
STEVE. CALL THE POLICE.

CHAPTER TEN

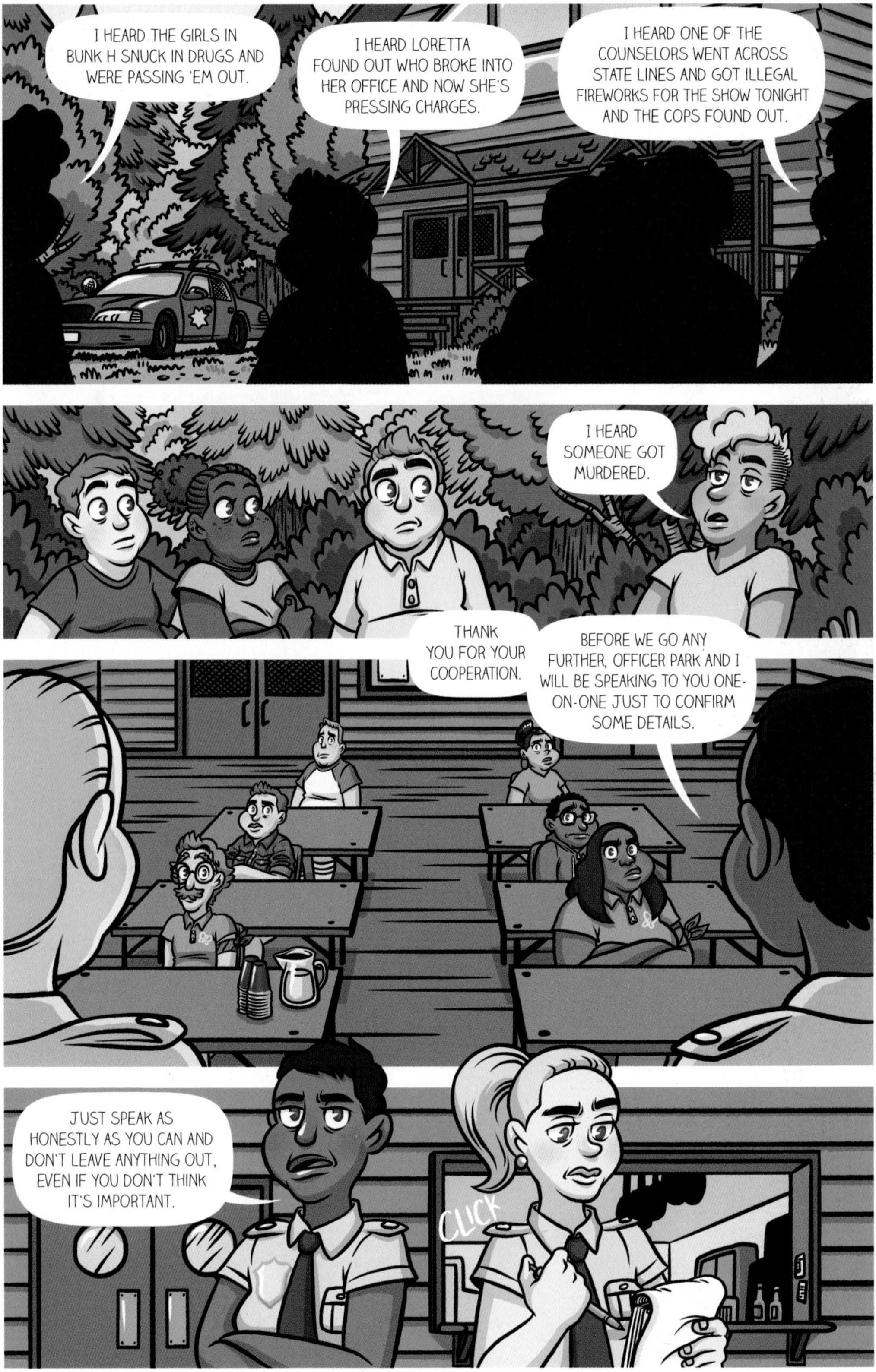
I HEARD THE GIRLS IN BUNK H SNUCK IN DRUGS AND WERE PASSING 'EM OUT.
I HEARD LORETTA FOUND OUT WHO BROKE INTO HER OFFICE AND NOW SHE'S PRESSING CHARGES.
I HEARD ONE OF THE COUNSELORS WENT ACROSS STATE LINES AND GOT ILLEGAL FIREWORKS FOR THE SHOW TONIGHT AND THE COPS FOUND OUT.
I HEARD SOMEONE GOT MURDERED.
THANK YOU FOR YOUR COOPERATION.
BEFORE WE GO ANY FURTHER, OFFICER PARK AND I WILL BE SPEAKING TO YOU ONE-ON-ONE JUST TO CONFIRM SOME DETAILS.
JUST SPEAK AS HONESTLY AS YOU CAN AND DON'T LEAVE ANYTHING OUT, EVEN IF YOU DON'T THINK IT'S IMPORTANT.
CLICK

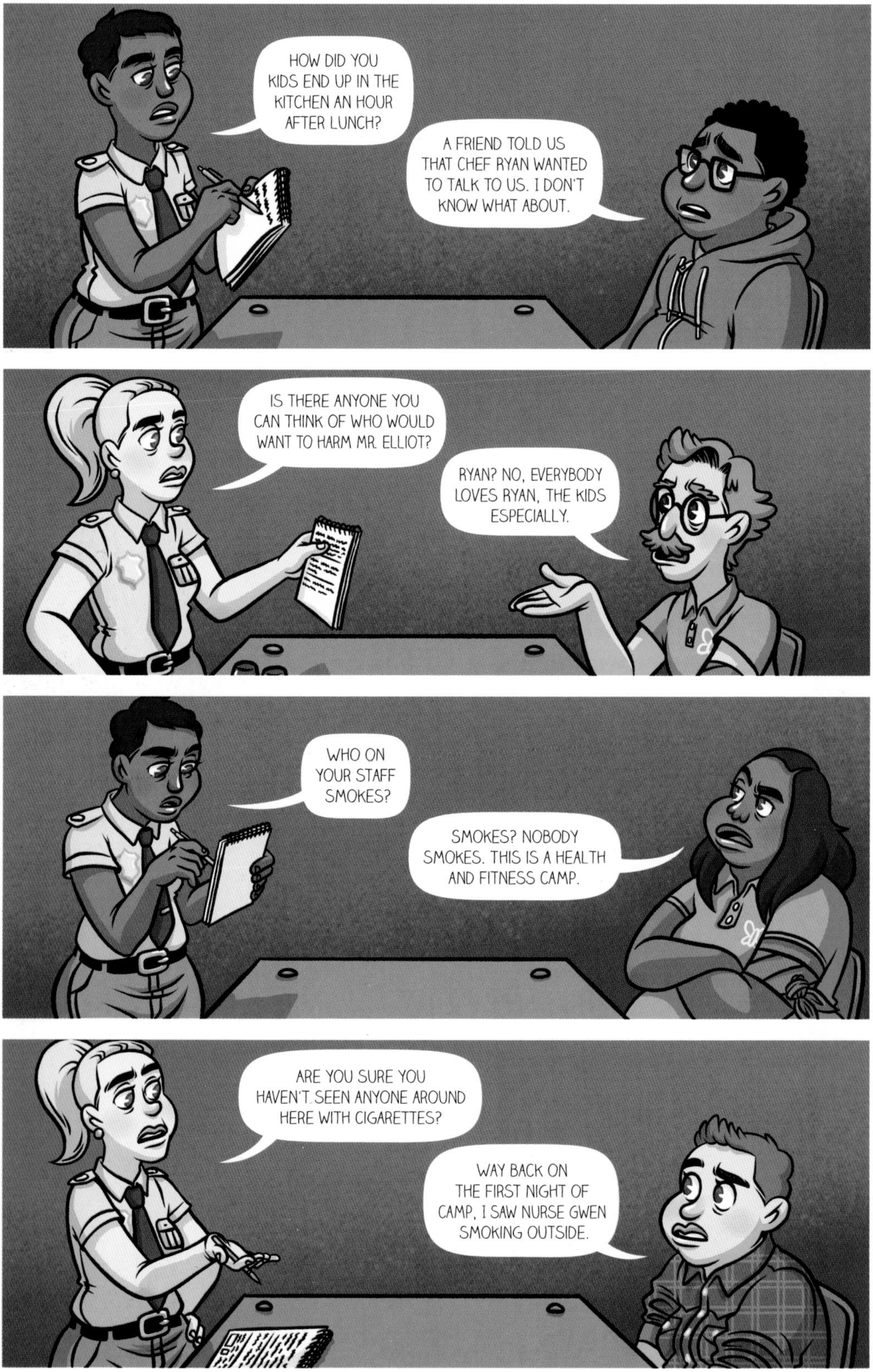
HOW DID YOU KIDS END UP IN THE KITCHEN AN HOUR AFTER LUNCH?
A FRIEND TOLD US THAT CHEF RYAN WANTED TO TALK TO US. I DON'T KNOW WHAT ABOUT.
IS THERE ANYONE YOU CAN THINK OF WHO WOULD WANT TO HARM MR. ELLIOT?
RYAN? NO, EVERYBODY LOVES RYAN, THE KIDS ESPECIALLY.
WHO ON YOUR STAFF SMOKES?
SMOKES? NOBODY SMOKES. THIS IS A HEALTH AND FITNESS CAMP.
ARE YOU SURE YOU HAVEN'T SEEN ANYONE AROUND HERE WITH CIGARETTES?
WAY BACK ON THE FIRST NIGHT OF CAMP, I SAW NURSE GWEN SMOKING OUTSIDE.

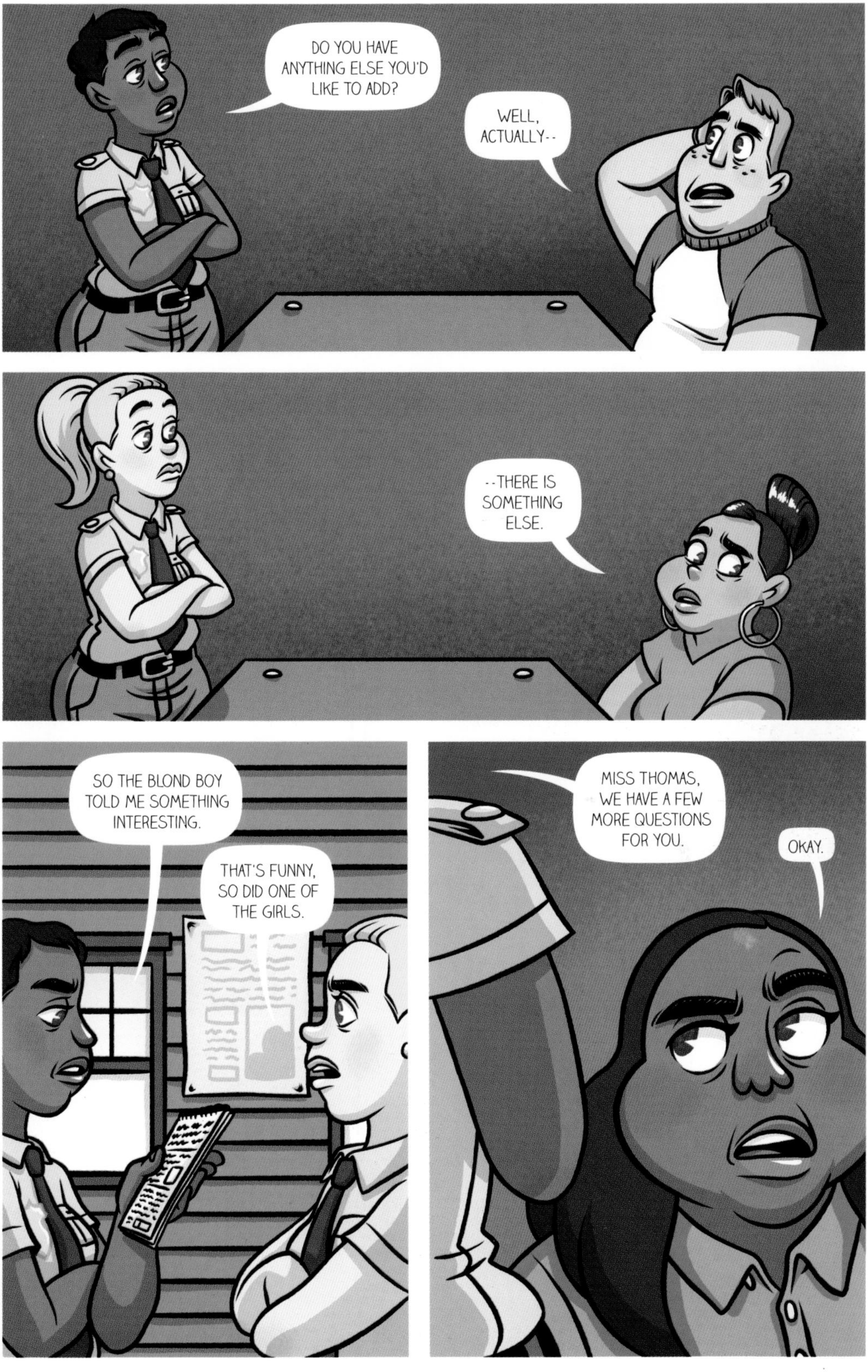

DO YOU HAVE ANYTHING ELSE YOU'D LIKE TO ADD?
WELL, ACTUALLY--
--THERE IS SOMETHING ELSE.
SO THE BLOND BOY TOLD ME SOMETHING INTERESTING.
THAT'S FUNNY, SO DID ONE OF THE GIRLS.
MISS THOMAS, WE HAVE A FEW MORE QUESTIONS FOR YOU.
OKAY.

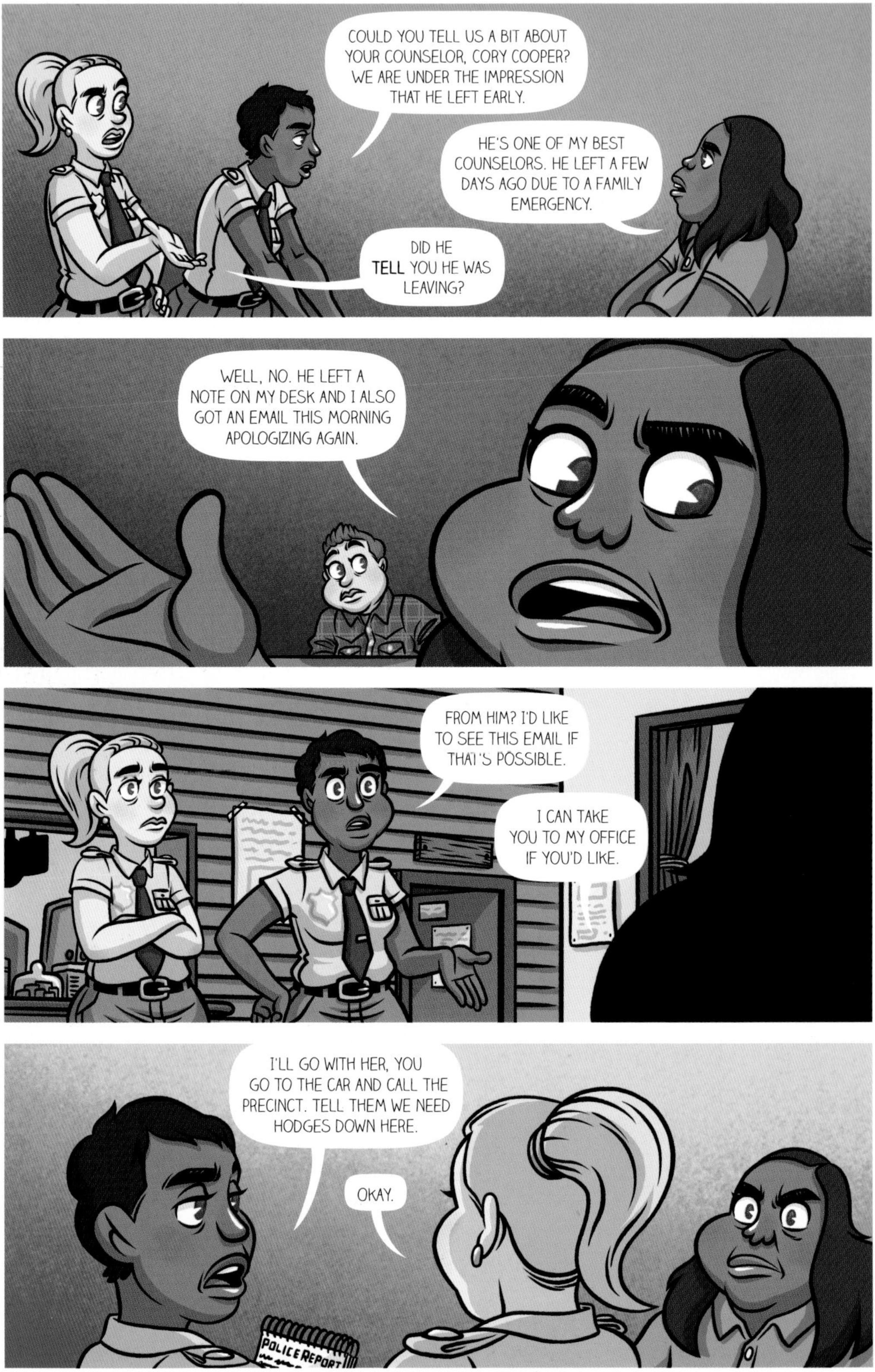
COULD YOU TELL US A BIT ABOUT YOUR COUNSELOR, CORY COOPER? WE ARE UNDER THE IMPRESSION THAT HE LEFT EARLY.
HE'S ONE OF MY BEST COUNSELORS. HE LEFT A FEW DAYS AGO DUE TO A FAMILY EMERGENCY.
DID HE **TELL** YOU HE WAS LEAVING?
WELL, NO. HE LEFT A NOTE ON MY DESK AND I ALSO GOT AN EMAIL THIS MORNING APOLOGIZING AGAIN.
FROM HIM? I'D LIKE TO SEE THIS EMAIL IF THAT'S POSSIBLE.
I CAN TAKE YOU TO MY OFFICE IF YOU'D LIKE.
I'LL GO WITH HER, YOU GO TO THE CAR AND CALL THE PRECINCT. TELL THEM WE NEED HODGES DOWN HERE.
OKAY.
POLICE REPORT

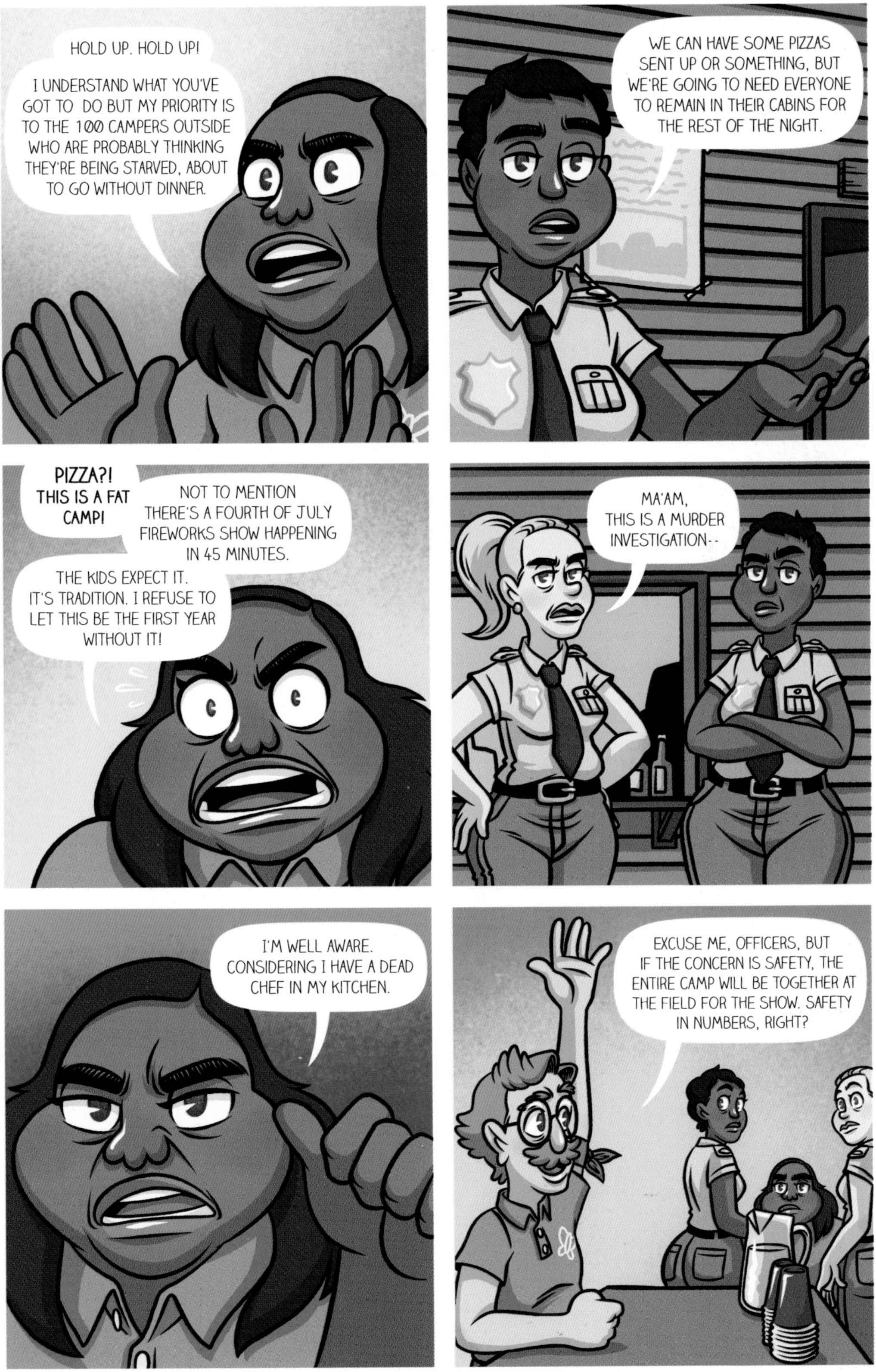
HOLD UP. HOLD UP!
I UNDERSTAND WHAT YOU'VE GOT TO DO BUT MY PRIORITY IS TO THE 100 CAMPERS OUTSIDE WHO ARE PROBABLY THINKING THEY'RE BEING STARVED, ABOUT TO GO WITHOUT DINNER.
WE CAN HAVE SOME PIZZAS SENT UP OR SOMETHING, BUT WE'RE GOING TO NEED EVERYONE TO REMAIN IN THEIR CABINS FOR THE REST OF THE NIGHT.
PIZZA?! THIS IS A FAT CAMP!
NOT TO MENTION THERE'S A FOURTH OF JULY FIREWORKS SHOW HAPPENING IN 45 MINUTES.
THE KIDS EXPECT IT. IT'S TRADITION. I REFUSE TO LET THIS BE THE FIRST YEAR WITHOUT IT!
MA'AM, THIS IS A MURDER INVESTIGATION--
I'M WELL AWARE. CONSIDERING I HAVE A DEAD CHEF IN MY KITCHEN.
EXCUSE ME, OFFICERS, BUT IF THE CONCERN IS SAFETY, THE ENTIRE CAMP WILL BE TOGETHER AT THE FIELD FOR THE SHOW. SAFETY IN NUMBERS, RIGHT?

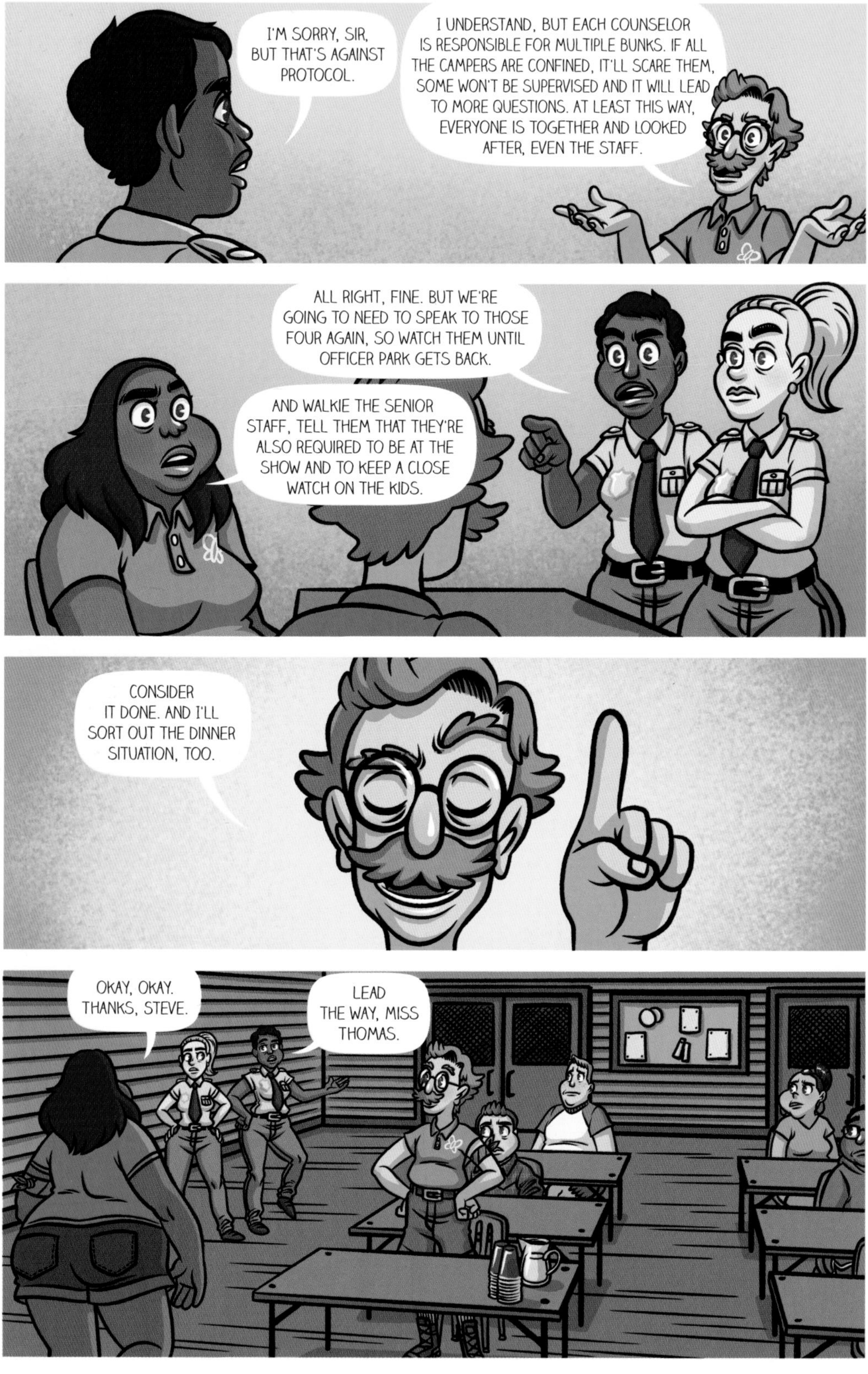
I'M SORRY, SIR, BUT THAT'S AGAINST PROTOCOL.
I UNDERSTAND, BUT EACH COUNSELOR IS RESPONSIBLE FOR MULTIPLE BUNKS. IF ALL THE CAMPERS ARE CONFINED, IT'LL SCARE THEM, SOME WON'T BE SUPERVISED AND IT WILL LEAD TO MORE QUESTIONS. AT LEAST THIS WAY, EVERYONE IS TOGETHER AND LOOKED AFTER, EVEN THE STAFF.
ALL RIGHT, FINE. BUT WE'RE GOING TO NEED TO SPEAK TO THOSE FOUR AGAIN, SO WATCH THEM UNTIL OFFICER PARK GETS BACK.
AND WALKIE THE SENIOR STAFF, TELL THEM THAT THEY'RE ALSO REQUIRED TO BE AT THE SHOW AND TO KEEP A CLOSE WATCH ON THE KIDS.
CONSIDER IT DONE. AND I'LL SORT OUT THE DINNER SITUATION, TOO.
OKAY, OKAY. THANKS, STEVE.
LEAD THE WAY, MISS THOMAS.

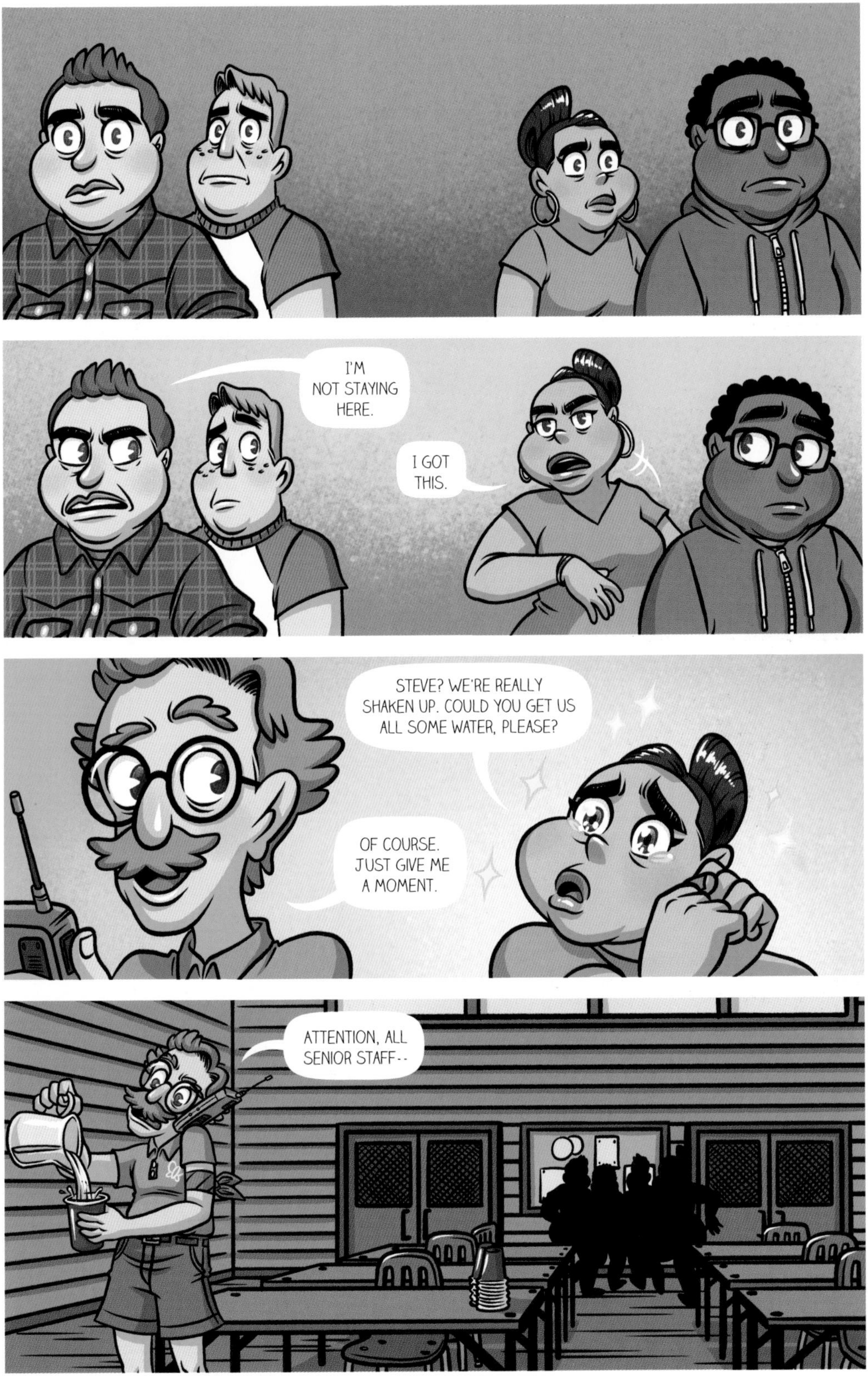

I'M NOT STAYING HERE.
I GOT THIS.
STEVE? WE'RE REALLY SHAKEN UP. COULD YOU GET US ALL SOME WATER, PLEASE?
OF COURSE. JUST GIVE ME A MOMENT.
ATTENTION, ALL SENIOR STAFF--

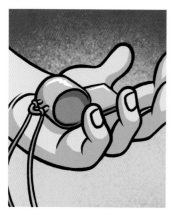

YOU GUYS, WE COUNTED GWEN OUT TOO EARLY. YOU TWO SAID SHE HAD AN ALIBI.

SHE DID! SHE WAS OUT.

YOU DIDN'T EVEN GO IN AND LOOK AROUND.

IF SHE HAD, I'M SURE NOAH WOULDN'T HAVE LEFT HER ALL ALONE.

EXCUSE ME?

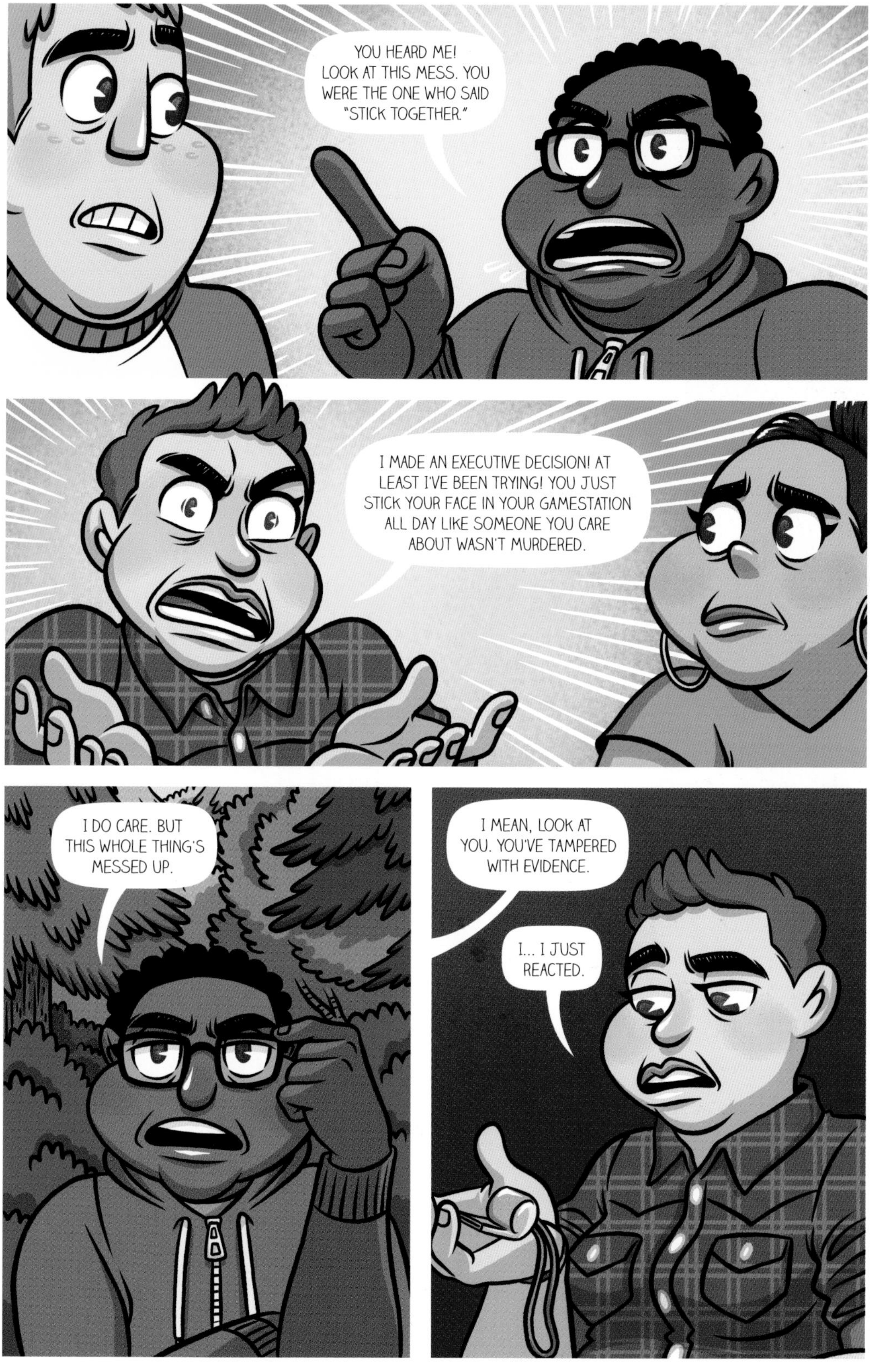
YOU HEARD ME! LOOK AT THIS MESS. YOU WERE THE ONE WHO SAID "STICK TOGETHER."
I MADE AN EXECUTIVE DECISION! AT LEAST I'VE BEEN TRYING! YOU JUST STICK YOUR FACE IN YOUR GAMESTATION ALL DAY LIKE SOMEONE YOU CARE ABOUT WASN'T MURDERED.
I DO CARE. BUT THIS WHOLE THING'S MESSED UP.
I MEAN, LOOK AT YOU. YOU'VE TAMPERED WITH EVIDENCE.
I... I JUST REACTED.

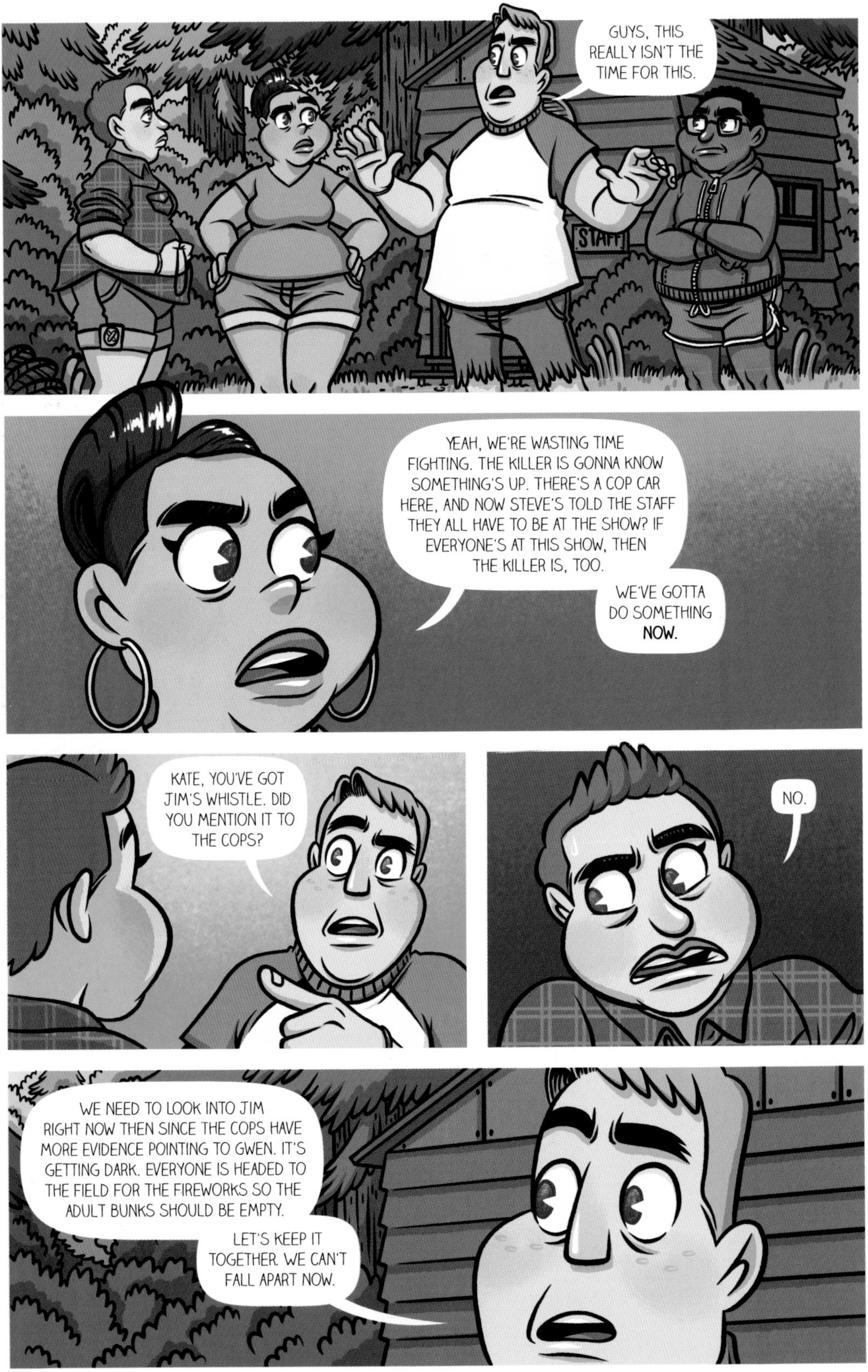
GUYS, THIS REALLY ISN'T THE TIME FOR THIS.
STAFF
YEAH, WE'RE WASTING TIME FIGHTING. THE KILLER IS GONNA KNOW SOMETHING'S UP. THERE'S A COP CAR HERE, AND NOW STEVE'S TOLD THE STAFF THEY ALL HAVE TO BE AT THE SHOW? IF EVERYONE'S AT THIS SHOW, THEN THE KILLER IS, TOO.
WE'VE GOTTA DO SOMETHING **NOW.**
KATE, YOU'VE GOT JIM'S WHISTLE. DID YOU MENTION IT TO THE COPS?
NO.
WE NEED TO LOOK INTO JIM RIGHT NOW THEN SINCE THE COPS HAVE MORE EVIDENCE POINTING TO GWEN. IT'S GETTING DARK. EVERYONE IS HEADED TO THE FIELD FOR THE FIREWORKS SO THE ADULT BUNKS SHOULD BE EMPTY.
LET'S KEEP IT TOGETHER. WE CAN'T FALL APART NOW.

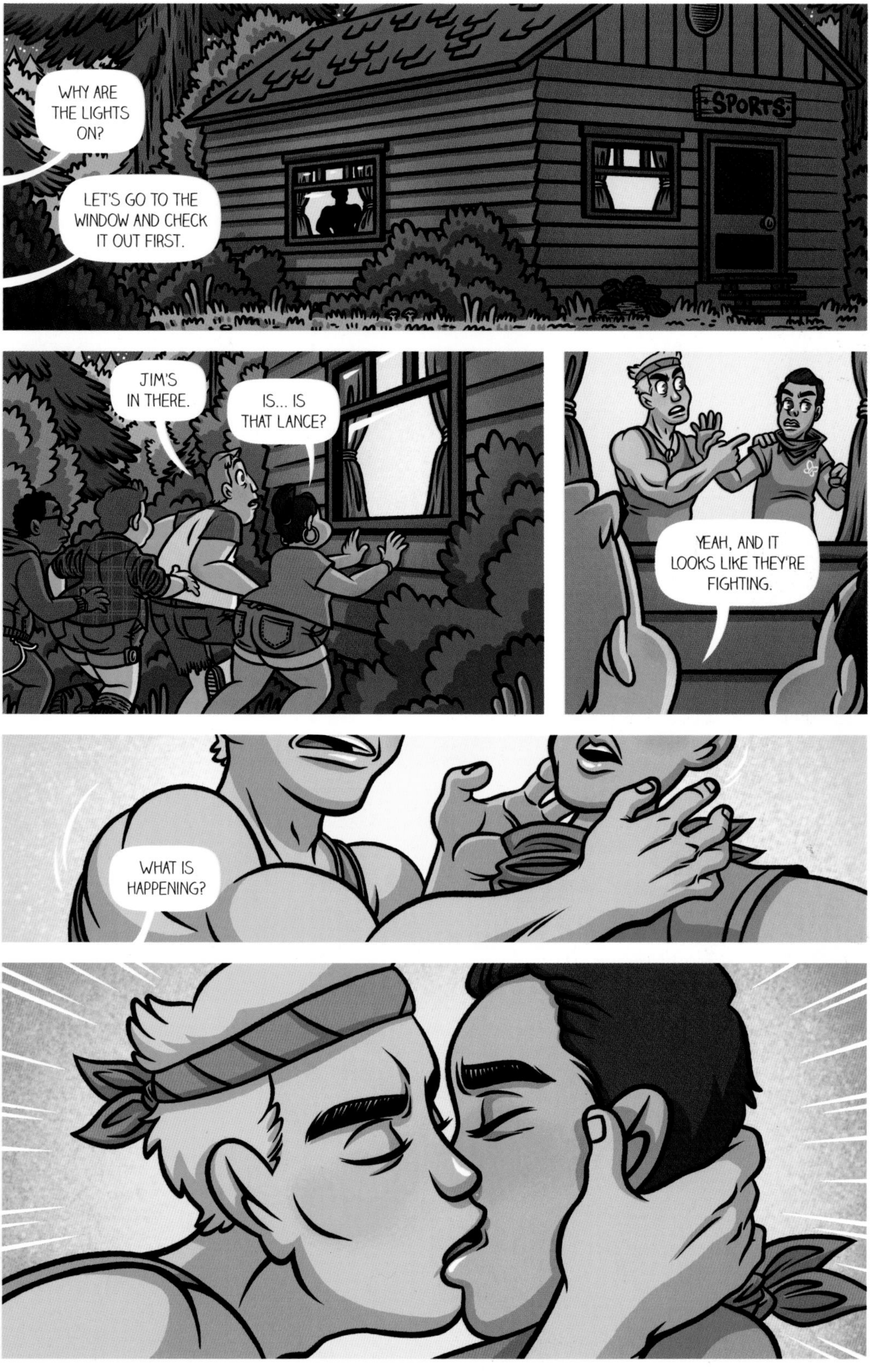

WHY ARE THE LIGHTS ON?
LET'S GO TO THE WINDOW AND CHECK IT OUT FIRST.
SPORTS
JIM'S IN THERE.
IS... IS THAT LANCE?
YEAH, AND IT LOOKS LIKE THEY'RE FIGHTING.
WHAT IS HAPPENING?

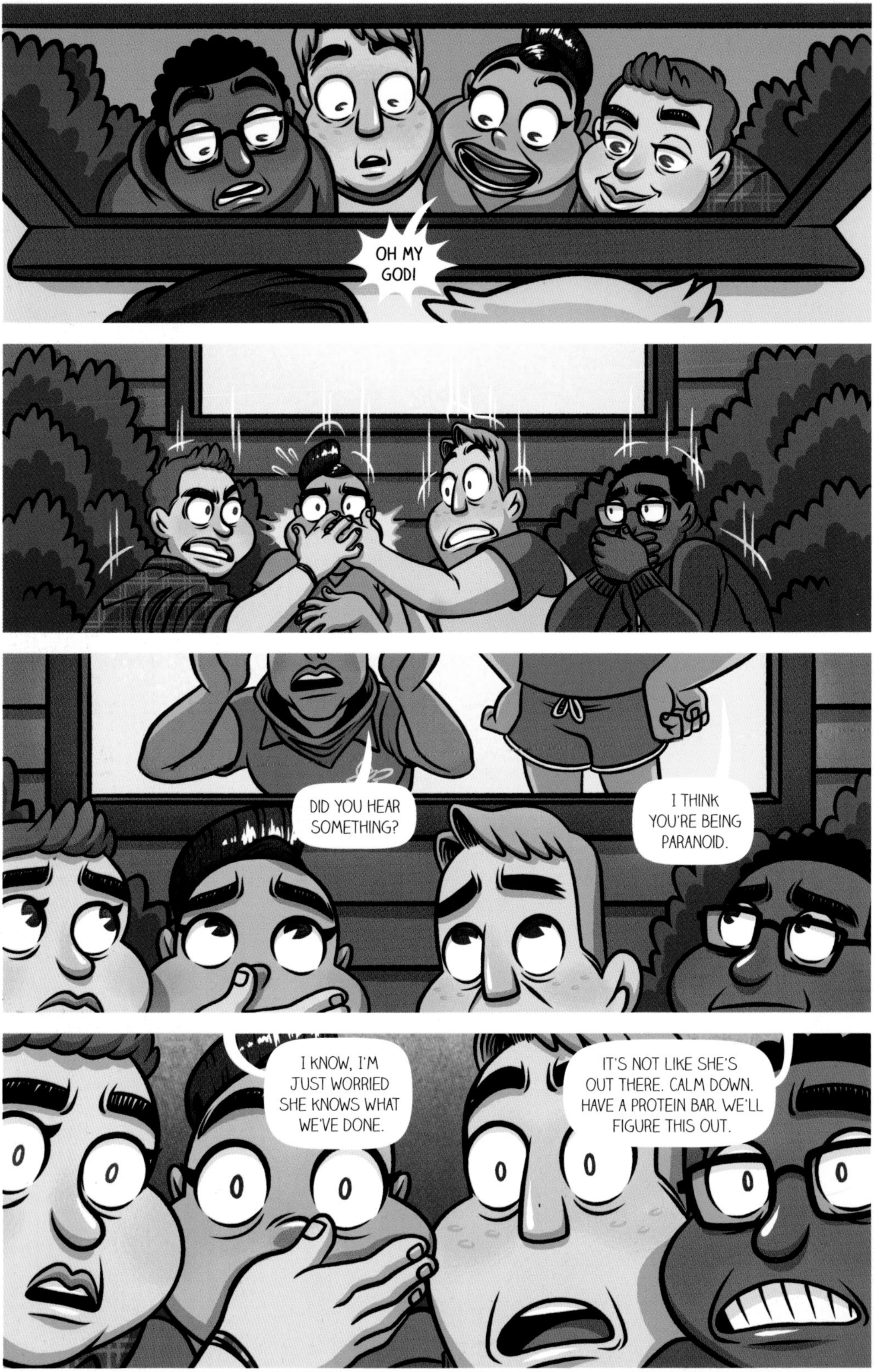
OH MY GOD!
DID YOU HEAR SOMETHING?
I THINK YOU'RE BEING PARANOID.
I KNOW, I'M JUST WORRIED SHE KNOWS WHAT WE'VE DONE.
IT'S NOT LIKE SHE'S OUT THERE. CALM DOWN. HAVE A PROTEIN BAR. WE'LL FIGURE THIS OUT.

CHAPTER ELEVEN

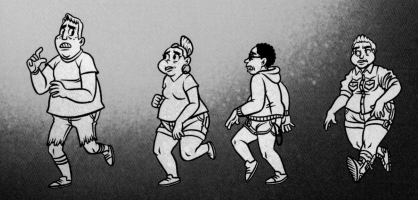

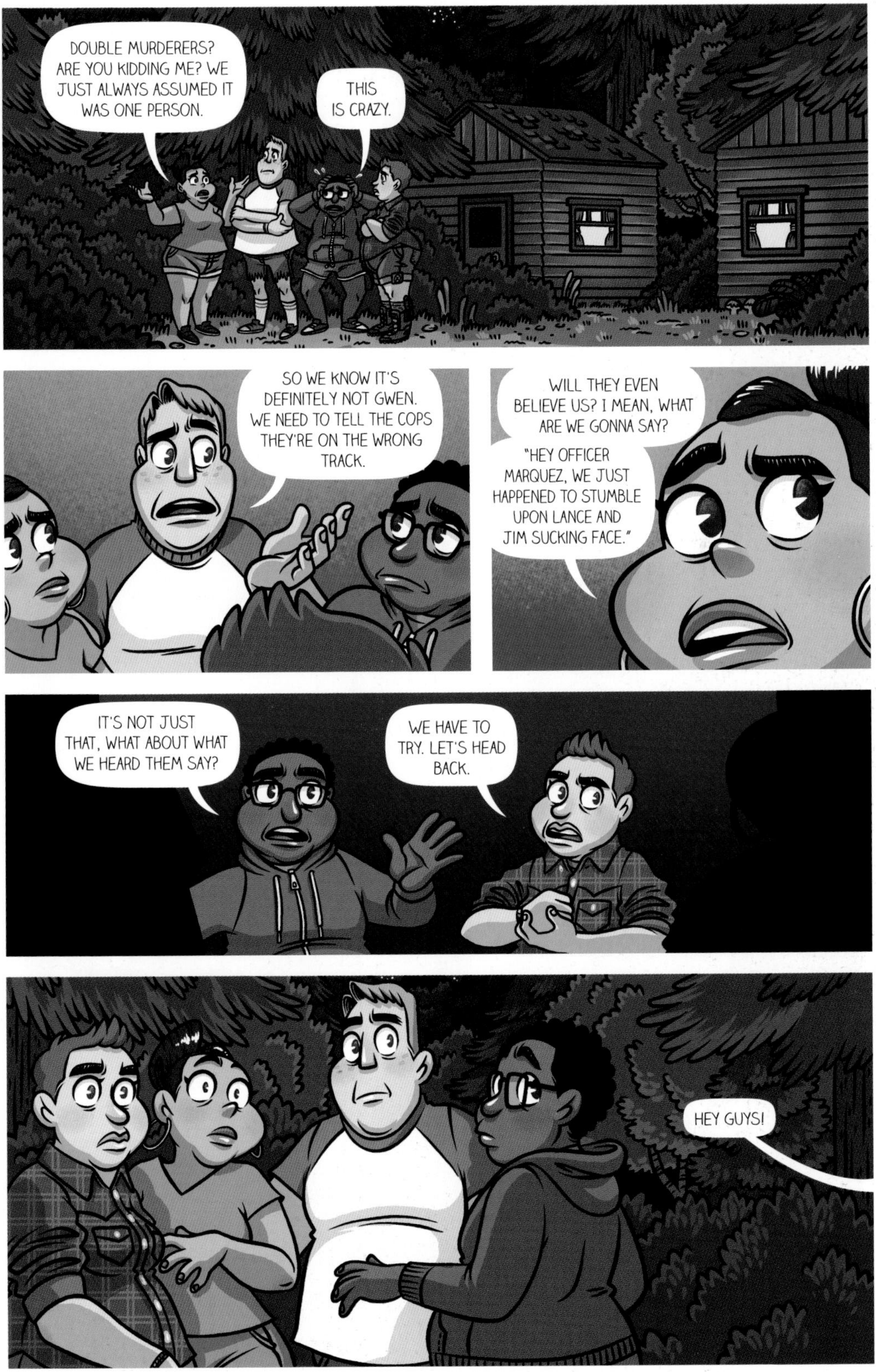
DOUBLE MURDERERS? ARE YOU KIDDING ME? WE JUST ALWAYS ASSUMED IT WAS ONE PERSON.
THIS IS CRAZY.
SO WE KNOW IT'S DEFINITELY NOT GWEN. WE NEED TO TELL THE COPS THEY'RE ON THE WRONG TRACK.
WILL THEY EVEN BELIEVE US? I MEAN, WHAT ARE WE GONNA SAY?
"HEY OFFICER MARQUEZ, WE JUST HAPPENED TO STUMBLE UPON LANCE AND JIM SUCKING FACE."
IT'S NOT JUST THAT, WHAT ABOUT WHAT WE HEARD THEM SAY?
WE HAVE TO TRY. LET'S HEAD BACK.
HEY GUYS!

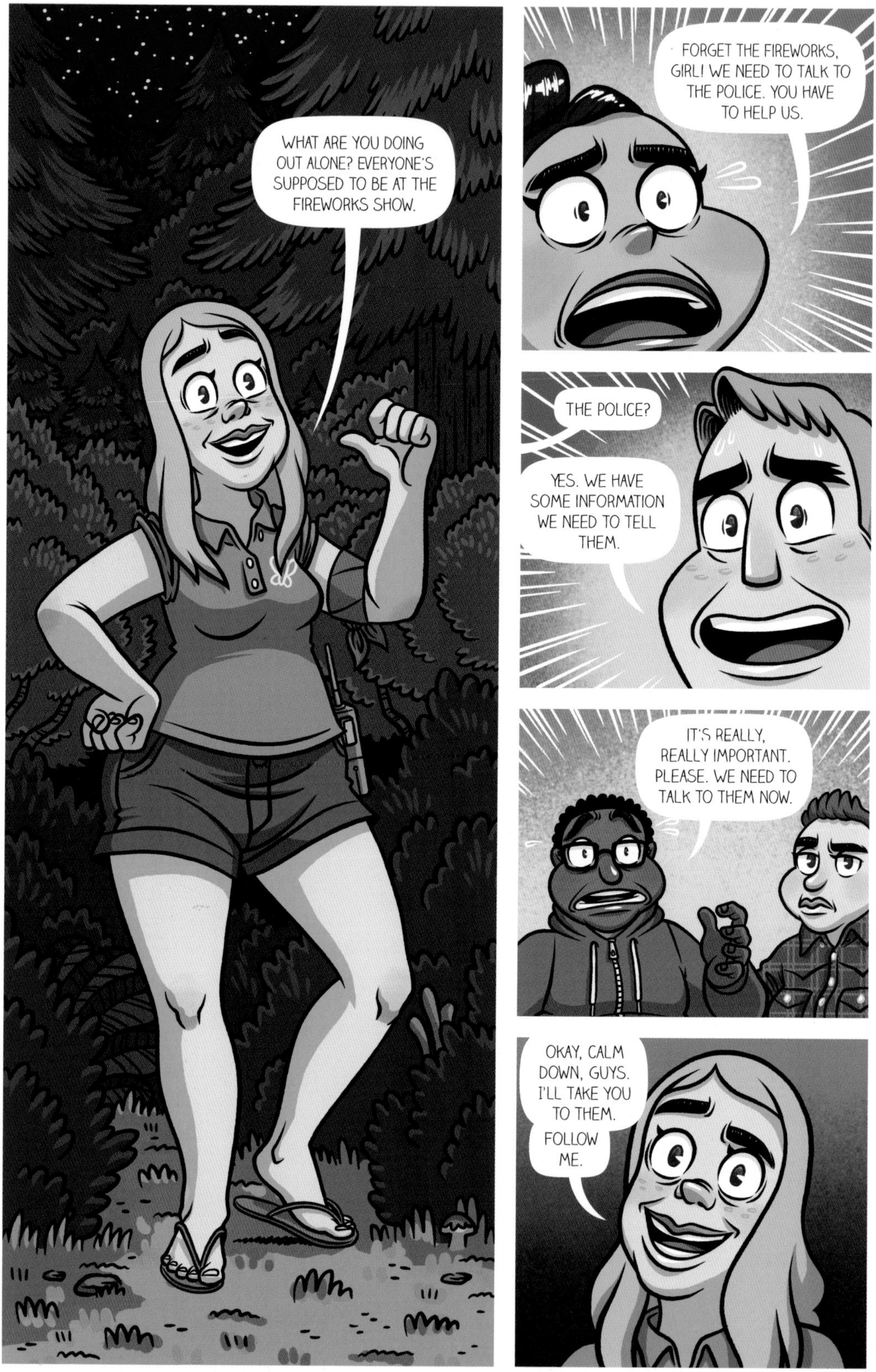
WHAT ARE YOU DOING OUT ALONE? EVERYONE'S SUPPOSED TO BE AT THE FIREWORKS SHOW.
FORGET THE FIREWORKS, GIRL! WE NEED TO TALK TO THE POLICE. YOU HAVE TO HELP US.
THE POLICE?
YES. WE HAVE SOME INFORMATION WE NEED TO TELL THEM.
IT'S REALLY, REALLY IMPORTANT. PLEASE. WE NEED TO TALK TO THEM NOW.
OKAY, CALM DOWN, GUYS. I'LL TAKE YOU TO THEM.
FOLLOW ME.

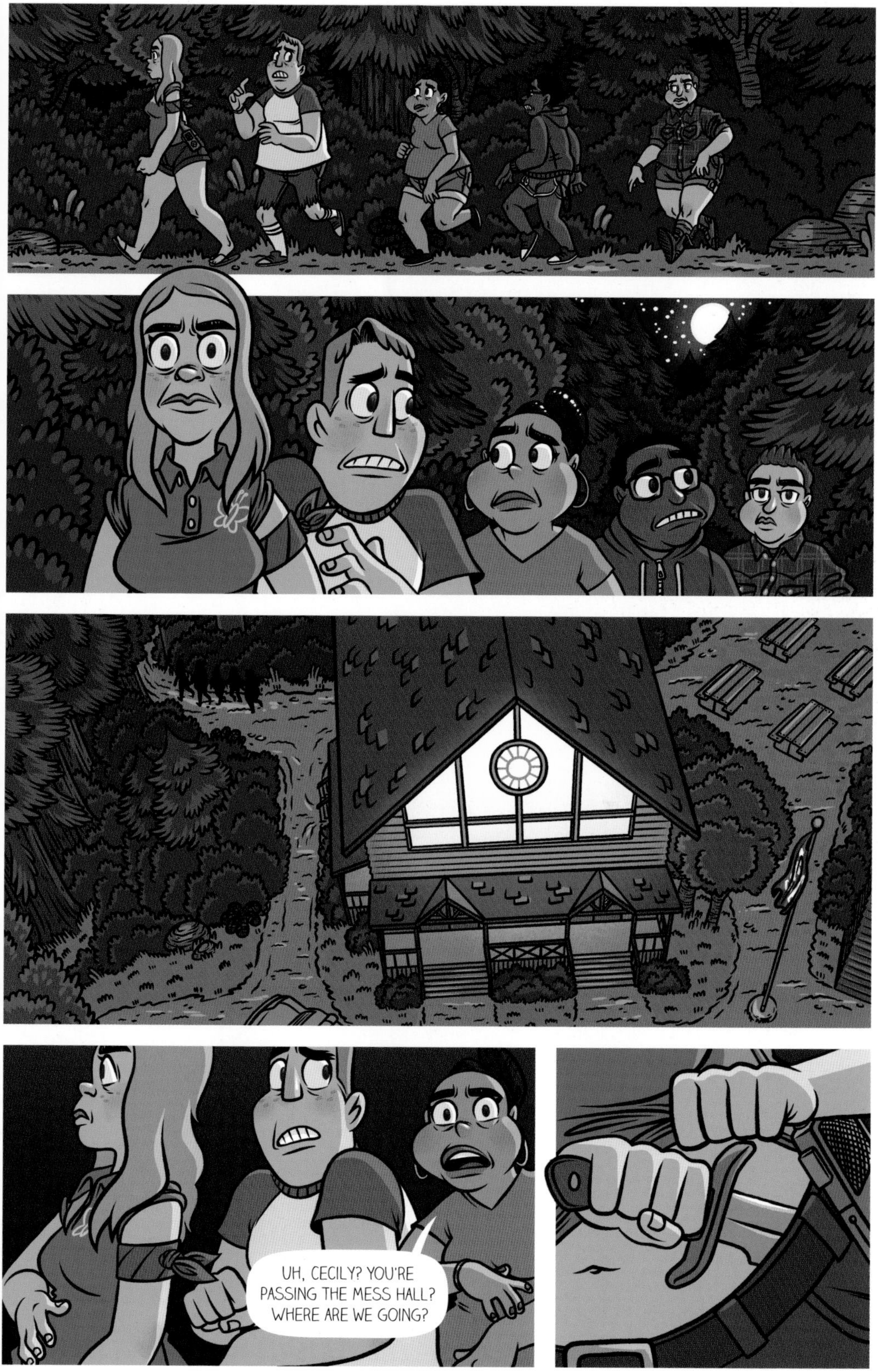
UH, CECILY? YOU'RE PASSING THE MESS HALL? WHERE ARE WE GOING?

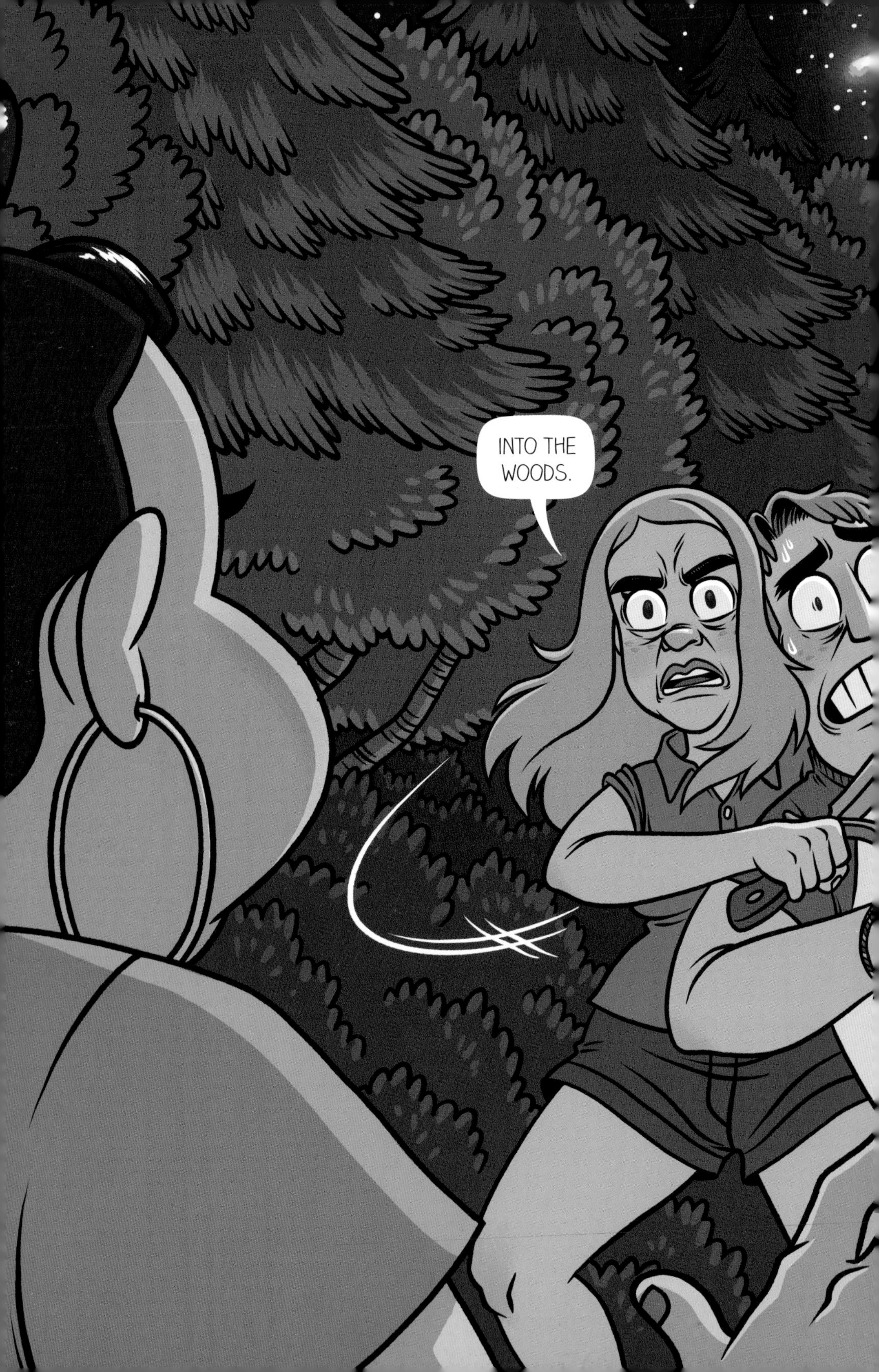
INTO THE WOODS.

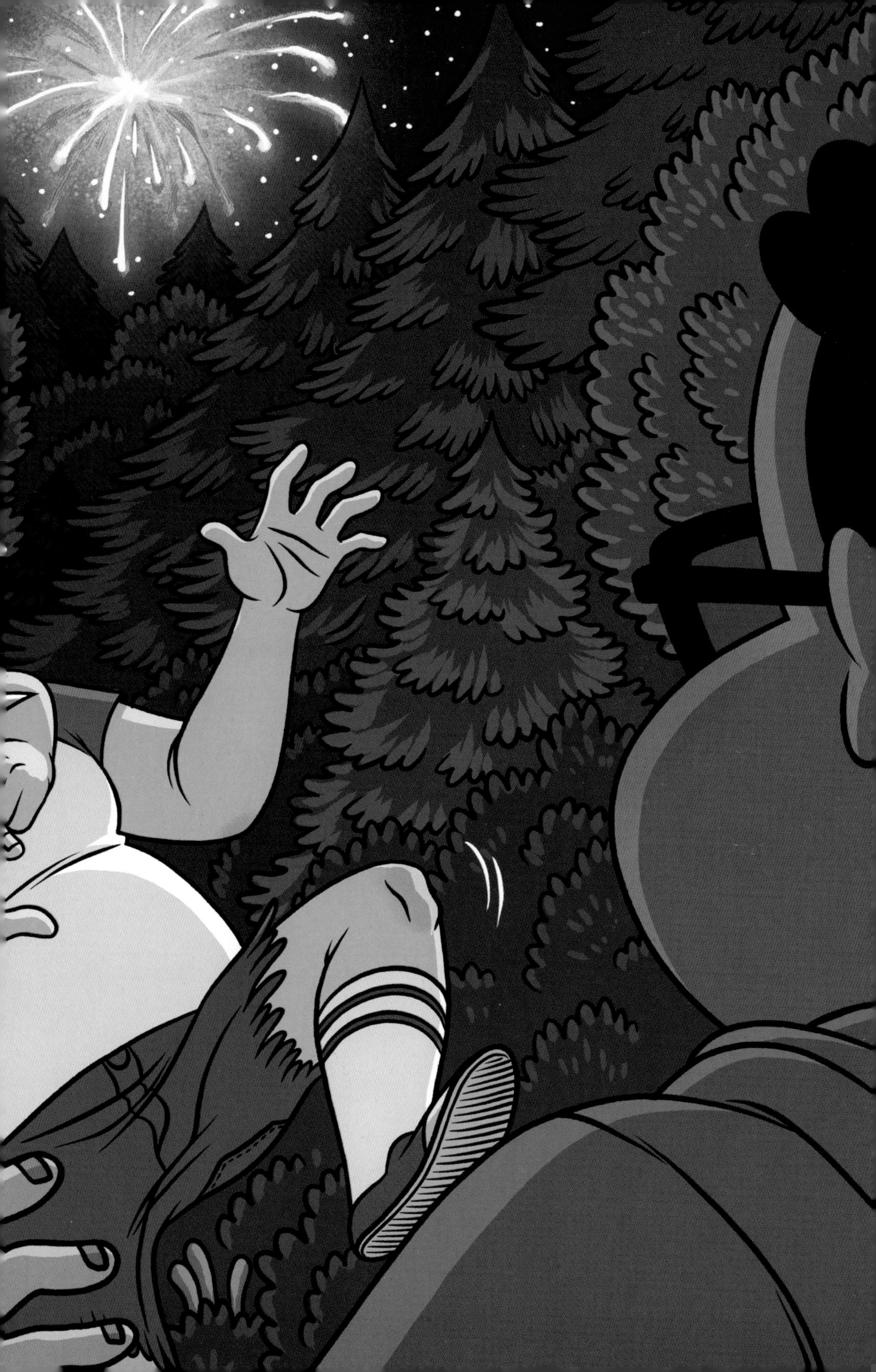

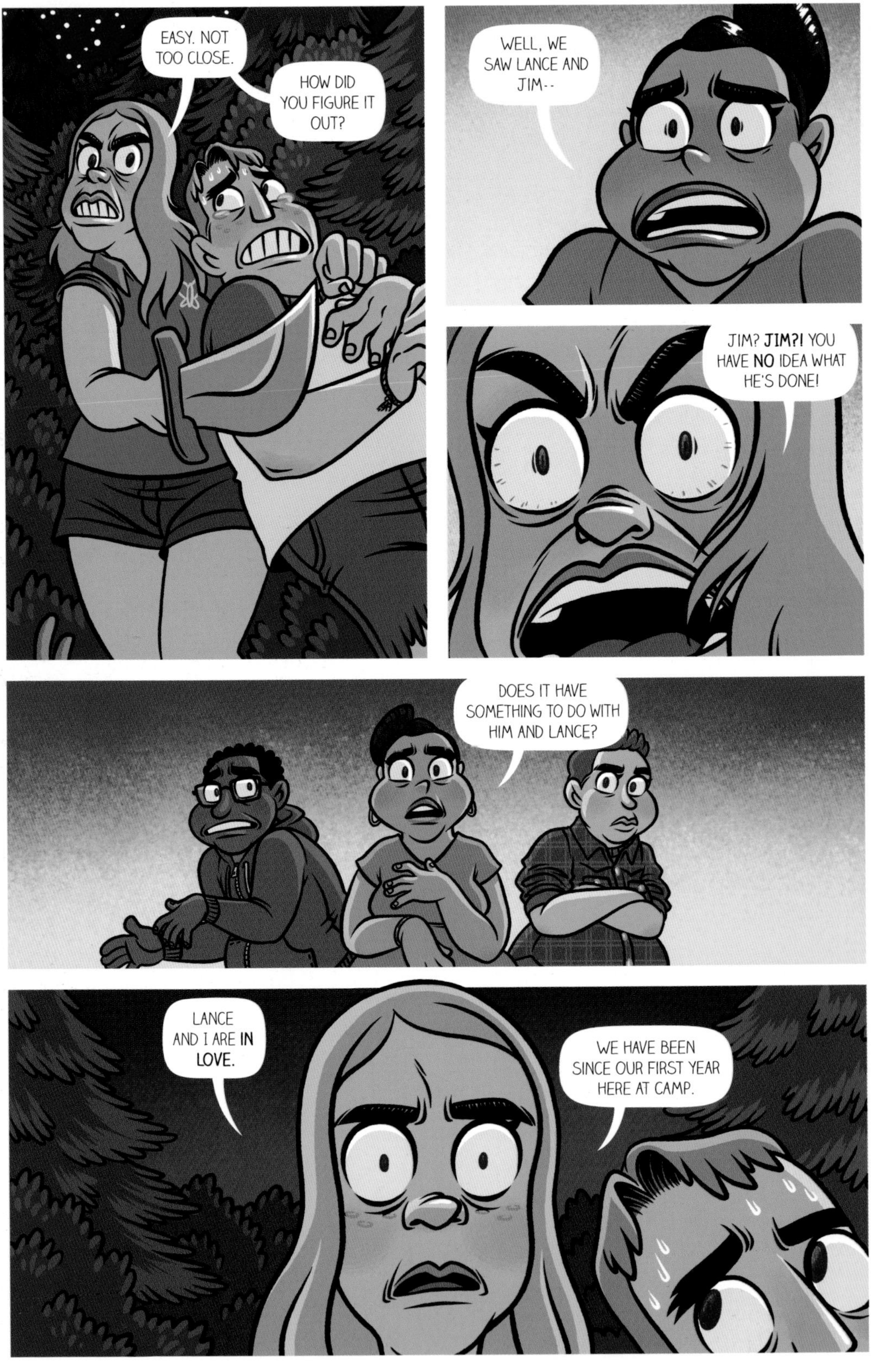
EASY. NOT TOO CLOSE.
HOW DID YOU FIGURE IT OUT?
WELL, WE SAW LANCE AND JIM--
JIM? JIM?! YOU HAVE NO IDEA WHAT HE'S DONE!
DOES IT HAVE SOMETHING TO DO WITH HIM AND LANCE?
LANCE AND I ARE IN LOVE.
WE HAVE BEEN SINCE OUR FIRST YEAR HERE AT CAMP.

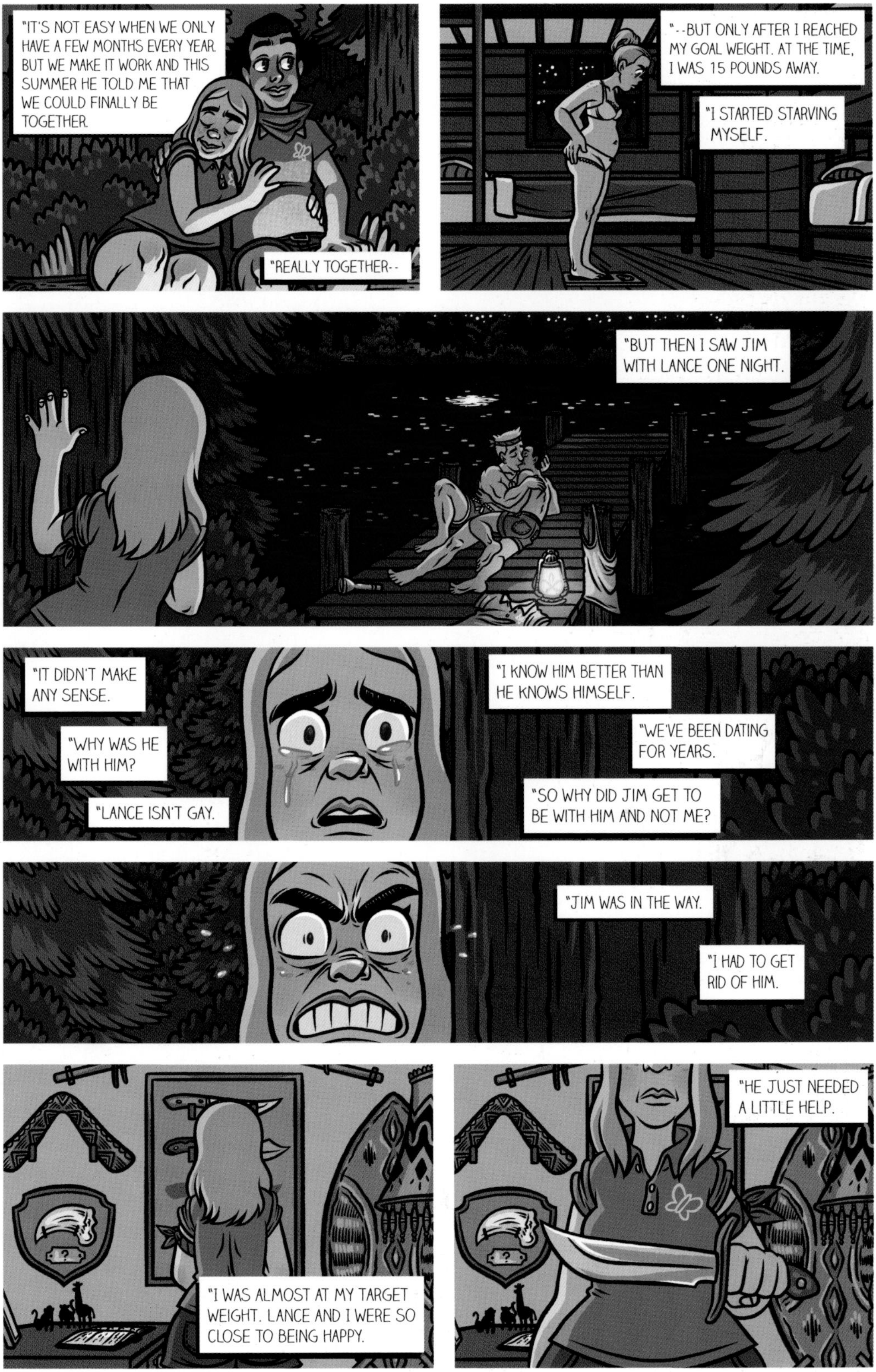
"IT'S NOT EASY WHEN WE ONLY HAVE A FEW MONTHS EVERY YEAR. BUT WE MAKE IT WORK AND THIS SUMMER HE TOLD ME THAT WE COULD FINALLY BE TOGETHER.
"REALLY TOGETHER--
"--BUT ONLY AFTER I REACHED MY GOAL WEIGHT. AT THE TIME, I WAS 15 POUNDS AWAY.
"I STARTED STARVING MYSELF.
"BUT THEN I SAW JIM WITH LANCE ONE NIGHT.
"IT DIDN'T MAKE ANY SENSE.
"WHY WAS HE WITH HIM?
"LANCE ISN'T GAY.
"I KNOW HIM BETTER THAN HE KNOWS HIMSELF.
"WE'VE BEEN DATING FOR YEARS.
"SO WHY DID JIM GET TO BE WITH HIM AND NOT ME?
"JIM WAS IN THE WAY.
"I HAD TO GET RID OF HIM.
"I WAS ALMOST AT MY TARGET WEIGHT. LANCE AND I WERE SO CLOSE TO BEING HAPPY.
"HE JUST NEEDED A LITTLE HELP.

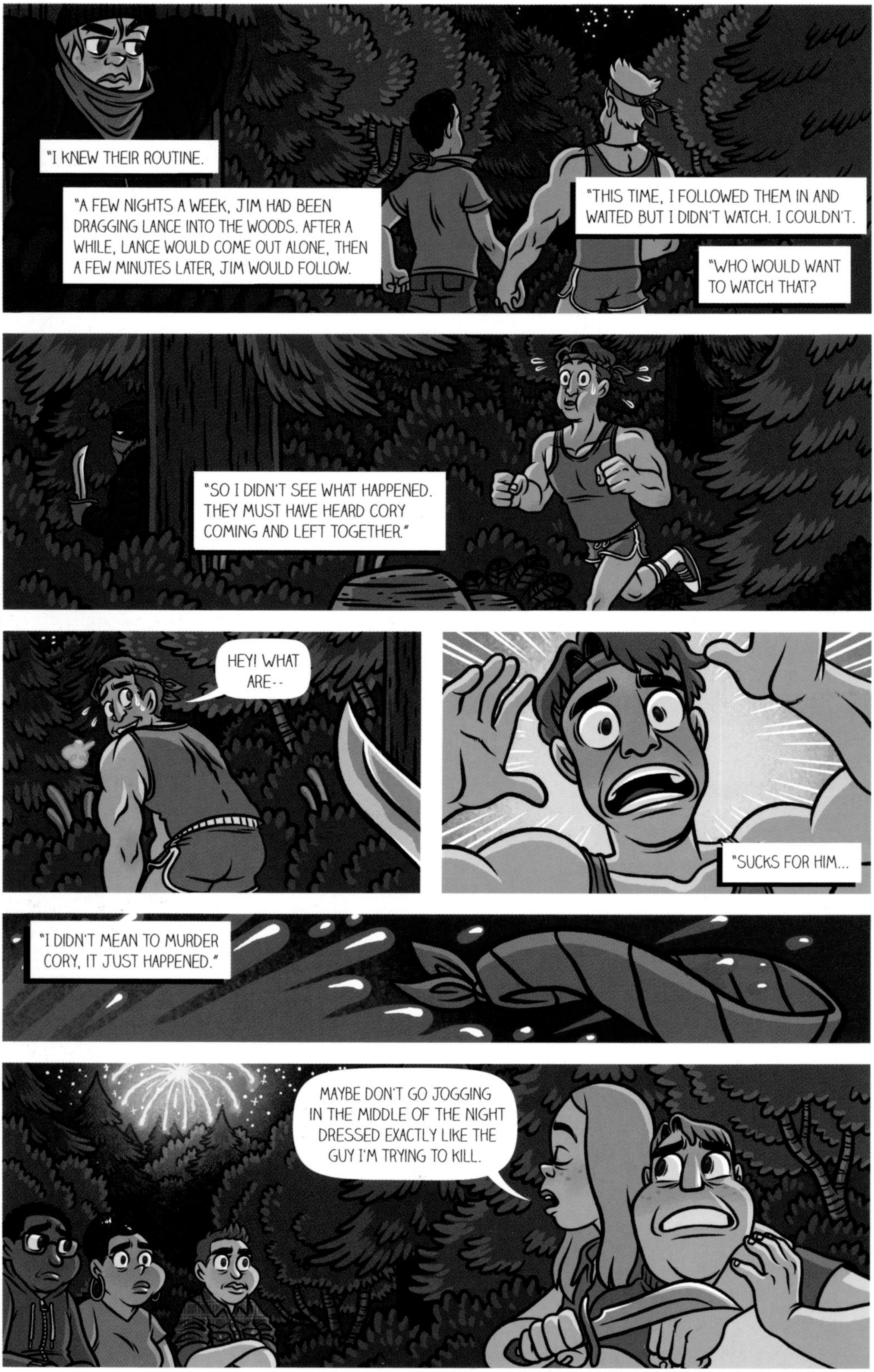
"I KNEW THEIR ROUTINE.
"A FEW NIGHTS A WEEK, JIM HAD BEEN DRAGGING LANCE INTO THE WOODS. AFTER A WHILE, LANCE WOULD COME OUT ALONE, THEN A FEW MINUTES LATER, JIM WOULD FOLLOW.
"THIS TIME, I FOLLOWED THEM IN AND WAITED BUT I DIDN'T WATCH. I COULDN'T.
"WHO WOULD WANT TO WATCH THAT?
"SO I DIDN'T SEE WHAT HAPPENED. THEY MUST HAVE HEARD CORY COMING AND LEFT TOGETHER."
HEY! WHAT ARE--
"SUCKS FOR HIM...
"I DIDN'T MEAN TO MURDER CORY, IT JUST HAPPENED."
MAYBE DON'T GO JOGGING IN THE MIDDLE OF THE NIGHT DRESSED EXACTLY LIKE THE GUY I'M TRYING TO KILL.

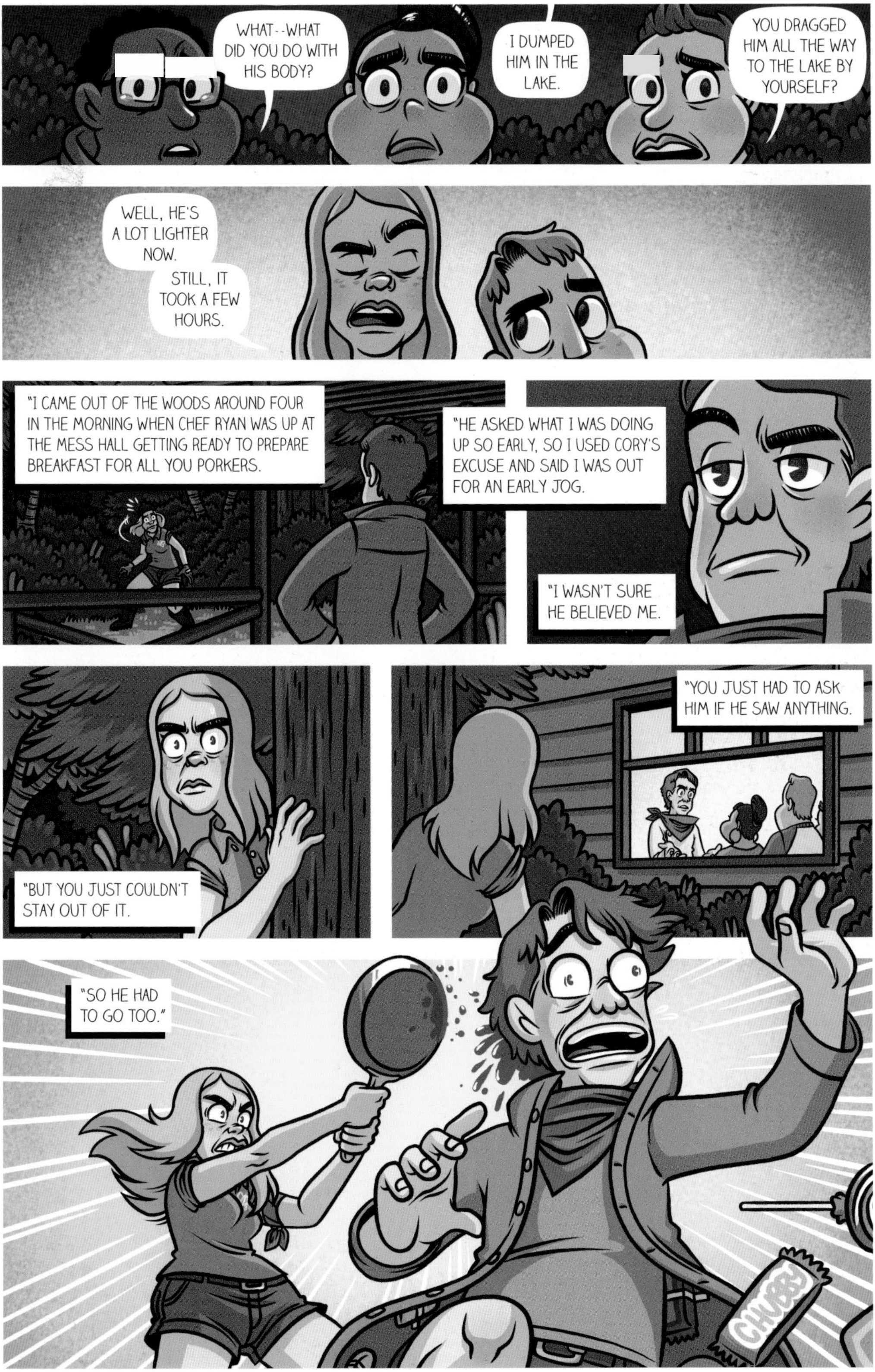

WHAT--WHAT DID YOU DO WITH HIS BODY?
I DUMPED HIM IN THE LAKE.
YOU DRAGGED HIM ALL THE WAY TO THE LAKE BY YOURSELF?
WELL, HE'S A LOT LIGHTER NOW.
STILL, IT TOOK A FEW HOURS.
"I CAME OUT OF THE WOODS AROUND FOUR IN THE MORNING WHEN CHEF RYAN WAS UP AT THE MESS HALL GETTING READY TO PREPARE BREAKFAST FOR ALL YOU PORKERS.
"HE ASKED WHAT I WAS DOING UP SO EARLY, SO I USED CORY'S EXCUSE AND SAID I WAS OUT FOR AN EARLY JOG.
"I WASN'T SURE HE BELIEVED ME.
"BUT YOU JUST COULDN'T STAY OUT OF IT.
"YOU JUST HAD TO ASK HIM IF HE SAW ANYTHING.
"SO HE HAD TO GO TOO."
CHUBBY

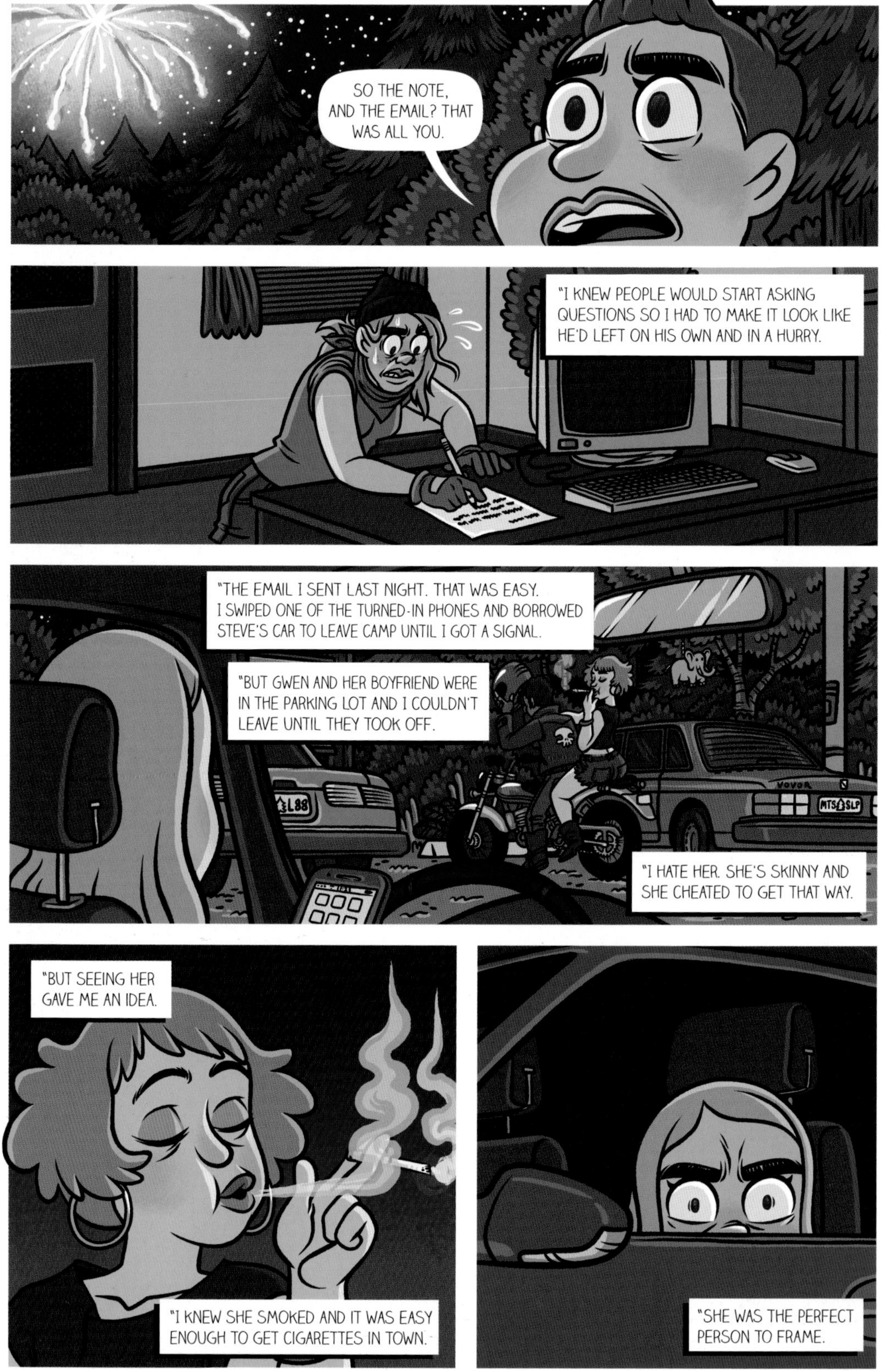
SO THE NOTE, AND THE EMAIL? THAT WAS ALL YOU.
"I KNEW PEOPLE WOULD START ASKING QUESTIONS SO I HAD TO MAKE IT LOOK LIKE HE'D LEFT ON HIS OWN AND IN A HURRY.
"THE EMAIL I SENT LAST NIGHT. THAT WAS EASY. I SWIPED ONE OF THE TURNED-IN PHONES AND BORROWED STEVE'S CAR TO LEAVE CAMP UNTIL I GOT A SIGNAL.
"BUT GWEN AND HER BOYFRIEND WERE IN THE PARKING LOT AND I COULDN'T LEAVE UNTIL THEY TOOK OFF.
"I HATE HER. SHE'S SKINNY AND SHE CHEATED TO GET THAT WAY.
"BUT SEEING HER GAVE ME AN IDEA.
"I KNEW SHE SMOKED AND IT WAS EASY ENOUGH TO GET CIGARETTES IN TOWN.
"SHE WAS THE PERFECT PERSON TO FRAME.

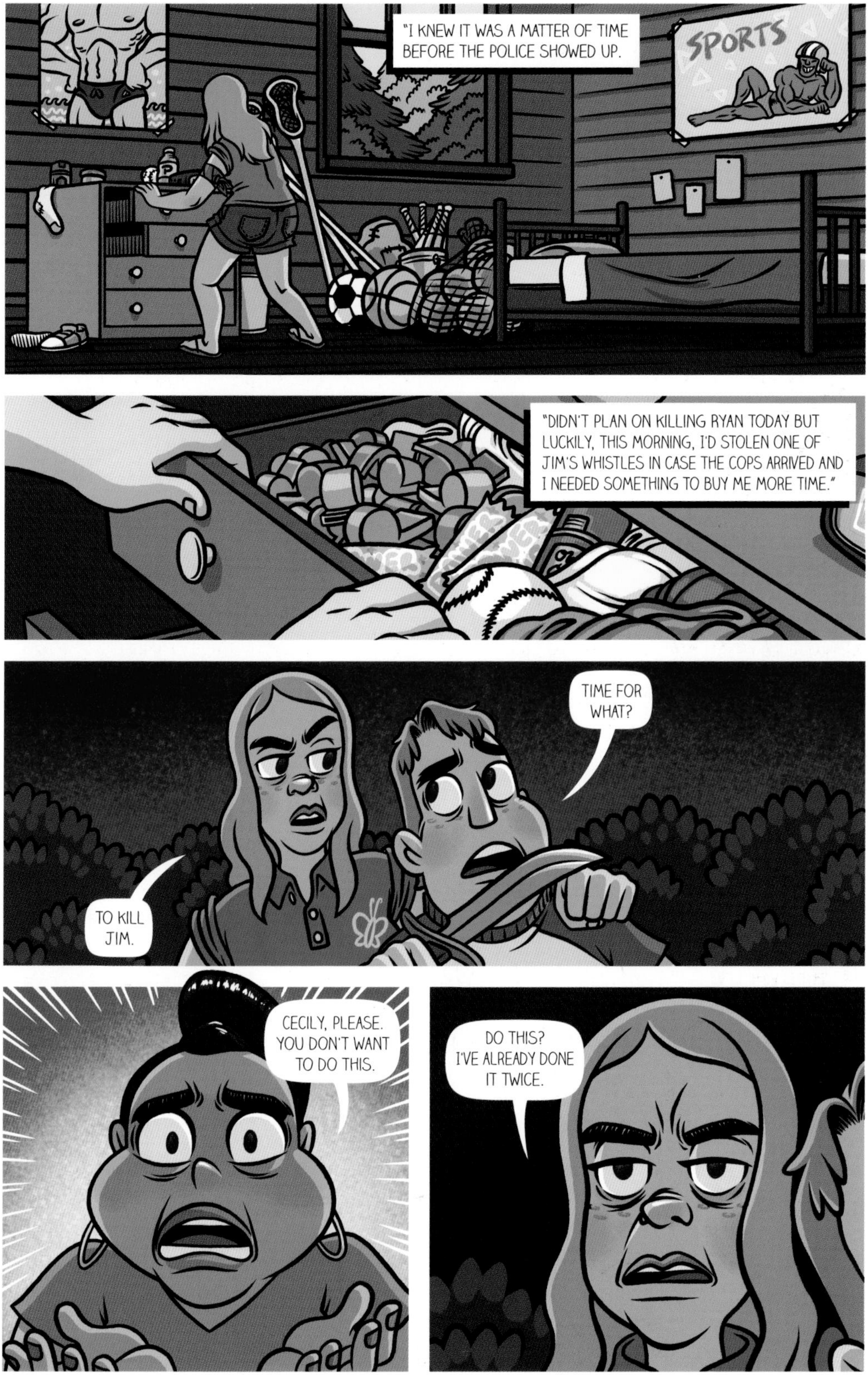
"I KNEW IT WAS A MATTER OF TIME BEFORE THE POLICE SHOWED UP.
SPORTS
"DIDN'T PLAN ON KILLING RYAN TODAY BUT LUCKILY, THIS MORNING, I'D STOLEN ONE OF JIM'S WHISTLES IN CASE THE COPS ARRIVED AND I NEEDED SOMETHING TO BUY ME MORE TIME."
TIME FOR WHAT?
TO KILL JIM.
CECILY, PLEASE. YOU DON'T WANT TO DO THIS.
DO THIS? I'VE ALREADY DONE IT TWICE.

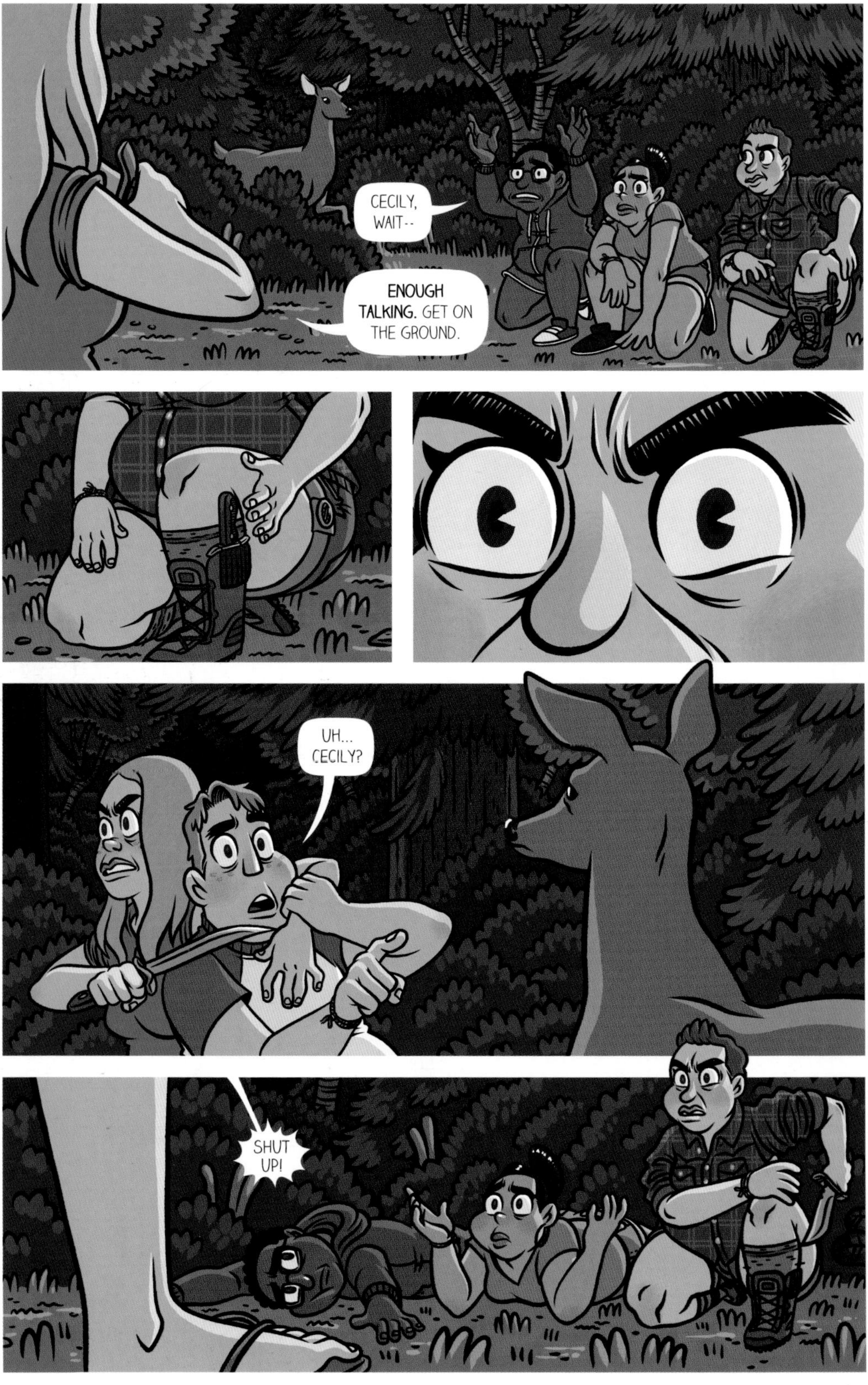
CECILY, WAIT--
ENOUGH TALKING. GET ON THE GROUND.
UH... CECILY?
SHUT UP!

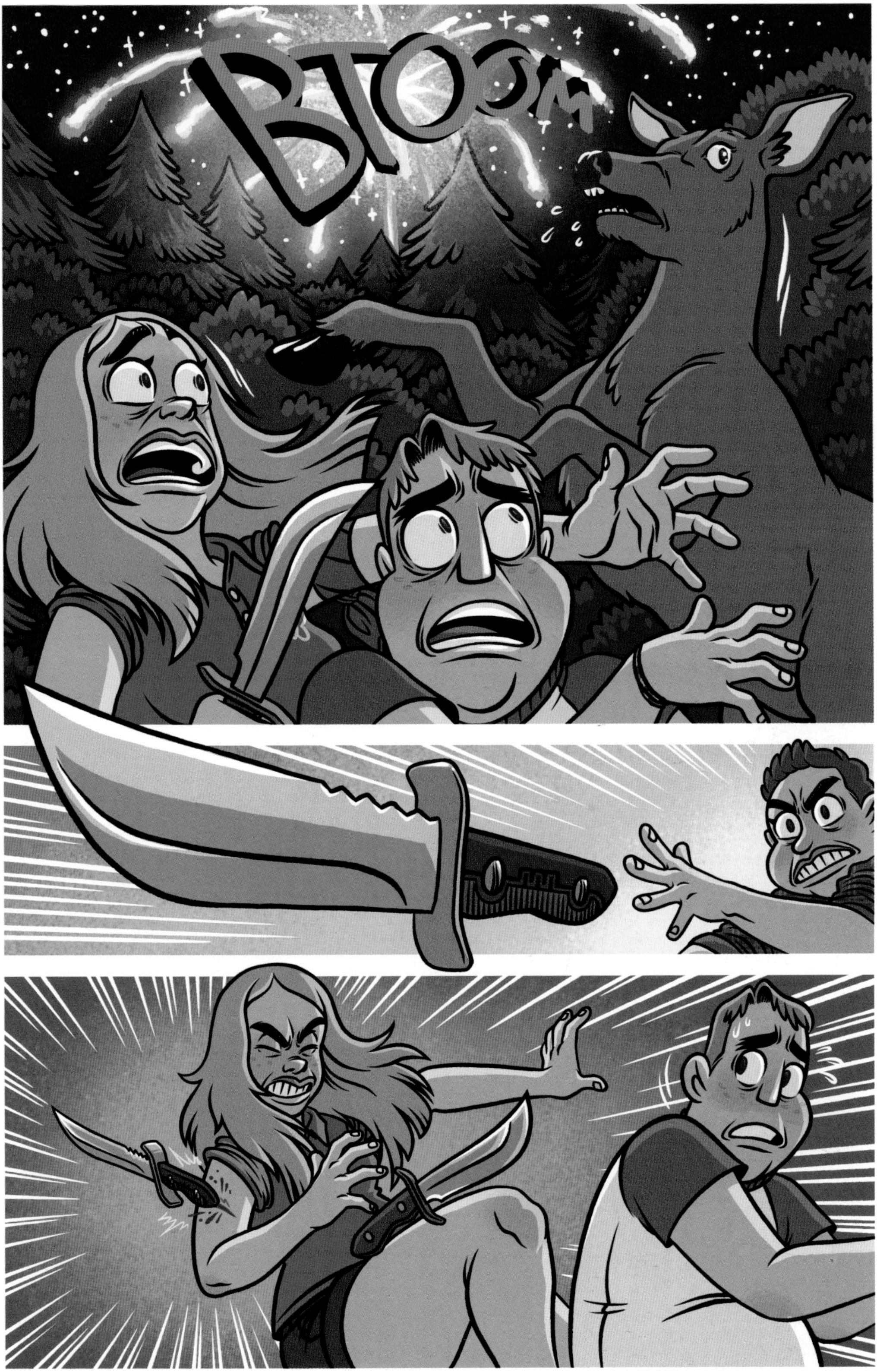
BTOOM

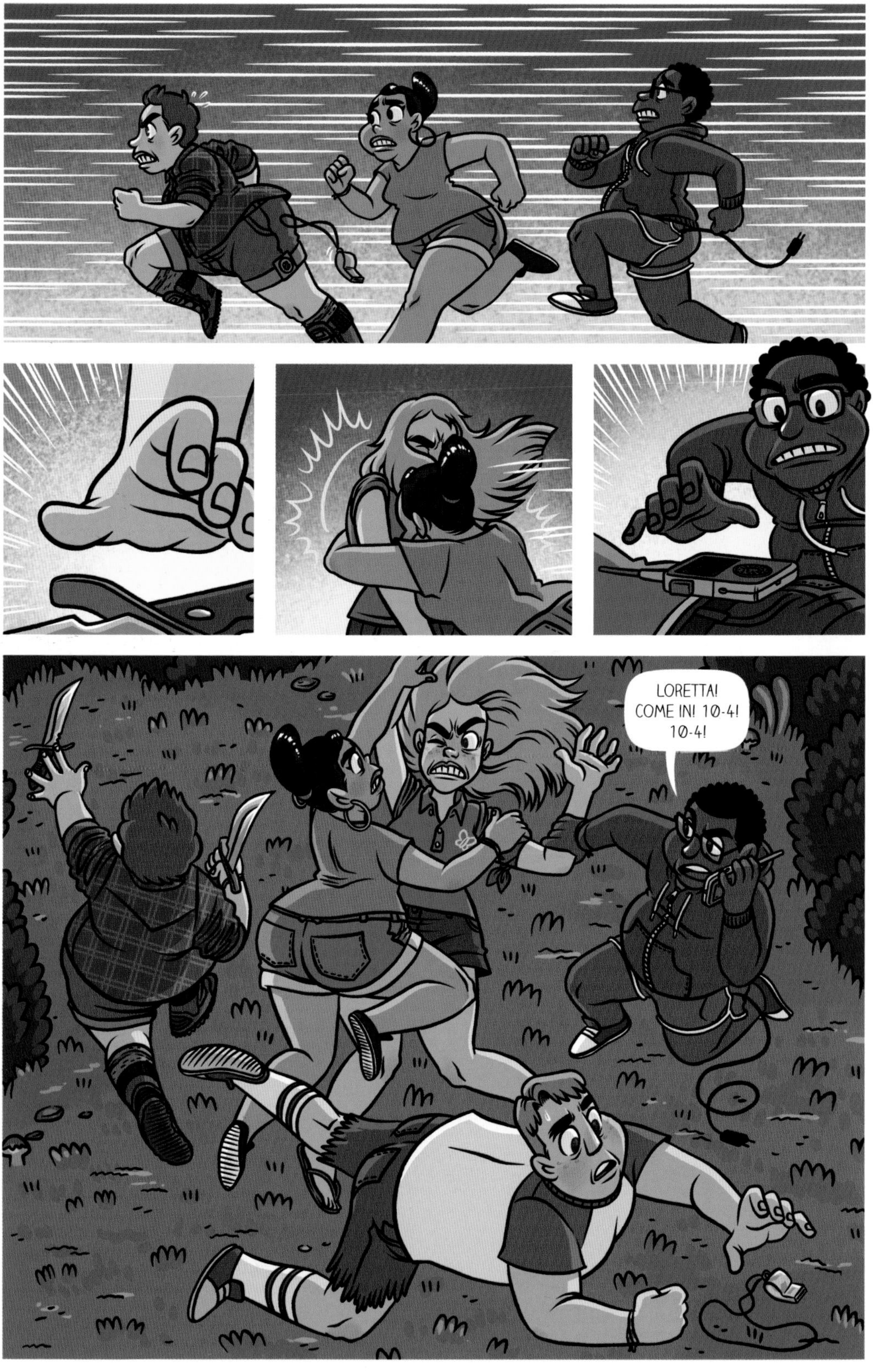
LORETTA! COME IN! 10-4! 10-4!

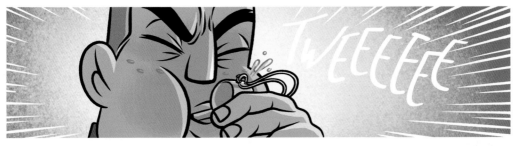

TWEEEEEE

LORETTA, BRING THE COPS! WE'RE IN THE WOODS! CAN YOU HEAR ME? DO YOU COPY? FOLLOW THE WHISTLE!

NO! GET OFF OF ME! LET ME GO!

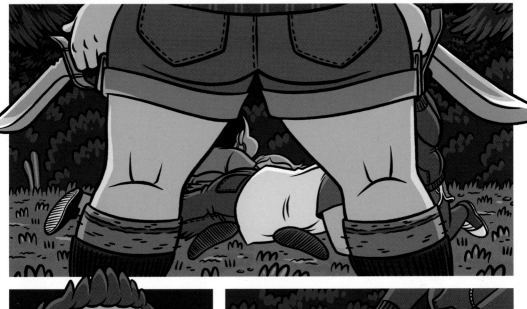

ROLL. OVER.

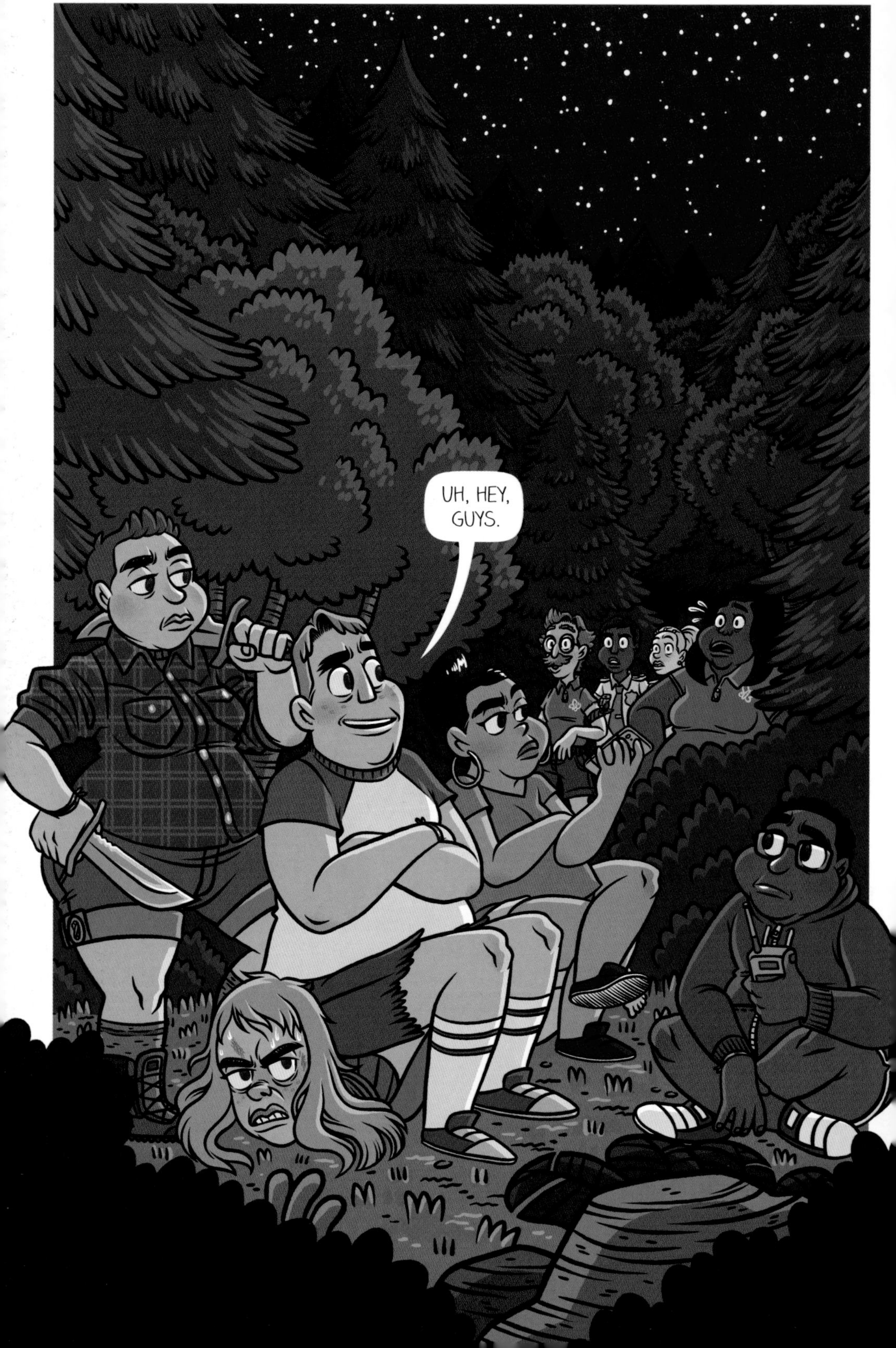
UH, HEY, GUYS.

CHAPTER TWELVE

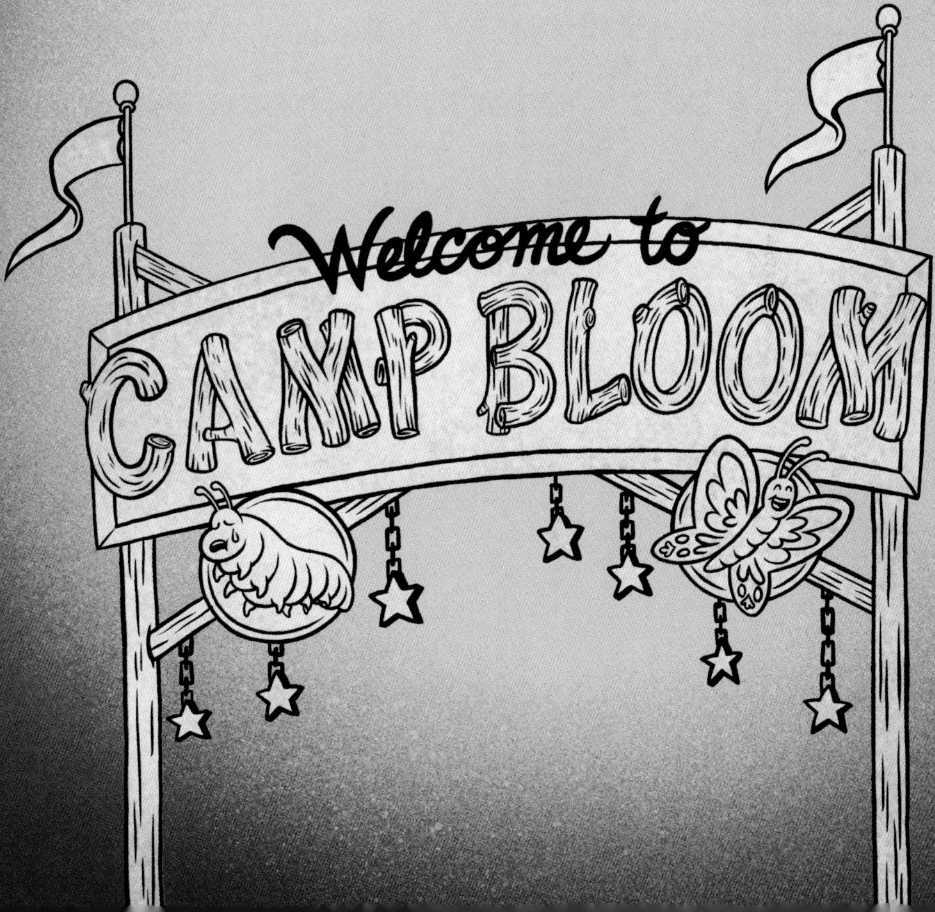
Welcome to
CAMP BLOOM

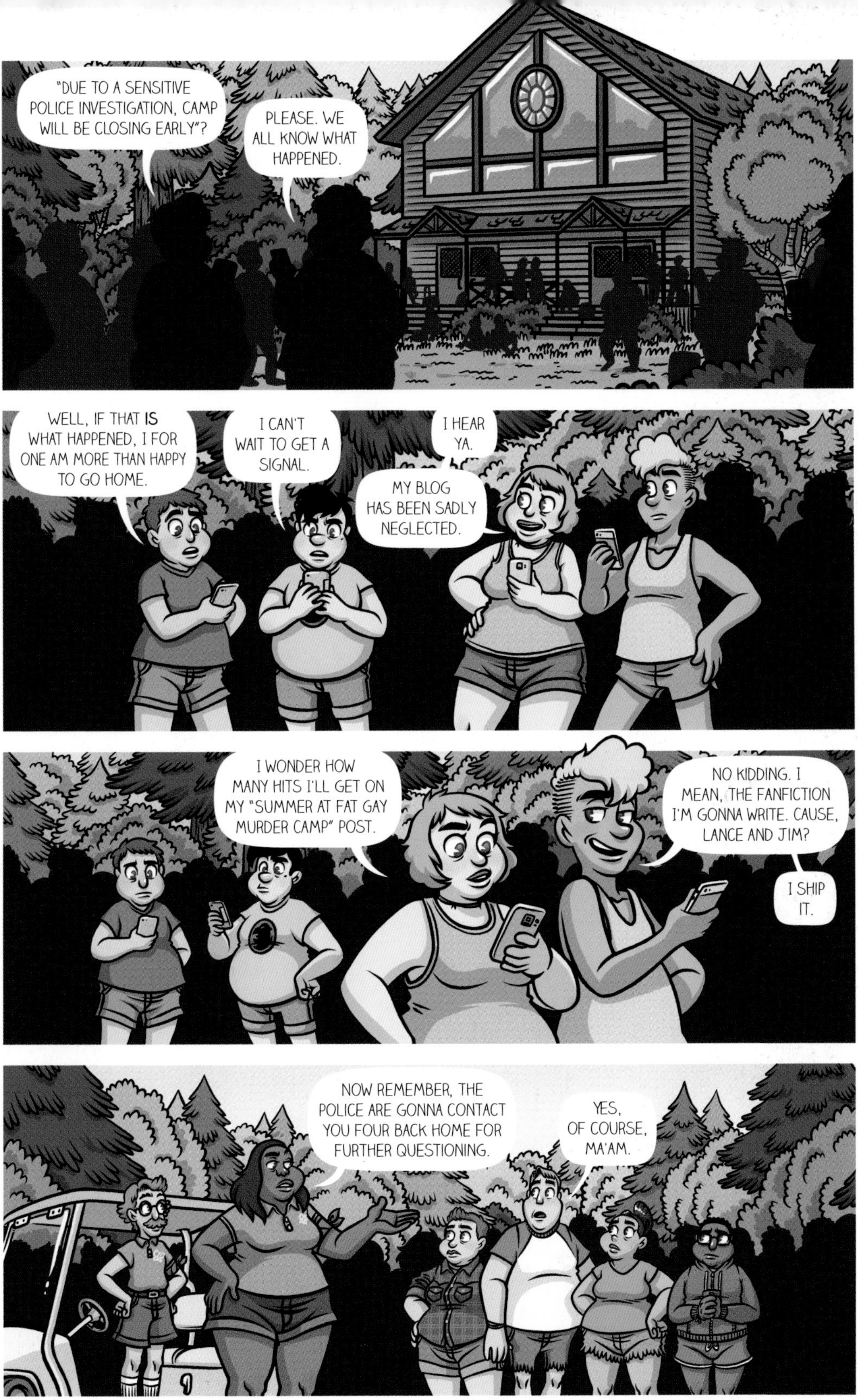
"DUE TO A SENSITIVE POLICE INVESTIGATION, CAMP WILL BE CLOSING EARLY"?
PLEASE. WE ALL KNOW WHAT HAPPENED.
WELL, IF THAT IS WHAT HAPPENED, I FOR ONE AM MORE THAN HAPPY TO GO HOME.
I CAN'T WAIT TO GET A SIGNAL.
I HEAR YA.
MY BLOG HAS BEEN SADLY NEGLECTED.
I WONDER HOW MANY HITS I'LL GET ON MY "SUMMER AT FAT GAY MURDER CAMP" POST.
NO KIDDING. I MEAN, THE FANFICTION I'M GONNA WRITE. CAUSE, LANCE AND JIM?
I SHIP IT.
NOW REMEMBER, THE POLICE ARE GONNA CONTACT YOU FOUR BACK HOME FOR FURTHER QUESTIONING.
YES, OF COURSE, MA'AM.

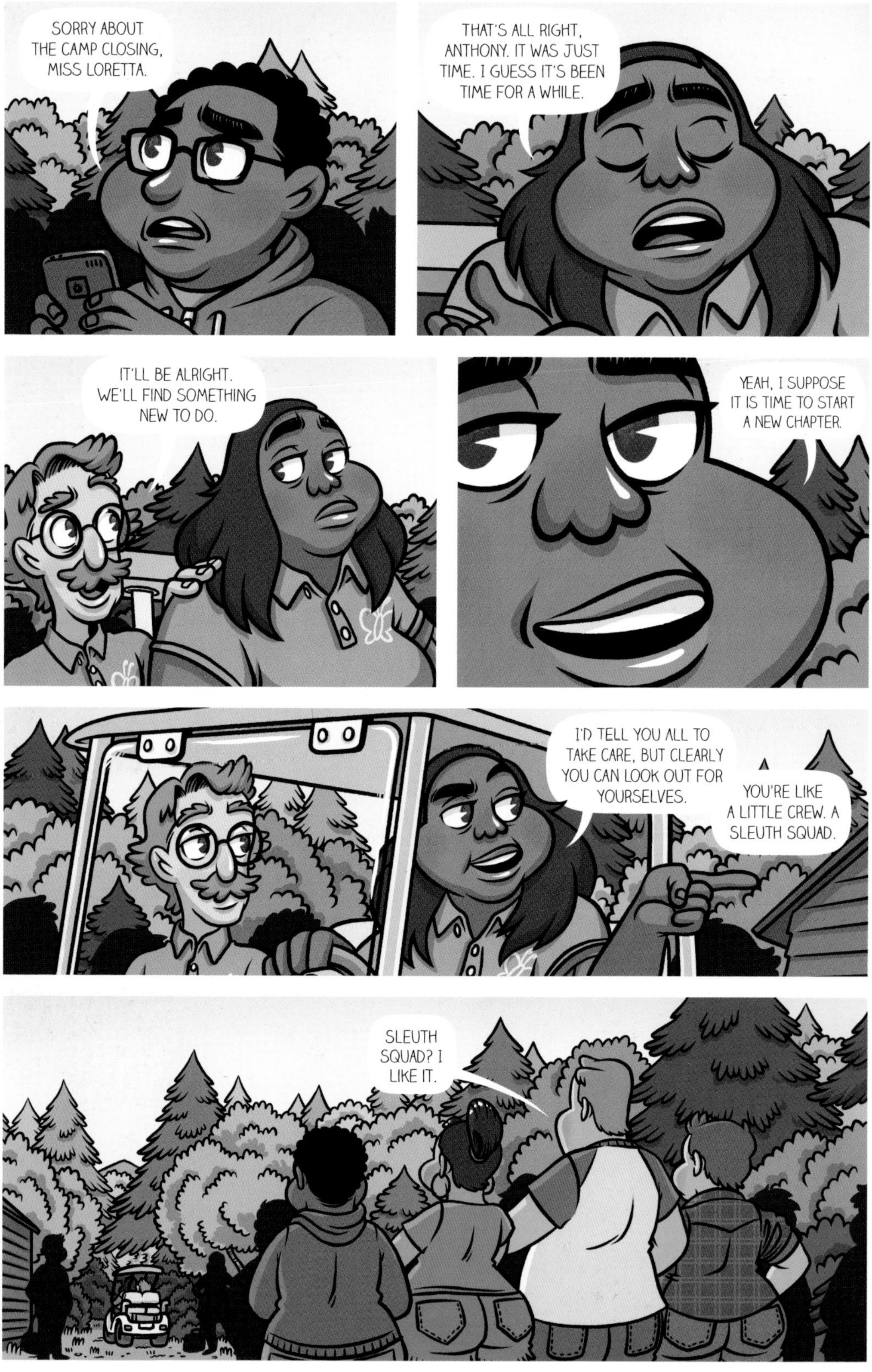
SORRY ABOUT THE CAMP CLOSING, MISS LORETTA.
THAT'S ALL RIGHT, ANTHONY. IT WAS JUST TIME. I GUESS IT'S BEEN TIME FOR A WHILE.
IT'LL BE ALRIGHT. WE'LL FIND SOMETHING NEW TO DO.
YEAH, I SUPPOSE IT IS TIME TO START A NEW CHAPTER.
I'D TELL YOU ALL TO TAKE CARE, BUT CLEARLY YOU CAN LOOK OUT FOR YOURSELVES.
YOU'RE LIKE A LITTLE CREW. A SLEUTH SQUAD.
SLEUTH SQUAD? I LIKE IT.

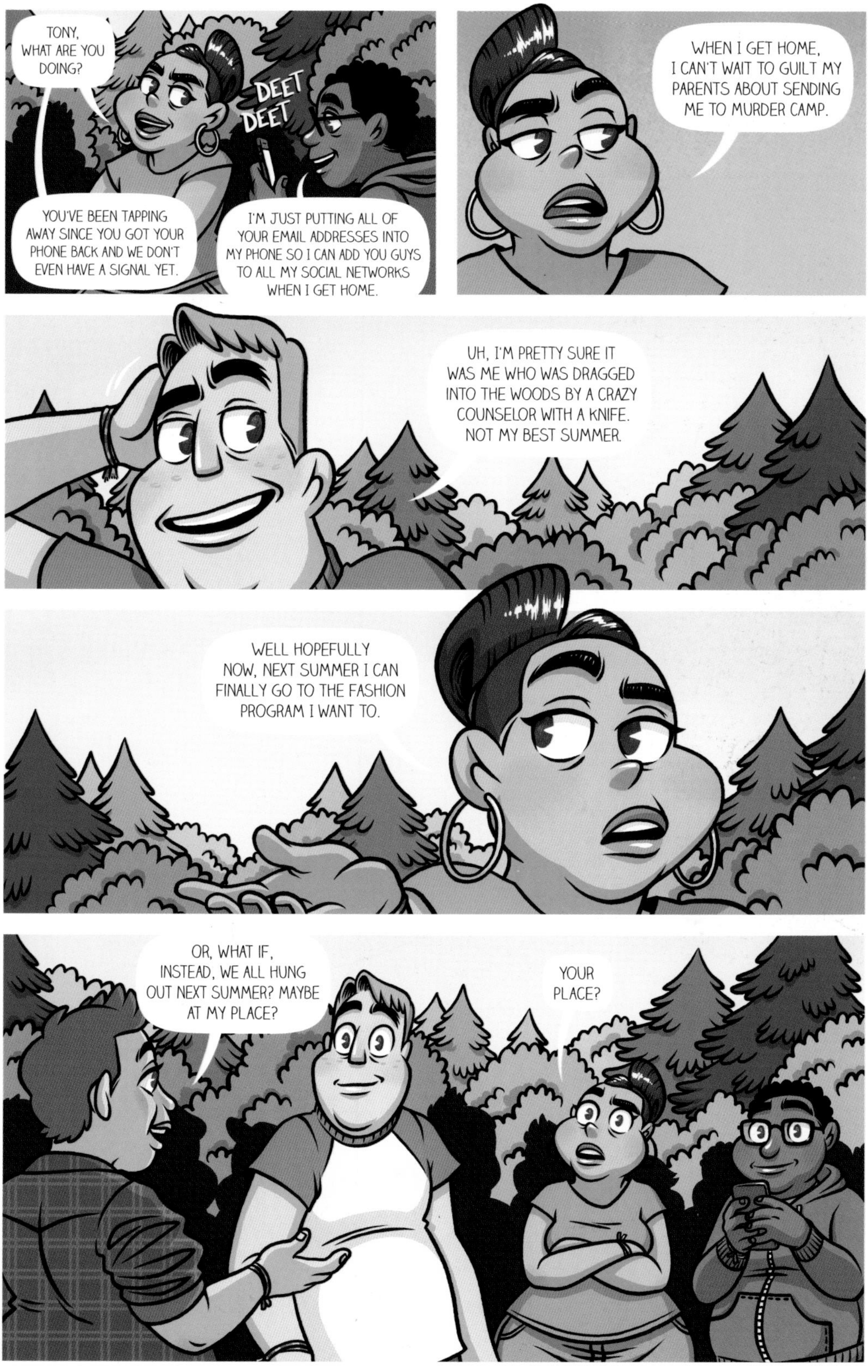
TONY, WHAT ARE YOU DOING?
DEET DEET
YOU'VE BEEN TAPPING AWAY SINCE YOU GOT YOUR PHONE BACK AND WE DON'T EVEN HAVE A SIGNAL YET.
I'M JUST PUTTING ALL OF YOUR EMAIL ADDRESSES INTO MY PHONE SO I CAN ADD YOU GUYS TO ALL MY SOCIAL NETWORKS WHEN I GET HOME.
WHEN I GET HOME, I CAN'T WAIT TO GUILT MY PARENTS ABOUT SENDING ME TO MURDER CAMP.
UH, I'M PRETTY SURE IT WAS ME WHO WAS DRAGGED INTO THE WOODS BY A CRAZY COUNSELOR WITH A KNIFE. NOT MY BEST SUMMER.
WELL HOPEFULLY NOW, NEXT SUMMER I CAN FINALLY GO TO THE FASHION PROGRAM I WANT TO.
OR, WHAT IF, INSTEAD, WE ALL HUNG OUT NEXT SUMMER? MAYBE AT MY PLACE?
YOUR PLACE?

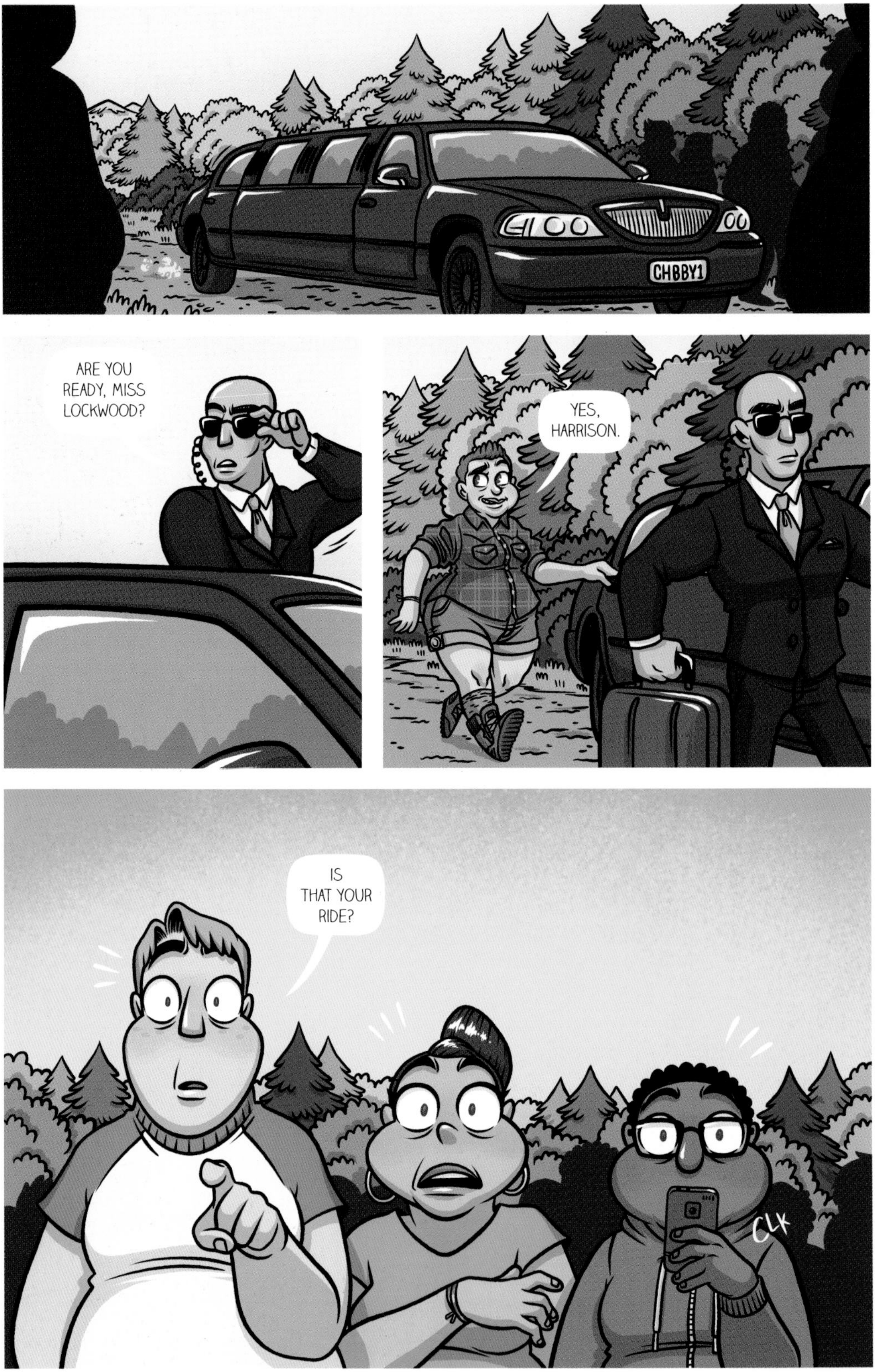
CHBBY1
ARE YOU READY, MISS LOCKWOOD?
YES, HARRISON.
IS THAT YOUR RIDE?
CLK

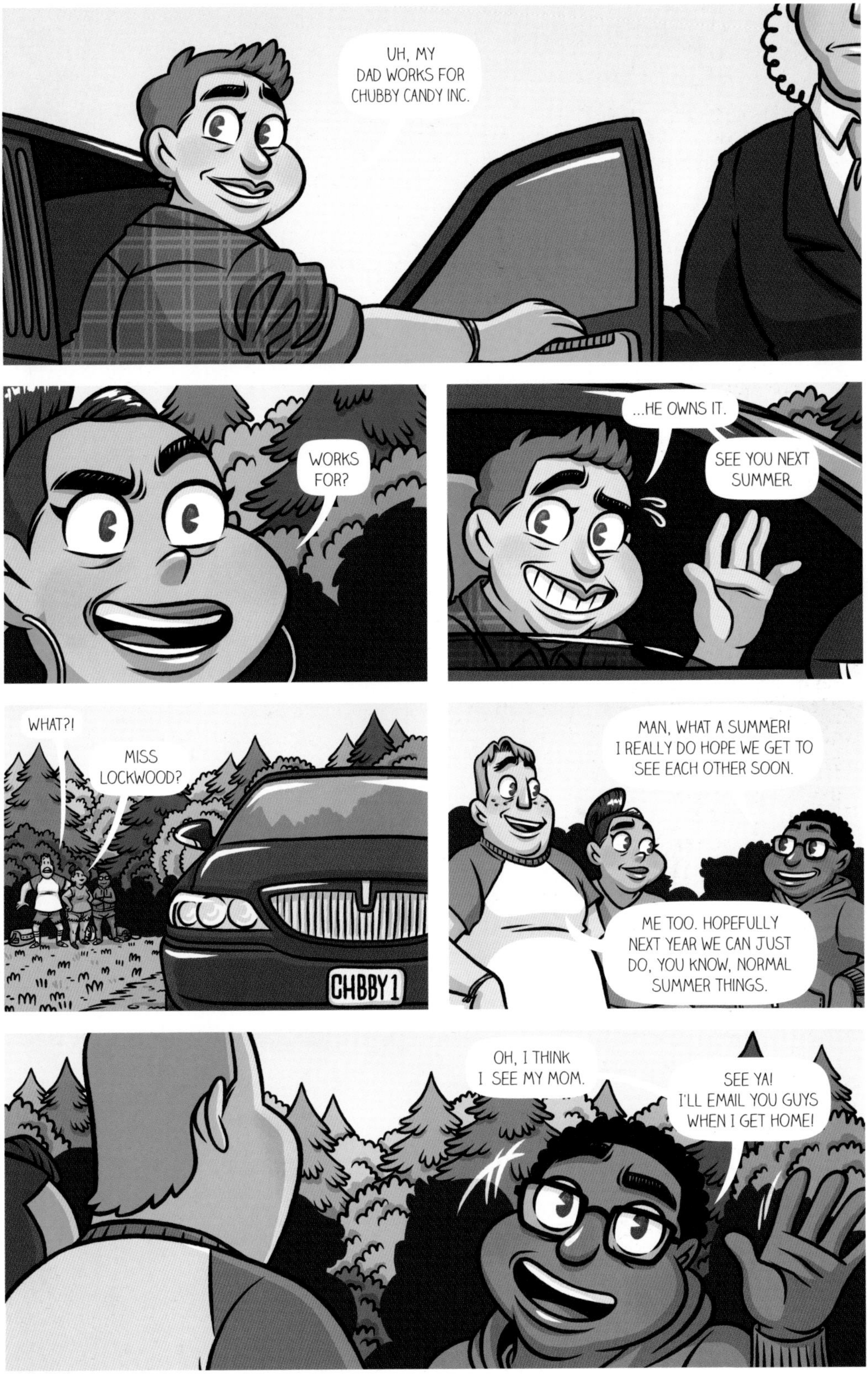
UH, MY DAD WORKS FOR CHUBBY CANDY INC.
WORKS FOR?
...HE OWNS IT.
SEE YOU NEXT SUMMER.
WHAT?!
MISS LOCKWOOD?
CHBBY1
MAN, WHAT A SUMMER! I REALLY DO HOPE WE GET TO SEE EACH OTHER SOON.
ME TOO. HOPEFULLY NEXT YEAR WE CAN JUST DO, YOU KNOW, NORMAL SUMMER THINGS.
OH, I THINK I SEE MY MOM.
SEE YA! I'LL EMAIL YOU GUYS WHEN I GET HOME!

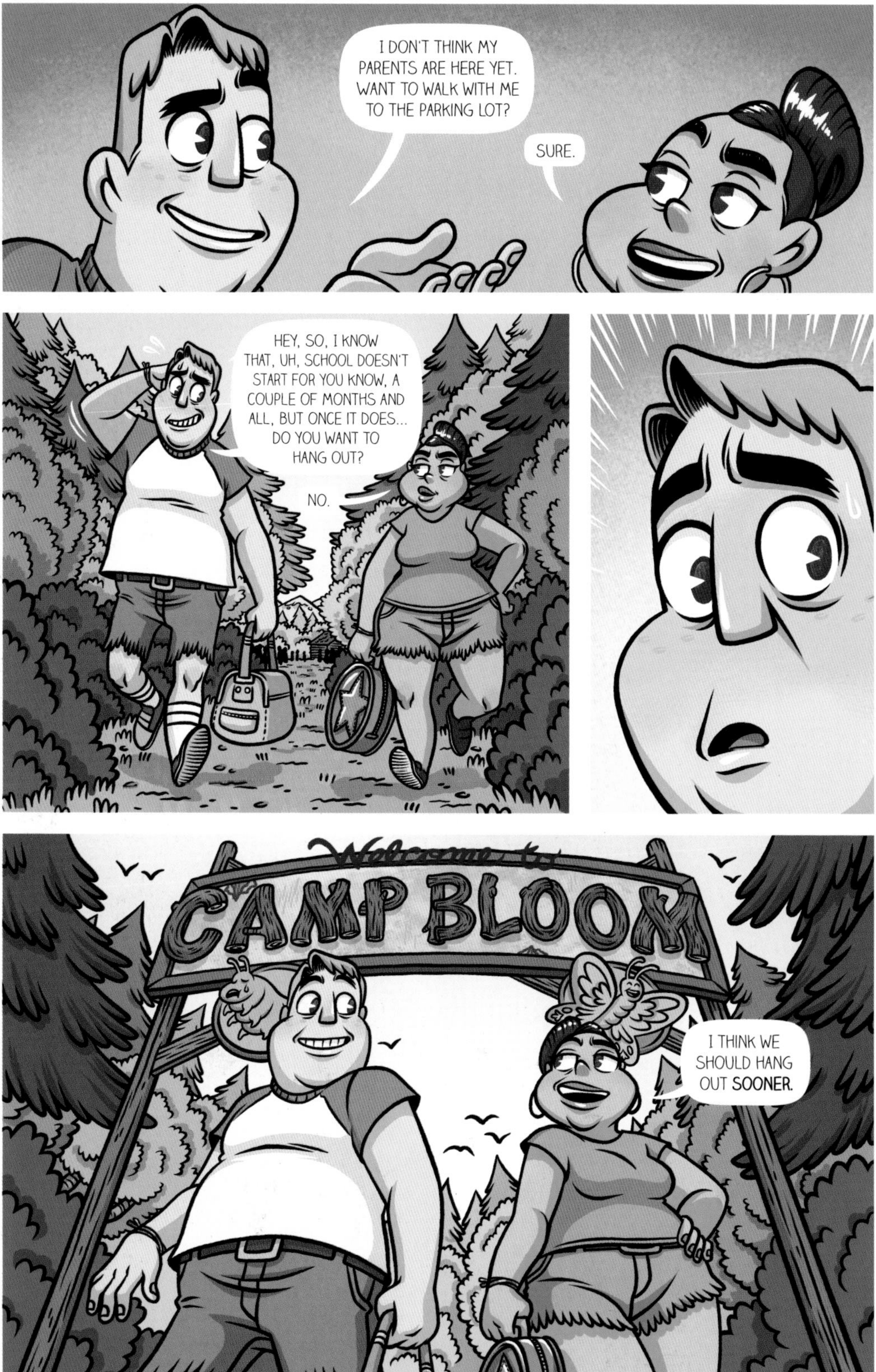
I DON'T THINK MY PARENTS ARE HERE YET. WANT TO WALK WITH ME TO THE PARKING LOT?
SURE.
HEY, SO, I KNOW THAT, UH, SCHOOL DOESN'T START FOR YOU KNOW, A COUPLE OF MONTHS AND ALL, BUT ONCE IT DOES... DO YOU WANT TO HANG OUT?
NO.
Welcome to
CAMP BLOOM
I THINK WE SHOULD HANG OUT **SOONER**.

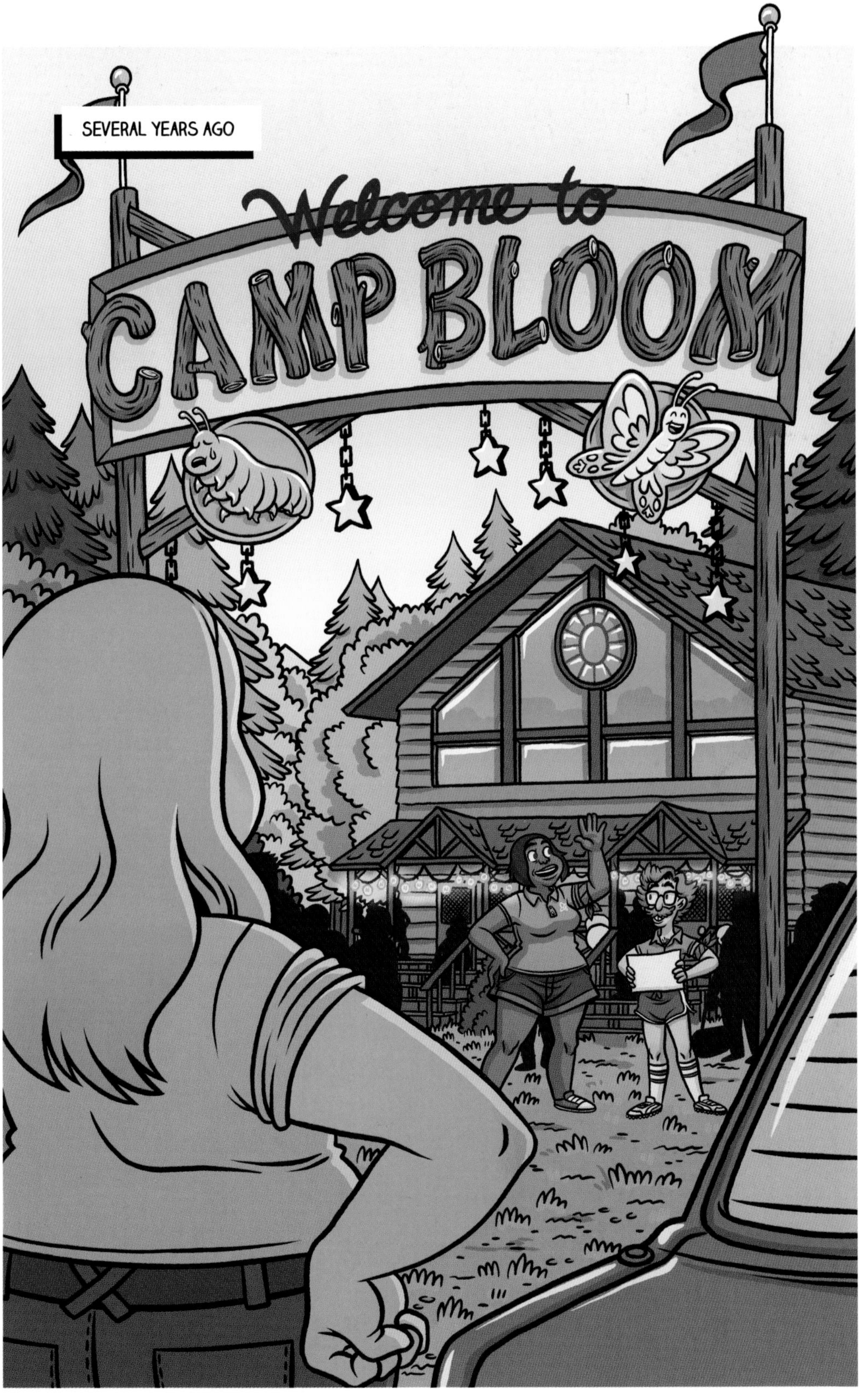
SEVERAL YEARS AGO
Welcome to
CAMP BLOOM

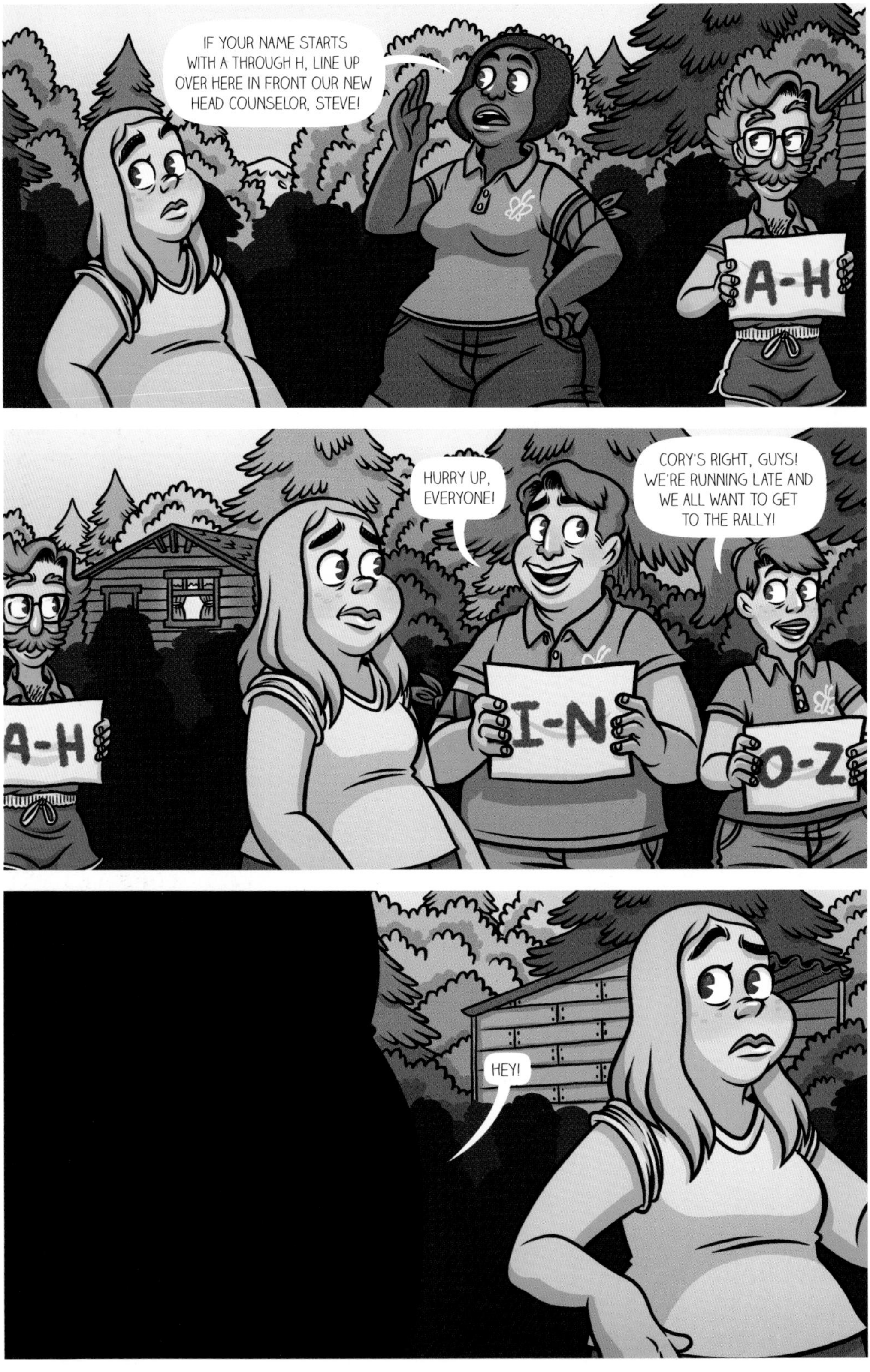
IF YOUR NAME STARTS WITH A THROUGH H, LINE UP OVER HERE IN FRONT OUR NEW HEAD COUNSELOR, STEVE!
A-H
HURRY UP, EVERYONE!
CORY'S RIGHT, GUYS! WE'RE RUNNING LATE AND WE ALL WANT TO GET TO THE RALLY!
A-H
I-N
O-Z
HEY!

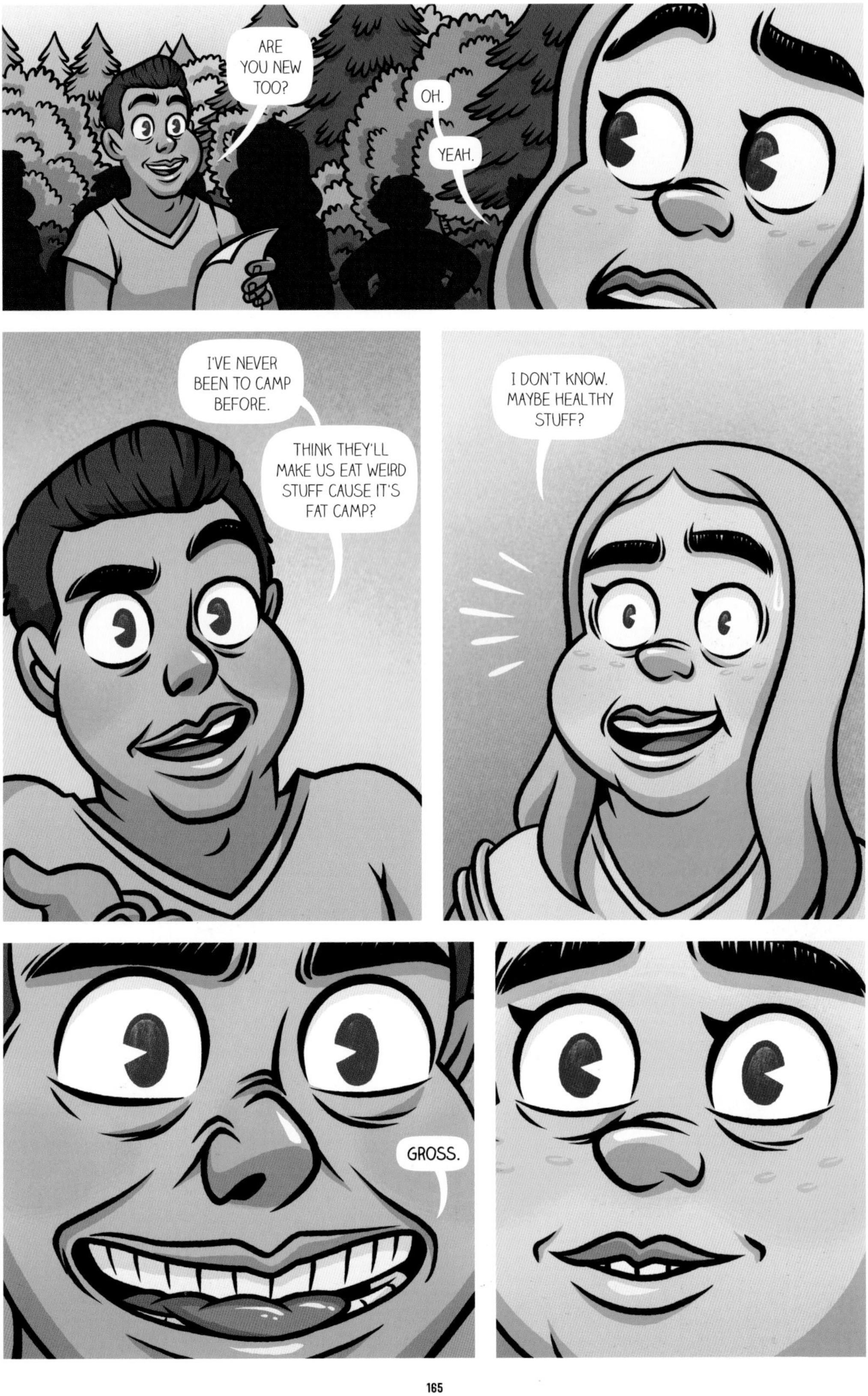
ARE YOU NEW TOO?
OH.
YEAH.
I'VE NEVER BEEN TO CAMP BEFORE.
THINK THEY'LL MAKE US EAT WEIRD STUFF CAUSE IT'S FAT CAMP?
I DON'T KNOW. MAYBE HEALTHY STUFF?
GROSS.

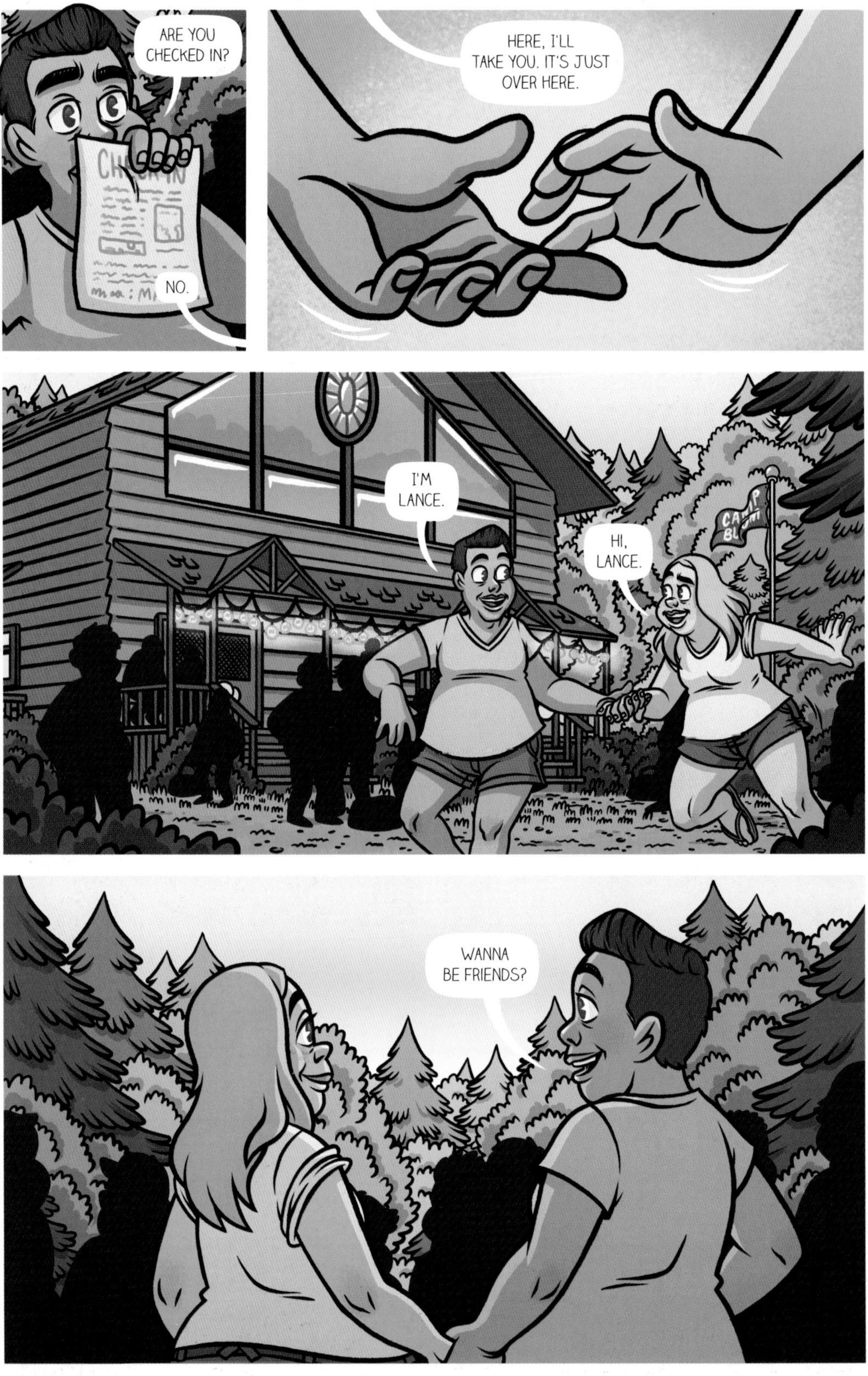
ARE YOU CHECKED IN?
NO.
HERE, I'LL TAKE YOU. IT'S JUST OVER HERE.
I'M LANCE.
HI, LANCE.
WANNA BE FRIENDS?

THE END

EXTRAS!

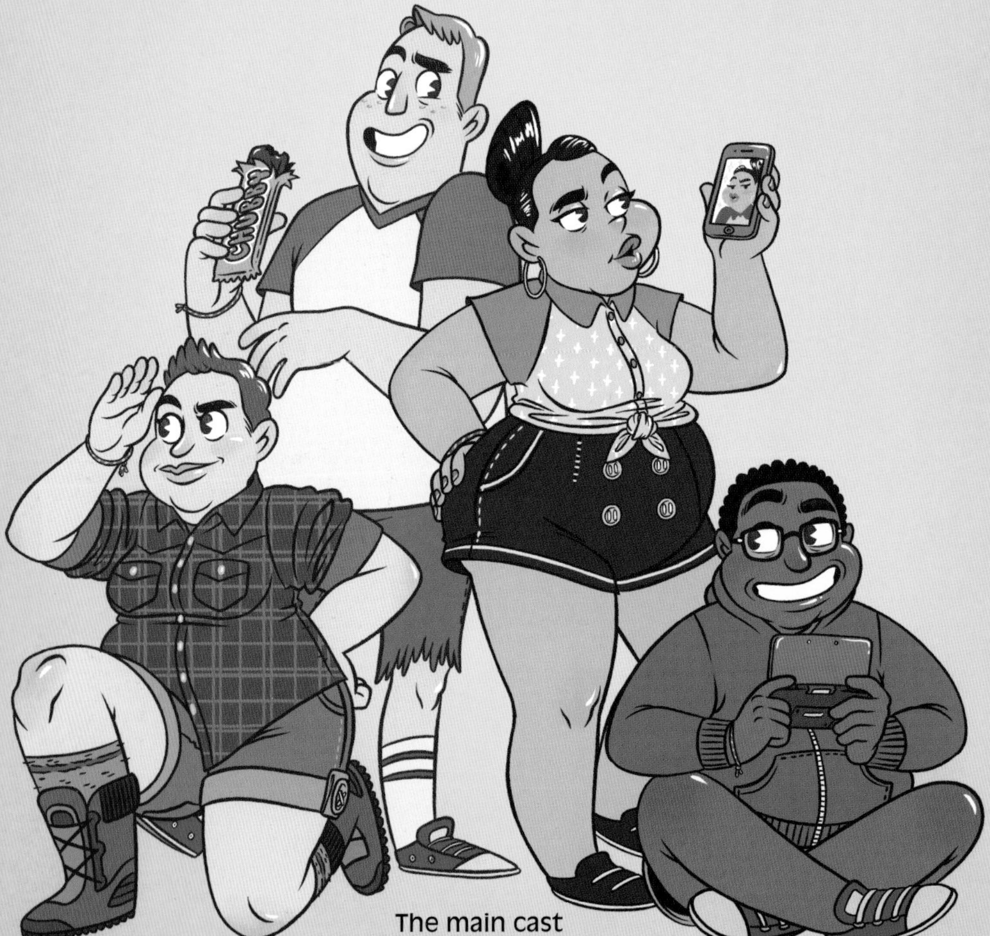
CHUBBY

The main cast
illustrated by Matthew Seely

THE STORY OF
CAMP BLOOM

MOLLY: If you told me ten years ago my first big project would be co-writing something, I would not have believed you. As much as I love doing things with friends, I've always been a bit of a loner when it comes to work. But after Terry and I plotted all of Dead Weight in a marathon four-hour Starbucks session, it was clear that we were on the same page, so to speak, and everything came surprisingly easily.

TERRY: The writing process Molly and I used consisted of a lot of dialogue creation and afternoon sandwich eating.

The process for me is more technical than anything. With a good synopsis we would plot out how many pages were needed for certain scenes and visually how they would look. Taking something from a synopsis into a comic script could turn a long description into just one panel.

MOLLY: I spent most of my teens and twenties consuming murder mysteries so the plot structure was my strength. Terry is great at creating characters that feel real and relatable. It made for a pretty good team.

TERRY: What I remember more than anything are the times Molly and I would consider whether or not we were writing characters with voices that seemed authentic to them. Benji seemed to come easy to us. Tony too. But it was important for us to have the characters sound and be distinct from one another.

MOLLY: The nice thing about working with another person is that it's very rare for both of you to get writer's block at the same time. It's easy to bounce ideas off each other and have two different perspectives on the story. When we were stuck on a line, one of us would say the preceding line of dialogue and the other would give a gut reaction. It worked pretty well. I was best at Noah, Terry best at Jesse. And in the very rare moments when we disagreed on something, usually something very small like a single line of dialogue, skipping it and coming back later always gave a fresh perspective and an easy answer.

TERRY: My favorite writing session was the day we wrote the scenes where most of the kids talk about why they are at camp. Each one was there for a different reason and once they were able to open up to one another I felt that they were a stronger team and had created a strong friendship. Ultimately that made the book stronger too.

MOLLY: There's nothing greater than crafting a story that you love and I got to do that with one of my best friends. Together with our lovely editor Robin, we were able to write something that means something and that's something I'll always be proud of.

CHARACTER ART

Seely first drew the four main campers: Jesse, Noah, Tony, and Kate, before moving on to the counselors. Blas gave lots of photo reference, so very few of the character designs needed to be tweaked.

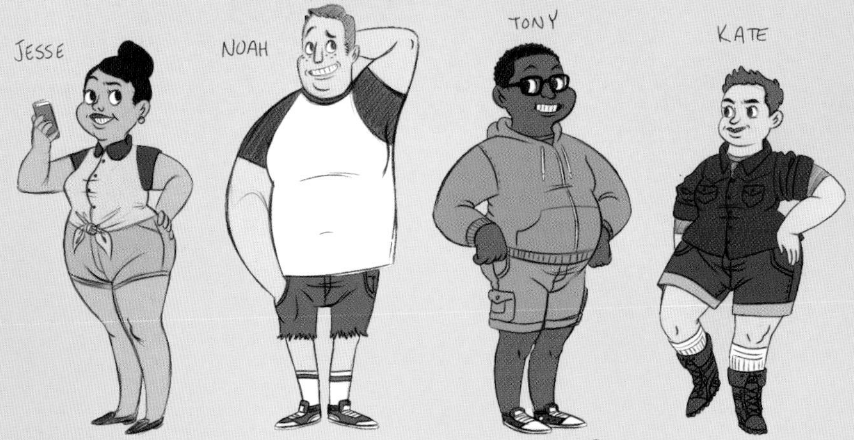
JESSE
NOAH
TONY
KATE

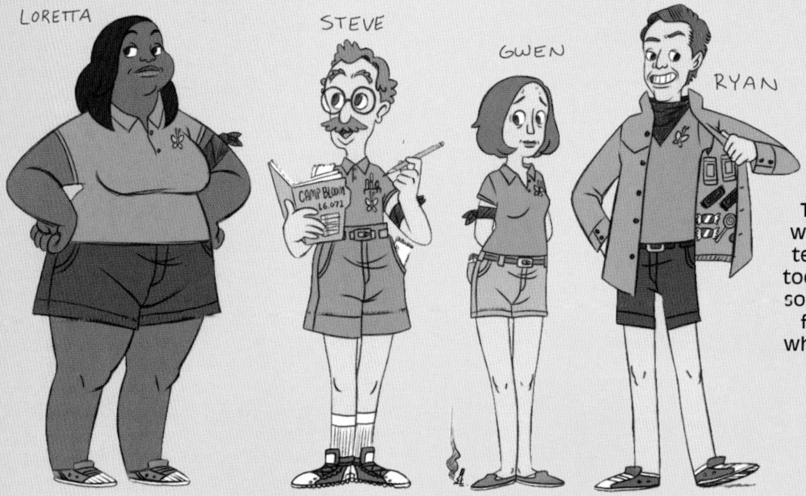
LORETTA
STEVE
CAMP BLOOM
GWEN
RYAN

The biggest change was in Gwen, who the team felt looked a bit too meek in the lineup, so Seely submitted the following redesign, which everyone agreed worked perfectly.

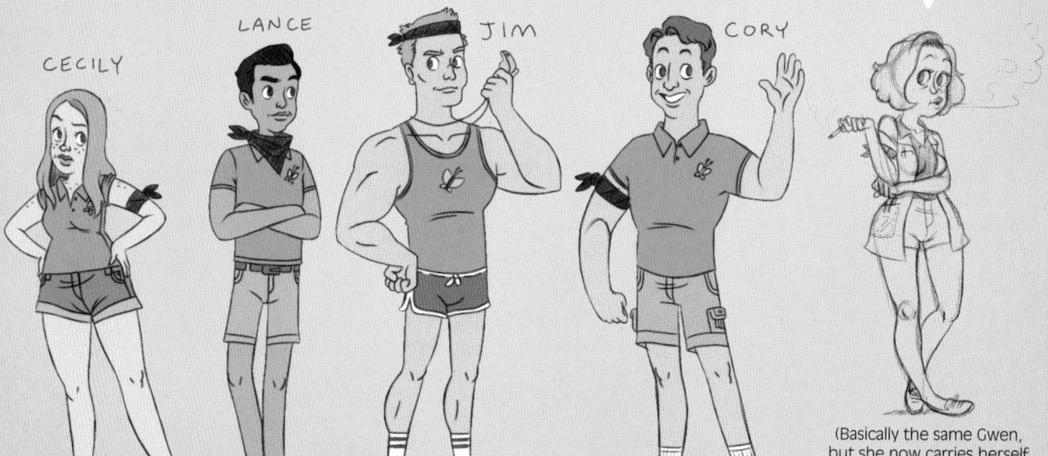
CECILY
LANCE
JIM
CORY

(Basically the same Gwen, but she now carries herself differently—and is worse at hiding her cigarette habit.)

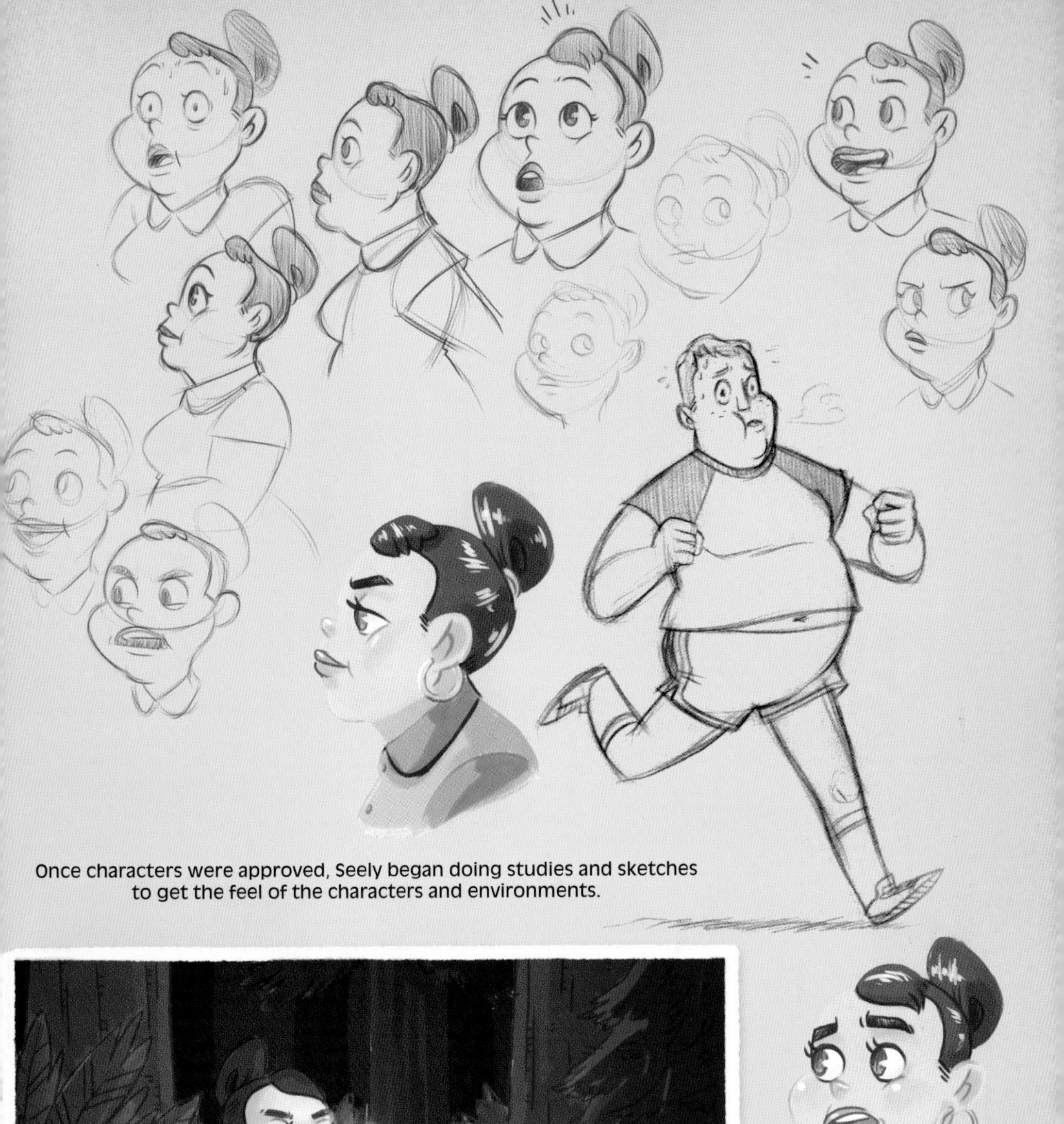

Once characters were approved, Seely began doing studies and sketches to get the feel of the characters and environments.

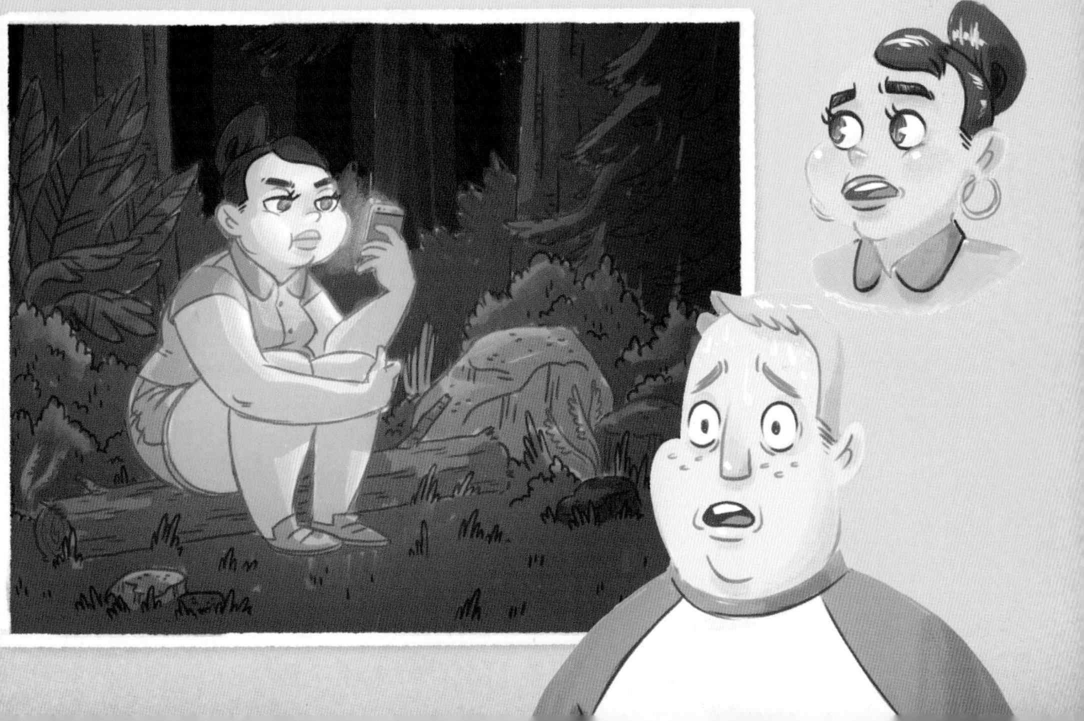

A typical comic page has four stages: thumbnails, where the artist jots down a quick but unrefined layout; pencils, where the artist works on a template to render more details; inks, where the artist creates the final linework on top of the pencils (either as a separate layer on a tablet or computer or with a brush/pen over pencils on paper); and finally, colors. As you'll see, Seely has a few steps involved in coloring—page 38 is below.

THUMBNAILS

Characters are recognizable. Balloons are drawn in at this stage to ensure there will be room for them, but are discarded in later stages.

PENCILS

Note that Seely has mostly only pencilled in the characters.

INKS

Final lineart has taken shape! This page is now ready for colors.

COLORS

First, flat colors are used to establish palette. No shading or rendering is done at this stage.

COLORS

This stage is where textures and highlights are added in and colors are selected for things like backgrounds. Note that the fire is now rendered.

COLORS

The final stage involves laying down tones and determining lighting. This is a night scene, but is heavily lit by a campfire, which makes it different from other night scenes. Since the fire is the light source, faces are lit from below.

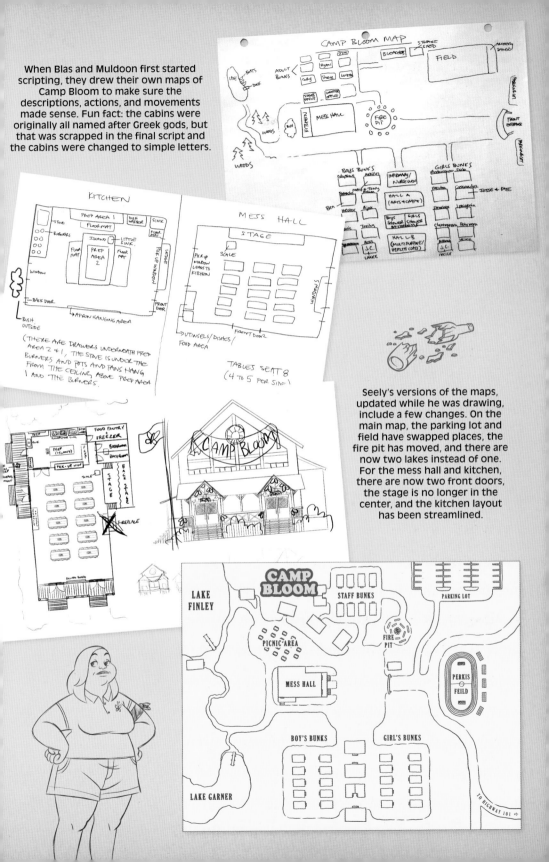

When Blas and Muldoon first started scripting, they drew their own maps of Camp Bloom to make sure the descriptions, actions, and movements made sense. Fun fact: the cabins were originally all named after Greek gods, but that was scrapped in the final script and the cabins were changed to simple letters.

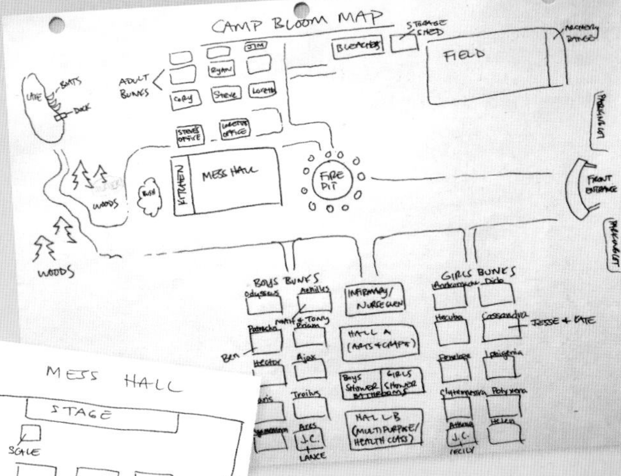

CAMP BLOOM MAP
STORAGE SHED
ARCHERY RANGE
BLEACHERS
FIELD
ADULT BUNKS
LAKE
BOATS
DOCK
Ryan
Cory
Steve
Loretta
STEVE'S OFFICE
LORETTA OFFICE
KITCHEN
MESS HALL
FIRE PIT
FRONT ENTRANCE
PARKING LOT
WOODS
BOYS BUNKS
GIRLS BUNKS
INFIRMARY/ NURSE GWEN
HALL A (ARTS + CRAFTS)
HALL B (MULTIPURPOSE/ HEALTH CLASS)
Hecuba
Cassandra
JESSE + KATE
Ajax
Hector
Troilus
Penelope
Iphigenia
Helen
J.C.
LANCE
CECILY

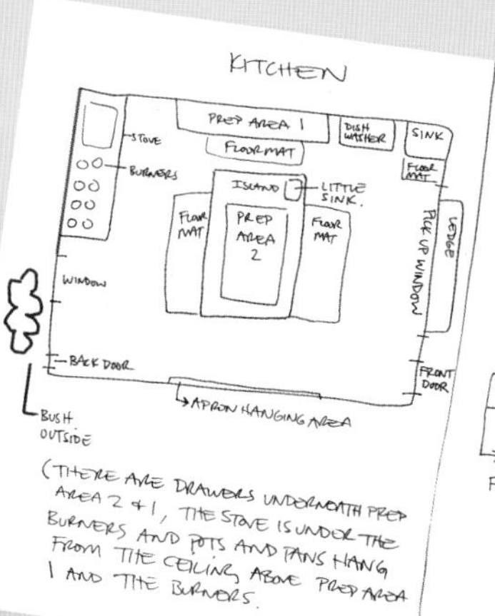

KITCHEN
PREP AREA 1
DISH WASHER
SINK
STOVE
FLOOR MAT
BURNERS
ISLAND
LITTLE SINK.
FLOOR MAT
PREP AREA 2
PICK UP WINDOW
LEDGE
WINDOW
BACK DOOR
FRONT DOOR
APRON HANGING AREA
BUSH OUTSIDE
(THERE ARE DRAWERS UNDERNEATH PREP AREA 2 + 1, THE STOVE IS UNDER THE BURNERS AND POTS AND PANS HANG FROM THE CEILING ABOVE PREP AREA 1 AND THE BURNERS.

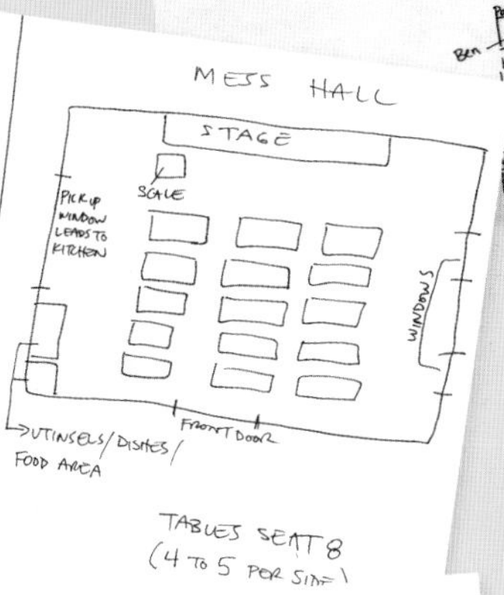

MESS HALL
STAGE
SCALE
PICK UP WINDOW LEADS TO KITCHEN
WINDOWS
FRONT DOOR
UTINSELS/DISHES/ FOOD AREA
TABLES SEAT 8 (4 TO 5 PER SIDE)

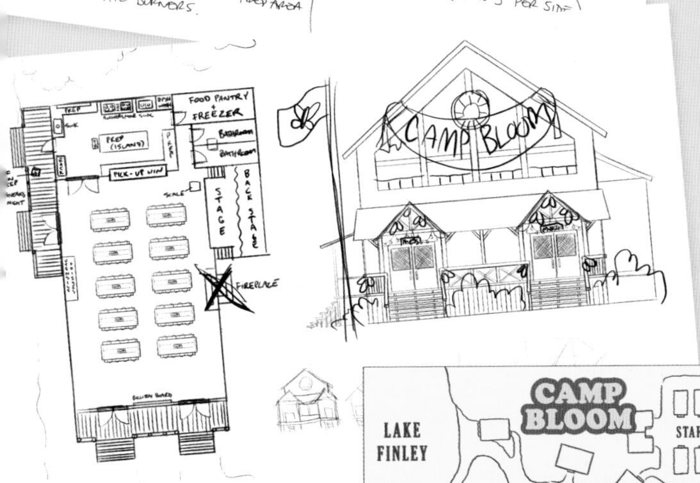

FOOD PANTRY + FREEZER
PREP
PREP (ISLAND)
BATHROOM
PICK-UP WIN
SCALE
STAGE
BACK STAGE
FIREPLACE
CAMP BLOOM

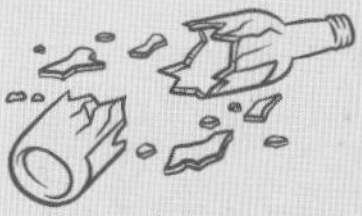

Seely's versions of the maps, updated while he was drawing, include a few changes. On the main map, the parking lot and field have swapped places, the fire pit has moved, and there are now two lakes instead of one. For the mess hall and kitchen, there are now two front doors, the stage is no longer in the center, and the kitchen layout has been streamlined.

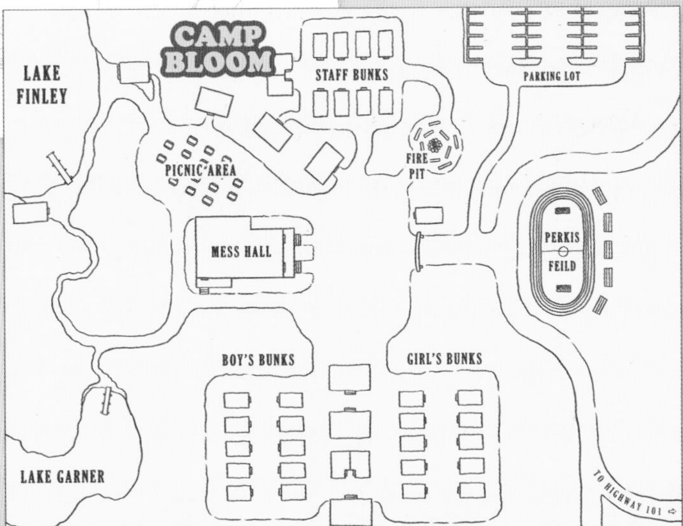

CAMP BLOOM
STAFF BUNKS
PARKING LOT
LAKE FINLEY
PICNIC AREA
FIRE PIT
MESS HALL
PERKIS FEILD
BOY'S BUNKS
GIRL'S BUNKS
LAKE GARNER
TO HIGHWAY 101

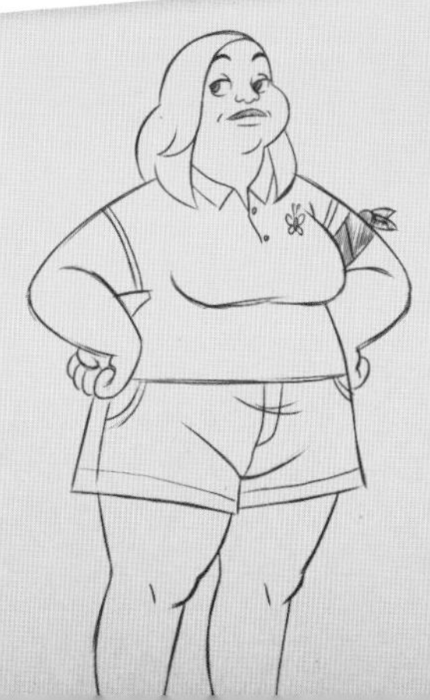

TERRY BLAS

Terry Blas is the illustrator and writer behind the webcomic *Briar Hollow*. His comics *Ghetto Swirl* and *You Say Latino* were featured on Vox.com, NPR and the *Huffington Post*. Some of his comic work includes *Regular Show*, *The Amazing World of Gumball*, *Rick and Morty*™, *Adventure Time*, and *Mama Tits Saves the World*. *Dead Weight: Murder at Camp Bloom* is his first graphic novel. He lives in Portland, Oregon where he is a member of Helioscope Studio.

MOLLY MULDOON

Molly Muldoon's high school superlative was 'Most Likely to Write Murder Mysteries." Well played, yearbook staff. Molly's a writer, editor, and newly-minted librarian who's always on the move with her *paw*tner-in-crime, Jamie McKitten.

MATTHEW SEELY

Matthew Seely is an animator, illustrator, and comic artist from Portland, Oregon. He's worked with ShadowMachine as Segment Director on *Dancing in the Dark* for season two of MTV's *Greatest Party Story Ever*, and has created multiple independent animated shorts. He's also written, drawn and self-published comics including *Robo-Boy vs. Boybot* and *Oswald the Orange*. In his free time, Seely enjoys playing music, listening to podcasts, and eating peanut butter and banana sandwiches.

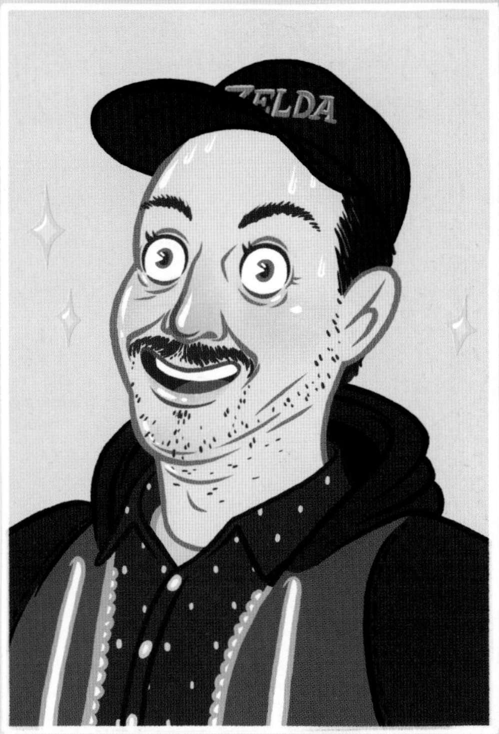
ZELDA

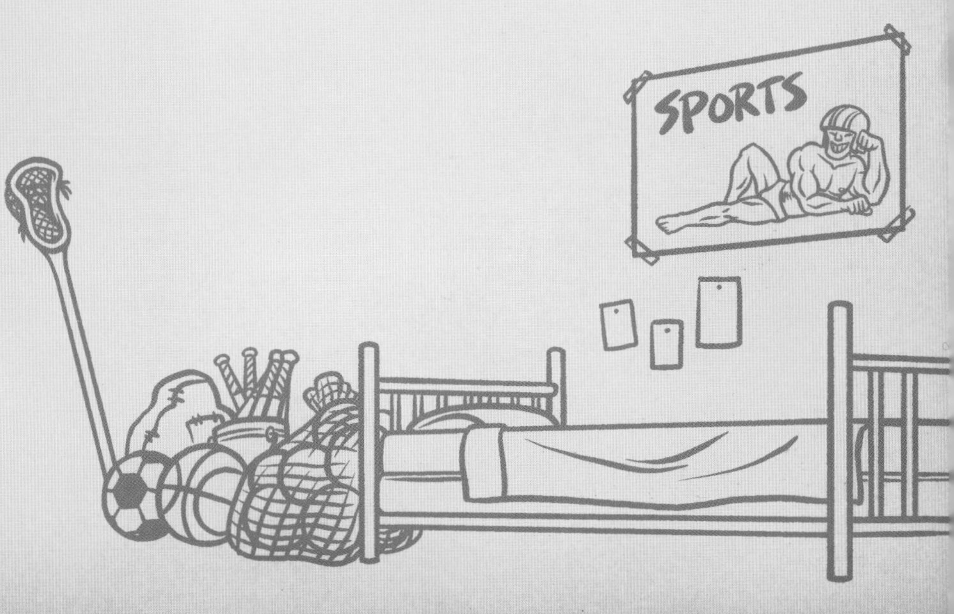
SPORTS